Y0-BOE-866

ERUPTION

MICHAEL CRICHTON
AND
JAMES PATTERSON

LITTLE, BROWN AND COMPANY

New York Boston London

The characters and events in this book are fictitious. Any similarity to real persons, living or dead, is coincidental and not intended by the author.

Copyright © 2024 by CrichtonSun, LLC and James Patterson

Hachette Book Group supports the right to free expression and the value of copyright. The purpose of copyright is to encourage writers and artists to produce the creative works that enrich our culture.

The scanning, uploading, and distribution of this book without permission is a theft of the author's intellectual property. If you would like permission to use material from the book (other than for review purposes), please contact permissions@hbgusa.com. Thank you for your support of the author's rights.

Little, Brown and Company
Hachette Book Group
1290 Avenue of the Americas, New York, NY 10104
littlebrown.com

Originally published in hardcover, June 2024
First trade paperback edition, July 2025

Little, Brown and Company is a division of Hachette Book Group, Inc. The Little, Brown name and logo are trademarks of Hachette Book Group, Inc.

The publisher is not responsible for websites (or their content) that are not owned by the publisher.

The Hachette Speakers Bureau provides a wide range of authors for speaking events. To find out more, go to hachettespeakersbureau.com or email hachettespeakers@hbgusa.com.

Little, Brown and Company books may be purchased in bulk for business, educational, or promotional use. For information, please contact your local bookseller or the Hachette Book Group Special Markets Department at special.markets@hbgusa.com.

Map by John Barnett

Book interior design by Marie Mundaca

ISBN 9780316565073 (hc) / 9780316577847 (large print)
9780538743157 (paperback)
LCCN 2023947317

Printing 1, 2025

LSC-H

Printed in the United States of America

E ko Hawai'i pono'ī:
No 'oukou i ho'ola'a 'ia a'e ai kēia mo'olelo, no ka lāhuikanaka o ka
pae 'āina e kaulana nei.

To Hawai'i's own:
This story is dedicated to you, the people of the
famed island chain.

THE BIG ISLAND
OF
HAWAI'I

N

W · E

S

NI'IHAU

KAUA'I

O'AHU

HONOLULU

MOLOKA'I

LĀNA'I

MAUI

KAHO'OLAWE

HAWAI'I

HILO

The Pacific Ocean

THE
HAWAIIAN
ISLANDS

HĀWĪ

KOHALA

MAUNA KEA

Mauna Kea
Observatory

WAIMEA

Ice Tube

Boiling Pots
Pe'epe'e Falls

Honoli'i
Beach
Park

WAIKŌLOA

Saddle Road

Military
Reserve

Wailuku River

HILO International
Airport

Mauna Loa
Observatory

HUALĀLAI

HILO

Port of Hilo

Mauna Loa Trail

Hilo
Botanical Gardens

Moku'aweoweo
Caldera

KAILUA-KONA

Summit Cabin

KĪLAUEA

MAUNA LOA

Hawai'i Volcanoes
National Park

Hawaiian Volcano
Observatory

NĀ'ĀLEHU

KA LAE
(SOUTH POINT)

PROLOGUE

This early part of the larger story about the volcanic eruption of Mauna Loa became classified information days after it happened in 2016 at the Hilo Botanical Gardens. It remained highly classified until recently.

ONE

Hilo, Hawai'i
March 28, 2016

Rachel Sherrill, thirty years old in a few days, master's degree from Stanford in conservation biology, rising star in her world, still thought of herself as the smartest kid in the class. *Just about any class.*

But today at the Hilo Botanical Gardens, she was trying to be the cool substitute teacher for a restless, wide-eyed bunch of fifth-graders visiting from the mainland.

"Let's face it, Rachel," the general manager of the botanical gardens, Theo Nakamura, had said to her early that morning. "Taking these undersized tourists around is a way for you to put your immaturity to good use."

"Are you saying I act like a ten-year-old?"

"On a good day," Theo said.

Theo was the fearless academic who had hired her when the

park opened last year. As young as Rachel was—and looked—she was very good at what she did, which was serve as the park's chief plant biologist. It was a plum job, and she loved it.

And to be honest, one of her favorite parts of the job was conducting tours for kids.

That morning's walk in the park was with some very lucky and well-heeled schoolkids who had traveled all the way here from Convent and Stuart Hall in San Francisco. Rachel was trying to entertain and educate the kids about the natural world surrounding them.

But as much as she wanted to lecture about what they were observing—orchid gardens; soaring bamboos; coconut palms; jackfruit trees; edible plants like breadfruit, kukui, and red pineapple; dueling hundred-foot-high waterfalls; hibiscus literally everywhere—Rachel had to compete for the children's attention with the two closest of the five volcanoes on the Big Island: Mauna Loa, the largest active volcano in the world, and Mauna Kea, which hadn't erupted in more than four thousand years.

These city kids clearly considered the twin peaks the highlight of their tour, the best sight they'd seen in the picture-postcard wonderland called Hawai'i. What kid wouldn't give anything to watch Mauna Loa erupt and spew out a stream of lava heated to over a thousand degrees?

Rachel was explaining that Hawai'i's volcanic soil was one of the reasons why there was so much natural beauty on the island, a PowerPoint example of the good that had come out of past eruptions, helping Hawai'i grow beans that produced coffee as delicious as any in the world.

"But the volcanoes aren't going to explode today, are they?" a little girl asked, her large brown eyes pinned to the twin peaks.

"If they even *think* about it," Rachel said, "we're going to build a dome over them like we do with those new football stadiums. We'll see how they like *that* next time they try to blow off a little steam."

No response. Crickets. Pacific field crickets, to be exact. Rachel smiled. Sometimes she couldn't help herself.

"What kind of coffee comes from here?" another straight A–student type asked.

"Starbucks," Rachel said.

This time they laughed. *One in a row*, Rachel thought. *Don't forget to tip your waiters.*

But not all the kids were laughing.

"Why is this tree turning black, Ms. Sherrill?" an inquisitive boy with wire-rimmed glasses sliding down his nose called out.

Christopher had wandered away from the group and was standing in front of a small grove of banyan trees about thirty yards across the lawn.

In the next instant, they all heard the jolting crash of what sounded like distant thunder. Rachel wondered, the way newcomers to Hawai'i always wondered, *Is a big storm coming or is this the start of an eruption?*

As most of the children stared up at the sky, Rachel hurried over to the studious, bespectacled boy who was looking at the banyan trees with a concerned expression on his face.

"Now, Christopher," Rachel said when she got to him, "you know I promised to answer every last one of your questions—"

The rest of what she'd been about to say collapsed in her throat. She saw what Christopher was seeing—she just couldn't believe her eyes.

It wasn't just that the three banyan trees closest to her had turned black. Rachel could actually see inky, pimpled blackness spreading like an oil spill, some terrible stain, except that the darkness was climbing *up* the trees. It was like some sort of upside-down lava flow from one of the volcanoes, but the lava was defying gravity, not to mention everything Rachel Sherrill knew about plant and tree diseases.

Maybe she wasn't the smartest kid in the class after all.

TWO

"What the shit—" Rachel began, then stopped herself, realizing that a fragile ten-year-old was standing right next to her.

She bent low to the ground and saw suspicious dark spots leading up to the tree, like the tracks of some mythical round-footed animal. Rachel knelt down and felt the spots. The grass wasn't moist. Actually, the blades felt like the bristles on a wire brush.

None of the blackness had been here yesterday.

She touched the bark of another infected tree. It flaked and turned to dust. She jerked her hand away and saw what looked like a black ink stain on her fingers.

"These trees must have gotten sick," she said. It was the best she could offer young Christopher. She tried another joke. "I might have to send them all home from school today."

The boy didn't laugh.

Even though it was still technically morning, Rachel announced that they were breaking for lunch.

"But it's too early for lunch," the girl with big brown eyes said.

"Not on San Francisco time, it's not," Rachel said.

As she ushered the kids back to the main building, her mind

raced to come up with possible explanations for what she'd just witnessed. But nothing made sense. Rachel had never seen or read about anything like this. It wasn't the result of the vampire bugs that could eat away at banyan trees if left unchecked. Or of Roundup, the herbicide that the groundskeepers used over-zealously on the thirty acres of park that stretched all the way to Hilo Bay. Rachel had always considered herbicides a necessary evil—like first dates.

This was something else. Something dark, maybe even dangerous, a mystery she had to solve.

When the children were in the cafeteria, Rachel ran to her office. She checked in with her boss, then made a phone call to Ted Murray, an ex-boyfriend at Stanford who had recommended her for this job and convinced her to take it and who now worked for the Army Corps of Engineers at the Military Reserve.

"We might have a thing here," Rachel told him.

"A *thing*?" Murray said. "God, you scientists with your fancy words."

She explained what she had seen, knowing she was talking too quickly, her words falling over each other as they came spilling out of her mouth.

"On it," Murray said. "I'll get some people out there as soon as I can. And don't panic. I'm sure there's a good reason for this...*thing*."

"Ted, you know I don't scare very easily."

"Tell me about it," Murray said. "I know from my own personal experience that you're the one usually doing the scaring."

She hung up, knowing she *was* scared, the worst fear of all for her: *not knowing*. While the children continued noisily eating lunch, she put on the running shoes she kept under her desk and ran all the way back to the banyan grove.

There were more blackened trees when she got there, the

stain creeping up from distinctive aerial roots that stretched out like gnarled gray fingers.

Rachel Sherrill tentatively touched one of the trees. It felt like a hot stove. She checked her fingertips to make sure she hadn't singed them.

Ted Murray had said he would send some of his people to investigate as soon as he could assemble a crew. Rachel ran back to the lunchroom and collected her group of fifth-graders from San Francisco. No need for anybody to panic. Not yet, anyway.

Their last stop was a miniature rainforest far from the banyan grove. The tour felt endless to her, but when it was finally over, Rachel said, "I hope you all come back someday."

A thin reed of a girl asked, "Are you going to get a doctor for the sick trees?"

"I'm about to do that right now," Rachel said.

She turned around and once again jogged back toward the banyan trees. She felt as if the entire day had exploded around her, like one of the volcanoes in the distance.

THREE

A voice came crackling over the loudspeakers—Rachel Sherrill's boss, Theo Nakamura, telling visitors to evacuate the botanical gardens immediately.

"This is not a drill," Theo said. "This is for the safety of everyone on the grounds. That includes all park personnel. Everyone, please, out of the park."

Within seconds, park visitors started coming at Rachel hard. The grounds were more crowded than she had thought. Mothers ran as they pushed strollers ahead of them. Children ran ahead of their parents. A teen on a bike swerved to avoid a child, went down, got up cursing, climbed back on his bike, and kept going. Smoke was suddenly everywhere.

"It could be a volcano!" Rachel heard a young woman yell.

Rachel saw two army jeeps parked outside the distant banyan grove. Another jeep roared past her; Ted Murray was at the wheel. She shouted his name but Murray, who probably couldn't hear her over the chaos, didn't turn around.

Murray's jeep stopped, and soldiers jumped out. Murray directed them to form a perimeter around the entrance to the grove and ensure that the park visitors kept moving out.

Rachel ran toward the banyan grove. Another jeep pulled up in front of her and a soldier stepped out.

"You're heading in the wrong direction," the soldier said.

"You—you don't understand," she stammered. "Those— they're my trees."

"I don't want to have to tell you again, ma'am."

Rachel Sherrill heard a chopper engine; she looked up and saw a helicopter come out of the clouds from behind the twin peaks. Saw it touch down and saw its doors open. Men in hazmat suits, tanks strapped to their backs, came out carrying extinguishers labeled COLD FIRE. They pointed them like handguns and ran toward the trees.

Her trees.

Rachel ran toward them and toward the fire.

In that same moment she heard another crash from the sky, and this time she knew for sure it wasn't a coming storm.

Please not today, she thought.

FOUR

The next day, Hilo's newspaper, the *Hawaii Tribune-Herald*, did not mention the evacuation at the botanical gardens. Neither did the *Honolulu Star-Advertiser*. Or any of the other island newspapers. There was no report in the *New York Times*.

None of the local newscasts brought up what had happened at the park the day before. There was no chatter about it on talk-radio stations, which were obsessed with Hawai'i's tourism being down for the first quarter of the year.

There were some mentions on social media, but not many, nothing viral, perhaps because the crowds had been relatively sparse at the Hilo Botanical Gardens on that particular Monday. Some Twitter posts described a small herbicide fire that had been successfully contained by the rapid response, though a few people did mention that they had seen a helicopter land on the grounds when they were leaving.

None of this was surprising. This was Hilo. This was laid-back Hawai'i, despite the fact that everyone here lived in the shadows of the volcanoes, this menacing constant in their lives, no one going very long without their eyes being drawn once again to Mauna Loa and Mauna Kea.

The park remained closed for two days.

When it reopened, it was as if nothing had ever happened.

ERUPTION

CHAPTER 1

Honoli'i Beach Park, Hilo, Hawai'i
Thursday, April 24, 2025
Time to eruption: 116 hours, 12 minutes, 13 seconds

D ennis!" Standing on the beach, John MacGregor had to yell so the surfer would hear him over the sound of the waves. "How about you don't go all *kūkae* on me, if that would be all right with you."

The kids that John MacGregor was coaching had heard the expression from him before, and they knew full well that it wasn't a compliment. *Kūkae* was a native Hawaiian word for "kook," and when John MacGregor said it, it meant that someone in the water was acting as if he'd never been on a board before. Or was about to end up underneath one.

Mac was thirty-six years old and an accomplished surfer, or at least he had been when he was younger, before his knees started sounding like a marching band every time he got into a crouch on his board. Now his passion for the sport was channeled into these tough fourteen-, fifteen-, and sixteen-year-old kids from Hilo, half of whom had already dropped out of school.

They came to this beach just two miles from downtown Hilo four afternoons a week, and for a few hours they were part of what islanders called the postcard Hawai'i, the one from the TV shows and the movies and the Chamber of Commerce brochures.

"What did I do wrong, Mac man?" fourteen-year-old Dennis said as he came out of the water.

"Well, to start with, that wasn't even your wave, it was Mele's," Mac said.

The two of them stood at the end of the exposed reef beach. Honoli'i was known as a good beach for local surfers, mostly because the strong currents kept swimmers away and the kids had the beach to themselves.

The last one out on the water was Lono.

Lono Akani, who had grown up without a father and whose mother was a housekeeper at the Hilo Hawaiian Hotel, was sixteen and Mac's favorite. He possessed a natural talent for this sport that Mac only wished he'd had at his age.

He watched Lono, into his crouch now on one of the Thurso Surf lancers Mac had purchased for each of them. Even from here Mac could see him smiling. Surely someday this boy would find fear in the ocean. Or fear would find him. Just not today as he flawlessly rode the inside curve of the wave.

Lono paddled in, put his board under his arm, and walked to where Mac waited on the beach. "Thank you," he said.

"For what?"

"For reminding me to always see the sets coming," the boy said. "It's why I was patient, *ya*, like you tell me to be, and waited for the wave I wanted."

Mac patted him on the shoulder. *"Keiki maika'i."*

Good boy.

They heard the rumble from the sky then. Heard it and felt the beach shaking underneath them, making them both stagger. The boy didn't know whether to look up or down. But John MacGregor understood what had happened—he knew a volcanic tremor, often associated with degassing, when he felt one. He looked up at the sky around the Big Island. All the kids were doing the same. It made Mac remember something one of his college professors had said about volcanoes and "the beauty of danger."

When the earth quieted, he felt the phone in his pocket buzzing. He answered and Jenny Kimura said, "Mac, thank God you picked up."

Jenny knew that when he was coaching his surfers, he didn't like to be disturbed with minor details from work. The press conference wasn't starting for another hour, so if Jenny was calling him, it wasn't about something minor.

"Jenny, what's wrong?"

"We've got degassing," she said.

No, not a minor detail at all.

"*Hōʻoʻopaʻoʻopa,*" he said, cursing like one of his surfer boys.

CHAPTER 2

Mac's eyes were drawn to the twin peaks again and again. They were like a magnet for people who lived here.

"Where?" he asked Jenny, feeling his chest tighten.

"At the summit."

"On my way," he said. He hung up and called out to the surfers, "Sorry, boys, gotta bounce."

Dennis whooped. "Bounce?" he said. "Never say that again, Mac man."

"Well," Mac said, "I need to haul ass and get back to work—how's that?"

"Rajah dat," Dennis yelled back at Mac, grinning. "You go grind, brah." All the boys occasionally slipped into pidgin; it was part of the teenage pose.

Mac walked toward his green truck, and Lono caught up to him, board still under his arm, wet hair slicked back. His eyes were serious, troubled.

"That wasn't Kīlauea, was it?" Lono said, referring to the smallest volcano on the island, keeping his voice low.

"No," MacGregor said. "How do you know that, Lono?"

"Kīlauea quakes—they're all shivery and quick, *ya*? Like a set of waves, one after another, then dying off. That was the big one, wasn't it?"

MacGregor nodded. "Yeah, kid," Mac said, "what we just heard came from the big one."

Lono leaned in and spoke in a low voice, even though no one was close enough to hear him: "Is there gonna be an eruption, Mac?"

MacGregor reached for the door of his truck. On it was a white circle with the letters HVO in the center and the words HAWAIIAN VOLCANO OBSERVATORY on the outside. But then he stopped. Lono looked up at him, eyes more troubled than before, a kid trying hard not to act scared but unable to carry it off. Lono said, "You can tell me if there is."

Mac didn't want to say anything that would scare him even more, but he didn't want to lie to him either. "Come with me to my press conference," he said, forcing a smile. "You might learn something."

"Learning all the time from you, Mac man," the boy said.

Of all the kids, Lono was the one Mac had most aggressively encouraged to become an intern at the observatory, recognizing from the start how fiercely bright this boy was despite average grades in school. He was always in search of approval from Mac that he'd never gotten from his father, who'd deserted him and his mother. It was why he'd done as much reading about volcanoes as he had and knew as much as he did.

But Lono glanced back at the other boys and shook his head. "Nah. You can call and tell me about it later. You gonna be here tomorrow?"

"Not sure right now."

"This is bad, isn't it?" Lono asked. "I can see you're worried even if you're not saying it."

"You live here, you always worry about the big one," Mac said, "whether it's your job or not."

MacGregor got in the truck, started the engine, and drove off toward the mountain, thinking about all the things he hadn't said to Lono Akani, primarily how worried he actually was—and for good reason. Mauna Loa was just days away from its most violent eruption in a century, and John MacGregor, the geologist who headed the Hawaiian Volcano Observatory, knew that and was about to announce it to the press. He'd always known this day would come, probably sooner rather than later. Now here it was.

Mac drove fast.

CHAPTER 3

Merrie Monarch Festival, Hilo, Hawai'i

Beneath the ribbed ceiling of Hilo's Edith Kanaka'ole Stadium, the Tahitian drums pounded so loudly that the audience of three thousand felt the vibration in their seats. The announcer cried the traditional greeting: "*Hookipa i nā malihini, hanohano wāhine e kāne,* distinguished ladies and gentlemen, please welcome our first *hālaus*. From Wailuku... Tawaaa Nuuuuui!" A burst of wild applause as the first troupe of women shimmied onto the stage.

This was the Hula Kahiko event during the weeklong Merrie Monarch Festival, the most important hula competition in the Hawaiian Islands and a significant contributor to the local economy of Hilo.

As was his custom, Henry "Tako" Takayama, the stocky chief of Civil Defense in Hilo, stood at the back during the event ceremonies in his trademark aloha shirt and ready smile, shaking hands and welcoming people from all over the Big Island to the annual performance of ancient-style dances by Hawaiian hula schools. Even though his was not an elected job, he had the air of the campaigner about him, like a man who was always running for something.

His upbeat manner had served him well during his thirty years as Civil Defense chief. In that time, he had guided the community through multiple crises, among them a tsunami that wiped out a Boy Scout troop camped on a beach, the destructive hurricanes of 2014 and 2018, the lava flows from Mauna Loa and Kīlauea that took out roads and destroyed houses, and the 2021 eruption on Kīlauea that created a lava lake in a summit crater.

But few people glimpsed the tough, combative personality behind the smile. Tako was an ambitious and even ruthless civil servant with sharp elbows, fiercely protective of his position. Anyone, politician or not, trying to get something done on the east side of Hawai'i had to go through him. No one could go around him.

In the stadium, Tako, chatting with state senator Ellen Kulani, felt the earthquake at once. So did Ellen. She looked at him and started to say something, but he cut her off with a grin and a wave of his hand.

"No big thing," he said.

But the tremor continued, and a low murmur ran through the crowd. A lot of the people here today had come from other islands and weren't used to Hilo's earthquakes, certainly not three in a row like this. The drumming stopped. The dancers dropped their arms.

Tako Takayama had fully expected earthquakes all during the festival. A week before, he'd had lunch with MacGregor, the *haole* head of the volcano lab. MacGregor had taken him to the Ohana Grill, a nice place, and told him that a big eruption from Mauna Loa was coming, the first since 2022.

"Bigger than 1984," MacGregor said. "Maybe the biggest in a hundred years."

"You have my attention," Tako said.

"HVO is constantly monitoring seismic imaging," MacGregor said. "The latest shows increased activity, including a large volume of magma moving into the volcano."

At that point it became Tako's job to schedule a press conference, which he did, for later today. He'd done it reluctantly, though. Tako thought that an eruption on the north side of the volcano wouldn't matter a damn to anybody in town. They'd have better sunsets for a while, the good life would go on, and all would once again be right in Tako's world.

But he was a cautious man who considered every possibility, starting with the ones that affected him. He didn't want this eruption to be a surprise or for people to think he had been caught off guard.

Eventually, being a practical man, Tako Takayama found a way to turn this situation to his advantage. He'd made a few calls.

But now he was in the middle of this awkward moment in the auditorium—drums silent, dancing stopped, audience restless. Tako nodded at Billy Malaki, the master of ceremonies, who was standing at the edge of the stage; Tako had already told him what to do.

Billy grabbed the microphone and said with a big laugh, "*Heya*, even Madame Pele gives her blessings to our festival! Her own hula! She got rhythm, *ya*!"

The audience laughed and burst into applause. Mentioning the Hawaiian goddess of volcanoes was exactly the right touch. The tremors subsided, and Tako relaxed and turned back with a smile to Ellen Kulani.

"So," he said, "where were we?"

He was acting as if he himself had ordered the tremors to stop, as if even nature obeyed Henry Takayama.

CHAPTER 4

Hawaiian Volcano Observatory, Hawai'i
Time to eruption: 114 hours

In the men's room, John MacGregor leaned over a sink, buttoned the collar of his blue work shirt, tugged up the black knit tie, and ran his fingers through his hair. Then he stepped back a few feet and looked at himself in the mirror. A dispirited face stared back at him. He tried to smile, but it looked painted on. John MacGregor sighed. He hated doing press conferences even more than he hated running budget meetings.

When he stepped out, he found Jenny Kimura waiting for him. "We're ready, Mac."

"They're all here?"

"Honolulu crew just arrived." Jenny was thirty-two, the scientist in charge of the lab. She was a Honolulu native with a PhD in earth and planetary sciences from Yale, well-spoken, very attractive. *Extremely* attractive, MacGregor thought. Ordinarily she did the press conferences, but she had flatly refused to do this one.

"Sounds like a Mac thing to me" was what she'd said.

"I'll pay you to make it a Jenny thing."

"You don't have enough money," she'd said.

Now MacGregor fiddled with the knot on his tie. "What do you think?" he asked her.

"I think you look like you're on your way to the electric chair," she said.

"That bad?"

"Worse."

"Does the tie make me look like a wimp? Maybe I should take it off."

"It's fine," Jenny said. "You just have to smile."

"You'll have to pay *me*," he said.

She laughed, took him gently by the elbow, and steered him into the changing room. They passed rows of lockers and a line of green heat-resistant jumpsuits that hung from wall hooks, each with a name over it.

"These shoes hurt," Mac said. He was wearing polished brown oxfords he'd thrown into the truck that morning. They squeaked as he walked, a shoe-store sound.

"You look very *akamai* for a *kama'āina*," she said. Sharp and with it—for someone who wasn't a native. "I've put the big map on an easel for you to refer to," she continued, back to business. "The rift zones are marked. The map's been simplified so it'll read clearly on TV."

"Okay."

"Will you want to use the seismic data?"

"Is it ready?"

"No, but I can get it for you in a blink. The past three months or all of last year?"

"Last year will be clearer."

"Okay. And satellite images?"

"Just MODIS."

"It's on poster board."

They came out of the changing room, crossed a hall, went down a corridor. Through the windows, Mac saw the other buildings of the Hawaiian Volcano Observatory, all connected by tin walkways. The HVO was built on the rim of the Kīlauea caldera, and even though no lava was flowing in the crater these days, there were always lots of tourists walking around, pointing down at the steam vents.

A fleet of TV trucks, most of them white with satellite dishes mounted on top, were in the parking lot. MacGregor sighed. It wasn't a happy sound.

"It'll be fine," Jenny said. "Just remember to smile. You have a very nice smile."

"Says who?"

"Says me, handsome."

"Are you flirting with me?"

She smiled. "Sure, go with that."

They walked through the data room, where computer techs were hunched over keyboards. He glanced up at the monitors suspended from the ceiling that showed views of various parts of the volcano. Sure enough, there was now steam coming out of the summit crater of Mauna Loa, proof that he'd been right, that he wasn't being alarmist—the eruption was only days away. He felt as if a ticking clock had begun its countdown.

As they went through the room, a chorus of voices wished him luck. Rick Ozaki's voice cut through the others: "Nice shoes, *ya!*"

Now Mac managed a real smile; he reached behind his back and flipped off his friend.

They went through another door and down the main hallway. In the room at the far end, he saw the podium and the map mounted on the easel. He heard the murmur of the waiting reporters.

"How many are there?" Mac asked just before they walked in.

"Everyone we expected," Jenny said. "Now go be your best self."

"I don't *have* a best self," he said.

Jenny moved to one side, and Mac stepped forward and felt the eyes of everyone in the room focus on him.

Tako Takayama had told him that when Mauna Loa erupted in December of 1935, George Patton, then a lieutenant colonel in the U.S. Army Air Corps, had been part of the effort to divert the lava flow. At this moment Mac felt like that kind of heat was rushing toward him.

Yeah, he told himself, *that's me, Old Blood and Guts MacGregor.*

CHAPTER 5

John MacGregor knew who he was and what his strengths were. Public speaking was not one of them. He cleared his throat and nervously tapped the microphone.

"Good afternoon. I'm John MacGregor, scientist in charge of the Hawaiian Volcano Observatory. Thank you all for coming today."

He turned to the map. "As you know, this observatory monitors six volcanoes—the undersea volcano Kama'ehuakanaloa, formerly Lō'ihi; Haleakalā, on Maui; plus four on the Big Island of Hawai'i, including the two active volcanoes, Kīlauea, a relatively small volcano that has been continuously active for over forty years, and Mauna Loa, the largest volcano in the world, which erupted in 2022 but has not had a major eruption since 1984."

On the map, Kīlauea was a small crater alongside the laboratory building. Mauna Loa looked like a huge dome; its flanks occupied half the island.

Mac took a deep breath and exhaled. The microphone picked up the sound.

"Today," MacGregor said, "I am announcing an imminent eruption of Mauna Loa."

The photographers' strobe lights were like flashes of lightning. MacGregor blinked away the white spots in front of his eyes, cleared his throat again, and kept going. He'd probably only imagined that the television lights had just gotten brighter.

"We expect this to be a fairly large eruption," he said, "and we expect that it will come within the next two weeks, perhaps much sooner than that."

He held up a hand to quiet the suddenly elevated noise level from the audience and pivoted toward Jenny, who put up the seismic data on an easel to his left. The image, which plotted the epicenters of all the earthquakes on the island during the last year, showed dark clusters around the summit.

"According to the data we have gathered and analyzed, this eruption will most likely occur at the summit caldera," MacGregor continued, "which means that the city of Hilo should not be affected. Now I'm happy to take any questions you have."

The hands went up. Mac didn't do a lot of major press conferences, but he knew the rules of the road, one of which was that local news always got the first question.

He pointed to Marsha Keilani, the reporter from KHON in Hilo. "Mac, you said a 'fairly large eruption.' Just how large, exactly?" She smiled. "Asking for some friends."

"We expect it to be at least as large as the 1984 eruption that produced half a billion cubic meters of lava and covered sixteen square miles in three weeks," he said. "In fact, this eruption may be much larger, perhaps as large as the eruption of 1950. We just don't know at this point."

"But you obviously have an idea about timing or we wouldn't be here," she said. "So *are* we talking about two weeks? Or sooner?"

"Could be sooner, yes. We've been combing through all the data, but there's still no way to predict the exact timing of an eruption." He shrugged. "We're just not sure."

Keo Hokulani from the *Honolulu Star-Advertiser* was next. "Dr. MacGregor, aren't you hedging a little? You have very sophisticated equipment here. You're quite sure of the size and timing, aren't you?" Keo knew that because he'd toured the HVO a few months earlier. He'd seen all the latest computer models and projections and knew his stuff.

"As you know, Keo, Mauna Loa is one of the most intensely studied volcanoes in the world. We have tiltmeters and seismometers all over it, drones flying thermal cameras, satellite data in thirty-six frequencies, radar, and visible- and infrared-light sensors." He shrugged and grinned. "Having said that, yeah, I am hedging." They all laughed. "Volcanoes are a little—or a lot—like wild animals. It's difficult and dangerous to predict how they'll behave."

Wendy Watanabe from one of the Honolulu TV stations raised a hand.

"In the 1984 eruption," she said, "lava came quite close to Hilo, and people felt threatened. So are you saying that this time there is no danger to Hilo?"

"That's correct," MacGregor said. "The lava in '84 came within four miles of Hilo, but the main lava flows were east. As I said, this time we expect most of the lava to flow away from Hilo." He turned and pointed at the map, feeling like a weatherman on the local news. "This means it will flow down the north slope into the center of the island, the saddle between Mauna Loa and Mauna Kea. This is a big and—fortunately—largely uninhabited area. Mauna Kea Science Reserve has several observatories at twelve thousand feet, and the army runs a large training area over there, at six thousand feet, but that's all. So I want to reiterate: This eruption will not threaten Hilo residents."

Wendy Watanabe put up her hand again. "At what point will HVO raise the volcano alert level?"

"While Mauna Loa is at elevated unrest, the level remains at advisory/yellow," MacGregor said. "We remain focused on the northeast rift zone."

A reporter he didn't recognize asked, "Will Mauna Kea erupt as well?"

"No. Mauna Kea is dormant. It hasn't erupted for about four thousand years. As you know, the Big Island has five volcanoes, but only two are currently active."

Standing by his side, Jenny Kimura gave a quiet sigh of relief and smiled. It was going as well as she could have hoped. The reporters weren't being sensationalistic, and Mac seemed comfortable, sure of himself and his information. He was speaking effortlessly, sliding past the issues they didn't want to cover. She thought he'd handled questions about the size of the eruption particularly well.

Mac had managed to stay on point and not stray into the weeds like he sometimes did. Jenny knew her chief's tendencies. Before coming to Hawai'i, John MacGregor had been a member of the United States Geological Survey advisory team, which was sent all over the planet to wherever there was an impending eruption. Starting in his student days, he'd been present at all the famous ones. MacGregor had been at Eyjafjallajökull and Mount Merapi in 2010, Puyehue-Cordón Caulle in 2011, Anak Krakatau in 2018, and Hunga Tonga-Hunga Ha'apai in 2022. And he had seen very bad things. All because, as he put it, "People waited too long, which means until it was too late."

MacGregor's experiences had left him with a blunt, chin-out, do-it-now attitude and a willingness to plan for worst-case scenarios. He was a cautious scientist but a quick, decisive administrator who tended to act first and worry about consequences later. He was that sure of himself.

Mac was extremely well respected at HVO, but sometimes Jenny was left to pick up the pieces after his shotgun decisions. She couldn't remember how many times she had said, "Uh, well…" after hearing one of his spontaneous ideas.

But no one could argue that he wasn't generous or didn't care about people. He'd been a troubled kid himself, which was why he'd become a surfing coach for local troubled kids. While coaching the boys, he tried to motivate some of them to work harder at school and others to stay in school; he'd even gotten a few of them into the intern program at HVO. And he always followed their careers after they left HVO for various universities.

And then there was his unmatched experience. Everybody else on the HVO staff had seen these famous eruptions on videotape. MacGregor had been there. If he was acting this quickly and decisively now, he had his reasons. He'd been there. He knew.

He also knew enough not to explain in detail that HVO was tracking the biggest eruption in a century—that would only have caused a panic, no matter which side of the volcano was going to blow.

There was one other thing that Mac knew and Jenny knew but the media didn't.

John MacGregor was lying his ass off.

He knew exactly when the eruption was coming, and it wasn't two weeks or even one.

Five days.

And counting.

CHAPTER 6

The press conference was winding down.

MacGregor had felt more relaxed the longer it had gone, knowing he was giving them more information than they needed. He explained now that the Hawaiian Islands were on a hot spot built by a mantle plume—a hole in the ocean floor, through which magma flowed intermittently. The magma cooled as it rose, making a dome of lava that slowly grew until it broke the surface of the ocean as an island. As each island was built up, the shifting of the Pacific Plate moved it north and west, leaving behind the hot spot, where a new island began forming.

This hot spot had produced a chain of islands stretching half-way across the Pacific Ocean. The Hawaiian Islands were merely the end of the chain. Once their volcanism stopped, the islands slowly eroded away, shrinking in size. Of the Hawaiian Islands, Niʻihau and Kauaʻi were the oldest and smallest, then Oʻahu, Maui, and Hawaiʻi.

John MacGregor was in his personal comfort zone now. The people in front of him might not feel back on firm footing after the quakes. But he was.

"In geological terms," MacGregor said, "the island of Hawaiʻi is brand-new. It's one of the few landmasses on our planet that is younger than mankind itself. Three million years ago, when small apes began to stand upright on the African plains, the island of Hawai'i did not exist. It was not until a million years ago, when *Homo habilis*, the descendants of the early ape-men, were living in crude shelters and starting to use stone tools, that the Hawaiian seas began to boil, revealing the presence of undersea volcanoes. Since that time, five different volcanoes have poured out enough lava to create an island above the surface of the ocean."

He paused, looking out at the audience. A lot of this was dense, he knew, but he still had their attention, although probably not for much longer.

He continued. "The eruptive pattern of the five volcanoes on the island of Hawai'i is the same pattern as the entire island chain." Of the five volcanoes, the one farthest north, Kohala, was extinct and badly eroded. It hadn't erupted for 460,000 years. Next northward was Mauna Kea, which hadn't erupted for 4,500 years. Third was Hualālai, which hadn't erupted in over 200 years, not since Jefferson was president. (Mac didn't bother telling them that Hualālai was the fourth-most-dangerous volcano in America. The tourists at Kona didn't need to hear that.) And then the two active volcanoes, Mauna Loa and Kīlauea.

And finally, he explained, in the ocean thirty miles to the south, the volcano Kama'ehuakanaloa, formerly Lō'ihi, was building a new island less than a mile underwater.

He grinned. "The midterm exam will be at the end of the week," he said. He glanced at his watch. "Anything else?"

He wanted to get out of here, but he had been taught not to leave if there were any hands still in the air.

"What are the chances this eruption will be violent?" another reporter he didn't recognize, an older man, asked.

"Very small. The last explosive eruption was in prehistoric times."

"What's the risk of avalanches to Hilo?"

"None."

"Hasn't lava reached Hilo in the past?"

"Yes, but thousands of years ago. The city of Hilo is actually built on old lava deposits."

"If lava flows toward Hilo, what can be done to stop it?" the older reporter asked, staying with Mac.

"We don't think it will flow that way. We think it will flow north toward Mauna Kea."

"Yes, I get that. But can flowing lava be stopped?"

MacGregor hesitated. He wanted to get the hell off the stage without alarming them, but it was a fair question, one that deserved an honest answer.

"No one has ever succeeded in stopping it," he said. "In the past, people on Hawai'i have tried bombing to divert the flows, bulldozing dikes to divert the flows, and spraying seawater on the lava to cool it and divert the flows. None of those tactics worked."

He glanced at Jenny, who came forward, nearly running, and said, "Are there any specific questions about this coming eruption?" She scanned the audience. "No? Then our thanks to Dr. MacGregor and thank you very much for being here. Any other questions, don't hesitate to call. Our numbers are on the press release."

She held up a hand as the reporters began to stir. "Now, I have a few announcements for the TV people. Once the eruption begins, you'll want B-roll and flyovers. Let me explain how it's going to work. If the eruption is large, flyovers will be forbidden because volcanic ash shuts down airplane engines. However, we'll send up three helicopter flights a day, and that tape will be provided to you. Filming from the ground is allowed during the eruption as long as you do it from designated safe points. If you want to film from another area, we'll send a geologist out with you. Don't go by yourself. And don't assume you can go to the same place you went yesterday because conditions change hourly. Please take these rules seriously, because in every past eruption we've had newspeople killed and we'd like to avoid that this time."

MacGregor watched as the reporters and camerapeople came forward to the edge of the stage and clustered in front of Jenny. He managed to slip quietly away.

He pulled off his tie as he went.

CHAPTER 7

Back in the data room, MacGregor was greeted with complete silence; it was almost as if everyone were making a concerted effort to ignore him.

Kenny Wong, the lead programmer, was busy typing and did not look up. Rick Ozaki, the seismologist, was busy enlarging the data on his screen. Pia Wilson, the woman in charge of the volcano alert levels, was busy working at the back of one of her monitors. MacGregor stood there a moment, waiting. He hadn't expected a standing ovation but he also hadn't expected to hear nothing but the tapping of keys.

He walked over to Kenny Wong, sat down, pushed Kenny's bag of potato chips and Diet Coke cans to one side, put his arms on the table, and said, "Well?"

"Nothing." Kenny shook his head, kept typing.

"There has to be something."

"There's not."

"Kenny..."

Kenny looked up at him with hard eyes. "Okay, here's something, Mac: Why didn't you tell them?"

"Tell them what?"

"That it's going to be the biggest damn eruption in a century."

"C'mon, man, you know we talked about this," MacGregor said. "They're reporters, and we both know they'd blow it out of proportion—they'd be the ones erupting. And I don't want to make a prediction like that and have it be wrong."

"But you know it won't be wrong," Kenny said. He was wounded and angry, and he made no effort to edit his words for his boss. "There's no *way* it could be wrong. The computer models have been consistent for thirty-seven straight weeks. *You* come on, Mac. Thirty-seven frigging weeks. That's longer than the baseball season."

"Kenny," MacGregor said. "In 2004, the head of HVO predicted an eruption of Mauna Loa that never happened. Don't you think his programmers swore to him that it was a sure thing?"

"I wouldn't know," Kenny said. "I wasn't even born yet."

"Yeah, you were," Mac corrected him. "And please stop being so dramatic."

Their lead programmer was twenty-three years old. Brilliant, frequently childish, given to fits of pique, particularly when he had been up all night. Which was most of the time.

Across the room, Rick called out, "Mac, you might want to look at this." The seismologist—thirty, bearded, heavyset, wearing jeans and a black Hirano Store T-shirt—was slow-moving and thoughtful, the opposite of the hotheaded Kenny Wong. Rick pushed his glasses farther up the bridge of his nose as MacGregor came over.

"What've you got?"

"This is the summarized seismic output for last month, filtered for artifact noise." The screen showed a dense pattern of squiggles, the data transmitted by the seismometers positioned around the island.

"So?" MacGregor shrugged. "These are typical tremor

swarms, Rick. High frequency, low amplitude, long duration. We have them all the time now. What am I missing here?"

"Well, I've been doing second order on this," Rick said, typing as he spoke. "The hypocenters cluster around the caldera and north slope. The fit to data is perfect. Like, *perfect*. So I think there's an opportunity that we ought to talk about—"

They were interrupted by a loud thumping sound that built rapidly, shaking the floor of the laboratory and rattling the glass. A helicopter appeared in the window, frighteningly close and low; it rushed past them and swooped down into the caldera.

"Sweet Jesus!" Kenny Wong yelled, running to the window to get a better look. "Who is that asshole?"

"Get the tail number," MacGregor snapped, "and call Hilo ASAP. Whoever that idiot is, he's going to give one of the tourists a haircut. Damn!" He went to the window and watched as the helicopter dropped low and thumped its way across the smoking plain of the caldera. The pilot couldn't be more than twenty feet above the ground.

Beside Mac, Kenny Wong watched through binoculars. "It's Paradise Helicopters," he said, sounding puzzled. Paradise Helicopters was a reputable operation based in Hilo. Their pilots ferried tourists over the volcanic fields and up the coast to Kohala to look at the waterfalls.

MacGregor shook his head. "They know there's a fifteen-hundred-foot limit everywhere in the park. What the *hell* are they doing?"

The helicopter swung back and slowly circled the far edge of the caldera, nearly brushing the smoking vertical walls.

Pia cupped her hand over the phone. "I got Paradise Helicopters. They say they're not flying. They leased that one to Jake."

"Is there any news at the moment I might like?" Mac said.

"With Jake at the controls, there is no good news," Kenny said.

Jake Rogers was an ex-navy pilot known for breaking the rules. After two FAA warnings in a year, he had been fired by his tour company, and now he spent most of his time in a seedy bar in Hilo. "Apparently Jake's got a cameraman from CBS with him, some stringer from Hilo," Pia said. "The guy's pushing for exclusive footage of the new eruption."

"Well, there's no eruption *in there*," MacGregor said, staring at the caldera. The Kīlauea caldera—what most people called the crater—had been a tourist attraction in Hawai'i since the nineteenth century; Mark Twain, among other notables, had stood looking down into the huge smoking pit. Today there was steam and sulfur and other evidence of volcanic activity, but there hadn't been an actual eruption from the caldera in twenty years. All the recent lava flows from Kīlauea had come from the volcano's flanks, miles to the south.

The helicopter rose out of the caldera, scattering tourists at the railing, roared above the observatory, and made a broad circle. Then it *thump-thump-thump*ed off to the east.

"Now what?" Rick asked the room.

"Looks like he's going to the rift zone," Kenny said. "And what good can come of that?"

"None," MacGregor said, still standing at the window.

Jenny Kimura came in. "Who is that guy? Is somebody calling Hilo?"

MacGregor turned to her. "Are the reporters still here?"

"No, they left a few minutes ago."

"Didn't I make it clear the eruption hasn't started yet?"

"I thought you made that abundantly clear, yes."

"Mac, this guy's a stringer," Rick said. "He wasn't at the press conference. He's trying to get ahead in the world. You know what they say: Don't worry about being right, just being first."

"Hey, Mac? You're not going to believe this." Pia Wilson, at the main video panel, flicked on all the remote monitors to show the eastern flank of Kīlauea. "The pilot just flew into the eastern lake at the summit of Kīlauea."

"He *what?*"

Pia shrugged. "See for yourself."

MacGregor sat down in front of the monitors. Four miles away, the black cinder cone of Puʻuʻōʻō—the Hawaiian name meant "Hill of the Digging Stick"—rose three hundred feet high on the east flank. That cone had been a center of volcanic activity since it erupted in 1983, spitting a fountain of lava two thousand feet into the air. The eruption continued all year, producing enormous quantities of lava that flowed for eight miles down to the ocean. Along the way, it had buried the entire town of Kalapana, destroyed two hundred houses, and filled in a large bay at Kaimūī, where the lava poured steaming into the sea. The activity from Puʻuʻōʻō went on for thirty-five years—one of the longest continuous volcanic eruptions in recorded history—ending only when the crater collapsed in 2018.

Tourist helicopters scoured the area looking for a new place to take pictures, and pilots discovered a lake that had opened to the east of the collapsed crater. Hot lava bubbled and slapped in incandescent waves against the sides of a smaller cone. Occasionally the lava would fountain fifty feet into the air above the glowing surface. But the crater containing the eastern lake was only about a hundred yards in diameter—much too narrow to descend into.

Helicopters never went inside it.

Until now.

"What the hell?" Jenny said.

Mac said, "That *is* hell."

CHAPTER 8

MacGregor kept staring at the image on the video screen. "Where's this feed from?"

"Camera's on the rim, pointing down."

Mac could see the helicopter hovering right above the lava lake. The cameraman was clearly visible through an open door on the port side, camera on his shoulder. The idiot was leaning out, filming the lava.

It was like some daredevil movie scene, complete with special effects, Mac thought. Except what they were watching was real.

"They're both crazy," he said. "With all the thermals around there—"

"If that thing fountains, they'll be fried *pūpūs*."

"Get 'em the hell out of there," MacGregor said. "Who's on the radio?"

Across the room, Jenny put her hand over the phone and said, "Hilo is talking to them. They say they're leaving now."

"Yeah? Then why aren't they moving?"

"They say they are, Mac. All I got."

MacGregor said, "Do we know gas levels down in there?" Near the lava lake, there would be high concentrations of sulfur dioxide and carbon monoxide. MacGregor squinted at his monitor. "Can you see if the pilot's got oxygen? 'Cause the cameraman sure doesn't. Both these idiots could pass out if they stay there."

"Or the engine could quit," Kenny said. He shook his head. "Helicopter engines need air. And there's not a lot of air down there."

Jenny said, "They're leaving now, Mac."

As they watched, the helicopter began to rise. They saw the cameraman turn and raise an angry fist at Jake Rogers. Clearly he didn't want to leave.

That meant Rogers's passenger was even more reckless than he was.

"Go," MacGregor said to the screen as if Jake Rogers could hear him. "You've been lucky, Jake. *Just go.*"

The helicopter rose faster. The cameraman slammed the door angrily. The helicopter began to turn as it reached the crater rim.

"Now we'll see if they make it through the thermals," MacGregor said.

Suddenly there was a bright flash of light, and the helicopter swung and seemed to flip onto its side. It spun laterally across the interior and slammed into the far wall of the crater, raising a tremendous cloud of ash that obscured their view.

In silence, they watched as the dust slowly cleared. They saw the helicopter on its side, about two hundred feet below the rim, resting precariously at the edge of a deep shelf below the crater wall, a rocky incline that sloped down to the lava lake.

"Somebody get on the radio," Mac said, "and see if the dumb bastards are alive."

Everyone in the room continued to stare at the monitors.

Nothing happened right away; it was as if time had somehow stopped moving when the helicopter did. Then, as they watched, a few small boulders beneath the helicopter began to trickle down. The boulders splashed into the lava lake and disappeared below the molten surface.

MacGregor said, in a voice no louder than a whisper, "It just keeps getting worse."

More rocks clattered down the sloping crater wall, then more—larger rocks now—and then it became a landslide. The helicopter shifted and began to glide down with the rocks toward the hot lava.

They all watched in horror as the helicopter continued its downward slide. Dust and steam obscured their view for a moment, and when it blew away, they could see the helicopter lying on its side, rotor blades bent against the rock, skids facing outward, about fifty feet above the lava.

Kenny said, "That's scree. I don't know how long it'll hold."

MacGregor nodded. Most of the crater was composed of ejecta from the volcano, pumice-like rocks and pebbles that were crumbly and treacherous underfoot, ready to collapse at any moment. Sooner or later the helicopter would fall the rest of the way into the lava lake. Probably within minutes, and certainly within hours.

From across the room, Jenny said, "Mac? Hilo still has contact. They're both alive. The cameraman's hurt, but they're alive."

MacGregor shook his head. "And what exactly are we supposed to do about that?"

No one spoke, but they were all looking at him. He felt as if he were back at the press conference, about to step up to the microphone.

Kenny said, "It's their own damn fault."

"Not exactly breaking news," MacGregor said, bending over to unlace his shoes.

Across the room, Jenny said, "No, it is not."

"How much daylight do we have left?" MacGregor asked her.

"An hour and a half at most."

"Not enough."

"Mac, we can call another helicopter, they can drop a line, pull 'em out."

Pia said, "It'd be suicide for somebody else to go in there, Mac."

"Call Bill, tell him to start his engine," Mac said. "Call Hilo, tell them to close the area to all other aircraft. Call Kona, tell 'em the same thing. Meantime I need a pack and a rig and somebody to stand safety. You decide who. I'm out of here in five, as soon as I get my boots back on."

"Wait," Pia said, incredulous. "Out of here in five to do what, exactly?"

"Pull the dumb bastards out," MacGregor said.

CHAPTER 9

Summit of Kīlauea, Hawaiʻi

The red helicopter lifted off the HVO helipad and headed south. Directly in front of them, four miles away, they saw the black cone of Puʻuʻōʻō, its thick fume cloud rising into the air.

He rechecked his equipment in his front seat, making sure he had everything. Jenny Kimura and Tim Kapaana were in the rear. Tim was the biggest of their field techs, a former semipro linebacker.

Over the headphones, Jenny said, "Mac? Hilo is saying they can get a Dolphin recovery helicopter over from Coast Guard Station Maui in thirty minutes, and it can perform the rescue. You don't have to do this."

MacGregor turned to Bill Kamoku, their pilot, a cautious, careful man. "Bill?"

The pilot shook his head. "It's an hour, minimum, for them to get here."

"By then it'll be almost dark," Mac said.

"Right."

"And they can't rescue in the damn dark."

"Hell, I don't think they can rescue in daylight, Mac," Bill said. "You get that big Dolphin thumping over the narrow crater, you're going to get landslides, and then it's game over."

Jenny said, "But, Mac—"

He turned to her. "Let's not kid ourselves. We wait, they die."

He stared out of the bubble. They were over the rift zone now, following a line of smoking cracks and small cinder cones in the lava fields. The collapsed crater of Puʻuʻōʻō was a mile ahead and just beyond it was the eastern lake.

Bill said, "Where do you want to put down?"

"South side is best."

They couldn't land too near the crater rim because it was filled with cracks and completely unstable. Both Mac and Bill knew that.

"Why do you think Jake went down there?" Mac asked.

Bill turned, his eyes hidden behind the black helmet's faceplate. "Money. I think he needed money, Mac. And there's one other reason."

"What's that?"

"He's Jake."

The helicopter set down about twenty yards from the crater rim. Immediately, the helicopter's bubble clouded over with steam from nearby vents. MacGregor opened his door and felt air both wet and burning on his face.

"Can't stay here, Mac," Bill said. "I've got to move downslope."

"Go ahead," Mac said, then pulled off his headset and stepped down onto the gray-black lava without hesitation, ducking his head beneath the spinning rotor blades.

* * *

Jenny Kimura could hear the pinging and cracking of the lava as its surface solidified, the rumbling of new lava breaking freshly formed rock. She saw two glowing red vents on the outside of the crater wall, one to the west, one to the north. The downed helicopter was at the opposite side of them, on a shelf above the lake. But its position was even more precarious now. The lava could spin at any moment, meaning the craft was perhaps seconds away from sliding down into the lava.

Mac had already zipped up his green jumpsuit. He cinched the harness tighter around his waist and legs. He could loosen it when he got down there and put it around another person.

MacGregor handed the ends of the rope to Tim.

"Please let me do this," Tim said.

"No." MacGregor hung one gas mask around his neck, placed two others in his backpack. "You can hold me from up here. I can't hold you."

He adjusted the radio headset over his ears, pulled the microphone alongside his cheek. Jenny had put on her own headset and clipped the transmitter to her belt, and she heard MacGregor say, "Here we go."

Tim moved several paces back from the rim and braced himself. The rope immediately tightened in his hands as MacGregor went over the side.

Jenny was sick with anxiety, though she was trying not to show it. There had been two fatalities that she knew of inside Puʻuʻōʻō crater. The first was in 2012, a daredevil American mountain climber who entered without authorization, was overcome by fumes, and tumbled into the lava lake. The second was in 2018, a stubborn German volcanologist who'd insisted on rappelling down to collect gas samples even as the crater was collapsing; he was caught in a gushing lava fountain—goodbye. Since then, no one else had been fool enough to enter the crater of the eastern lake.

Jenny adjusted her headset. Through the earphones, she heard the crackle of voices from Hilo control, then the sound of coughing coming from the helicopter below.

Jenny watched as Mac descended slowly and carefully into the crater.

CHAPTER 10

The lava lake was nearly circular, its black crust broken by streaks of brighter and more incandescent red. Steam issued from at least a dozen vents in the rocks. The walls were sheer, the footing uncertain; Mac stumbled and slid as he went down.

Suddenly his extended leg hit a solid surface, like he was a base runner sliding into second.

Although he was only a few feet below the rim, he could feel the searing heat from the lake. The air shimmered unsteadily in the convection of rising currents. Between that and the sulfurous odors swirling from the crater, he began to feel slightly nauseated.

Inside his heat-resistant jumpsuit, he was sweating. Thin Mylar-foam insulation sewn between layers of Gore-Tex kept sweat off the skin, because if the temperature went up suddenly, the sweat would turn to steam and scald his body, meaning almost certain death. Several scientists had died that way, most recently his friend Jim Robbins at the Anak Krakatau volcano in Indonesia.

Mac lost his balance again and slid several yards in the hot dust, then quickly scrambled to his feet.

On the radio Jenny said: "You all right?"

"Piece of cake."

He knew, because it was his business to know these things, that sixty-seven scientists around the world had died working within a thousand yards of volcano summits. Three of them, along with forty nonscientists, had been burned to death in an instant at the Unzen volcano in Japan in 1991. That was the single worst accident in recent history. And there had been other incidents. Six scientists had died at Cotopaxi in Ecuador when the volcano suddenly exploded while they were taking measurements.

He pushed those thoughts out of his head and kept going, descending along the sheer wall. The helicopter was off to his right, a hundred yards or so away. MacGregor was approaching it from the side so that his own descent would not cause another slide.

On his radio he heard groaning and then a crackling transmission from the pilot, his words garbled.

"Mac." Jenny again.

"I'm here."

"Did you copy that?"

"No."

"It's the pilot." She paused. "He's worried that they might be starting to leak fuel."

"Then I need to pick up the pace."

"You know that's not safe!"

"I was afraid you'd say something like that."

The helicopter hung only fifty yards above the lava lake. Below the crust, the glowing lava was around 1800 degrees Fahrenheit, and that was at the low end. The only good news was that if the helicopter had started to leak fuel, it would have blown up already.

"Mac," Jenny said, "the Dolphin copter is on the way from Wailuku. You sure you don't want to reconsider this?"

"I'm sure."

Sometimes wrong, never in doubt, they said about Mac back at HVO.

Through the shifting plumes of steam, Mac could see deep scratches and dents on the helicopter. The tail rotor had torn free.

"Mac, I'm patching you to the pilot."

"Okay."

There was another crackle. Through his headset, Mac heard more groaning. He said, "Hey, Jake. How you looking?"

Jake coughed. "Truth, brah? Been better."

"Try cruise, *ya*?" Mac said. Meaning *Take it easy.*

Mac heard something between a cough and a laugh.

"Not like I have much choice," Jake Rogers said. "You feeling me on that?"

CHAPTER 11

Jake Rogers, on his side and in a tremendous amount of pain, looked straight down at the lava lake and heard the hissing of the gas escaping from the glowing cracks. He saw spatters of lava, like glowing pancake batter, thrown up on the sides of the crater.

Jake didn't think his leg was broken. The cameraman—Glenn something—was in worse shape, moaning in the back seat that his shoulder was dislocated. He rocked in pain, which rocked the helicopter.

Jake swore at him again and told him to stop before he killed them both, but the guy just kept moaning and rocking like a baby.

Over the radio, MacGregor said, "How's the cameraman?"

"*Pau*, Mac." Finished. "Busted shoulder. Acting real funny *kine*."

From the back, the cameraman said, "Who're you talking to?"

"There's a guy coming down for us."

"Great!" the cameraman cried; he lurched across the back seat to look out the window, and the sudden shift of weight sent the copter sliding downward again, throwing Jake's head against the Plexiglas bubble.

The cameraman began to scream.

Only twenty yards away now, MacGregor watched helplessly as the helicopter began a rumbling descent. He heard yelling from inside, and it must have been the cameraman, because Jake Rogers swore at the guy and told him to shut the hell up.

The helicopter slid another twenty feet toward the lava, then miraculously stopped again. The struts were still facing outward; the twisted rotors were buried in the scree. The passenger door was still facing upward.

"Mac?" said Jake. "You still there?"

Cautiously, MacGregor moved forward along the slope. "Yeah, I'm here. Lucky for you I got nowhere else to be."

"This guy's a piece of work, Mac."

"Look who's talking." Mac heard the cameraman moaning in pain. "Can you move, Jake?" Mac asked.

He was close enough to the copter that he could see Rogers.

"Yeah, I think so."

MacGregor gestured with a Spark gas mask, offering it to Jake. Rogers shook his head.

"You need to unlock the passenger door for me," MacGregor said. "Don't open it, just unlock it."

Jake raised himself up and fumbled with the latch. Mac heard a metallic click. Then another. Jake was frowning with effort, struggling.

"Son of a *bitch*! It's jammed."

"I guess we know what's next," Mac said.

CHAPTER 12

Up at the rim, Jenny Kimura, looking through her binoculars, saw Mac suddenly step back and then begin moving around to the front of the copter.

She said, "Mac, what are you *doing*?"

"Just trying to get the toolbox."

"That's crazy!"

"I need it."

Jenny turned to Tim. "Where's the toolbox on those things?"

"Port side." He shook his head. "Or in this case, the lava side."

"I knew it!" Jenny said. "Mac's going *underneath* the goddamn helicopter!"

Mac eased himself beneath the helicopter, just forty yards above the lava lake. He could see the red glow reflected in the metal over his head. He carefully pulled the ring on the panel, not wanting to jar the helicopter further, and it opened.

The metal toolbox was strapped firmly inside.

He released the canvas buckles and yanked the box toward

him, but it had shifted slightly in the crash and was stuck in there. He tried to dislodge it without disturbing the helicopter.

"*Come... on,*" he said, pulling harder.

He was running out of time, but he needed this box.

"*Come on, you piece of—*"

The box came loose.

Jenny turned to Tim, covered her microphone, and said, "How long has he been down there?"

"Eighteen minutes."

"He's not wearing his mask. That may help him communicate clearly, but it's going to get to him soon. We both know that."

She meant the sulfur dioxide gas, which was concentrated near the lake. Sulfur dioxide combined with the layer of water on the surface of the lungs to form sulfuric acid. It was a hazard for anyone working around volcanoes.

"Mac?" she said. "Did you put your mask on?"

He didn't answer.

"Mac. *Talk to me.*"

"Kind of busy at the moment," he answered finally.

She looked through the binoculars, saw that Mac was moving again. He was above the helicopter now, about to lean down on the bubble. She couldn't see his face but saw straps across the back of his head, so at least he was wearing the mask.

She saw him drop to his knees and crawl gingerly onto the bubble.

Crouched down, he opened the box, took out what looked to be a forged pry bar, and began to work on the door. He managed to open the metal lip six inches on either side of the lock.

Through the plastic, Jake looked up at him, a very tough guy unable to hide the fear and pain he was clearly feeling. The bubble was beginning to cloud over as the sulfuric acid in the air etched the plastic.

Mac picked up a short crowbar and started trying to pry open the door. He saw Jake pushing up on the Plexiglas from inside. He heard the cameraman whimpering. MacGregor strained against the crowbar, using all the leverage he had, until, with a metallic *whang*, the door sprang open wide and clanged hard against the side panel. MacGregor held his breath, praying that the helicopter wouldn't begin to slide again.

It didn't.

Jake Rogers stuck his head up through the open door. "I owe you, brah."

"Yeah, brah, you do." MacGregor reached out a hand, and the pilot grabbed it and clambered onto the bubble. Once he was out, MacGregor saw that his left pants leg was soaked in blood; it was smeared all over the Plexiglas dome.

MacGregor asked, "Can you walk?"

"Up there?" Jake pointed to the rim above. "Bet your ass."

Mac unclipped one of the ropes and handed it to him. Jake clipped it to the belt at his waist. Mac bent over the door and looked inside.

In the back, the photographer was huddled in a ball at the far side of the helicopter. Still whimpering. A *haole* guy, late twenties, skinny, his face the color of paste.

"He got a name?" Mac asked Jake.

"Glenn." Jake was already starting up the slope.

"Glenn," MacGregor said. "Look at me."

The cameraman looked up at him with vacant eyes.

"I want you to stand up," MacGregor said, "and take my hand."

The cameraman started to stand, but as he did, the lava lake below began to burble, and a small fountain spit upward with a hiss. The cameraman collapsed back down and started to cry.

Over the headset, Mac heard Jenny say, "Mac? You've now been down twenty-six minutes. You know better than anyone what that means. Glenn and Jake already have pulmonary restriction. You've got to get out of there before you do."

"I got this," MacGregor said, looking at the lake through the bubble. Everything he'd learned from everywhere he'd been in the world of volcanoes told him he wasn't fine at all.

"We're gonna die here!" Glenn yelled, tears streaming down his cheeks.

"Just hang on," Mac barked.

Then he climbed down into the helicopter.

CHAPTER 13

Jenny Kimura shivered as she studied Mac through the binoculars, trying to will him out of the copter and back up to safety. The connection she had always felt between them—though they'd never discussed it—was more powerful than ever.

"What's he doing now?" Tim said, holding the ropes.

"He went all the way inside."

"He *what*?"

"He went inside the damn helicopter," she said, shaking her head.

"*Why?*"

"You know why," Jenny said. "Because he couldn't *not* go in."

"A cowboy to the end," Tim said.

"If it's all the same to you," she said, "let's not talk about the end."

The helicopter slowly rotated on its axis. Mac gripped the seat, trying to keep his balance, watching helplessly as the world outside spun, the Plexiglas bubble closer than ever to the glowing surface.

Then it stopped, and the Plexiglas started to blister and melt, and smoke filled the interior of the helicopter.

MacGregor reached out with the Spark gas mask. "Put this on," he said.

"*I can't!*" the cameraman said. "I'm afraid I'm gonna be sick!"

No point in arguing with him; MacGregor just had to get him out of here, with or without the mask. They were minutes away from the helicopter exploding.

"Grab my hand, for Chrissake," Mac said to the cameraman. "*Now.*"

In the main room at HVO, Rick Ozaki watched the monitor and said, "He takes more chances since Linda left with the boys."

"Oh, hell," Pia said, "he's always taken chances. Taking chances is part of his damned genetic code."

"I hear that's why Linda finally left him."

"Nah, man, she left him because of her law practice."

Rick said, "Seriously? You want to talk about Mac's marriage *now*?"

"Sorry."

"He's a pain in the ass," Rick said. "But he's our pain in the ass."

Alarms suddenly went off. A red warning light flashed repeatedly across the bottom of Pia's screen: DATA CONTAMINATION. Rick looked away from the monitor and said, "What the hell is happening now?"

Across the room, Kenny Wong was staring at his own monitor. "I think it's the gas analyzers in the crater," he said.

"What's wrong with them?" Pia asked.

"They're picking up something new inside the crater," Kenny said. "Monoxide, dioxide, sulfides, the usual, and..."

"What else?"

"Looks like a new complex—high carbon, lots of ethylene, methyl groups all over the place."

Pia Wilson crossed the room and peered over his shoulder. "Damn," she said.

"Do you know what that is?"

"Yeah," Pia said. "Aviation fuel."

Inside the helicopter, Glenn finally managed to reach out with his good hand. MacGregor grabbed it and pulled the man slowly toward him.

"Just try to keep your balance so you don't jar this thing," Mac said.

The cameraman stepped between the seats, coughing because of the smoke, moving as if in a daze.

They were just a few feet above the lava lake. Small sparks were spattering up. MacGregor stepped out, drew Glenn after him.

He tried to ignore the smell of fuel.

Nearly out of time.

Glenn followed him outside.

"You got this," Mac said, steadying him as his feet slid.

"I'm scared of heights," Glenn said, keeping his eyes fixed on the rim of the crater, away from the lava.

MacGregor thought: *You should have thought of that before, you jackhammer.*

Mac looked up, saw Jake about ten yards above them, reaching for Tim. Down here, the sharp odor of aviation fuel was stronger than ever.

Mac spoke soothingly to Glenn, trying to distract him. "Almost there."

The cameraman said, "We have to stop."

"No," MacGregor said.

They kept moving. The guy looked around and said, "Hey, what's that smell?"

Too late to lie to him, too close to the top. "Fuel," John MacGregor said.

His radio crackled, and he heard Jenny say, "Mac, the lab says the concentration from the fuel vapor is going up."

Mac looked back and saw the Plexiglas bubble of the helicopter had begun to burn; flames licked upward along the fuselage.

His headset crackled again. "Mac, you're out of time—"

But in the very next moment Tim was grabbing Glenn in his big arms and pulling him over the side. He quickly did the same for Mac, who glanced back and saw the helicopter enveloped in flames. Glenn tried to move back to the crater, but Tim shoved him hard toward their copter.

"We're safe now," the cameraman said. "What's the freaking rush?"

The helicopter exploded.

There was a roar, and the force of the explosion nearly knocked them all to the ground. A yellow-orange fireball burst up beyond the crater rim. A moment later, hot, sharp metal fragments clattered onto the slope all around them as they hurried to the red HVO helicopter.

"That's what the freaking rush was, asshole," Mac said to Glenn the cameraman.

CHAPTER 14

Hawaiian Volcano Observatory, Hawai'i

The doors of the ambulance slammed shut. MacGregor watched as it pulled out of the parking lot and headed around the caldera, lights flashing in the growing darkness. He turned to Jenny. "We going to get press on this?"

She shook her head. "I doubt it. I don't think Jake or that cameraman is particularly eager to publicize this." She reached up and touched his cheek, unable to stop herself. "I thought I was going to lose you," she said.

"You know better than that."

"Not today I didn't," she said.

For a moment, Mac thought she might cry. He felt a sudden urge to pull her into an embrace but fought it, not knowing who was watching them.

They walked back toward the main laboratory building. The

night was clear, and Mauna Loa loomed high above them, the line of its dark slope just visible against the deep blue sky.

Jenny said, "Rick and Kenny want to talk to you about something."

MacGregor looked at his watch. "Can't it wait until tomorrow?"

"They say it can't."

When Mac and Jenny walked into the data room, Rick Ozaki wasn't afraid to hug him. Mac was grinning when he stepped back.

"Any longer and we'd be picking out furniture," he said.

Rick grinned back. "Kiss my ass."

"And here I thought we were having a moment."

"Listen," Rick said. "I'll make this short."

MacGregor sat beside him and stared at the screen. The monitor showed a computer-generated cutaway view of Kīlauea and Mauna Loa that rotated slowly in three dimensions. Beneath the volcanoes, the magma pipes and reservoirs were outlined in pale gray, the image courtesy of hundreds of optimally positioned sensors. "So," Rick began, "from seismic and ground-deformation data, we get our model of the internal structure of Mauna Loa, down to about forty kilometers underground. As you know, we've been refining this model for ten years."

Rick zoomed in, enlarging the image. Beneath Mauna Loa the gray magma structures reminded MacGregor of a tree: a central lumpy trunk rising upward, splitting into thick branches, and then, near the top, fanning out into a series of horizontal magma reservoirs like leaves.

"These are the locations of the magma transport system inside the volcano," Rick said. "We had this ten years ago. What's different is now we know that it's accurate. Here is the full data series for six months, and you can see how tremor epicenters align with the magma pipes." Black squares representing earthquake centers dotted the vertical magma columns. "Okay?"

"Okay," MacGregor said. "But I think—"

"Let me finish telling you what *I* think," Rick said. "Here's the inflation data from the GPS net."

"Yes, yes." MacGregor sighed. He found himself looking at Rick's bulging waistline. MacGregor was old enough to remember when being a volcanologist meant being in shape. To members of the field team, like Tim Kapaana, hiking across the slopes of mountains to make observations, tending the monitoring stations, pulling colleagues out of dangerous spots—all of that was a rush. MacGregor heard nothing but complaints whenever he ordered the systems and data analysts into the field. It was hot out there, hiking across the lava fields was difficult, and the sharp lava cut their boots and melted the rubber soles. For better or worse, this new generation of scientists was entranced with computers, addicted to them the way kids were to their phones. They were content to sit in the lab and manipulate data on monitors. MacGregor believed that led to a kind of computer arrogance. He saw it in Rick Ozaki's attitude.

Rick said, "Mac, Kenny and I and some of the others have been talking."

"Shocker."

Rick let the word die between them and continued. "Look, everything is sharper now. When old Thomas Jaggar started this observatory in 1912, he used to predict eruptions within a range of a few months. Later scientists could predict them within a few days. Now we can predict them within hours."

"I'm well aware."

"And I'm aware that you are," Rick said. "We have a better grasp of timing, but we also have a much better idea of where exactly an eruption will occur. Before the '84 eruption, they knew within a square mile where it would happen, and everybody stood out in the field and looked for the lava. The 2022 eruption was a small one, but we learned from it. Kenny and I believe we can predict the sites lava will erupt from within ten meters."

MacGregor nodded. "Go on."

"So we've been thinking, Mac. We've got the predictions down—we can say when and where the lava is going to come out—so maybe it's time for the lab to take the next logical step."

"Which is?"

Rick paused, then said, "Intervene."

"Intervene?"

"Yes. Intervene in the eruption. Control it."

MacGregor frowned. "Rick, listen, you know I respect your opinion—"

"And you know how much we all respect yours, even with all the smack we like to lay on you," Kenny said, coming over. "But we think we can set explosive charges at specific places along the rift zone and vent the volcano."

"Really."

"Yes."

MacGregor barked out a laugh.

"We're serious, Mac."

"*Vent the volcano?*"

"Why not?"

MacGregor didn't answer. He just turned and walked up the stairs to the observation deck, located above the main laboratory. Rick and Kenny followed him.

"Seriously, Mac," Rick said. "Why the hell not?"

MacGregor stared at the vast outline of Mauna Loa, a dark shape against the darkening sky. The volcano filled the horizon. "*That's* why not," he said, pointing.

"Yeah, I know, it's big," Kenny said, "but—"

"Big?" MacGregor said. "What you can see of that beast in

the distance is big. If you measure it from its base on the ocean floor, that volcano is almost six miles high—more than three miles underwater, two and a half miles above. It is by far the largest geographical feature on this planet. And it produces fantastic volumes of lava—a billion cubic yards in the past thirty years. The eruption in 1984 wasn't particularly large, but it produced enough lava to bury Manhattan to a depth of thirty feet. For Mauna Loa, that was hardly a belch. And then there's the speed. In 2022, lava production was between fifty and one hundred cubic yards per second. That's enough lava to fill one Manhattan apartment every second.

"And you're talking about *venting* the sucker? You guys have been spending too much time in front of your screens. That mountain isn't some false-color satellite image that you manipulate with a couple of keystrokes. It's a goddamn gigantic force of nature."

In the darkness, Kenny and Rick tried to remain patient while Mac corrected them as if they were schoolchildren. "We understand that, Mac," Kenny said. "We're big boys."

"*Do* you understand? When was the last time you were up there?" MacGregor said. "It takes four or five hours just to walk around the caldera. It's a big-ass mountain, guys."

"Actually, we've spent quite a lot of time up there lately," Rick said. "And we think—"

"What we're really thinking about," Kenny said, interrupting him, "is not Mauna Loa, Mac. It's *that*." He pointed away from the volcano, toward the ocean and the glowing lights of Hilo. "Lava has threatened Hilo four times in the past century. Jaggar himself tried diversions, dams, and bombing to stop it. None of it worked."

"No," MacGregor said. "But the lava never reached Hilo either."

"The '84 flows came within four miles," Kenny said. "We

know that sooner or later, they'll go all the way. Nearly fifty thousand people live in Hilo now. And there are more every year. So the question is, Mac, the next time an eruption threatens Hilo, how are we going to stop it? What good is all our knowledge if we can't even protect the nearest big town?"

"That's right," Rick said. "I mean, let's face it—the day will come when we're going to be asked to control the lava flow, and the only practical way to do it is by venting. By directing the flow of magma from the deep reservoirs to the surface"—he paused for dramatic effect—"toward the places that *we* choose."

MacGregor sighed, shook his head. "Guys—"

"We think it should at least be considered," Rick said. "And the perfect place to try it is up on the saddle, where it doesn't matter whether we succeed or fail. There's nothing in the saddle except that army base, and they won't care. They explode stuff all the time up there."

"And what do you plan to explode to vent the volcano?" MacGregor asked.

"Not that much. We think that a sequence of relatively small explosions can mobilize preexisting rift zones to open a vent that—"

"Preexisting rift zones? No. I'm sorry, I can tell you've given this a lot of thought, but this is just total BS."

"Maybe not, Mac. In fact, the Defense Department did a feasibility study on this back in the seventies and concluded it would be possible in the future," Kenny said. "It was a DARPA project, run through the Army Corps of Engineers. We found a copy of the report in the files. Maybe you'd like to see it—"

MacGregor shook his head. "Not so much."

"Well, here it is, Mac." Kenny thrust a faded blue folder into his hands. The word VULCAN was printed in large type; underneath it, in smaller type, were the words *Defense Advanced Research Projects Agency.* MacGregor flipped through the pages. The paper was yellowing. He saw black-and-white line charts, typewritten paragraphs. Very seventies.

Mac shook his head. "Guys, you're not hearing me."

"And you're not hearing us," Kenny said. "At least take the time to read it."

"All right. When I catch my breath." He closed the blue file. The two men were looking at him as if they had just presented him with a unique opportunity. He felt, as he often did with the younger scientists, like a parent with small children. "Okay, look," he said. "Tell you what. Take the next twenty-four hours to do your own feasibility study."

"You mean it?" Rick asked.

"As a matter of fact, I do."

"Great!" Kenny said.

"You two go out on the volcano, walk the rift zones, trace the route of those giant cracks that extend below the seafloor and send the magma to the surface. Then decide exactly where you think we should place explosives. Draw up a detailed map and a plan, and then we'll talk."

"We'll have it for you tomorrow!" Rick said.

"That's fine," MacGregor said. He knew exactly how this little exercise would end. Once they started walking the lava, they'd see the magnitude of the project they were proposing. Hell, just walking the length of the northeast rift zone one way was a full day's hike. "And now, if it's all right with you two, I'm going home to fix myself a stiff drink," he said. He looked down at the palms of his hands. They were still red, still hot, as if the fire had followed him here.

"You sure you're okay, Mac?" Kenny asked as Mac walked toward the data room.

"I am," John MacGregor said. "But I can't lie, boys. I've had just about as much fun as I can handle for one day."

CHAPTER 15

Kīlauea Rim, Hawai'i
Time to eruption: 110 hours

MacGregor pulled into the carport of his house on Crater Rim Drive, behind the tourist facility at Volcano House. There were six National Park Service houses on Crater Rim Drive, all rented by HVO staff. When he got out of his car, he heard the shouts of Rick Ozaki's kids playing on the lawn in front of the brightly lit house down the road.

His own house was dark and silent. He went inside, turned on the lights, and walked into the kitchen. Brenda, his housekeeper, had left him a bowl of saimin—Hawaiian noodle soup—for supper. He clicked on the TV. It had been nearly a year since Linda moved back to the mainland, and he kept promising himself he would move out of the home they'd shared. It wasn't that large, but it still held too many memories. He glanced into the twins' bedroom, which he hadn't changed since their departure. For a while, he'd kept thinking they would come back, but they never did. They were eight now. Second grade. Charlie and Max.

They should have been outside making as much noise as Rick's kids were.

He'd come home early one afternoon and found the twins sitting in the living room dressed in their good clothes and Linda packing in the bedroom. She said she was sorry, but she couldn't take it anymore: the constant rainy weather, the isolation up on the mountain, the absence of her friends and family. She said that MacGregor had his work and it was fine for him to go around the world to strange places chasing volcanoes, but she was a lawyer and she couldn't practice here in Hawai'i, couldn't do anything here; she was going crazy being only a mother, and she had tickets for the five o'clock plane to Honolulu.

She said the boys didn't know yet—they thought they were going on a quick trip to see Grandma.

He said, incredulous, "Were you just going to leave without telling me?"

"I was going to call you at the office."

"And then, what, send me a Hallmark card?"

"Please don't make this any more difficult than it already is."

"Of course not," he said. "I wouldn't want to upset *you*."

They were only a few feet apart, but the distance that she was about to put between them existed already.

"So you weren't even going to let me say goodbye to the boys?"

"I didn't want you to upset *them*."

Somehow, he managed not to lose his temper. There was no point in arguing with her or trying to change her mind. They both knew this had been coming for a long time, but they had no way to prevent it. Even though he'd given up his place on the USGS advisory team when he married her, they still moved every few years. He'd been in Vancouver for two years, then

Hawai'i for five years, and he'd be leaving here next year. But Linda wanted to practice law, and for that she needed to move to a city and stay there so she could build a practice.

When they'd first married, none of this seemed important. She'd talked about doing pro bono work, said his travel didn't matter. But of course it did matter. For his part, MacGregor had said he was willing to take a university position and settle down. But of course he wasn't. He was a research volcanologist by training and temperament. That meant being in the field. He felt good only when he was in the field. He got restless if he spent too much time indoors. It was one of the reasons the guys in the data room called him a cowboy.

There had been a time after the twins were born when they might have worked it all out, made the necessary compromises. But they'd waited too long, had become more and more removed from each other.

That day, he had watched her pack for a while, and then he'd gone to hug the boys and—

The screen door slammed behind him, jolting him out of his thoughts.

"Are you trying to torture yourself? What's next, you take out the home movies?"

It was Jenny. She'd caught him standing in the doorway to the boys' room, saw him blinking back tears as he turned around.

She said, "I thought you were going to move out."

"I am."

"When, the twelfth of never?" She headed toward the kitchen. "I brought you the checklist for all the extra personnel we're going to need in case you want to go over that tonight. Last big eruption, they had forty extra park rangers. We'll need at least that many, and we'd better requisition them. And extra police, Hilo and Kona, for additional traffic control. And we need to set up an infirmary with a full-time doc, paramedics, and a standby ambulance...there's a lot to arrange."

Despite himself, he smiled. This was Jenny being Jenny.

He followed her into the kitchen. "Want some saimin?" he asked, putting it in the microwave.

She wrinkled her nose. Despite being a Honolulu native, Jenny didn't like the local food. "Got any yogurt?"

"I think so." He opened the refrigerator. "Strawberry?"

She looked at him suspiciously. "Don't take this the wrong way, but how old is it?"

"Not that old." He managed a smile. "And is there any other way for me to take a question like that?"

He got the yogurt out of the refrigerator, fished in a drawer for a spoon.

"What's this?" Jenny said, pointing to the blue folder on the kitchen table.

"Some old Defense Department study that Rick and Kenny dug up and wanted me to look at."

" 'Vulcan,' " she read aloud, sitting down. "The Roman god of fire."

The microwave beeped and he removed the steaming bowl of noodles. He sat down at the table and, with chopsticks, picked out the floating pieces of Spam and set them aside on a plate. The dirty little secret about island saimin was that it was made with Spam, and although MacGregor had told his housekeeper multiple times that he didn't like it, she kept using it.

Jenny thumbed quickly through the folder. She paused and frowned, then turned the pages more slowly.

MacGregor asked, "What is it?"

"Mac, have you read this?"

"No."

"What's vent deflection?"

He shook his head. "Never heard of it."

"Well, this whole report is about vent deflection." She flipped back to the first page. "Here it is…Project Vulcan and mechanisms of vent deflection."

MacGregor got up and read over her shoulder.

PROJECT VULCAN (VENT DEFLECTION)
BACKGROUND TO PROJECT

In response to the threat of a potentially disastrous eruption of Mauna Loa following the July 1975 eruption, local authorities requested that federal military agencies prepare contingency plans for lava diversion. Four methods to divert lava were investigated: dikes, seawater application, bombing, and vent deflection.

Dikes have invariably failed in the past. Even when they are notably strong and high, i.e., 25 to 40 feet (8 to 12 meters), they are overrun.

Seawater cooling has succeeded only in Iceland; there, the lava flowed near the sea, so pumping was manageable. In Hawai'i, pumping seawater up a 13,000-foot mountain is not practical.

Bombing was carried out in 1935 and in 1942, with questionable results. In 1935, the lava was already halting of its own accord and most observers felt bombing had no effect. In 1942, bombing clearly failed to halt the lava.

"We know all this already," MacGregor said.

"Yes," she said, "but did you know the army ran bombing tests back in the seventies?" She turned the page, kept reading.

To acquire detailed information on direct bombing effects, in 1976 the U.S. Army conducted tests on the north slope using 2,000-pound (900-kilogram) MK-84 bombs. This ordnance produced craters 10 meters wide and 1.8 meters deep, which were deemed too small to divert flows. Attempts to break open lava tubes failed. The 1976 tests suggest that aerial bombing will never succeed and should be abandoned.

Vent deflection remains the only possible method for control of lava flows. Procedures to accomplish this are limited by a lack of knowledge of subsurface geography and magma flows prior to eruption. However, such data may be available in the future. This report considers three potential methods of vent deflection that may be employed in the future.

"It seems," Jenny said, "they're talking about placing explosives around a potential vent to control its behavior."

In a modified form, the idea wasn't entirely new. A bombing contingency plan had been drafted ahead of Mauna Loa's 1984 eruption but never used. Since lava seemed to be unstoppable once it got going, there had been a lot of discussion about trying to modify the vents—the openings through which lava appeared on the slopes. Some scientists believed that you could bomb the vents and divert the lava right at the mouth.

But this was different. It was more like the technique used in 1992 during the eruption of Italy's Mount Etna, when engineers detonated eight tons of explosives to expand a channel for flowing lava and save a village in its path. This report suggested that a vent could be opened at will and that the eruption could be directed, could be controlled...

MacGregor leafed through the report and saw page after page of dense calculations—explosive zone effects, shock-wave propagation in basalt, target conduit expansion rates.

He nodded in genuine admiration. "They really went into this."

"Looks like it," Jenny said. She turned to a series of detailed maps of the caldera and the rift zones where placements for explosives had been marked. There were also ground photographs of proposed rift-zone sites.

MacGregor's eyes settled on one paragraph.

> Current tunneling technology (TK-17, TK-19, etc.) permits the drilling of narrow cores (less than one meter in diameter) to a depth of four kilometers beneath the surface, deeper if significant thermal effects are not encountered. On an emergency basis such cores can be drilled in 30 to 50 hours. The effect of appropriate ordnance in narrow cores has been studied previously (cf. Project Deep Star, Project Andiron). Furthermore, the recent success of precise detonation timing (PDT) suggests that the resonant-shock phenomenon (RSP) will greatly amplify any ordnance effect within a core.

"So this is what the boys were talking about," MacGregor said, frowning. "But I don't get it. I mean, I get that somebody spent a lot of money to do this study. I'm just not sure why."

Jenny shrugged. "DARPA does cutting-edge projects. They started developing the internet back in the 1960s, remember?"

"Ah, our tax dollars at work."

"Local officials must have asked for this," Jenny said.

"True," MacGregor said, "but back then, Hilo was a town

of—what? Thirty-five thousand? That doesn't justify a study costing a couple of million dollars. It still doesn't make sense to me."

"Could be strictly political," Jenny said. "So many studies for Hawai'i, so many studies for California and Oregon. Like that."

"Maybe."

"Didn't HVO get some funding from this?"

"Not sure. I'd have to check." He drummed his fingers on the table. "There's something we don't know." Still frowning, he flipped to the last page, the summary.

SUCCESS PROBABILITIES

Estimation of success for Project Vulcan is difficult given the degree of uncertainty surrounding major project variables. These cannot be weighted in the absence of an actual eruption. A succession of simulations using the STATSYL program for statistical analysis suggests a likelihood of success ranging from 7 percent to 11 percent.

However, based on the past 200 years of eruptions, the likelihood that lava will reach any given site is a function of distance from the eruptive region and is, on average, 9.3 percent. This suggests that Vulcan's likelihood of success is no greater than chance—that is, it is entirely ineffective. In the absence of further technological advances, we recommend that attempts at vent deflection be abandoned.

We conclude that the only practical method to protect populations from flowing lava is to evacuate them before its advance.

MacGregor laughed.

"What is it?" Jenny said.

"Our boys didn't give away the ending."

"What are you talking about?"

"They didn't tell me that the report concluded it wouldn't work."

"But they think it can?"

"It's like they're trying to talk themselves into it," he said. "And talk me into it."

"Have they?"

He grinned. "Have you ever seen them talk me into anything?"

"Always a first time," Jenny said. She kissed him on the cheek quickly and left.

Mac spent an hour or so researching dikes and seawater cooling, trying to get to where Rick and Kenny wanted him to be. Surprisingly, the most compelling argument came from J. P. Brett, billionaire tech guy, in a long op-ed piece in the *Los Angeles Times*. Brett, Mac knew, was as obsessed with volcanoes as other rich billionaire types were with space travel. Rockets were rich-guy phallic symbols.

But Brett knew his stuff. One of the events he referenced was the 1973 eruption of Eldfell in the Vestmannaeyjar archipelago in Iceland. Brett focused on seawater pumped in to cool the lava and a twenty-five-meter-high artificial dike built at the end of the lava tongue. A handful of scientists believed that pumping in seawater would significantly slow the lava and stop it from flowing into the town, but only if extremely powerful pumps were used and only if that equipment was there within one week. The pumping equipment was delivered, but not until two weeks later. As for the dike, although the lava traveled slowly at first, by the time it reached the dike, it was more than twice its height and easily overtopped it. After the fact, scientists concluded that even if the seawater pumping equipment had been brought in much sooner, it still would not have stopped the powerful lava flow or saved the town.

Brett disagreed. Vehemently. He noted that now, half a century later, friends of his could build their own rockets, so Brett was certain that one of his companies could produce sophisticated and powerful pumping equipment and build a dike that would survive a nuclear attack.

Mac sat in the quiet of his den and reread the article, then printed it out. Now he would have that drink. "Well, I'll be damned," he said, raising his glass in a toast to the boys. "Maybe they can talk me into this."

But he sure wasn't going to make it easy for them.

CHAPTER 16

Later that night, MacGregor flipped through the channels on the TV, looking for local news. When he got to KHON, he heard the reporter say, "We'll have updates on that pending eruption of Mauna Loa, so be sure to stay tuned. In the day's sports news—"

MacGregor's phone rang. Or, rather, phones—landline and cell simultaneously. He glanced at his watch as he answered it. The HVO had an automated telephone alert system that kicked in whenever there were significant changes in the field-monitoring devices. He half expected to hear the flat computer-generated voice calling him back to work, but instead a male voice said, "Dr. John MacGregor?"

"Yes. Speaking."

"This is Lieutenant Leonard Craig. I'm a staff physician at the Kalani VA Hospital in Honolulu."

"Yes?" His first thought was that this must be about Jake Rogers or the cameraman he had fished out of the crater. Or both. Had they been so badly injured that they were taken to Honolulu? "Is this about the helicopter crash?"

"No, sir, it's not. I'm calling about General Bennett."

"Who?"

"General Arthur Bennett. Do you know him?"

MacGregor frowned. "No, I don't think so."

"He's retired now. Perhaps you met him in the past. General Bennett was in charge of all army training installations in the Pacific from 1981 to 2012."

"I wouldn't know him, then. I didn't come here until 2018," MacGregor said.

"That's very odd, because he definitely seems to know you."

"Did he say he knows me?"

"Unfortunately, the general suffered a stroke that left him with one-sided weakness and an inability to speak. But his cognitive functions are still intact. That's why we thought you might know him. Or know about him."

Mac took the phone away from his ear and stared at it for a moment. He wondered if Lieutenant Craig had dialed him by mistake.

"I'm sorry," MacGregor said. "Do you have the right person? I'm a geologist with—"

"The Hawaiian Volcano Observatory. Yes, sir. We know who you are. Sir, do you know a Colonel Briggs?"

"No, I don't know him either," MacGregor said. "What is this about?" He glanced at the television—they were showing footage from the Merrie Monarch Festival's hula competition in Hilo.

There was a knock at his front door. MacGregor glanced at his watch and said, "Can you hold on? Someone's at my door."

"That will be the car we've sent for you, sir."

"The *car* you've sent for me?" *What the hell?*

"Colonel Briggs has arranged transportation for you from Lyman. The car will take you there now. Colonel Briggs will see you in an hour."

"See me where?"

"Honolulu, sir. Thank you in advance for your cooperation."

In the empty house, his voice sounded much too loud when he said, "Yes, *sir*."

CHAPTER 17

Kalani VA Hospital, Honolulu, Hawaiʻi
Time to eruption: 108 hours

R ain drummed on the roof of the blue sedan as it drove through the stone gates and up the long drive. Through the sweep of windshield wipers, MacGregor saw the lights of the main building directly ahead. When the car pulled up under the canopy, three uniformed men stood waiting. They opened the door for MacGregor, and the senior man extended his hand.

For the second time that day, John MacGregor felt as if he were traveling into the unknown. Despite what he did for a living, he hated surprises. This, he thought, was a different kind of crater.

"Dr. MacGregor? I'm Major Jepson. This way, please."

Jepson was a short, trim man with an equally trim mustache that could have been military-issue. He walked briskly down the corridor, glancing at his watch.

When they reached a room at the end of the corridor, Jepson opened the door.

"General Bennett?" he said in a tone that suggested he was delivering the day's best news. "I have somebody special to see you, sir." He motioned for MacGregor to follow him in.

General Arthur Bennett looked as frail and slender as a leaf; he was deathly pale, propped up in bed on enormous pillows. An IV line was in his arm. His head hung down, and he stared at the floor; one side of his face was slack, and his mouth hung open. The room smelled of disinfectant. The TV was on but muted.

"General, I've brought Dr. MacGregor."

He sounds like he's telling a five-year-old that he's brought Santa Claus, Mac thought.

The old man raised his eyes slowly, as if it took all the strength he had.

"How are you, sir?" Mac asked.

Almost imperceptibly, Bennett shook his head. His gaze dropped down to the floor again.

"Do you recognize him?" Jepson asked.

"No," Mac said, terse. He was damp from the rain and tired from the flight and from trying to contain his annoyance at being brought to a room to see someone who was barely here himself.

Maybe Jepson sensed his annoyance, because he backed off.

"Well, Colonel Briggs is on his way in now. Let's see how General Bennett reacts to this."

"To what?"

"The eleven o'clock news." Jepson crossed the room to the television and turned up the volume. "Let's see if it happens again."

There was a musical fanfare, then an excited voice announcing the *Eyewitness News* team, all news all the time. MacGregor saw three newscasters at a curved table with a backdrop of Honolulu skyscrapers.

General Bennett remained motionless, his head drooping. Mac thought he might be asleep. Perhaps permanently.

"Tonight's top stories: The governor says no tax cut this year. Another woman is found murdered in Waikiki. Restaurant workers will not strike after all. And on the Big Island, reports of an impending eruption from the volcano Mauna Loa."

At last, General Bennett stirred. His right hand moved restlessly in the direction of the IV line.

Major Jepson said, "There it is."

There what is? Mac thought. *Proof of life?*

Mac saw his own picture flash up behind the newscasters. One of them said that Dr. John MacGregor, the chief volcanologist at Kīlauea, had held a news conference confirming the impending eruption of the volcano. As he continued, the general became more agitated. His arm moved in erratic jerks across the starched bedsheet.

"Maybe he recognizes you," Jepson said.

"Or maybe he's just processing the news," Mac said.

He was vaguely aware of the newscaster saying that scientists were predicting a new eruption in the next few days, but it was expected to take place on the uninhabited north slope, and there was no risk to any residents of the Big Island.

General Bennett gave a low moan, and his hand moved again, as if he were frantic to get the attention of the man delivering the news.

"The strange thing is," Jepson said, "he always moans at exactly the same point—whenever a reporter says there's no risk to local residents from the eruption." He turned back to General Bennett. "You want to write, General?"

A nurse who'd just come in lifted the general's left hand from the bedside table and slipped a sheet of paper under it. She put his hand back on the paper, placed a pencil in his hand, and closed his fingers around it.

"There he goes," Jepson said, nodding. "First letter is always an *I*…"

The nurse held the paper down. Slowly, the frail, elderly man scrawled.

"Then *C*… *E*…"

MacGregor got closer to the bed, but the writing was difficult to make out.

Jepson frowned. "It's a little different this time… *I-C-E-T-O-B-B*."

MacGregor, frowning himself, said, "Wait—is that an *O* or a *U*?"

"Hard to say."

The general seemed to be listening. He drew a large semicircle, running his pencil over it again and again.

"Looks like he's saying it's *U*."

"Icetubb?" MacGregor said.

"Does that mean anything to you?" Jepson asked.

"No."

With the heel of his hand, the general pushed away the paper. He seemed to be irritated. The nurse removed that paper and placed a fresh sheet on the table.

"Now let's see if he draws the symbol," Jepson said.

The general drew again: a lopsided circle surrounded by arc-shaped lines. *Like a sort of halo*, Mac thought.

"We can't figure that out either," Jepson said.

Again, the general pushed the paper away. He gave a long sigh and went limp. The pencil fell from his fingers and clattered to the floor.

"If this is frustrating for us," Jepson said, "imagine how frustrating it is for him."

The nurse picked up the pencil. With his head drooping to the side, almost as if it might roll off his shoulders, General Bennett watched her, eyes blank. But then his hand began to move in a restless motion, as if he were conducting an unseen orchestra.

"Ah, this is something new," Jepson said to Mac. "Usually, he's done." To Bennett he said, "General? You want to write more?"

The nurse gave the old man another sheet of paper and placed the pencil back in his hand.

"We're trying to understand, sir," Jepson said, leaning close to him.

General Bennett shook his head slightly and drew again. They all watched as the pencil began to move.

A circle.

Then straight lines coming out from the circle and looping back.

Three lines in all.

Jepson said, "Petals on a flower? Propeller blades? A fan?" Like this was some kind of quiz show.

It certainly looked like a fan, Mac thought. Blades of a fan sticking out from a central rotor. But the old man was shaking his head. And something was nagging at the back of John MacGregor's mind. Just three blades.

He was sure he knew what that image was...

General Bennett began to draw again. This time, his hand described big loops.

"This is new," Jepson said. "What is it? That's a lowercase *a*...and that's a capital *B*...and—what's that? It's just a loop...is it a *d*?"

In a flash of insight, Mac saw it. "No," he said. "It's Greek. It's a gamma."

The general gave a sigh, nodded, and slumped back against the pillow, exhausted.

MacGregor said, "He's drawn the first three letters of the Greek alphabet: alpha, beta, gamma. But—"

"That is correct," said a voice behind them. MacGregor turned and saw a man in his sixties, white-haired, trim, and fit. He introduced himself as James Briggs. "I was General Bennett's adjutant for the last nine years of his command before he retired. Dr. MacGregor?"

"Call me Mac." They shook hands.

Briggs leaned over Bennett and placed his hand on his shoulder. "I know what you're trying to tell us," Briggs said. "And don't worry, we'll take care of it. You just rest now, sir."

Then he carefully collected all the pieces of paper the general had drawn on, folded them, and put them in his pocket.

He motioned for Jepson and MacGregor to step outside. In the hall, Briggs said, "Major, I want that nurse and everyone else who's had anything to do with General Bennett confined to the hospital grounds for the next two weeks. Call it a quarantine, call it whatever the hell you want, but keep 'em here. Clear?"

"Yes, sir, but—"

"They get no cell phones, no laptops, no email, no nothing. If they need to notify their families, you do it for them."

"Yes, sir."

"Military security will close the hospital tomorrow to all visitors at oh eight hundred hours and will shut down communications at that time. And let me remind you that everything you have seen and heard in that room is strictly confidential. Is that clear?"

Major Jepson blinked. "Sir, what exactly *have* I seen?"

"Nothing at all," Briggs said. He turned back to Mac. "Dr. MacGregor, please come with me." He left. Mac followed, noting that Jepson looked slightly bewildered.

When they were down the hall Briggs said to Mac, "You've obviously heard the term *military secrets*."

"Everybody has."

"Well, Dr. MacGregor, if you're in the military, keeping

those secrets is a way of life. Revealing those secrets can result in the loss of life. In that way, they're more than secrets. They're part of our code."

Mac waited.

"You're in the military now," Briggs said. "You didn't enlist—you were drafted. Nonetheless, from now on, that code of silence is your code too. Understood?"

"Yes," Mac said.

"Have you had any sleep tonight?" Briggs asked after he'd led Mac back down the hall.

"Not yet," Mac said.

"I'll arrange for a bed here. You can get a few hours before it's time to leave."

"Leave for where?" McGregor said.

CHAPTER 18

Agent Black

U.S. Military Reserve, Hawaiʻi
Friday, April 25, 2025
Time to eruption: 100 hours

The Black Hawk helicopter descended through thick clouds at nine thousand feet, and suddenly the landscape opened beneath them, a vast expanse of black lava in the dawn light. To the right, the broad northern flank of Mauna Loa with the silver buildings of the NOAA observatory far above them; to the left, the dark peak of Hualālai volcano. Directly ahead was the broad, flat saddle, the uninhabited region in the center of the Big Island; the military training area was located at the base of Mauna Kea.

Colonel Briggs pointed out the window. "So you expect the lava to flow in this area?"

"Yes," Mac said. "But Mauna Loa eruptions originate higher up, at the summit and rift zones."

"What time frame?"

"Four days plus or minus one."

"Jesus," Briggs said, shaking his head. "And it'll be a large eruption?"

"Very large," MacGregor said. "A volcano swells before it erupts, and we measure that. Inflation over the past few months is greater than the inflation that occurred before the 1950 eruption. That one produced three hundred seventy-six million cubic meters of lava."

"And that much lava will flow a long distance?"

"Yes. I expect it'll go down the mountain and across the saddle right up to the base of Mauna Kea. That's a little over twenty miles."

Briggs frowned. "How fast?"

MacGregor shook his head. "There's no way to predict. Might take days. More likely just a few hours."

"A few hours," Briggs said.

There was a short silence between them.

MacGregor said, "Are you going to tell me what all this is about?"

Briggs said, "It would be better if I showed you."

The Military Reserve was built along the base of Mauna Kea mountain, Hawai'i's highest peak, which rose up to the north. Permanent structures were sparse: a small airstrip, a rickety wooden tower with flaking paint; a handful of Quonset huts streaked with red dust; a parking lot with cracked asphalt. The general impression was of desolation and neglect.

A camouflage jeep pulled onto the pad as the helicopter

touched down. MacGregor and Briggs got in and were driven through the compound toward the mountain.

The driver was Sergeant Matthew Iona. Young guy, tall, skinny, a native, and dressed in fatigues. He said, "Dr. MacGregor, I need to know your glove and shoe size."

MacGregor told him. Ahead was a small area surrounded by rusted chain-link fence. The driver got out, unlocked the gate, opened it, drove through, locked it again behind them.

Directly ahead in the side of the mountain MacGregor saw a large steel door, ten feet high. The steel was painted brown to blend in with the mountain.

Briggs said, "That's the old entrance. We won't go in there. It's no longer safe."

"Why not?"

Briggs didn't answer. The jeep abruptly turned left and went down a concrete ramp that took them twenty feet below ground level.

They pulled under a corrugated tin port alongside a small concrete bunker. The driver unlocked the bunker door, and they all went inside. There were bright yellow suits and gold helmets with glass plates hanging on the wall. Briggs pointed to one. "That's yours."

Briggs stripped to his underwear, climbed into his suit, and zipped it up. Mac did the same. He remarked on how heavy the suit was.

"It *is* metal," Briggs said, but he didn't explain further.

The gold boots were also heavy. They attached with Velcro to the pants, which came down over them. Briggs told him to make the seal tight because it needed to be waterproof. Then Briggs helped MacGregor put on the helmet. The glass faceplate was at least an inch thick.

The driver came over and slipped a red plastic tag into a slot on the chest of Mac's suit. MacGregor could see the tag was marked RADOSE and had three yellow blades around a central circle—the international symbol for radiation.

"So *that's* what the general was drawing," Mac said. "The radiation symbol. And the alpha, beta, and gamma—that must have meant alpha and beta particles and gamma rays. Types of radiation."

"That's part of what he was trying to tell us," Briggs said, inserting his own tag. "Now, let's get going. It's hot as hell in these things." He went to a metal door at the end of the shed, punched in a code, and turned the handle. The door hissed open.

"This way," Briggs said and led Mac into the darkness.

CHAPTER 19

The Ice Tube, Mauna Kea, Hawai'i

They were in a cave about twelve feet in diameter with smooth walls.

MacGregor said, "This is a lava tube."

"We've always referred to it as the Ice Tube," Briggs said. "At one time, it was cold enough to have ice on the walls in winter. Goes into the mountain about half a mile."

During eruptions, lava flowed in channels down the flanks of the volcano. The surface of the lava flow cooled and formed a crust, while the lava below the hardened surface continued to flow. At the end of an eruption, the lava drained out, leaving empty tubes behind. Most lava tubes were only a few yards wide; some, though, were large caves. The HVO had mapped more than eighty tubes, and many of them were very deep.

Mac hadn't known that this one, at the base of Mauna Kea, existed.

They went past massive air coolers with fans six feet in diameter. But John MacGregor could still feel the heat radiating from the depths ahead.

They were now walking on a metal deck covered in thick foam. On either side were stacked metal lockers, each four feet square and padlocked. Up ahead, pale blue light reflected off the ceiling.

MacGregor said, "What is this place?"

"Storage facility."

"And what are you storing?"

Briggs opened a heavy grate door. It creaked open. "Look."

On both sides of the walk were row after row of cylindrical glass canisters, each glowing a deep, unreal blue. The canisters were identical: five feet high and capped at either end by a heavy foam block.

"Technically," Briggs said, "this material is gel-matrixed compound HL-512. It's high-level radwaste, stored in lead-glass canisters."

"You're telling me this is radioactive waste?"

"Of a kind."

MacGregor looked at the glowing canisters stretching away into the distance. He could feel his chest constrict, like a fist closing. "How much have you got here?"

"Six hundred and forty-three canisters," Briggs said. "All together, about thirty-two thousand pounds of material. And we can't risk lava coming anywhere close to it."

No kidding. MacGregor frowned. "Where'd the canisters come from?"

"Possibly from the Hanford Site in Washington State, the original plutonium production facility for the U.S. nuclear weapons program. Before that, maybe from Fort Detrick, U.S. Army Environmental Command, in Maryland."

MacGregor said, "You're telling me you're not certain who sent it here?"

Briggs nodded. "And we don't know where it was from originally."

Mac felt as dizzy as he had inside the crater. "So you have six hundred forty-three canisters of radioactive waste and you don't know where it came from?"

"That's correct."

Mac bent to look at the nearest canister. The glass was about an inch thick. Behind the glass there seemed to be a liquid containing suspended particles. Up close, he saw that the glass was not clear but covered with a spidery network of fine white lines. The foam bases were dusty. There was a thick layer of dust on the floor.

"How long has this stuff been here?" he said.

"Since 1978."

They walked down the cave past the rows of canisters. "Back in the 1950s," Briggs said, "it was standard procedure to dispose of radioactive waste by dumping it in the ocean. We did it until 1976; the Russians did it until 1991. Everybody did it. By 1977, the material had been sent to the Hanford Site in Washington State. When Hanford's facilities became too crowded, the stuff was shipped to Hawai'i to be encased in concrete blocks and deep-sixed in the ocean. We don't know who put a stop to that, but somebody did. The canisters were kept in a Honolulu warehouse, but nobody liked having them so close to a large population center. Finally," Briggs continued, "they told us to store the waste on one of the outer islands until a new disposal plan could be agreed on."

Briggs's shoulders rose and fell in what appeared to be resignation. "So in 1978 or so, it came here to the Big Island. In 1982, the Nuclear Waste Policy Act was passed, and in 1987, the Department of Energy designated Yucca Mountain in Nevada as the national disposal site. But Washington decided that this particular material could not withstand a trip stateside, which is why the canisters are still here."

"Wait—there wasn't a protest?" MacGregor asked.

Briggs smiled behind his glass faceplate. "There wasn't a protest because nobody knew it was here."

"And nobody found out?"

"It was the 1970s," Briggs said as if that explained everything. "Another world back then. Until 1959, Hawai'i wasn't even a state. It was a trust territory. The military's strong presence on all the islands continued, and this corner of Hawai'i was basically one big military base, so it wasn't a problem to put it here. And here it has remained ever since."

"And the military never tried to remove it?"

"Of course we tried," Briggs snapped, sounding defensive. "The army wanted to get rid of it. But the Senate Appropriations subcommittee wouldn't authorize funding, and we couldn't make a public fuss because the state of Hawai'i wanted it kept secret. Sometime in the 1980s, state officials learned this stuff was here, and they wanted it gone, but they didn't want any headlines. You know, 'Radioactive Waste Removed from Hawaiian Island Site.' That would be bad for tourism."

"Jesus," Mac said. "You *think*?"

Briggs said, "Sadly, the cost of removal got higher every year." He pointed to the canisters. "Those glass tubes were supposed to be encased in concrete. They were never meant to stand in the air for decades. Over the years, the decay heat from radioactivity has changed the qualities of the glass. You noticed the fine white lines all over the canisters?"

"Hard to miss."

"Well, those are cracks."

"Jesus," MacGregor said again.

"Yes. The glass is now extremely friable. It's not impossible to remove them, but at this point it'd be very difficult and very dangerous."

"And what exactly is in them?" Mac said.

"There is some dispute about that."

"Dispute?"

"We know that the material contains large amounts of unusual isotopes, in particular iodine-143, and that confused the experts we consulted. Portable proton scanning gave us unclear results."

MacGregor said, "No offense, sir. But how can this possibly be?"

"No offense taken," Briggs said. "Blame it on modern technology. Unfortunately for us, the relevant data was stored on computers."

"And that's a problem in the modern world?"

"In this case it is," Briggs said.

As they walked out of the cave, he explained. In the 1980s, the military, like most modern American organizations, used mainframe computers to keep track of their data. "Everything from personnel pay schedules to PX orders to nuclear warhead locations," Briggs said. "It was all on big mainframes. The programs that manipulated the data were written in Ada, the language chosen by the Department of Defense for the embedded systems used in military projects. There were no hard drives back then. Data was stored on eight-inch floppy disks that were kept in sleeves in air-conditioned rooms."

"Those were the days," Mac said.

Briggs ignored him. "But each year," he continued, "there was more stored data. And with each upgrade, it became more and more expensive to transfer the old data. On top of that, a lot of the old data wasn't relevant anymore. Who cared how much canned tuna was put aboard the USS *Missouri* in May 1986? Tanks and airplanes from that time had been decommissioned. Eventually, the military decided not to transfer the old data unless it was needed. So the old disks were left in storage for decades."

"And?"

"One night Mauna Kea was struck by lightning that generated an electromagnetic field so powerful it degaussed the disks and erased all the information stored there."

"There were no backups?"

"The backups were unreadable too."

"And that's why you don't know what this material is?"

"Well, we didn't," Briggs said. "For twenty years, we had no idea."

He paused and looked directly at Mac.

"We found out when we had an accident," Briggs said.

CHAPTER 20

W hat kind of accident?" Mac asked.

"One of those canisters cracked about nine years ago. All hell broke loose for a week, but that was how we found out what this stuff really is."

"And what is it?" MacGregor said.

"It's herbicide."

"Radioactive herbicide?"

"Well, it wasn't originally radioactive. They did that later."

"Who did that?"

"The scientists at Fort Detrick, in Maryland." Briggs sighed. "Have you ever heard of Project Hades? Agent Black?"

Back in the 1940s, the army had tested chemicals for defoliant properties. By the 1950s, these programs had become much more sophisticated and the chemicals much more powerful. This was the research that led to dioxin, Agent Orange, Agent White, and the other defoliants used in Vietnam.

"The program was called Project Hades," Briggs said. "The work was carried out in a series of labs in Building A-14 at

Detrick. In one lab, they found an unusually powerful chemical that killed a whole range of plants and trees very rapidly. Because the chemical turned the plants a smoky gray-black color, it was called Agent Black and earmarked for field testing."

At Detrick A-14, all the labs had houseplants. Lots of them. They were the equivalent of canaries in coal mines. Although the testing of Agent Black had been done in closed containers, houseplants around the lab began to die.

"Gee, I wonder why," Mac said.

"The head of the lab was a guy named Handler," Briggs said, "and he kept these rare orchids in his office, which was across the hall from the main lab. The orchids died too."

At first everybody assumed it was due to contamination—that somehow the herbicide had been carried by the lab workers to other plants. But when they tested the dead plants, they found no trace of herbicide. Why they had died was a mystery.

Then, in other labs, more plants turned black and died. Again no trace of the herbicide.

"All this happened in the course of a week," Briggs continued. "No one in that building knew what the hell was happening. They didn't even know whether it was safe to go home to their families at night, since plants all around them were dying for no apparent reason. They did know that the stuff was dangerous as hell, but they were afraid to burn it, because at that time there was no closed incinerator capable of handling large quantities of hazardous material. They knew they couldn't bury it. And they couldn't leave it sitting there. So they decided to mix the bomb contents with radioisotopes."

Briggs explained this approach had several advantages. First, the Detrick scientists had begun to suspect that Agent Black wasn't just a chemical herbicide, that it contained some kind of living material, probably bacteria, and if that was so, the radiation would kill it. In addition, radioactivity would mark the material as dangerous. And finally, if any of it escaped into the environment, they could trace it through the radioactivity.

By 1989, it became possible to bring a portable incinerator to the Big Island and burn the canisters—or it would have been possible if they hadn't been radioactive. To be burned, they would have to go back to Hanford, but that same year Hanford was decommissioned.

It was already clear that the glass canisters were starting to degrade because of the decay heat produced by the radioactive material. Since there was still no funding to remove the canisters, the army decided, as a temporary measure, to place them in cooling pools of water; this was standard procedure for high-level radioactive materials. It hadn't been done in the Ice Tube because nobody had expected the material to remain there so long.

A contract to construct five concrete-lined pools was put out for public bidding, as required by law. The project was referred to vaguely as a "hazardous waste facility." The French Greenpeace organization in Tahiti got word of it and sued to block construction. There were pamphlets and headlines about the "U.S. Toxic Paradise." So Hawai'i pulled the plug, and the contract was withdrawn. Greenpeace declared victory and went away.

But the canisters continued to decay.

Then, in 2016, there was the accident.

The increasing brittleness of the glass worried everyone, so the army decided to cap each end of the canisters with impact-cushioning foam blocks and place the blocks on a multi-padded floor. The idea was that the foam and flooring would absorb minor shocks. This was admittedly an inadequate solution, but there was no funding for anything more substantial. Explosive ordnance disposal teams, skilled at handling hazardous materials, were deployed to mount the canisters in the foam blocks. The work was carried out over twelve weeks.

While one canister was being set in blocks, it began to leak. Only a small amount of material escaped before the cylinder was encased in sealant and repackaged for permanent removal. However, one of the EOD workers involved in this incident apparently performed inadequate washdown, failing to thoroughly clean the soles of his boots as he left the cave. A small quantity of the material was tracked into the locker room and picked up on the bottom of the worker's own shoes. A few days later, this worker visited the Hilo Botanical Gardens wearing those shoes, and he tracked the material into a grove of banyan trees.

"What happened to him?"

Briggs's face didn't change expression. "He died," he said. "Like the banyan trees."

"How was that explained?"

"It wasn't. The guy had no family. Lived alone. It was like he was never here."

He described the scene from the botanical gardens; Mac vaguely remembered hearing about it when he came to HVO. Something about an herbicide spill. Little did he know.

"Long story short," Briggs said, "we sent a team and cleaned the spill up with these modern fire extinguishers called Cold Fire."

"And that was the end?"

"Yes. We stopped it. But Detrick took back samples of dead grass and tree bark. And they finally figured out what the mechanism of action was."

"You just going to leave me hanging, Colonel?"

Briggs glanced at his watch. "I believe we've arranged a demonstration for you in about ten minutes."

CHAPTER 21

The Demonstration

Military police stood outside the building and at all the interior doors, although the room itself reminded MacGregor of an old classroom: gray walls, pale green splashboard.

There were several windows looking out at the slopes of Mauna Loa, but the only furniture was a long battered wooden table with chairs around it. Six men in shirtsleeves sat at the table, very erect, eyes turned to the presentation. MacGregor had been introduced to them but couldn't remember a single name. All he knew was that they were young army scientists.

At the far end of the room, standing in front of an ancient blackboard, a young man in uniform who introduced himself as Adam Lim and said he was a geneticist began speaking.

Mac wasn't entirely sure why a geneticist was there.

A side door opened, and two men walked in carrying a bonsai tree in a glass case. They carried it as if it were a precious jewel and set it carefully on the table. At first Mac thought it was a display case, but then he saw the gas gauge mounted near the thick base. A projector was slid over the plant, and a light turned on. A large video image of the tree appeared on the screen.

Lim said, "This plant was sprayed five hours ago with Agent Black. As you see, it appears quite normal." He paused. "For the moment."

Lim pulled a tab at the base, and a small window opened. A black fly flew into the case.

Lim explained that Agent Black was an insecticide consisting of 2,4-dichlorophenoxyacetic acid and 4-amino-tetrachloroco-linic acid. The substances mimicked plant hormones and killed the plant by disrupting its metabolism.

Mac looked down and realized he was squeezing his hands together tightly; his knuckles were white. He took in a deep breath through his nose and exhaled through his mouth, trying to relax despite what he was hearing.

"Agent Black," Lim continued, "is therefore a fairly ordinary herbicide—except for one interaction. When the common housefly *Musca domestica* lands on a sprayed leaf, it will lick the sticky material from its legs, because, as you may know, its feet are important sensors. You can see that happening now."

Someone handed MacGregor a magnifying glass. He walked over and leaned close to the case. The fly was indeed licking its legs.

"The herbicide now enters the fly's gut," Lim lectured, "where it is broken down by enzymes. The original herbicide is reduced to fragments. Just like human beings, *Musca domestica* maintains a particular ecology within the gut, a mixture of bacteria and viruses."

Mac had met scientists like Lim often in his career. Sometimes he was one of those smart-ass scientists himself. *I know things that the rest of you don't.*

Lim went on. "If the fly has been exposed to a pesticide, its gut ecology has changed. The fly now carries increased numbers of tobacco mosaic virus, a plant virus common in the environment. One particular fragment of broken-down 2,4-D adheres to the coat of that virus. This coated virus almost immediately irritates the gut, so the fly excretes its intestinal contents onto a leaf. This entire process takes only a few seconds; you can see the fly lick its legs and then excrete."

MacGregor *could* see it. There was a small white dot on the leaf, about the size of a pencil point, near the rear of the fly, which now buzzed away.

"The excreted virus enters a leaf cell," Lim said, "where it does what all viruses do—it takes over the cell's machinery and forces it to produce new viruses until it bursts. Within the plant cell, the 2,4-D fragments are incorporated into the genome of some viruses. When the cell breaks open, these viruses containing the fragment are released into the environment. The viruses are extremely aggressive and reproduce quickly on any plant they come in contact with. The process is so fast that you can watch the blackness move across the plant. You may see it starting now. Even a large tree will die within forty-eight hours."

Even a banyan tree, Mac thought.

He squinted at the leaf through the magnifying glass. A tiny black dot appeared on the leaf. Then another dot, and another. It was as if an invisible black rain was falling on the leaves. Some of the dots were beginning to enlarge and grow toward each other.

"Holy shit, it's fast," Mac said.

"Too fast." Lim rolled his shoulders. "Questions?" He seemed about to add, *Class dismissed*.

From the back, Briggs said, "Thank you, Adam. Now I think it's time to tell Dr. MacGregor what will happen to the material in the canisters during the eruption."

The fun just never stops, Mac thought.

Lim sat down, and a new man stepped to the front of the room. Robert Daws was stocky and muscular and had a crew cut.

But although he looked like a bouncer, he had a precise, almost fussy way of speaking. He said he was an atmospheric scientist.

Daws said, "We've assumed source lava at twenty-two hundred degrees Fahrenheit, and we assume negligible cooling for seventy-two hours. Surface crust may fall to a thousand degrees, but the temperature of material beneath the crust is essentially unchanged. Yes?" he asked Mac.

"That would be my assumption, yes," Mac said.

"This means," Daws said, "that the heat of the moving lava front is more than sufficient to make the canisters burst and release their contents. We assume the contents will still be chemically active and will oxidize at an extremely rapid rate. A frightening rate."

"Are you telling us this stuff will explode if the lava comes close enough?"

"Yes, sir, it will."

"How close?"

"Anywhere on the army base's side of Mauna Loa," Daws said.

MacGregor sighed. "What a goddamn mess."

"Yes, sir, it is," Daws said. "Contact with lava will generate an explosive cloud of steam and organic debris rising nine to fifteen thousand feet into the air. That of course is stratospheric levels, which means global circulation. We anticipate most of the particulate material will fall back to the island of Hawai'i within a few hours, but forty-three percent of the material will be carried off by the jet stream, where it will circulate for as long as twelve months."

Now Daws was the one who sighed. "By and large, however, most of it will slowly descend to lower altitudes over a period of weeks and eventually come down to the ground like rain."

Mac said, "Sounds more like acid rain to me."

"I guess you could think of it that way." Daws swallowed. "The distribution of the fly *Musca* is worldwide. The infectivity of the tobacco mosaic virus is very broad-based. We do not know its full range. It does not kill every plant, but we believe that this process of fragment incorporation will occur in other plant viruses. As a result, all, or nearly all, plants in the biosphere will die."

There was an almost kinetic energy to the silence in the room now. Mac felt the urge to get up and open a window, though he suspected that if he did, one of the soldiers outside would arrest him. Or shoot him.

"Given several years of research, it would be possible to develop resistant plant strains," Daws continued. "But we do not have years. The viruses will kill every plant on Earth within two months. All animal life, including human life, will die of starvation soon after. A conservative forecast is one point four billion death events in the first five weeks, and three point one billion in the first eight weeks. Nearly everyone will be dead by four months. A few isolated individuals may be able to hold out by hoarding, but not for long."

Mac said, "I understand what happens if the virus escapes those canisters and what it will do to the biosphere. But what happens if humans are somehow contaminated before that? Can it be transmitted from one person to another?"

"You mean if a spill happens before lava ever gets near those canisters?"

"Yes."

"We're going to make sure that doesn't happen."

"But *if* it does," Mac said.

"We believe that the results would be a variation of typical radiation poisoning, affecting some more quickly than others. Some might die immediately, as if their personal biosphere had been poisoned. It might take close contact; it might not. It might take longer for some than for others. But they're all going to die from the same black death."

Mac stared at Robert Daws, trying to comprehend the magnitude of what he was hearing. Daws had delivered the information as dispassionately as a weatherman reporting that a cold front was moving in. Mac looked around at the scientists seated at the table. They hadn't even reacted. Because they already knew.

So this is how the world is going to end.

"But if it is released into the atmosphere, in five months or thereabouts, no life-forms will exist on the planet except some insects and bacteria," Daws said. "The Earth will essentially have died."

Now he was done. No one spoke for over a minute. Finally Mac took it upon himself to state the obvious, if only for his own benefit: "We have to find a way to stop or divert the flow of lava."

Daws nodded. "Before the end of the week," he said. He was looking directly at Mac now, as if it were just the two of them in this room. "Do you have any other questions?"

"Just the one I keep asking," Mac said. He turned to the men at the table. "How in God's name was this allowed to happen?"

CHAPTER 22

The men at the table stared back at him.

"Excuse me?" one of them finally said.

"You heard me," Mac said.

Briggs cleared his throat. "Listen," he said, "there's plenty of blame to go around. Blame the army. Blame the Cold War. Blame your congressperson for not appropriating the money. Blame Hawai'i for protecting its tourist trade. Blame the tree-huggers for blocking the construction of dump sites forty years ago when we could still have moved this stuff out. Blame all the people who looked at one piece of the puzzle and not the whole problem. We've inherited this mess from the 1950s, with plenty of help from the '70s and '80s. The whole thing has been a slow-moving train wreck."

They all looked through the window and watched as six U.S. Army CH-47 Chinooks—tandem-rotor, heavy-lift helicopters—slowly descended, mini-excavators hanging beneath and backhoes in the cargo bays.

Briggs said, "We're going to build a dike."

He sounded like Noah announcing he was going to build an ark.

"How big?"

"Twenty feet high, maybe a quarter of a mile long."

Mac shook his head. "Not big enough," he said. "It needs to be fifty feet high and half a mile long. At least."

"Fifty feet?" Briggs said. "That's the height of a four-story building. You're joking, right?"

"With all due respect, Colonel, do I look like I'm joking?" Mac pointed to the dark slope of Mauna Loa. "It doesn't look steep out there, but it is," he said. "The lava flow is very liquid, especially when it's hot. It flows like a swollen river. You'll have lava coming down at you in flows that are going to be ten, fifteen feet high. Like a tsunami. They'll flow right over a twenty-foot wall."

"So would a fifty-foot wall work?"

"Probably not," MacGregor said. "But you should build it anyway."

Briggs said, "And I suppose bombing—"

Mac cut him off. "Won't work."

There was a moment of silence, the air even heavier than before.

Briggs said, "You may know there was a DARPA study about venting the volcano—"

"One that concluded that it won't work."

Quietly Briggs said, "There must be *something* we can try."

MacGregor watched the helicopters maneuvering, bringing in the big equipment. He frowned, bit his lower lip.

"Give me an hour," MacGregor said.

"To do what?"

"To come up with a plan so we don't have to kiss our asses goodbye," he said.

CHAPTER 23

Hawaiian Volcano Observatory, Hawai'i

Mac came into the data room at eight o'clock. The team was already there. Rick Ozaki was huddled with Kenny Wong at one monitor. Pia was working on the remote cameras with Tim Kapaana, who was out in the field, adjusting settings. From there, he'd deploy drones with thermal cameras to find the areas where lava was coming toward the surface.

Jenny fell into step beside Mac. "You might want to touch base with Tako Takayama," she said. "You know how he gets his panties in a wad when he feels like he's not in the loop."

"Later," Mac said. He lowered his voice and asked, "How soon I can get the latest satellite imagery?"

"What do you want?"

"Visible and infrared will do."

She went to a monitor and typed, her fingers flying across the keys as she called up the orbit schedules for the Terra satellite.

Mac watched over her shoulder. The Terra satellite passed over the Big Island once every forty-eight hours, and HVO could access its MODIS data.

"The satellite passed over at two forty-three a.m.," Jenny said. "It probably hasn't been downloaded." She kept typing.

"How long is this going to take?" Mac said impatiently.

She gave him a look. "Would five minutes ago be soon enough, Your Excellency?"

"Not the right tone, I'm guessing?"

"Not even close."

But then she leaned over her screen, looked back up at him, and smiled.

"Actually, we're in luck," she said. "The data's already down. I can probably have it for you in ten minutes."

"Tell me when you do. And thanks, pal."

"*Pal?*"

Now he smiled. "Bosom buddy?"

"Beat it, smooth talker, and let me work."

Mac went over to Rick and Kenny. "Okay, boys," he said, taking a seat next to them. "Show me what you got."

Kenny did most of the talking. He explained that he'd run his program against all the data for each of the past five Mauna Loa eruptions, all the way back to 1949. They showed Mac how their data sets corresponded to a rotating three-dimensional display of the magma structures beneath the volcano. Additionally, there were sets about gas monitors and GPS three-axis inflation, thermal and satellite images. All of this was delivered rapid fire, as if the scientists didn't even need the information on their screens, as if they had it memorized, a flow of what Mac thought of as the inside baseball of their world.

The world that might be about to blow.

That one.

"Then we get to predictive output," Rick said, and there on

the screen was data on eruption probability, eruption volume, various locations, coolants, and dikes.

Finally, this:

ESTIMATED TIME TO ERUPTION: 4 days plus or minus 11 hours

When they were finished, they looked at Mac. Rick said, "What do you think?"

"I think it's crap," Mac said.

"You're joking, right?" Rick asked.

Mac remembered Colonel Briggs saying the same thing. "Both of you, look at me," Mac said, "and then decide if you think that's a question you want to ask."

"But we've run and rerun the numbers," Kenny said, sounding defensive. "This is solid."

"If you torture data long enough," Mac said, "you can make it tell you whatever you want it to. What you guys are giving me is a false hard."

He wasn't actually sure that's what they were doing, but he always made them defend their findings with everything they had. He would make them do it now, and he was not worried about hurting anyone's feelings. In the past there had been room for error, lengthy back-and-forth debate, and even handholding. But not today.

"What happened when you ran the model against past data?" Mac said. Before they could answer, he added, "Did your program predict the 2022 eruption, for instance?"

"Yeah, Mac, it did, actually," Kenny said.

"How close?"

"Within two hours."

"How about the one in 1984?"

"Nine hours."

"I'm telling you, the program works, Mac," Rick said.

Mac said, "Can you predict ground temperature around the summit?"

Rick and Kenny looked at each other.

"We've never done it before," Rick said. "We'd need to do some calculating."

Mac said, "I've got the latest satellite infrared image, taken at two forty-three this morning. I need to see how closely your model matches it."

"Give me ten minutes," Kenny said.

"And you both think dikes can work?"

"I stand by my data," Kenny said.

"Same," Rick said.

"Shocker," Mac said. "You stand by the data on coolants too?"

"On all of it."

"Then you better be right," Mac said.

Mac walked away. When Kenny thought Mac was out of earshot he said, "Who shoved the stick up his ass?"

"Still here," Mac called.

He was glad they couldn't see him smiling.

It ended up taking Rick and Kenny fifteen minutes.

But now they all studied an image on the screen showing an aerial view of the island of Hawai'i in false colors, with Mauna Loa in blues and browns, increasing to orange and yellow toward the summit. There was a line of bright orange spots, like a string of pearls, along the northeast rift. There were also some black patches around the summit.

To Mac, they were as ominous as storm clouds. He called out to Jenny across the room. "Give us the near-infrared, please."

"Coming up."

A moment later, in a corner of the screen, the satellite image taken earlier that day appeared. At first glance, it looked roughly similar to Rick and Kenny's image.

"That's what I'm talking about!" Kenny said, pumping his fist.

"Not so fast. Overlay it."

Kenny enlarged the satellite image, made it translucent, and moved it over their image.

"Now opaque it," Mac said. "And flip them."

Kenny flipped back and forth between the two images, the first computer-generated, the second taken by the satellite. He and Rick watched MacGregor hopefully, like kids waiting to see if they'd get a pat on the head.

"I gotta admit," Mac said, nodding in appreciation, "it's not half bad."

"Gee," Rick said. "Thanks, Dad."

Mac grinned. "The only difference I see is that the satellite is showing a hot spot in the ocean just off the west coast of the island, and you don't show that."

"Not our territory," Kenny said.

"Today it is, Sparky."

"You know we don't have sensors on the west coast, Mac," he said.

Mac ignored that. "Okay," he said, standing. "Pack it all up on a laptop and be ready in twenty minutes. There are some people who have to see this."

CHAPTER 24

County of Hawai'i Civil Defense Building, Hilo, Hawai'i

Henry Takayama stormed into his office and slammed the door behind him, knowing the sound would send tremors across the desks outside because everyone assumed it meant he was upset about something. And he was. It was only eight thirty in the morning and already he was having a very bad day.

First of all, representatives from both Paradise Helicopters and Mauna Loa Helicopter Tours had called him, demanding to know why they couldn't take tourists over the volcanoes. The airspace over Mauna Loa and Kīlauea had been closed the night before—Henry knew about that *'ōkole* pilot Rogers and his damn-fool stunt—and was still closed in the morning, and the companies wanted to know what Takayama was going to do about it. Henry had said it was a mistake and promised he would fix it, mostly because Henry Takayama saw himself, first and foremost, as a fixer.

So he called the tower at General Lyman Field/Hilo International Airport. Bobby Gomera was running Access Control, which Henry saw as great good fortune. Henry had known Bobby since he'd met him at his family's luau when Bobby was one year old.

But that got him nowhere today. Bobby informed him there was nothing he could do about the airspace because the army command had ordered it closed.

"I'm willing to do a lot for you, 'Anakala Tako," Bobby Gomera said, using the Hawaiian word for "uncle." "But I can't go to war with the United States Army."

The army sometimes closed the airspace around the volcano but never without giving advance notice to the Civil Defense office, and Henry had gotten no advance notice. This was not just a breach of what he considered island protocol—it was extremely strange.

Worse, he would now have to call the helicopter guys and tell them that he, Henry Takayama, couldn't open the airspace even though he'd promised he'd do it. He would blame the army, of course, a perfectly good default position in almost any matter involving them. But Henry did not like going back on a promise. Not because he saw keeping promises as some kind of moral imperative. No. Because breaking promises made him look bad. And that, to Henry Takayama, was a sin against everything he considered holy.

He asked Bobby if the army was staging maneuvers at the military base.

"I don't think so," Bobby said. "But *something* is happening."

"Why do you think that?"

Bobby told him that the HVO guy MacGregor had flown in one very big hurry to Honolulu on a military transport the night before. No one knew why. And MacGregor hadn't come back yet.

Or maybe he had, because an army helicopter had entered Big Island airspace early that morning and landed at the military base. It had given Gomera a call designation of Romeo-Vector-Three-Niner. That meant army brass was on board.

An hour after that, an army helicopter had landed at Lyman and six guys had come out, not in uniform but wearing short-sleeved shirts. They'd been driven from Lyman to the UH campus in Hilo. Bobby told Takayama he'd overheard some of their radio transmissions. They were going to the computer science department at the university. They'd arranged for it to open early. They were clearly techies of some kind, Gomera said. Maybe engineers.

In addition, he told Takayama, six helicopters had recently entered the airspace from the west, the Kona side. Gomera had monitored their radios and discovered they were C-17 Globemaster III cargo aircraft bringing earthmoving equipment to the military base.

"Sounds like maneuvers to me," Henry said.

"I don't think so," Bobby said. "The army guys left the computer science department in Hilo and went up the mountain by helicopter. To the NOAA observatory near the summit." He paused. "There's more."

"Am I going to like it?" Takayama said.

"Doubtful," Gomera said.

He told his uncle Tako about the helicopter going to HVO from the military base.

"I heard another transmission after that," Gomera said. "The brass is coming in for some kind of summit. Something to do with a programmer named Wong and another guy, Ozaki. Apparently, they worked all night on something big."

Gomera was right, Takayama thought after he hung up. He didn't like anything about this. Whatever those two had been up all night working on, a summit had been convened, very hastily, to discuss it. At the summit of Mauna Loa.

Henry Takayama leaned forward on his desk, his fingers clasped tightly in front of him. *Last night MacGregor announces an eruption. Today he meets with the army at the summit. It's obviously something about the eruption*, Henry thought, though he couldn't imagine what. But whatever it was, important things were happening fast.

And he had not been informed.

"Those bastards!" Takayama said.

He had never liked MacGregor. A mainlander who acted as if he were doing Takayama a favor every time they had a meeting, as if he always had something more important to do, someone more important to see. Guys like MacGregor made him *ho'opailua*.

Made him want to puke.

He pushed the button on his intercom. He still used one; he considered it stupid to send a text to an assistant seated just outside his door. "Has HVO called me?"

"No, Henry, not yet," Mikala Lee said.

"Any calls from the army?"

"Not yet. No."

He paused, organizing his thoughts about what to do next. The easiest thing would be to alert a reporter; Kim Kobayashi at KHON owed him a lot of favors. But with the Merrie Monarch under way, that might be the wrong move. Takayama didn't know what was going on, and he didn't want alarming news to get out. For the moment, he would just obtain as much information as he could.

"Put in a call to MacGregor," he said. "And call Colonel Briggs."

"Right away."

He sat back and almost immediately leaned forward again and jabbed at the intercom button. "Never mind. Cancel the calls."

There was something else to consider. If he started asking questions, he'd probably get answers today. But what about tomorrow? And the day after? These men had already demonstrated their indifference to Civil Defense by keeping him out of the loop on whatever they were doing. Henry couldn't very well call them every day, hat in hand, pleading for intel. What he needed was an ongoing flow of information. From the inside.

He needed a contact inside HVO.

The trouble was, everybody up there was loyal to MacGregor. All of them, whether they were newly arrived *haole* or *kama'āina*. Like that Kimura girl from Oah'u who acted like a snob because of her fancy mainland education. There wasn't a chance in hell that she'd inform Tako of anything. And the other techs were just foot soldiers.

He needed to put a source in place. A reliable source.

There were only two people in the world who could help him.

One more time, he pushed the intercom button. "Do we know where the Cutlers are?" he asked his assistant.

"No, but I can probably find them by following their bread crumbs on social media."

"So find them," Takayama said.

CHAPTER 25

NOAA Mauna Loa Observatory, Hawai'i

A half hour before the morning meeting, everyone from HVO had been packed into the belly of one Chinook copter. Now they were all clustered around Kenny Wong's laptop. Alongside it was the laptop belonging to one of the six young guys from the military base. The six guys immediately began swinging away at Kenny and Rick's calculations.

They were doing it politely, but that didn't matter. They were relentlessly carving up his work into what he imagined were bite-size morsels. It made Kenny want to hide under his desk. Rick Ozaki was sitting next to him breathing heavily and painfully, like a wounded bear. Kenny didn't dare look around for Mac.

It turned out these guys were part of a geophysical modeling team from AOC, Army Ordnance Corps.

And, Kenny had to admit, they were damned good.

They had been to UH and reviewed Kenny's stored data. They had run their own calculations on the data. And they seemed to have dozens of additional programs that they were running and rerunning on the spot.

Finally, the head of the team, a George Clooney look-alike named Morton, said, "I think we need to go outside now. All of us."

Kenny, Rick, Mac, Jenny, Briggs, and the army guys all walked outside, shoes crunching on black lava. It was sunny up there at eleven thousand feet, with a light, fluffy cloud layer about five thousand feet below them.

"I'm sorry, boys," Morton said, "but the stress-load calculations are very clear. Even if you have magma within a kilometer of the surface—and most of it is much deeper than that—there is no way to open a one-kilometer vent in a mountain with conventional explosives. This mountain is too big; the forces are too big. It would be like trying to move a jumbo jet with a swizzle stick."

Kenny said, "Even with resonant explosives?" Resonant explosives were a recent innovation. The idea was to use small, precisely timed charges to set up resonant movement in large objects, the way giving small pushes to a swing gradually made it go higher and higher.

"Even resonant explosives won't do it," Morton said. "Computer-controlled timing can produce very powerful effects. But we're still orders of magnitude too small. Even if we wanted to go nuclear—and I'm going to assume we don't—it probably wouldn't be enough."

No one spoke right away. The only sound was the wind.

During the discussion, something had nagged at Mac. He gazed at the summit now, shielding his eyes against the glare of the sun, looking past the engineers and Colonel Briggs and Jenny and the guys from the data room to where steam vents hissed into the air.

He had been thinking about steam all day.

Whenever the volcano began degassing, there was always the question of whether it was gas released by magma or groundwater being heated to steam. Steam eruptions had occurred on multiple occasions in the past, and Mac knew the dangers they presented, and not just to the environment.

"Hold on a minute," he said.

They all turned to him.

"We're thinking about this wrong," Mac said.

Morton, who was standing next to Briggs, said, "How so?"

"We're thinking about ways to control the volcano," Mac said. "But we can't."

"Right," Morton said. "We don't have the explosive power to open a vent, and we can't generate enough energy to do it."

"But the volcano itself has plenty of energy," Mac said.

He felt them all staring at him.

"What if we can make the volcano do the work for us?" Mac asked.

Briggs said, "Wait…*what*?"

Mac said, "How far down can you place explosives?"

"That depends on the thickness of the basalt and the presence of thermal effects," Morton said. "But that doesn't alter the basic—"

Mac ignored him and addressed Briggs. "Those helicopters you have carrying the bulldozers—"

"Chinooks," Briggs said.

"Can they also carry water?"

Rick Ozaki dropped his head. He was sure he knew what his boss would say next. Quietly he murmured, "Please, God, no," to his boots.

Jenny Kimura was shaking her head. "John MacGregor," she said.

It was never good when she used his full name. But she also knew where he was headed with this.

Briggs said, "Yes, they can carry water. They've occasionally been used for firefighting."

"How *much* water?" Mac said.

"I'd have to check. Water's heavy. But I'm guessing three thousand gallons each."

"How many helicopters can you get?"

"I'd have to check that too. I think we've got five at Barking Sands on Kaua'i. There's probably fifteen or twenty on all the islands. Why?"

"This summit—this whole mountain—is dotted with lava tubes and air chambers," Mac said. "Most of them are sealed over by the eruption that created them, and some of them are very large. We knew they were there, but we didn't know exactly where until we started mapping using high-resolution magnetometry. Anyway, you could break into the underground pockets and place your explosives, then you could fill them with water and seal them."

"Which would do what, exactly?" one of the army engineers finally asked.

"Keep the detonation wave under high pressure. Restore the explosive capacity. Instead of moving magma up, you'd just have to move water down to contact the magma."

"Where it makes steam and hisses out for a few hours," the engineer said.

"Only if the contact is slow. But if you make a sudden contact..." Mac said.

"I hear you!" another one of the AOC men said. He turned to the others on his team. "You could use quad arrays in multiples."

"We'd need a lot of on-site calculations..."

"I know," the AOC man said, "but I believe it *is* possible."

"And how would you get the arrays to communicate?" another man asked Mac.

"You don't," Mac said. "You make them autonomous."

The AOC team huddled together. Mac could hear them talking excitedly, although they kept their voices low. One of them picked up a chunk of lava. Someone said something about porosity and sealant pressures.

Rick and Kenny walked over to Mac; Mac could see the concern on Rick's face.

"Mac," Rick said, "you know what you're saying, right? You're talking about making this volcano explode."

"You know something, though? It just might work," Kenny said.

"And that's exactly what I'm afraid of," Rick said. "We're talking about trying to make a *nuée ardente*. An avalanche of fire. The most dangerous volcanic phenomenon there is."

"Pretty much," Mac said.

CHAPTER 26

Glowing volcanic avalanches had destroyed Pompeii in AD 79 and had flattened whole islands near Krakatoa in 1883, but they remained a phenomenon unknown to science until 1902, when the volcano Mount Pelée erupted on the Caribbean island of Martinique.

Pelée had been restless for months, but no one was prepared when, at 7:52 a.m. on May 8, 1902, an avalanche of red-hot gas and ash roared down the mountain at five hundred kilometers an hour; it destroyed the town of Saint-Pierre and most of the ships anchored in the harbor.

Twenty-nine thousand people died, many almost instantaneously.

The handful of surviving eyewitnesses—the lucky ones on boats far enough out to sea to avoid the gas cloud—described a scene of hellish destruction. Photographs of the town reduced to smoking ruins made the front pages of newspapers around the world.

The avalanche that had caused this instantaneous destruction was termed a *nuée ardente*, or "fiery cloud." It ripped through three-foot-thick concrete walls, smashed whole buildings, tore heavy cannons from their mountings, and snapped a lighthouse in half like a twig.

These avalanches were now termed *pyroclastic flows* and were the focus of intense study by volcanologists. Numerous attempts had been made to model their behavior in laboratories. Jenny Kimura had worked on it one summer at the Osservatorio Vesuviano near Naples, part of a team that made models of hot lava flows in a sloped laboratory tank, and she had also done computer modeling of these flows. She knew more about pyroclastic flows than anyone at HVO, including Mac, but she didn't say anything at first. It was one of the things Mac liked about her, sometimes loved. Jenny let the game come to her.

"Okay, let's think this through," Rick said. "Let's say you succeed. Then what?"

"Then we'll have blown open the vent and released the lava," Mac said.

"And sent a pyroclastic flow racing toward Hilo." Rick pointed down the mountain.

"It'll never get there."

"You hope."

"Rick, I'm telling you it won't," Mac said. "The slope is too gentle; the avalanche can't sustain. It'll die out in three or four kilometers."

"But isn't how far it goes a function of the initial blast, Jen?"

Mac wanted to smile. Rick was challenging them the way Mac always challenged him.

Jenny shook her head. Now she was ready to engage. "Mac's right. It'll never get to Hilo."

"For now," Briggs said, "we don't want Dr. MacGregor to just tell us how his plan might work. We want him to show us. With the understanding that we in the United States Army have not ruled out the building of walls at this time."

"Fair enough. Follow me," Mac said. He was the one giving the orders now.

Mac led them all over jagged lava fields for half a mile, then got down on his hands and knees in front of a hole that was just big enough to squeeze through.

"This one's a typical lava tube opening," he said to the group. "Just be careful when you come through. And don't keep going forward. Move to the right."

He crawled through the hole, and the others followed him one by one.

Once inside, Mac switched on his phone's flashlight app because the tube was pitch-black. As the others came through, they switched on their phones. Yellow beams crisscrossed like searchlights.

They found themselves in a domed pocket the size of a high-school gym. The ceiling was smooth, almost shiny, but the floor was rough black lava.

"This is a typical air chamber," Mac said, his voice echoing. "It's a bit like being inside a bubble. The magma releases gases as it rises, and if those collect in a big bulge, you get this smooth surface that you see above us. The lava flows continuously beneath this air pocket and often forms a second and even a third chamber. The ceilings of those chambers may break open, making a large pit. If you move carefully forward, you can see down into the pit here. Just don't get too close to the edge—it's thin. And it's a long drop."

"That's putting it mildly," someone behind him said, shining the light down.

The pit was a hundred meters deep, perhaps more. It was hard to be sure; the light beam vanished into the blackness of the lava tube as if it had been swallowed up.

One of the AOC men said, "Exactly how many chambers like this are there, Dr. MacGregor?"

"Dozens," Mac said. "Maybe more than that. We just have to choose the right ones."

The critical issue, Mac told them, was whether the HVO really was able to pinpoint the exact location of the magma beneath the surface. If they knew the location of the magma pipes within a few hundred meters, they could choose three or four air chambers that were directly above the rising magma, place explosives, then fill them with water.

"All in four days," he said. "Or the whole thing is pointless."

He looked at them, their faces illuminated by the various phone flashlight apps.

Earlier, as he was talking, the AOC team had produced some nylon line, and now they started lowering one of the men into the pit.

"They don't waste any time, do they?" Rick said.

"We have none to waste," Briggs said. He turned to Mac.

"We might be able to do this in four days," Mac said. "It'll be tight, but I think we can."

Briggs nodded. "There's no way in hell to keep this job a secret. You're talking about a lot of personnel, a lot of equipment on this mountain. You can't hide it."

Jenny Kimura said, "Couldn't you say the army is doing something up here? Something of a positive nature?"

"Like what?"

"I don't know. Repairing our access roads. We've lost some crucial access roads and the army is helping repair them."

"You really think we can sell that?" Briggs asked.

"The visuals alone can sell it," Jenny said. "This is the age of social media. All anybody cares about these days is how things look." She turned to Mac. "You know that big fissure on jeep trail four at about nine thousand feet?"

"The one that's been around since Truman was president?" he asked.

"Since 1950, to be exact," she said. "It's a good twelve feet deep and maybe eight feet wide. You show that in the afternoon when it's in shadow, and it's very dramatic."

"There's also a road that skirts around it."

"Right. But it skirts wide, and it's black-on-black lava. If we take the reporters up by helicopter from the Kīlauea side, they'll never see the bypass road."

"You want to take reporters up and show them a seventy-five-year-old vent?" Mac asked.

"They'll love it for the pictures alone, Mac." She turned to Colonel Briggs. "Do you have your uniform with you, sir? We'll need you in uniform."

"For what?"

"For the photo of you and Mac standing at the edge of the fissure, talking about the repairs. It'll look like you're standing at the edge of the world."

"I'd rather not appear." Briggs seemed uneasy. "I'm not the CO on the Big Island."

"Well, we'll need someone in uniform talking with Mac," Jenny said. "To make it into a movie moment."

"Let me make some calls," Briggs said.

The AOC team came back from the pit. Morton said, "We've been over this, and we've concluded there is a high probability it can work."

No shit, Sherlock, Mac thought.

Morton continued, "We're assuming five locations on the mountain, each with chain-linked resonant charges set as far as we can drill into the thick basalt. The sequencing begins with small charges that detonate very rapidly, like firecrackers. Then they get slower and slower until they're every quarter second or so."

He turned to address Briggs. "The problem is that these arrays have to be self-timed, using sensors within the blast material to give feedback to the computers that control the sequencing. So once it starts, it just keeps going."

"And you can get this ready in four days?"

"No, sir, we can't. We need a minimum of seven days for computer programming."

Briggs said, "We don't have seven days."

"I've been listening, sir. I'm aware that we don't."

"So what are you telling me?"

"We need to outsource this job. A few commercial demolition companies have proprietary software for sensors. They don't need programming time because their computers are hard-coded to do it themselves."

"Whom do you suggest?"

"We think the best is Cruz Demolition, out of Houston. They've done a lot of work for the army, and they're fast as hell."

"How long to get them here?"

"Actually, sir, they have a team on-island now."

"What? Here?"

"Honolulu. I believe they're blowing up a building next to a shopping center."

CHAPTER 27

Ala Moana Center, Honolulu, Hawai'i

O ne minute and counting, Becky."

Rebecca Cruz sighed and shook her head as she spoke into her microphone to her brother David.

"You know better than anyone, because I've punched you out over this more than a few times, that I hate being called Becky," she said.

"Why do you think I do it?" he asked.

"I'd like to be even closer," Becky said.

"You always want to be as close to the action as possible," he said. "But any closer than this and it's not safe."

"Safe is no fun," Becky said.

"Shut up," David Cruz said.

It was pounding rain in Honolulu; water was running in a continuous stream off her baseball cap. She felt as if she were standing underneath a waterfall. And Rebecca Cruz didn't like this one little bit.

She was standing in the huge upper parking lot of Ala Moana, staring up at the building they were about to blow. Ordinarily she liked rain on these jobs. Kept the dust down and the crowds small. But at the moment, there was no crowd at all, so the rain that had been falling for the past fifteen minutes could just freaking stop now.

She felt completely alone, a slender young woman wearing an orange construction slicker. With her pretty face and dark ponytail, she would have looked like a high-school cheerleader if it weren't for her wire-frame glasses, which she wore more for effect than for the slight improvement in her distance vision. She thought they made her look older and more serious. More like the boss that she was.

The glasses were spattered with water now, and she didn't even bother trying to clean them. She just lowered her plastic safety goggles over the glasses.

Ala Moana was the biggest outdoor shopping mall in the United States and now—*Stop me if you've heard this one before,* Rebecca thought—it needed room to grow. That was why Cruz Demolition was about to take down the Kama Kai office tower next to the mall. The fifteen-story structure had been built in the 1990s, a quick-and-dirty job by a local contractor who'd bribed officials liberally, enabling him to use construction techniques that David said he wouldn't even call substandard because that would be insulting to substandard techniques.

They had hardwired this job, mostly because they'd had no choice with so many radio taxis around. But that meant using about six miles of electrical cables held together by a lot of screw connectors. And if just one cable lying in a rain puddle shorted out—

Her radio headset clicked. David again.

"Sis, we have a problem here." David was all business now.

"What is it?"

"It's the water weight."

"I know. We're still going."

Another voice said, "I think we need to hold, Rebecca."

The voice belonged to their cousin Leo, who ran the computers. It always worked the same way with those two: When David got nervous, so did Leo. If David sneezed, Rebecca half expected Leo to reach for his handkerchief.

"Why?" she asked.

"I'm worried about connections."

"We're not holding."

Leo said, "But if the computers—"

That was as far as he got before Rebecca snapped, "Will you *shut up*!" She took a breath. "Pretty soon there'll be more people around here, more traffic, more problems. More risk."

David said, "That's true, but—"

She cut him off. "And the rain's hitting the east side of the building more than the other sides," she continued. "We know that that concrete is porous crap."

"More like an old sponge than concrete," David said.

"Right. So the longer we hold, the more weight the rain adds to one side. Right now the computers can handle the change. Later, maybe they can't."

"Let the rain stop," David said. "Let the building dry."

"*David.*" She hit his name hard. "It may do this for days."

Her brother wasn't thinking straight, but she couldn't tell him that. Once they had the building completely wired, they had to go. They ordinarily took buildings down on Sunday mornings, since that was when cities were least crowded. That was their routine, and they finished up their prep work the day before.

Just not this time.

This time they weren't able to wait until Sunday; they had to go on Friday. Every building had its surprises, but the Kama Kai was so shoddy, it seemed ready to fall down on its own. And that was a problem. A big-ass problem. It was much easier to take down a well-engineered and well-constructed building because you could predict what would happen. With a heap of Legos like the Kama Kai, there was always uncertainty.

Too much, in this case. And pushing things back added more.

"Give me the count," she said.

"We're at fifteen seconds, Rebecca." Leo again. He sounded unhappy, like Rebecca was punishing him by making them go ahead. But when they got this close to detonation, Rebecca knew, unhappiness was her cousin's natural state.

Go time, she told herself.

"Lock it and go off radio," she said. "Let's blow this puppy."

She started counting backward to herself. *Seven...six...five ...four...*

Rebecca waited, staring through the rain coming sideways now at the building.

At four seconds, she heard the preliminary *crack-crack-crack-crack* of the small calibration charges, the ones that the computer used. Ordinarily, it took the computer three seconds to make its final calculations.

Out loud, she said, "Three...two...one."

She heard no detonation.

In fact, nothing happened.

The Kama Kai tower still stood in the slashing rain.

Rebecca began counting forward. "One...two...three..."

Still nothing.

Rebecca Cruz was thirty and she had been working in the family business—the formal name was Cruz Demolition and Trucking—ever since she'd graduated from Vassar. It was best to keep this kind of work in the family, her brothers had told her when she talked about various other careers. It demanded too much patience, too much attention to detail, too much trust for them to invite outsiders into the tent.

This job is like a marriage, her older brother, Peter, used to say, *just a lot more stressful.*

By now she had worked on some fifty buildings around the world and been the lead on at least half of them. *Should have been the lead on all of them,* she told herself, *even when I was fresh out of college.*

But in the past few years, she had seen the business change. Contracts were shorter. The pace was much faster. The days when they could take three weeks to study a building were over. Now clients expected a building to be taken down and carted away in a matter of days, not weeks, and this was true even when they were working hazardous sites.

But the faster pace suited Rebecca's personality. Her brothers were more cautious—too cautious, to her mind, and too timid sometimes for a dangerous business like theirs. Rebecca Cruz wanted to keep pushing forward and get the job done, wherever in the world the job was. She was able to push forward, and push back, in several languages; she spoke Japanese, German, some Italian, a little Korean, a little Mandarin.

But pushing so hard was one of the things about her that pissed her brothers off, and royally.

She didn't believe she was reckless; she just didn't hesitate. By now even her brothers knew enough to get out of her way.

David couldn't lead on a job. If she left things to him, nothing would get taken down. David worried things to death.

Rebecca wasn't a worrier. She was always too busy getting things done, basically.

But she was worrying now.

She had counted to twenty and still nothing had happened.

Of course the computer would take a certain amount of extra

time to recalculate the blast timings because one side of the building was wet, and that changed the calibration impacts. But not twenty damn seconds. That could only mean one thing:

They had a short.

So Leo's fears were justified this time.

Damn it, she thought.

They would have to go back in. But she didn't want to be in that building again, with its scored I-beams, chopped floors, the possibility of live...

Forget about Legos. It was like a house of cards.

She heard a soft *whump!*

Sawdust burst outward from the lower floors' windows.

"*All right!*" she yelled, pumping her fist.

The walls of the upper stories gently folded inward. A perfect implosion; the building slid to the ground almost in slow motion. There was a final, much louder *whump!* as the roof crashed down.

And it was over.

Rebecca clicked her radio back on and waited for the congratulations from the others. Apparently, they hadn't turned their radios on yet.

No matter. They would celebrate with beers very soon; she didn't care how early it was.

As she turned to go find them, a dark brown van squealed to a stop in front of her, so close that it nearly clipped her.

Two men in dark raincoats jumped out. One of them said, "Rebecca Maria Cruz?" He held up some sort of badge.

"Yes."

"Come with us, please."

For one crazy moment she thought she was being arrested. Demolition without a license? But they didn't touch her; they just held open the door to the van.

"What is this?" she said.

"Please get out of the rain, ma'am," one of them said. "If you don't mind."

As she started to climb into the van, she saw that David and Leo were already inside. So were Don McNulty and Ben Russell. The whole team.

"Could somebody please tell me what's going on here?" Rebecca said.

Nobody answered.

She felt strong hands on her back, shoving her forward.

"Hey!" she yelled as she stumbled into a seat.

"Sorry, ma'am," one of the men said. "We have a schedule." The door slammed shut, and the van shot off into the rain, tires squealing.

CHAPTER 28

Hawaiian Volcano Observatory, Hawai'i
Time to eruption: 95 hours

Lono Akani wanted to be more than just Mac's star student surfer. He wanted to be his star intern at HVO too, wanted to feel like a *kāpena* of that team also.

Captain.

So Lono had decided to spend all day at the observatory up the mountain. His mother had dropped him off at school, but as soon as she was gone, he hitched a ride to HVO.

When he got there, he saw all these army guys. But why? He knew Mac wasn't here because his car wasn't in the parking lot. He saw Betty Kilima, the librarian, going down the hall, and he hurried after her. His station was on the other side of the room from hers.

"Why all the army guys?"

"I heard they're helping us rebuild the jeep roads."

"What's wrong with the roads?" Lono asked. "I never heard Mac say anything about the roads." He jerked his head in the direction of the men. "This looks like an invasion."

"I guess he's worried that they're in bad shape and we can't move around fast enough to take readings during the eruption."

He didn't think that was true. Just his gut instinct. Too many army guys. This was about more than roads, and he knew it. There seemed to be an atmosphere of excitement at the observatory, almost tension. It was in the air all around him.

Betty said, "Ready to work?" She raised her eyebrows. "Why aren't you in school?"

"Got permission," he said.

"Really?" she said suspciously.

He put his hand over his heart. "*Ho'ohiki wau*—I swear."

Most days he helped her sort data files for an hour or so. These were mostly satellite pictures that had to be cataloged by the acquisition time and spectrum covered before they were shipped down to UH for storage. It was grunt work, but Mac always said that details were part of the process. That was all Lono had needed to hear, even though the process was boring. Mac's word was law.

Betty's intercom buzzed. Lono was close enough to recognize the voice: Rick Ozaki, the seismic specialist. He was working in the data room.

"Betty? We need help," Rick said. "Can you get me the most recent mag data?"

Lono knew immediately what he was talking about. Rick wanted high-resolution magnetometry pictures showing Moku'āweoweo.

The summit crater.

"Sure," she said. Betty glanced over, saw Lono watching her. "What do you need?" she asked Rick. "GEM Systems?"

Lono knew that GEM's GSM-19 Overhauser magnetometer

delivered data that was very high quality. Rick often wanted GEM data because it had excellent resolution.

"No problem. Lono's right here with me."

"Is that right? Hey, Lono, what are you doing there?"

The boy grinned. "I know you can't make a move without me."

"Well, get data starting backward from present," Rick said. "I'm looking for an image that shows those dark areas around the summit, you know?"

"The air pockets?"

Rick said, "Yeah. The field team just walked the area to map new pockets. Find the pictures from the ground-level magnetic surveys." He meant the ones that came from a magnetometer a tech carried inside a nonmagnetic backpack, the device fitted to a boom six feet above the ground.

"The total magnetic strength above the lava tube complex?" Lono asked.

"Just see what you can find."

Lono was suddenly glad he had come to the observatory today, even without permission; he had a sense of mission, of something important to do. And he'd heard the urgency in Rick's voice.

A few minutes later, searching through the drive, he said to Betty, "Does this have to do with the roads?"

"Not sure. Maybe he's working on something else," she said.

Lono had a feeling she knew the answer but wasn't going to tell him. He hated being treated like a child, but he was used to it with her.

Lono pulled up the GEM file and scanned the database of stored images. The field team had walked quasi-parallel lines perpendicular to the locations estimated to be the walls of the lava tubes. He was looking specifically for a common magnetic pattern where lower magnetic field values ran the length of each tube.

The intercom buzzed—Rick again. "You still there, Lono?"

"Yes, Rick."

"What've you got?"

"I need a few more minutes."

"Let me know." Rick clicked off.

Lono went back to the GEM list now. The data acquisition was continuous, but deviations around brush and other natural obstacles were frequent. He wanted an image showing a positive magnetic anomaly.

He found five.

He was going through them when the intercom buzzed again.

"Lono?" Rick said. "I don't mean to jam you up, but if you don't have it, I have to arrange a flyover and acquire it today."

Rick had Lono's interest now. Big-time. Lono knew an aircraft flyover was expensive. The observatory did it from time to time, but only when there was a special reason.

After another fifteen minutes, Lono found the image he needed. In shades of purple, yellow, and green, it showed the summit crater and the northern rift zone curving off to the right. He zoomed in; the image softened and began to blur, but he saw the dark patches around the summit that indicated the air chambers.

He shipped it over to Rick and sat back, feeling the tension in his shoulders.

The intercom buzzed again. "Lono?"

"Yes, Rick."

"Is this it? Just one?"

"That's right," Lono said. "Unless you want me to look farther back than—"

"No, no, it has to be recent." Lono heard rustling papers, the soft murmur of other voices in the data room. Rick said to someone at his end, "Why don't you show this to the army guys? I

mean, they're the ones that have to place the damn explosives."
Then he spoke directly into the intercom. "Hey, Lono? Good
job."

And clicked off.

They're the ones that have to place the damn explosives. Had he
actually heard that right?

Lono wanted to open the intercom channel again. He knew
there was an intercom built into the computer system that connected all the workstations at the observatory. There was also a
voice-recognition system that converted voice to text. It was old
and outdated and not very good. Nobody used it much. But Lono
knew it existed.

If he could just remember how to turn it on...

He poked around on the drive. Pretty soon he found it. A
window came up; he typed in his password.

Rejected.

He glanced back at Betty. She was still going through her
papers.

Lono typed in her name and password; he knew what it was
because she always used the same one. The screen changed.
It asked who to link to. He hesitated, then typed JK, for
Jenny Kimura, figuring she would be with Mac and not at her
monitor.

He heard voices speaking and immediately clicked the button
for TEXT. His computer was silent. For a moment nothing happened, and then text began to flow.

```
KENSAY ***UP ***SO***


HAVE TO OPEN THE CHAMBERS IS THE
POINT AND YOU NEED AN EFFICIENT WAY
TO DO THAT
```

```
WE NEED FODAR MAPS TO DECIDE WHERE
TO OPEN UP

WHY

HOW MUCH EXPLOSIVE GOES IN EECH PIT

AN ARRAY IS TWENTY THOUSAND KEELOS
TIMES FOUR

THAT MUCH

ITS KNOT VERY MUCH WE WILL HAVE A
MILL YEN POUNDS OF EXPLOSIVE ON
THAT MOUNTUN IN THE NEXT TWO DAYS

BETTER YOU THAN ME
```

He signed off before Betty noticed what he had done, his mind racing as he tried to figure out why the army needed a million pounds of explosives to fix some bad roads.

As he was heading toward the main entrance to see if anything was going on outside, he heard a loud banging on the front door. One of the army guys opened it, and Lono saw a pretty, dark-haired woman wearing shorts and a T-shirt, hard hat under her arm, walk in like she owned the place. Two men, also carrying hard hats, were right behind her.

"Well, boys," she said to the army guys, "looks like you got something you can't handle and you had to ask for help."

The army guys laughed and started shaking hands with the two men behind her. Everybody seemed to be old friends, acting like this was some kind of reunion.

This isn't about roads, Lono thought. *Definitely not about roads.*

Then Lono heard the helicopter.

A few minutes later Lono saw Mac coming down the hall with an older, white-haired army man who looked like a commanding officer.

"Hey, Mac," Lono said. "What the heck is going on?"

Mac did not seem pleased to see him. The army man looked even less pleased.

"Who the hell is this?" the army man said.

"You need to leave, Lono," Mac said. "If you'd called, I would have told you not to come. I'm suspending interns until further notice."

"Why?"

Mac ignored the question. "Anyway, you should be in school," he said.

"I got permission," Lono lied.

"How'd you get here?"

"I hitched."

Mac blew out air, obviously pissed, and shook his head. "Well, Jenny Kimura's going to town in a few minutes, so she can give you a lift back. Get your stuff together and meet her in front. You can't be here today."

Mac and the army man hurried away, leaving Lono standing there.

Lono was just a kid, but he knew when people were lying to his face. The story about roads was a crock. Why would Mac suspend interns at HVO without even giving a reason to the intern standing right in front of him?

Maybe the island wasn't so safe after all.

He went outside to look for Jenny and saw a big army van parked in the lot. It was the size of a small school bus and painted a drab green, the color of seaweed. A bunch of antennas were sticking up from its roof, and two satellite dishes were mounted on the front.

Lono walked around to the back of it. The door was open, and he could see a lot of electronic equipment inside and men sitting in front of monitors wearing headphones. One man was talking as he punched away at a keyboard.

Another man turned and saw Lono. He got up, glaring at him, and slammed the van door in his face.

All of a sudden Lono felt like he was behind enemy lines.

CHAPTER 29

The data room of HVO had been transformed into an electronic command post.

Rebecca Cruz's team brought their portable consoles in on rolling tables and put them in the center of the room, then got down on their hands and knees, arranged big, insulated cables on the floor, and put beveled metal covers over them. This required some of them to crawl beneath Rick Ozaki's table, and he made no attempt to hide his unhappiness with that.

"I suddenly feel like a speed bump," Rick said to Mac.

"Would you like me to ask them to leave because they've invaded your personal space?" Mac said. "You should have figured out by now that it's all hands on deck."

"How are we supposed to do our work with all this going on around us?" Rick asked.

Rebecca came over and placed her hand on Rick's shoulder. "I am *so* sorry we're in your way. It must be very annoying."

Rick actually blushed. Mac wouldn't have believed it if he hadn't seen it with his own eyes. He grinned. The world might be about to explode, but guys were guys.

Rick went back to work, still blushing slightly, as if he'd just been noticed by the prettiest girl in class.

The Cruzes—Rebecca and her brother and her cousin—were clearly good at their job, Mac had to admit. They were competent and demanding, and they completely took over the room. They refused to plug into the existing HVO power supply—Rebecca said the current wasn't stable enough.

The team's own generators, now chugging away in the parking lot, were incredibly noisy. And they had placed backup batteries in the hall, turning it into an obstacle course.

There was no question who was in charge at Cruz Demolition.

"I know it's annoying," Rebecca told Mac, "but the batteries can't be more than five meters from the computers. It's a timing issue."

She shrugged and produced a dazzling, world-class smile. Her energy was as appealing as she was, Mac thought; she was a power source all by herself. Mac was looking for ways to prolong the conversation when Jenny came over then and asked if they were going to continue with their plan for an ambulance and a medical infirmary. She told him the army people said they needed the space for helicopter landings. Mac said she should ask Briggs.

He could tell Jenny had more to say, but his cell phone rang again—Betty wanted to know if the library should pull up the most recent satellite pictures to find hot areas where lava was coming close to the surface. Then Henry Takayama's assistant called to say that Tako couldn't meet Mac for coffee, but perhaps they could meet in an hour at the pier—would that work? Mac said it would and stuffed his phone back in the pocket of his jeans.

Tako Takayama.

His day just kept getting better.

From time to time, Mac glanced over to the corner of the

room where Colonel Briggs was standing, watching the activity in front of him, listening to the constant chatter. He was obviously feeling the hum of the place and quietly smiling.

Like they were all in the army now.

His.

Briggs understood the situation better than anyone else in the room. He knew he had opened himself up to criticism by trying to distance the army from a crisis they'd created.

But he knew, as a practical matter, that his job right now was to prevent widespread panic and present this operation as a civilian undertaking for which the army was providing support.

Then there was the problem of finance, which was no small thing. In order for the army to fund its involvement in this operation, Briggs needed approval from Hawaiian Command. But experience told him that if he'd attempted to get approval, it would have been delayed or simply denied. That was why the old army man looked at Cruz Demolition as the cavalry riding over the hilltop. Briggs could authorize that; later, if they pulled this mission off, the army could be reimbursed for assisting a civilian operation.

It was in this same spirit that Briggs urged MacGregor to talk to Takayama and keep the army as far in the background as possible.

He also encouraged MacGregor to continue his ordinary routine, including surfing practice in Hilo.

"The less feeling of crisis there is, the better," Briggs said. "Appearances matter, Dr. MacGregor. Trust me on that."

"But I'm needed here," MacGregor said.

"You're needed more down there to show people you're living your life."

"At least you didn't say living my best life," Mac said.

"I might not have the best people skills in the world," Briggs said, "but I'm not an idiot."

It was Briggs who deftly orchestrated the closing of the park to the public, which would be done in stages over the next forty-eight hours. Working with Jenny Kimura, Briggs had all the press releases for the coming days ready on the first day. And it was Briggs who encouraged MacGregor to bring in other high-profile experts as advisers.

"Don't take this all on your own shoulders," he said. "Spread it around."

"So I can spread blame around later?" Mac asked. "Is that the army way?"

The two men stared at each other in silence. Mac knew he had probably overstepped, but he wasn't any more worried about Briggs's feelings than he was about his own staff's. Something else Mac always told Rick and Kenny and even Jenny: *It's a hard-ball league. Wear a helmet.*

Briggs was the one who blinked first.

"I've heard concerns about pyroclastic flows," he said. "Are there experts in that area we could call in?"

"There are people we could call in," Mac said. "But we're not going to."

"Why is that?"

"Because either you trust me or you don't, Colonel," Mac said. "That's why."

Briggs gave him the cold-eyed stare again. Maybe he was surprised when Mac didn't go into a dead faint.

"Just so we understand each other," Mac said.

"I'm starting to think I couldn't possibly understand you better if I tried, Dr. MacGregor."

Mac walked over to where Rebecca Cruz was working, thinking, *What's he going to do, court-martial me?*

CHAPTER 30

Eventually so many people were at the observatory that someone made a call and had lunch brought in. A tent with tables and chairs was set up in the visitors' lot about fifty yards from where the green army satellite van was parked.

Rebecca Cruz fell in step with Mac as he made his way to the front door. "Can I join you for lunch, Dr. MacGregor?"

"Call me Mac."

"Can I join you for lunch, *Mac*?" she asked.

"I'd like nothing better, believe me," he said. "Unfortunately, I have a meeting in town."

"Must be important."

"He thinks it is," Mac said. "Henry Takayama. Lord of Civil Defense."

She laughed. "That pompous gasbag? You poor thing."

"I know," he said. "I've got to check with Briggs to see how much I can tell him. But dealing with Henry is the cost of doing business around here."

"Been there," Rebecca said, "done that."

"You've blown up buildings in Hilo?"

"And dreamed about having old Tako in them," she said.

He was liking Rebecca Cruz more and more by the minute. "After I meet with him, I've got practice for some high-school surfers I've been working with."

"So it's *Coach* Dr. MacGregor?"

"You can still call me Mac."

"Well, if you can't buy a girl lunch," she said, "how about dinner later? The ball of fire isn't going to come rolling down the hill tonight."

"Dinner it is," Mac said.

They exchanged phone numbers. Mac felt himself grinning.

"What?" she said.

"This feels like high school," he said.

"Relax, Doc," she said. "Saving the world is a lot less complicated than high school ever was."

CHAPTER 31

Fagradalsfjall Volcano, Iceland
Time to eruption: 93 hours

Huge white clouds blasted upward with a continuous, deafening roar. Standing by the giant circular steel vents, Oliver Cutler looked up to watch the steam clouds boil in the sky; his wife, Leah, was next to him. The camera guy and sound guy who frequently traveled with them, Tyler and Gordon, were a few yards away.

But the Cutlers had never required much direction from them; they had an instinct about the best way to be framed when they were staring down at another volcano. They were there as highly paid consultants, though their critics said the Cutlers' real job was being famous.

Oliver and Leah Cutler were well aware that Bear Grylls had spun his *Man vs. Wild* TV show into international celebrity as an adventurer, and they were doing something similar—they were the husband-and-wife team chasing volcanoes, like the one in front of them.

"I'm ready for my close-up," Leah Cutler said to her husband.

"You've been ready for your close-up your whole life," Oliver said, eyeing Leah's long red hair that he liked to describe as being the color of lava when it began to heat. His own wavy gray hair fell over the collar of the bush jacket that was his field-work uniform, no matter where in the world they were.

The ground beneath their feet vibrated even more power-fully. A louder rumbling filled the air. And as dangerous as they knew all this was, feeling the power of the volcano was part of the essential thrill of what they did; they felt a rush of excitement every time they showed up at a place like this.

And this volcano, one of twenty in Iceland, was relatively peaceful, though it had erupted in 2021 and 2022, filling the valley with blue-tinged volcanic gas.

They were standing on a brown hill above the Meradalir Valley on the western end of Reykjanes Peninsula. All around them, a network of pipes carried steam over the hill to the nearby Svartsengi geothermal power plant.

Oliver needed to shout to be heard by Birkir Fanndal, a friend acting as guide for this trip: "Will you ever use it?" Oliver asked.

"The steam?" Birkir shouted back.

Oliver nodded.

"Oh, yes. Eventually."

But Oliver and Leah Cutler, trained volcanologists and acknowledged experts in their field despite being celebrities, knew full well that the vents were too powerful to be har-nessed; that was why they were left open to release steam to the sky.

The young blond photographer from the Reykjavík news-paper circled them as they talked, working around the camera crew, taking pictures. As if on cue, Oliver Cutler flung his right arm skyward, pointing at the steam. He knew it would make a good picture. He was right, as usual.

"You like that one?" he asked, leaning close to his wife.

"You know I do," she said.

"I'm a giver."

The Cutlers had been invited by Iceland's government to tour the nation's geothermal sites. This country, including its capital city, Reykjavík, was powered almost entirely by geothermal energy; Iceland had exploited this resource more successfully than any other country in the world.

"Do you have enough?" Birkir called to the newspaper photographer.

The woman nodded.

"Then back to the car," Birkir said.

Oliver, Leah, and Birkir drove off in their Land Rover, leaving Tyler and Gordon to pack up and head out in their own rented car.

The Land Rover crossed a high earthwork dam overlooking the acres of black lava that marked the most recent eruption of Fagradalsfjall. The dam, the Cutlers saw, was man-made.

"Where'd this come from?" Leah asked.

"Built it for the last eruption," Birkir said. "We didn't want the lava to reach the power plant."

"And it worked?" Oliver said.

"Don't know if it would've or not," Birkir said. "The lava never got that far."

Oliver's cell phone rang. Even in the middle of the Icelandic countryside, cell phones worked. "Cutler."

"Please hold for Henry Takayama."

Now there's a name from the past, Oliver Cutler thought.

He and Leah had met Tako Takayama five years earlier on a consulting visit to Hilo; Takayama, the head of Civil Defense, had invited them. Oliver wondered if he still had the same job. As soon as he had that thought, he smiled. Of *course* Takayama still had the same job. He was the type. Oliver was sure of it—Tako Takayama would die in that job.

"Oliver, how the hell are you?" Takayama said when he came on the line.

"Very good, Tako."

Oliver saw curiosity register on his wife's face when she heard the name, obviously remembering him too.

Oliver raised his eyebrows and shrugged helplessly. But in that moment, a nearly forgotten phrase from the islands came back to him: "Long time, no smell."

He heard Takayama laugh. "Listen, I'm calling because I need your advice, Oliver. There's something going on at the observatory, and I think it could mean big trouble."

"Well, you know trouble's our business," Oliver Cutler said.

"I'm serious."

"Actually, Tako, so am I." Oliver winked at Leah.

"They're predicting an eruption at Mauna Loa," Takayama said.

"I figured that mountain was about due."

"Yes, but there is some big operation up there and the army is heavily involved. All sorts of heavy equipment, helicopters, and earthmovers."

"I'm listening."

"They *say* all they're doing is repairing the roads."

Cutler considered that. Finally he said, "You know, they could be. I remember those roads, actually. The jeep trails have been bad for years."

"So bad you need a hundred engineers and twenty helicopters up on the mountain? So bad you need to close the airspace for a week? Does that make any sense?"

"No, it does not."

Even from across the world, Oliver could hear the concern in

Takayama's voice. And the irritation. Tako was a powerful civil servant in Hilo, but the army was apparently excluding him from whatever was going on. To someone like Takayama, less power was as bad as no power.

Clearly there was a problem, at least from where Takayama sat. Maybe a big one.

"Oliver," Takayama said. "You still there?"

"I'm here."

Cutler was trying to process what he'd been told and what he was intuiting. If Takayama was calling, he didn't just have a problem with the army; he had a problem with HVO. And that likely meant a problem with MacGregor, the guy running it. That hothead. He didn't know as much as he thought he did and, worse, didn't know what he *didn't* know. A loner and an all-around pain in the ass. It had taken only one day in Hilo for Oliver and Leah to figure that out.

Oliver had recently heard that MacGregor's wife had left him; the news made Oliver happy.

"So how can I help?" Cutler asked.

"I was wondering if maybe you could come for a visit."

"Tako, that sounds like a marvelous idea, given where we are at the moment. But where we are at the moment is Iceland."

"It wouldn't have to be a long visit."

"Just a long goddamn trip to get there," Cutler said.

"Oliver," Takayama said. "I wouldn't be calling you if this weren't important to me. The city of Hilo has an interest in what's going on. I'm afraid that interest is being neglected. There'll be an eruption in a few days, which gives our city a perfectly legitimate reason to invite you and Leah here as official advisers."

"I need to give you a heads-up on something before we go any further," Cutler said. "We haven't gotten any cheaper since we were last there."

"I'll pay the ransom," Takayama said.

Oliver Cutler saw his wife smiling as she listened to his half of the conversation. She mouthed the word *Aloha*.

"How soon do you need us there?"

"How about yesterday?" Takayama said.

CHAPTER 32

Kīlauea Rim, Hawai'i
Saturday, April 26, 2025
Time to eruption: 76 hours

Mac had ended up postponing his dinner with Rebecca Cruz the night before. He'd asked for a raincheck and headed back to the office, where he'd pulled a college-like all-nighter with Jenny and Rick Ozaki and Kenny Wong. They'd finally left HVO around four o'clock in the morning. Somehow Mac had managed to get to sleep around five.

But an hour later, for some reason, he was wide awake. When he came out of the shower, he saw he'd missed a call from the Military Reserve. He was about to return it when Jenny phoned and told him she'd be at his house in fifteen minutes. The army had called her when they couldn't reach Mac.

"Our presence is requested, even though it didn't sound like a request," Jenny said. "The guy even used the word *stat*."

"Where are we going?" Mac asked.

Jenny said, "The Ice Tube."

"They say why?" Mac said.

"Colonel Briggs's man said it was easier to show us than tell us," Jenny said. Then she added, "You get any sleep?"

"'Ain't no slumber party,'" Mac said. "'Got no time for catching z's.'"

"Another one of your old songs?"

"You calling Bon Jovi old?"

"I know he's cute," she said, "but he looks like my dad now."

It was a short ride from Mac's house to the Military Reserve. The guy who'd called Jenny was the same sergeant who'd driven Mac and Briggs to the Ice Tube the day before, Matthew Iona. He met them at the base, dressed in fatigues, and they all changed into what Mac thought of as their spacesuits and got into Iona's jeep.

"You ready to tell me what this is all about?" Mac asked.

"It's like I told Dr. Kimura, sir. It's easier to show than tell."

They made the bumpy ride up the mountain in tense silence after that. When they arrived at the entrance to the cave, Mac said, "How many people at the base know what's inside here?"

"Not many," Iona said.

"But you're one of them."

Iona shrugged. "Just lucky, I guess." He looked at Mac. "You feeling lucky, Dr. MacGregor?"

"Not recently," Mac said.

Then they were back inside the cave, beams from the flashlights they'd brought with them crisscrossing in the semidarkness. They walked slowly, almost as if they were making their way across a minefield, the only sound in the Ice Tube the crunch of the lava rock underneath their feet and the breathing they heard behind their glass masks.

At one point Jenny stumbled and grabbed Iona's arm to keep from falling.

"You okay, ma'am?" he asked.

"Peachy," she said.

"Just a little farther," Iona said.

Mac knew that the dimensions of the cave hadn't changed since the last time he was here; it hadn't shrunk. But it seemed like it had. He didn't know why—he had spent his career in confined spaces like this and had never once suffered from claustrophobia.

But he felt like these walls were closing in on him.

They moved along the foam-covered deck, passing the massive coolers Mac remembered. Finally, they reached the grate door, and Iona unlocked it and opened it. The sudden creak of that in the quiet around them seemed jarring. Mac saw Jenny jump back.

"I feel like I'm in a freaking haunted house," she said. She looked at Iona. "Sorry. I'm usually not like this."

"No need to apologize, ma'am. We're all a little jumpy these days. I didn't know when I joined the army that I was signing up for this."

They went through the door and saw the canisters lined up on both sides of them. Mac was unable to shake the feeling that he was looking at miniature nuclear bombs.

"There," Sergeant Matthew Iona said, pointing to the right.

The walls seemed to press in closer.

CHAPTER 33

The Ice Tube, Mauna Kea, Hawai'i

Mac and Jenny squinted into the weird blue light coming from the canisters as if trying not to see what Sergeant Matthew Iona was showing them:

Two canisters with clear, well-defined cracks like quake fissures, cracks that hadn't been there when Mac came into the cave with Colonel Briggs.

"So there it is," Iona said.

Mac's breathing sounded louder than ever behind his mask; he was surprised the faceplate wasn't fogging up. His suit seemed much heavier than it had when he'd put it on back at the base. He felt like he was suddenly carrying the weight of the world.

He saw Iona sag as if he were feeling the same weight Mac was, and Mac knew Jenny Kimura surely felt it too.

"It's like they're time bombs," Jenny said, her voice sounding tinny from behind her mask. She stared wide-eyed at the canisters. "They've just been waiting half a century to explode."

Iona said, "We have to hope that the lava doesn't come anywhere near here and that we can find a safe way to remove these things and do it faster than Colonel Briggs says is humanly possible. We probably need a Hail Mary."

"Full of grace," Mac said quietly.

Mac and Jenny had spent all of last night listening to Rick and Kenny spell out their new projections in painfully precise detail. Mac had challenged them the way he always did, wanting to poke holes in their data, wanting them to be wrong. But gradually—and painfully—he'd come to the conclusion that they weren't.

"These cracks are pretty much a nightmare for us," Iona said.

"For all of us," Mac said.

The ground underneath them began to shake in a way it wasn't supposed to within these walls. The canisters right there in front of them shook too, and so did the walls.

As if they might come tumbling down.

CHAPTER 34

Honoli'i Beach Park, Hilo, Hawai'i

From where he stood on the Hilo beach, a place he'd begun to think of as his own private beach, Lono Akani watched with awe—there was no other way to describe it—as the cool members of the Canoe Club knifed across the water in their long boat.

Lono and his three friends were out here this early on a Saturday morning because Dennis Lee had checked the surf forecast the night before and promised them that this was when the waves would be fastest-breaking, with just the perfect chop in the water for the best possible rides.

But the guys rowing in the distance, they were training like they did almost every day, getting ready for the all-island regatta coming up in June, getting after it while Lono and Dennis and Moke and Duke ate the doughnuts they'd picked up in town.

Dennis had made them stop at Popover because he said there was no way he was surfing on an empty stomach.

"Your brain might be empty," Moke told him, "but your stomach hardly ever is."

Lono was barely listening. His eyes were focused on the rowers. It wasn't just awe that he felt; there was something else, something more—a powerful sense of envy at the teamwork he was witnessing. Mac liked to tell them that he thought of his surfers as a team, but Lono knew better. In surfing, it was every man for himself.

Lono had called Mac this morning to ask if he wanted to come watch them. But that was just his cover story. A head fake. With everything he'd seen and heard at HVO yesterday, Lono hoped that if he pressed hard enough, Mac might tell him what was really going on.

Mac didn't answer his phone, though, and Lono didn't leave a message.

So they'd come to surf without him for a change. While they waited for the waves, Lono told his friends about what had happened yesterday at HVO and how Mac had blown him off when he tried to ask questions about it.

"I'm telling you, they're gearing up for the Big One," Lono said.

"You decided that because of what you *think* you heard?" Duke asked.

He was the biggest of their group, and he looked older, a tight end and linebacker on the Hilo High varsity football team. He was rocking a Mohawk haircut.

"I *know* what I heard and what I saw," Lono said. "These guys are *scientists*. They know what they're talking about."

"*Haole* scientists," Dennis said.

"Right," Lono said. "Got it. Because you're native, so maybe we should call you a *kamaʻāina* meathead instead of just a plain old meathead."

Moke gave Lono a playful shove toward the water. "C'mon,

you think the Big One is coming when somebody's car engine makes a loud noise," he said.

Lono shook his head. His friends either weren't listening to him or just didn't want to believe it. Maybe because they were high-school kids and it was too perfect a morning on the Big Island for them to worry about anything except the waves they were about to catch.

"I told you the same thing before Mauna Loa blew a few years ago," Lono said.

"And we're still here, aren't we?" Dennis asked.

"I'm telling you, they were talking about something *loa* big," Lono said. "And *loa* bad."

"My grandmother always told me that eruptions are just the Earth's way of speaking to us," Dennis said.

Lono, *kama'āina* like his friends, knew all the myths and legends about volcanoes, the way old people like Dennis Lee's grandmother thought of them as powerful living creatures who were not to be interfered with for fear of their response.

"My *kupuna wahine*," Moke said, referring to his own grandmother, "tells me that eruptions are a way that the Earth is reborn."

"Until one comes along and kills us all," Lono said.

"Hey, are we gonna surf now?" Dennis asked Lono. "Or do you want me to take you home so you can hide under the covers and wait for your mommy?"

Before Lono could say anything, the sand underneath their feet began to shake so hard that the boys were afraid the beach might open wide and swallow them up.

He and his friends ran with their boards under their arms, but not toward the water.

They ran away from it.

* * *

Moke dropped Lono and Dennis off at Dennis's house, and the boys sat on the small couch in Dennis's living room trying to ignore the tremors that were still coming every few minutes, like rolling thunder.

They tried to play Dennis's new video game Riding the Lava, but they gave up when the walls of the small ranch house refused to stop shaking, both of them finally tossing their controllers onto the coffee table.

"When I was little and it got like this," Dennis said, "I used to tell my mother to make the *hekili* go away."

The native word for "thunder."

Lono somehow managed a smile, despite the nerves that were tying his stomach in knots. "So where's your mom when we need her?" Lono asked.

"She left for the office before Moke picked me up this morning," Dennis said.

"She's working on a Saturday?"

Dennis's mother was the assistant to Mr. Takayama, the head of Civil Defense in Hilo. "She said big things were happening," Dennis said.

"The Big One is happening, that's what," Lono said. "Whether you want to believe me or not."

The house shook with the biggest jolt yet; it felt like there had been a lightning strike on Dennis's block.

Dennis Lee looked at Lono. "They've always stopped before," he said. "Why won't they stop today?" He grabbed his controller from the coffee table, pointed it like a gun in the direction of the big living-room window, and furiously pressed buttons.

"What are you doing?" Lono asked.

"Trying to pause this," Dennis said.

He was the funniest kid of all of them, the one who didn't take anything seriously, except maybe the girls at Hilo High. But

Lono could see the fear in his eyes now—he wasn't even trying to hide it.

Lono tried to remember the excitement they'd felt an hour before when they'd gotten to the beach and the whole morning was spread out in front of them.

But that feeling was gone.

Lono realized something as the walls of the small house started shaking again: The Earth wasn't just talking, the way Dennis's grandmother said it did when the thunder came up out of the ground this way.

It was shouting at them and refusing to stop.

CHAPTER 35

When they'd felt the first tremors inside the lava tube, Mac saw Iona turn and take a step back toward the entrance.

Mac stopped him by putting a hand on his arm. He grinned as he did it, not wanting the move to seem overly aggressive.

"You know, son," Mac said, "they shoot deserters in the army."

"Hey, hold on—"

"Just kidding. But you need to relax."

"*Relax?*" Iona said. "You felt the same thing I did."

"And with your EOD training, *you* ought to know that quakes aren't our biggest concern in lava caves," Mac said.

"It's why the canisters are here, Sergeant, am I right?" Jenny asked.

Before Iona could respond, Mac said, "There's something else you should know, if you don't know it already. The shock waves produced by earthquakes are largely unable to travel through the air. These caves are structurally sound, at least generally, because most of the loose rocks have fallen during the formation process. So the fact is, even though this place does look spooky as hell, these caves are pretty goddamn solid when it comes to absorbing shock waves like the one we just felt."

"We shouldn't have felt anything at all in here," Iona said stubbornly.

"That just means the magma is on the move," Mac said. "But we knew that already, didn't we?"

Mac knew how much force magma exerted on rocks as it moved through the crust; it was what generated most of the earthquakes in volcanically active areas like theirs. Eventually, the fluid pressure from the rising magma caused cracks in the rocks, the lava making space for itself. These were earthquakes related to ground swelling, and they were rarely larger than a magnitude of 5 and usually less than a 3.

What they'd just felt, Mac explained, might have been a volcano tectonic quake or something else, perhaps a long-period quake, which could be an indicator that the magma had moved into the shallower parts of the volcano. Or it might have been some kind of hybrid of the two. And there were other possibilities, of course, though less likely, including the volcanic tremor he was certain he'd felt the other day at the beach with Lono and the other surfers.

But at this point, none of that really mattered. The only thing that mattered was that the magma *was* on the move and it had just sent that message powerfully enough that they had felt it even in here.

When he finished with his brief tutorial on volcano-related quakes, he told Iona what their next stop needed to be.

"Really?" Iona asked.

"Really."

"You think that's a good idea?" Iona asked.

"Probably not," Mac said.

"If it's all the same to you, sir, I think I'll sit that one out."

Mac grinned. "Not really a request, soldier."

"All due respect, sir," Iona said, "you're not my superior officer."

"All due respect," Mac said, "I am today."

Now Jenny was the one putting a hand on Iona's arm. She pointed at Mac with her other hand.

"My guy here is a fireman at heart," she said. "When others are running out of the building, he's running in."

"Let's go," Mac said, leading them toward the entrance.

When they were outside, he grabbed his cell phone from where he'd tossed it in the jeep, called Rick Ozaki, told him where they were, and asked him to meet them at the base. As soon as Rick got there, Mac said, they were going to take a ride.

"Do I want to know where?" Rick asked.

"We're going up the mountain," Mac said. "Big Mauna is sending us a message."

CHAPTER 36

Mauna Loa, Hawai'i
Time to eruption: 73 hours

A few hundred yards from the rim, Mac, Jenny, Iona, and Rick got out of the jeep. As soon as they stepped out, they felt the full force of the heat coming down the mountain at them. It was like an oven door had been flung open.

"I thought we were moving closer to heaven," Rick said. "Not hell." Rick fixed his eyes on the summit. "You said Big Mauna was sending a message," he said to Mac. "And I know what it is: *You people get the hell off my island.*"

They could hear the roar from inside the caldera. The earth suddenly shook with a harmonic tremor. Sometimes it was called a volcanic scream; it felt like the hum of a giant bass. They all held on to the jeep to keep from falling, and for a fleeting moment Mac worried that the jeep might tip over.

But the tremor passed.

"I thought I'd be used to the quakes by now," Jenny said.

"Trust me," Mac said. "You never get used to them."

"To repeat the question Sergeant Iona asked a little while ago: Is this a good idea?"

"We're fine," Mac said, trying to sound more confident than he felt.

"Fine?" Rick said. "Check it out." He pointed down at the wheels of the jeep at the same moment Mac smelled the burning rubber.

They all looked down and saw the wheels beginning to melt.

"Everybody, wait here," Mac said. He jumped behind the wheel, gunned the engine, made a hard right turn, and, tires skidding as they spit up lava rock and dirt, drove the jeep back down the mountain.

He stopped at least a quarter of a mile below where he'd parked before, then ran hard toward them, leaning forward to take some of the steepness out of his climb.

"He acts like this is some kind of triathlon," Jenny said to Rick.

"What's next, a swim in the lava?" Rick asked.

"You guys ready?" Mac said when he was back with them, not even out of breath.

"Oh, hell no," Rick said.

The heat became more intense the closer they got to the rim, as did the noise. Even Mac had never heard this part of the mountain so loud—it was as if the caldera had come to a full boil. They all had to shout to be heard above the din.

The heat became more suffocating as they made their way up through the rocks and brush. But Mac knew they needed to do this and do it now. The reality was that they were fast running out of time. Rick and Kenny and the rest of them could do all the projections they wanted about the rate of the rising magma.

But John MacGregor was here because of what he considered the cardinal rule of his job: You had to be there.

They kept making their way through the rough terrain, the soil rich with iron and magnesium, the once green crystals of olivine transformed into the orange mineral known as iddingsite. Most of the basalt rocks from previous eruptions were dark gray, sometimes black; some were a brighter rust color.

The closer they got to the rim, the more Mac wanted to stop and look around at this area so near the summit of the volcanic mountain that took up nearly half this island. He was overwhelmed as he always was by the thought of that, and by the reality of nature's beauty, and its potential fury.

But the big clock kept counting down.

Mauna Loa had two rift zones, on its northeast and southwest. Their group was on the northeast side today. There was no more conversation as they made their way the last fifty yards or so to the rim. The roar from the caldera had built up even more, and the sky had darkened somewhat, clouds lower than the top of Mauna Loa.

"I've never heard it like this!" Jenny had to shout even though she was inches from Mac's ear.

He was about to tell her that neither had he when he suddenly felt like his feet were on fire.

He looked down at his hiking boots and saw the thick soles with their wide treads were beginning to curl up and melt away, the way the tires of the jeep had a few minutes ago.

Mac saw Jenny and Rick and Iona staring down at their own boots, which were detaching at the soles.

"That's it!" Iona yelled. "I'll see you guys back at the jeep." He stared hard at Mac. "You want to tell my bosses I deserted, go right ahead."

He started back down the mountain.

"When the going gets tough," Mac said as he watched him go.

"The tough really do get going," Jenny said.

"Just curious, Mac. Are we still fine?" Rick Ozaki asked, furiously stamping his feet on the ground and extracting from his pocket a roll of duct tape to repair his boots.

Mac shrugged. "We've come this far."

Then the three of them were looking down at a lava lake, the heat shimmering off the silver surface.

"This lake...it's new, right?" Jenny yelled to Mac.

Mac nodded. The opening of a new lava lake near the northeast summit confirmed that the lava would head in the direction of Mauna Kea and the Military Reserve.

On the other side of the lake, small amounts of lava were pushing through cracks, and tiny geysers shot lava toward the sky.

"If I could still breathe," Jenny said, "this might actually take my breath away."

"Mac," Rick yelled, "we need to get out of here or we're going to be walking barefoot on hot coals back to the jeep."

"Gimme one more minute," Mac said, taking out his cell phone. "I need to take some pictures."

"For what?" Rick said. "The top of your casket?"

Then he watched as Mac scrambled up and over the rim.

CHAPTER 37

Hawaiian Volcano Observatory, Hawai'i

Rebecca Cruz waited for Mac and his crew at the observatory. He'd called her from his car and asked her to meet him there, said they were on their way back from the army base, where they'd gone after leaving the caldera.

When he told Rebecca about the trip to the summit, she pronounced it the second-dumbest stunt ever. "What's the first?" Mac asked.

"I don't know," she said, "but there must be one."

She heard him laugh. *At least somebody around here has a sense of humor*, she thought. "One more thing," she said.

"What's that?"

"Next time you better take me with you," Rebecca said.

What little she knew of him so far, she liked, starting here: He was sure of himself in an almost cocky way, and he was clearly used to being the smartest guy in the room.

Same as me, Rebecca thought. *May the best person win.*

He told her he wanted to get his team with her team at HVO, not the Military Reserve, and he had pointedly not asked Colonel Briggs to join them.

"I'll fill him in later," Mac said. "For now I'm proceeding on the fairly safe assumption that the army is resistant to independent thinking."

"Well," she'd said, "until they need it."

"Yeah," Mac said, "to get them out of what the natives call a *huikau*. One they helped create, incidentally."

"*Huikau?*"

"'Mess' is a rough translation."

"Is there no Hawaiian word for 'clusterfuck'?" Rebecca Cruz asked.

Mac told her that they needed to present their plan by the end of the afternoon. And he told her why. And to whom it would be presented.

"We've got to pitch our plan to *him*?"

"We do," Mac said. "I'm told the president asked him to come here and make sure the fiftieth state wasn't about to disappear into the Pacific."

A half hour later, they had all assembled in HVO's second-floor conference room. Rebecca's team was there: David, Leo, Don McNulty, Ben Russell. So was Mac's: Jenny, Rick, Kenny Wong, Pia Wilson.

"First off," Mac said, "I've been asked by Colonel Briggs to remind everybody that everything you hear in this room stays in this room, without exception," Mac said. "What we don't want to do is cause a panic because of what is about to happen and what Rebecca and I are proposing to do to deal with that."

"What exactly *are* you proposing?" Rick asked. "We've only heard pieces of it so far."

"You know we're really good at blowing up things, right?" Rebecca said to Rick. She paused.

"Well, this time we need to talk about blowing up a volcano," she said.

Mac went and stood in front of the map as Jenny pointed her remote at the map on the screen behind him, which featured a detailed schematic of the Big Island. Most of the island was in dark green, with the exception of Mauna Loa and Mauna Kea, which were highlighted by much lighter shades of green. There were various landmarks dotted throughout, all the way down to Hawai'i Volcanoes National Park, south and west of the town of Hilo.

They didn't waste time talking about anything other than blowing huge holes in the largest active volcano on the planet. "I'm going to show you where I think our main point of attack should be," Mac said.

"Northeast flank," Rebecca said.

Mac and Jenny nodded.

"The only thing that makes sense for us, and by 'us' I mean HVO and Cruz Demolition, is a man-made eruption on that side of the mountain," Mac said, pointing. "Or a series of them. I've taken a hard look at our various gradient maps, and I've determined what the steepest descent path is, because it is essential that we divert the lava there."

"But if we do that," Jenny said, "won't the lava flow right into Hilo?"

"Right down Kīlauea Avenue," Mac said, "if it makes it that far."

"Which it won't," Jenny said.

"As some of you know and the rest of you can see," Mac said,

"Mauna Loa, because it's such a gigantic shield volcano, has fairly gentle slopes in most places."

Rebecca looked at her brother but didn't speak.

Mac said, "We're going to need to have conduits in place, ones we're confident will hold, to draw the flow to the east. But mostly to the east. Gentler slope, longer distance from the town. Canals, really. Venice with lava."

"But whether the canals and conduits hold won't matter without precise, strategic bombing," Rebecca Cruz said. "If the explosives get too hot, they'll detonate before we want them to."

"And the lava flowing through the canals won't trigger those explosives?" Jenny asked.

A quiet alarm went off in Mac's head then—he realized he'd been ignoring Jenny. And he hadn't missed the looks she'd given Rebecca Cruz. He turned to her now. "Jenny, I know you've got some thoughts about the way this needs to work," he said.

"If we *are* going to successfully divert the lava," she said quickly, as if she'd been waiting for a chance to jump in, "we actually want it to move rapidly enough through our new channels that it won't cool into rock and clog those same channels."

Jenny pointed her remote at the screen, and now even more detailed fodar imagery appeared. The photogrammetry technology turned aerial photos into a high-resolution map showing specific elevations, angles of slopes, and locations of the various caves on Mauna Loa, Mauna Kea, and even Hualālai, northwest of Mauna Loa, the third youngest of the volcanoes on the Big Island.

"At the end of the day," Jenny said, "what we're trying to do with these explosives is not only use gravity but basically make our own."

Rebecca shrugged. "So there you have it," she said. "We're going to try to do with this mountain of yours what we do when we blow the hell out of a building."

"And what do you do?" Jenny asked.

"Tell it where we want it to go," Rebecca said.

"It sounds pretty simple when you put it that way," Pia Wilson said.

"You're confident this plan you and Mac have come up with will work?" Kenny Wong asked Rebecca.

"Actually, I'm scared silly," she said. "I've done a lot of dangerous things in a lot of places, but I've never done anything this dangerous in my life."

She looked briefly at Mac and then at the rest of the people seated around the table. She took a deep breath and forced a smile.

"But then, no one has," she said.

CHAPTER 38

Hilo International Airport, Hilo, Hawai'i

The two jets arrived roughly thirty minutes apart, both on runway 8-26, the longer of the airport's two runways.

The first to land, at 2:00 p.m., was a Peregrine, a modified Gulfstream G550 business jet, one of the many jets that belonged to billionaire tech legend J. P. Brett, friend and occasional business partner to Oliver and Leah Cutler.

On this Saturday, the Cutlers and their film crew were on board. They'd been picked up in Iceland after Oliver Cutler called Brett and explained why they needed to get to Mauna Loa as fast as humanly possible.

"Is it dangerous?" Brett had asked.

"I wouldn't be calling if it weren't," Oliver Cutler told him. "And we wouldn't be going if it weren't."

"You want company?"

"Always, my friend."

"Then I'll get there as soon as I can," Brett said, "as soon as I wrap up some business with my friend Zuckerberg."

"Do it quickly," Oliver Cutler said.

"I always do with that particular gentleman."

When the Cutlers deplaned, Henry Takayama was there with the Rivian R1T truck Oliver Cutler had requested that would take them all to the new Four Seasons property and the villa that Leah Cutler had requested, although Takayama knew that *request* wasn't the right word.

The crew packed their equipment into an SUV Takayama had rented for them. There was another new resort in Hilo, the Lani, but the crew were staying at the Hilton.

There were no reporters waiting to speak to the Cutlers at the airport, although they had initially "requested" the press. Takayama had managed to talk them out of that, at least for now.

He needed the Cutlers—they were his way of finding out what was going on inside the army and at HVO. The Cutlers wanted to be even more famous than they were, the heroes of this particular drama.

Henry Takayama wanted to be more powerful than he had ever been and to once again feel like the biggest guy in town.

When they had all settled into the crew cab of the electric pickup truck that handled like a sports car, Leah once again raised the possibility of a press conference *before* they met with the big brass.

Or the biggest brass, in this case.

"There will be enough time for the spotlight later," Takayama told her.

"There's never enough time for the spotlight, Henry," Oliver said. "By the way, is that asshole MacGregor still running point on this?"

"None other," Takayama said. "It's one of the biggest reasons why the two of you are here. The arrogant son of a bitch doesn't know it yet, but you're about to outrank him."

Takayama smiled a self-satisfied smile. "And so am I," he said.

As they drove off, a second Peregrine landed at the airport, this one carrying J. P. Brett.

CHAPTER 39

Hawaiian Volcano Observatory, Hawai'i
Time to eruption: 66 hours

General Mark Rivers, chairman of the Joint Chiefs of Staff, had been appointed by the previous president and stayed on when his successor took office. Rivers had offered to step down; the new president had refused to accept his resignation. That was partly due to his competency but mostly due to his popularity, not just with all branches of the armed forces but with the public. Rivers was being considered for a fifth star because of his leadership in both Iraq wars and in Afghanistan.

The current president had joked, more than once, that he served at the pleasure of General Rivers, not the other way around.

Rivers was six feet six inches tall and had the silver hair and rugged good looks of the actor Pierce Brosnan. He had been a star tight end at the United States Military Academy and had risen through the ranks to become the youngest army chief of staff; before that, he had been the youngest commander of Central Command in army history. It was widely assumed in his party's political circles that if he wanted to run for president when the man presently occupying the Oval Office concluded his second term, the nomination was his.

He was as comfortable in the field as he was on the Sunday-morning talk shows, and he dominated any setting in which he found himself. That included the Oval Office.

Now he was seated at the head of a long table on the second floor of HVO in the largest and most private conference room the place had. He was in full uniform, despite the heat outside. Briggs sat to his right, Sergeant Matthew Iona next to Briggs. Rebecca Cruz was the only one in the room representing Cruz Demolition. Mac had Jenny and Rick Ozaki with him.

Oliver and Leah Cutler with Henry Takayama between them were at the far end of the table, across from Rivers. Mac and Oliver Cutler had barely more nodded at each other.

"I just want to make something clear before we start," Rivers said. "I'm aware that I'm going to be presented with three plans for dealing with our problem. I could have asked for written proposals, but I don't operate that way and never have. I like to look people in the eye. It's why I'm here. And I'm sure as hell not walking out of here without a plan."

Mac looked around. General Mark Rivers had everybody's complete attention.

"There's an old army expression about success not being final and failure not being fatal," Rivers said. "But this time it might be." Rivers crossed his arms and leaned back slightly in his chair.

"Welcome to the dream team," he said.

CHAPTER 40

Briggs made the first presentation, with occasional input from Iona.

The colonel spoke as plainly as he could; he seemed to be deathly afraid that Rivers wouldn't follow all the seismological data.

The basic army plan was to dig trenches perpendicular to the lava flow, dig containment pits and ponds downslope from the trenches, and erect walls beyond the ponds.

Colonel James Briggs described the man-made channels to be built in the next forty-eight to seventy-two hours, channels that would eventually guide the bulk of the lava around the town of Hilo, with more containment ponds built as close to the town as possible.

"We'll use drills for the basalt, which will be difficult for even our heaviest equipment to move," Briggs said. "That's mostly near the bottom of the volcano, where the slope is the shallowest."

He stopped talking, poured himself some water from a pitcher, and took a sip. "Questions before I resume?" Briggs asked.

"One," Mac said. "I've brought this up before: Do you really think you can accomplish all this in two days? Because I don't."

"With all due respect, Dr. MacGregor," Briggs said, his voice rising, "you have absolutely no idea what the U.S. Army can do once it sets its mind to something."

He leaned toward Mac, the veins in his forehead suddenly visible.

"Have you ever served?" Briggs asked.

"You know I haven't, Colonel," Mac said.

"Then please don't lecture me about what the army can and cannot do."

"Let's take it down a notch, Colonel," Rivers said quietly. "We are all on the same team here."

Mac let it go. Arguing with Briggs got him nowhere, particularly with Rivers in the mix. And he wanted Rivers on his side, because he knew in his heart, even before he heard what that self-serving asshat Oliver Cutler had to say, that his plan was the only one that could work.

"Will your plan protect the Military Reserve?" Rivers asked Briggs.

Mac understood that although Rivers was talking about protecting the facility, what he really wanted was to protect the canisters in the Ice Tube and avoid the doomsday consequences of a spill once the eruption occurred. Rivers and Briggs knew about those canisters. Briggs had trusted Mac with the information and was aware that Mac trusted Rebecca and Jenny enough to tell them. But Briggs knew that telling the Cutlers would be tantamount to hiring a skywriter to announce it over the summit. Same with a bigmouth like Henry Takayama.

They were here to solve the problem of the lava hitting Hilo. Those were high enough stakes, as far as Colonel Briggs was concerned.

"The rest of them don't need to know what they don't need to know," he'd told Mac more than once.

"How many crews will we need?" Rivers asked.

"Three crews," Briggs said. "Each one building a different line of defense: trenches, pits, wall. Always with the priority of the base first and, obviously, the town."

"I'm just curious, Colonel Briggs," Oliver Cutler said, "why is protecting the military base somehow more important in the eyes of the army than protecting the town?"

"I'll handle that one," Rivers said. "Because the army says so, that's why. The nonmilitary personnel on this team are here serving at the pleasure of the government of the United States. If anybody has a problem with that, feel free to leave now."

"I have no problem with it," Oliver Cutler said, then quickly added, "I'm sorry if you and Colonel Briggs took it that way."

Mac looked at Rivers admiringly. The general was refusing to defer to the Cutlers' celebrity. The couple had leveraged their fame to see plenty of volcanoes, but Mac knew that getting funding was the hardest part of science.

Briggs finally got around to describing the expensive, complicated, and risky process of building the trenches even as the lava made its way down the mountain; the crews would basically be racing to stay ahead of it until it was finally diverted away from Hilo.

"There are more details, of course," he said. "Sergeant Iona and our geologists can lay them out for you when you get back to base, sir. But we believe this is the best way to save the base, save the town, and save this island from unimaginable destruction."

Rivers said, "Anything you care to add, Dr. MacGregor?"

"Just this," Mac said. "It won't work."

"Because it's not your plan?" Briggs snapped.

"Because you're not factoring in the problems you'll face

when you try to do this kind of construction work in the rainforests on that mountain," Mac said. "And that's provided the locals will even allow you to touch those areas. And then there's this: Just how long is this wall of yours going to be?"

"Seven miles," Briggs said.

"You're going to build a seven-mile wall in two days?" Mac said.

"Is that feasible, even for the army?" Rivers asked.

"We have no choice, sir," Briggs said. "There are two arms of Hilo. One is a mile wide, the other is about two and a half miles wide. We've talked about building walls to protect those two arms. But if either one of them splits, the lava could funnel right through it. It's why we think the longer wall is our best shot."

Rivers asked Briggs if he had anything else to add. Briggs said he did not. Oliver and Leah Cutler stood up to begin their own presentation; Mac had chosen to go last.

And then it was happening again.

This was the worst quake of the past few days, the worst Mac had ever felt in Hilo. The heavy table in front of them began to shake violently, as did the walls of HVO. Mac's people knew that this building had been built and then rebuilt to withstand earthquakes just like this, but nonetheless, they heard glass shattering.

For a brief moment, as crazy as the thought was, Mac imagined that Rebecca Cruz and her team had decided to blow up this building and it was about to collapse on top of them.

General Mark Rivers calmly instructed everybody in the room to get under the table. Most of them did, without another word. But Rivers stayed right where he was. So did Mac.

The chairman of the Joint Chiefs grinned at Mac, almost as if they were sitting next to each other on an airplane and merely experiencing some turbulence.

"Force of habit, Dr. MacGregor," he said. "A variation of first in, last out, I guess you could say."

"I'm the same way with volcanoes," Mac said. "So I get it, General." He shrugged. "Even though I never served," he added.

"You're serving now," Rivers said.

When the world stopped moving, everybody came out from under the table and sat down again, although all of them, even the Cutlers, appeared much shakier than they had when they'd arrived.

Rivers said, "Now, where were we?"

CHAPTER 41

Oliver Cutler immediately tried to make the whole thing about him, as Mac had known he would.

"Before I explain why I believe we need to blow holes in the side of this volcano of ours," Cutler began, "I have to tell you as a matter of full disclosure that the plan you're about to hear was coauthored by a friend of Leah's and mine."

"One he met online?" Rebecca whispered to Mac.

"Am I allowed to ask who the friend is?" Rivers said.

"J. P. Brett," Cutler said.

And there it is, Mac thought.

Rivers pushed his chair back slightly and turned to face Oliver Cutler, as if he were directing onto this TV personality the full force of his own personality.

"Let me see if I understand this," Rivers said, as if genuinely curious about what he'd just heard. "You have brought a grandstanding rich man like Brett into this top secret and potentially life-threatening situation? And done that on your own?"

"Leah and I have worked with him before in dangerous situations," Cutler said, "and found him to be more than useful and extraordinarily generous."

"This isn't one of your shows," Rivers said.

"I know that, sir," Cutler said. "I just assumed that since this is an all-hands-on-deck situation, the army would welcome the kind of support Mr. Brett can and is more than willing to provide."

"You *assumed*," Rivers said. "Much in the same way you assumed it was all right to reach out to Mr. Brett in the first place."

Cutler started to say something. Rivers held up a hand.

"You will learn very quickly, or perhaps you just have," Rivers said, "that you don't make assumptions with me. You make *suggestions*, ones that I either accept or reject." Rivers folded his arms across his chest without disturbing his multiple service medals. "Am I making myself clear?"

Cutler nodded. "Again, sir, I just assumed that with a man of Mr. Brett's wealth and ability to get things done in a hurry—"

"There we go, assuming again," Rivers said, shaking his head sadly. "Please continue."

Everybody in the room listened intently as Oliver Cutler explained the specifics of blowing holes in the sides of the volcano.

And doing that from the air.

"You're talking about targeted bombing?" Rivers asked.

"Yes, sir, we are," Cutler said, and he began to show the places on the map where he thought the bombs would be most effective.

"I have to admit," Rivers said, "you've done a lot of homework in very little time."

Cutler smiled. "I didn't want you to think Leah and I had fallen off a Learjet full of turnips," he said.

There was no reaction from Rivers, but Mac hadn't expected one. The chairman of the Joint Chiefs was a tough room.

"We feel this is the best way for us to do battle with nature," Cutler said. He made a sweeping gesture toward the map. "We firmly believe that with the air support that both the army and Mr. Brett can provide, we can effectively neutralize this volcano, and do it in a timely manner."

Cutler addressed Mac then. "Any comments, Dr. MacGregor?"

"I'll save them until you're finished."

"Almost there," Cutler said. "Obviously, we want to drop the bombs near where the lava is coming out, opening vents in the process, with the goal of making the lava exhaust itself faster. Then we come in with *more* planes to spray down the entire area with seawater, tag-teaming that effort with hoses extending from the tank trucks on the ground. And all of *that* will be supported by tankers in the bay pumping the seawater to the trucks."

"*Whose* tankers?" Rivers asked.

"J. P. Brett's tankers, sir."

"You're telling me they've already arrived in Hilo?" Rivers asked.

"On their way," Cutler said. "J.P.'s philosophy in just about any endeavor in which he's involved is to get out ahead of things."

"He can begin by having a conversation with me," Rivers said.

"I'll make that clear to him."

"You do that," Rivers said. "Now wrap this up, please. I want to hear Dr. MacGregor's plan."

"Our ultimate goal is to wage a two-front war—in the air and on the ground." Then Oliver Cutler added, "A war that we are here to help the United States Army win."

Should I applaud? Mac wondered.

Instead, he raised a hand.

"I don't want to be the one making assumptions," Mac said, "but I trust you're aware of the potential risk of aircraft-engine failure when there's ash and gas in the air."

"Naturally, we're aware of the risk," Cutler said. "But experienced pilots will know how and when and where to pick their spots. And I trust that *you're* aware, Dr. MacGregor, that you need to weigh risk against reward in an operation as complicated as this one is shaping up to be."

"I am."

"May I ask what you think of my plan?" Cutler said.

"As a matter of fact, I find it very sound," Mac said.

He could see the surprise on Cutler's face. He glanced across the table and saw the same looks of surprise from his team.

"You're saying you like it?" Cutler asked.

"I'd be crazy not to, wouldn't I?" Mac said. "After all, most of it is mine, Ollie."

CHAPTER 42

Mac saw he'd offended Cutler and quickly said, "Come on, lighten up, Ollie. I was just making a joke—a clunker, apparently—about great minds thinking alike."

"I frankly like the suggestion that my work isn't my own about as much as I like being called Ollie," Cutler said.

"I wouldn't either if I were you," Mac said, grinning at him.

Mac and Rebecca stood up and breezed through their own presentation, hitting the same PowerPoint slides they had in front of their teams. Mac noted that he and Rebecca were basically in agreement about the need to blow substantial holes over an area spanning a full square mile on the east side of the mountain, not the south side, which would push the lava toward Kīlauea and Route 11. And he stressed how much manpower would be required, especially since they would need to switch crews almost hourly because of the sweltering heat of the black rock, the volcano, and the sun.

"I can't state strongly enough that the whole ball game here is controlling the lava as much as humanly possible," Mac said. "Everything else is just noise."

"And if we can't effectively stop the lava?" Rivers asked.

"General, I'm a scientist," he said. "I deal in facts, even when we've got as many variables as we have here. In the end, what we're ultimately trying to do is redirect a tidal wave of lava and make a long-shot bet pay off."

"And what bet is that?" Rivers asked.

"That we can impose our will on the fury of the natural world," Mac said.

"We have to. Or else," Rivers said.

"Or else," Mac said.

No one spoke for a moment. Mac looked at Rivers and said, "So which of the three plans are you going to use, sir, if I might ask?"

"All of them," Mark Rivers said.

Then he added, "Now let me say one more thing before I tell you all about *my* plan."

CHAPTER 43

Edith Kanaka'ole Stadium, Hilo, Hawai'i
Time to eruption: 63 hours

The press conference had been going on for half an hour before General Rivers, Mac, and the Cutlers—both of whom were wearing the silver jumpsuits they favored for television appearances—joined Henry Takayama on the stage. Takayama had just finished explaining to the crowd of media and Hilo residents that the chairman of the Joint Chiefs of Staff, General Mark Rivers, had arrived on the Big Island and wanted maximum transparency going forward as they all prepared to confront the impending eruption at Mauna Loa.

Mac knew that was mostly bullshit—full transparency was the last thing Rivers wanted. But Rivers was confident that he could win these people over, so here they were.

Rivers stepped up to the microphone. "There is a problem

here and we all know it," he said. "But with your help, I can and will solve it."

Mac watched him and thought: *Now we've got a Patton of our own.*

"I have been sent by the president to assure everyone in this community that we have a plan to contain the situation and keep Hilo safe," he said. "Again, we can do this only with your full cooperation. And trust."

"Let's see you earn our trust!" a voice called out.

That touched off a lot of shouting from the audience, more people yelling out questions and others telling them to show some respect.

Rivers held up his hands for quiet.

"You all felt the tremors and quakes of the past few days," he said. "That's why I was sent here by the president—to show you that the fiftieth state is a number one priority for him. Our experts have indicated that a major event is imminent, most likely within the next forty-eight to seventy-two hours."

"Define *major*, General!"

The people in the crowd were starting to sound like spectators at a sold-out sports event, and Mac wondered, not for the first time, if this had been the best decision General Rivers could have made, putting himself out there.

He once again raised his hands for quiet. "But I can assure you, as long as you follow the instructions from Mr. Takayama of Civil Defense"—he pointed to Takayama, now seated next to Rebecca Cruz—"and the army, Hilo will stand strong against this eruption the way it has against the eruptions of the past."

"Says the *haole* man from the army!" It was a woman's voice this time. "Why should we believe an outsider like you?"

Rivers stared at the woman, who was standing against the wall to his right, for what felt like to Mac like a full minute.

"Because I give you my word," he said solemnly.

He gestured to the people sitting behind him on the stage. "We have assembled a dream team of experts. Some of them, the people from the army and from the Hawaiian Volcano Observatory, have been studying the mountain for years. Oliver and Leah Cutler, world-renowned volcanologists, are also here. J. P. Brett, who has worked with the Cutlers previously, will be arriving shortly."

Someone near the television cameras yelled, "J. P. Brett eats shit!"

A new voice shouted, "Nevertheless," and the crowd turned to see J. P. Brett walking from the rear of the room toward the stage.

CHAPTER 44

Mac watched as Brett took his time making his way down the center aisle, acting as if this were an orchestrated part of the show; he even high-fived some of the citizens reaching out to him.

Brett was dressed in a tight black T-shirt and skinny jeans and sneakers, the unofficial uniform of the billionaire boys' club. Mac figured Brett was probably in his fifties somewhere, but he was trying hard to look younger—his short hair was as black as his T-shirt.

When he reached the front of the room, Brett waved to the crowd; he was greeted by a burst of applause. He yelled, "I'm here to help," which got another cheer.

At the sight of J. P. Brett, Henry Takayama had jumped up and grabbed an empty chair from the end of his row. He'd had it next to Mac before Brett walked up the steps to the stage.

"I'm Brett," J. P. Brett said to Mac, extending a closed fist for Mac to bump.

"Of course you are," Mac said. He turned his attention back to the podium.

Rivers said, "I'll take a few questions before handing things over to our experts."

Marsha Keilani of KHON stood.

"General, you haven't told us how major an eruption we're talking about," she said. "Are you and your people anticipating something bigger than the one in 1984? Perhaps the biggest ever? My sources tell me it might be the biggest in a hundred years."

Takayama, Mac thought. *That's exactly what I told him.*

It meant there was a second leak. The first, about the bombing sites, could only have come from Mac's team.

Maybe I'm fighting a war on more than two fronts now.

"It's simply not prudent to speculate at this point," Rivers said.

"But *you're* here, sir," Marsha Keilani said, staying with him. "Mr. Brett is here. I'm told the Cutlers flew in from Iceland. Why shouldn't everyone on this island be alarmed?"

A large man, obviously a native, stood up in the back row and pointed at Rivers. "Tell us the truth!"

More people in the back rows were standing now; it was like the room was erupting.

Rivers waited until everyone had settled down before speaking. "No one should be alarmed, partly because we *are* all here, and partly because, if history tells us anything, it's that Hilo can survive eruptions. And I assure you, Hilo will survive this one."

Reporters shouted more questions, but Rivers ignored them. "With that," he said, "I would like our experts to weigh in."

Mac was already out of his chair when Rivers added, "Let's start with Mr. Brett."

Mac couldn't decide whether he was more embarrassed or more pissed off that Rivers was presenting this rich man as being the same kind of expert on volcanoes and the looming danger of Mauna Loa as Mac was. He sat back down.

Brett stood; Rivers walked over to him, extending his right

hand for a real handshake, not a fist bump. Brett had no choice but to take it. Rivers leaned close to him, not releasing Brett's hand, and spoke in a low voice that only Mac and Brett could hear. "You're in Hilo because I think you can help," the chairman of the Joint Chiefs said. "But don't fuck with me."

CHAPTER 45

J. P. Brett had been close enough for her to touch before he got a good laugh with "Nevertheless" and walked up to the stage. He replaced the silver-haired general from central casting at the podium and then, just like the general had, did his level best to cover his ass.

Rivers and Brett weren't technically lying, but they weren't telling the truth either. Rachel Sherrill was convinced of that.

At least, they weren't telling the *whole* truth.

Excellent timing, Rachel, girl, she told herself. *It's your first trip back to Hilo since you got fired from the botanical gardens, and this time a lot more than a grove of your precious banyan trees might get blown sky-high.*

Rachel walked out the door while Brett was still speaking. She needed some air and some time to think, knowing this particular show wasn't even close to being over.

It had been nearly a decade since her own world blew up. The decision to fire her, she was convinced, hadn't been made by her bosses at the botanical gardens. She'd gotten nothing but praise and support from them since the moment she'd taken the job.

But after what happened in the banyan grove that day, she had been persistent with her questions about why the army had reacted with such a frightening show of force. Eventually she was told that the board members of the botanical gardens were "going in a different direction"—the corporate version of a soon-to-be-ex-boyfriend saying, "It's not you, it's me."

But Rachel Sherrill, Stanford graduate and no one's fool, suspected that "going in a different direction" wasn't the reason she'd been fired. And she'd always wondered what Henry Takayama did or didn't know about what happened in the banyan grove that day.

All she really knew for sure was that the army had buried news of an event that had turned her trees to ashes.

How very biblical, she'd told herself at the time. *Ashes to ashes, dust to dust.* The dust being her career.

She'd never gotten to speak to Henry Takayama about it. Ted Murray had phoned her just before she left and said, "They know I'm your friend and that I talked to you. But I'm done with this now, Rachel. *Done.* Don't ask me about it again unless you want to get me fired too."

"Get fired from the U.S. Army?" she'd asked.

"Have a nice life," Murray had said, and he hung up.

A few months later Rachel was back on the mainland, vowing never to return to Hawai'i. She took an associate's job at the Bellevue Botanical Garden in Washington State. Got married; got divorced. Moved to Portland, got a job at the Hoyt Arboretum. But she was still full of regrets and anger about the way her dream job in Hawai'i had ended.

And still full of questions about what had happened that day in Hilo all those years ago, even though, according to public records, nothing had actually happened that day.

But a month ago, she'd made a spur-of-the-moment decision.

She announced to her boss at Hoyt that she was taking all her vacation time, then she booked a flight to Hawai'i. She was staying in the hotel nearest to the botanical gardens.

The moment she arrived at Hilo International, the earth began to shake. She knew about quakes from when she'd lived here. But this was different. *These* were different—more powerful and more persistent than anything she remembered.

But she hadn't come this far to turn around and head back to the mainland.

She went to the botanical gardens and walked all the way out to where the poisoned banyan trees had stood. She saw only a wide expanse of beautifully manicured lawn—it was as if the army's scorched-earth assault had never happened.

Almost as if the trees had never been there.

Almost as if I were never here.

Standing there, she felt the most powerful quake yet. It nearly knocked her to the ground and made her wonder if coming to Hawai'i had been an even bigger mistake than she'd feared.

Back in her hotel room that afternoon, she had a couple of glasses of wine to settle her nerves and told herself she would leave tomorrow, that it really had been crazy for her to come back in the first place.

Then she'd seen the announcement on social media about what sounded like a combination press conference and emergency town hall meeting. Rachel was curious enough to drive over to the Edith Kanaka'ole Stadium. She'd arrived just in time to see the by God chairman of the Joint Chiefs step up to the microphone. Dr. John MacGregor, whom she'd recently seen on television talking about the coming eruption at Mauna Loa, was on the stage with him, as were the Cutlers, the two divas dressed like comic-book heroes.

Then J. P. Brett had arrived, and that's when she'd stepped out for some air.

When she returned to the auditorium, MacGregor was talking about lava flow and the speed of it and trenches and pits. But Rachel found herself wondering what Dr. John MacGregor *wasn't* telling them, her mind flashing to what might happen if an epic lava spill somehow combined with the incident she remembered at the botanical gardens.

Rachel wondered if the by God chairman of the Joint Chiefs was here for something more than an eruption.

And she wasn't just angry now.

Rachel Sherrill was scared.

CHAPTER 46

Rivers and Brett, trailed by Colonel Briggs, left the stage in animated conversation.

Rivers's exit through the door behind the stage indicated that the press conference was over. Oliver and Leah Cutler, who had made only brief remarks earlier, stepped off the stage and into the auditorium, where, as Mac assumed they'd expected, they were immediately surrounded by reporters and cameras.

With Rivers and Brett gone, they now had the spotlight to themselves.

The object of the game, Mac thought. He leaned against the side of the stage, out of sight but close enough to hear what they were saying.

"Welcome to this week's episode of *Volcano Chasers*," Oliver Cutler said. "As usual, my lovely wife and I will be your hosts."

The line got a laugh, but it stopped abruptly when Edith Kanaka'ole Stadium was rocked by another quake, the kind that had been occurring on what felt like an hourly basis all week.

Then another quake.

And another.

The crowds had already been moving toward the exit doors at

the other end of the hall. Now people began to push one another. Mac heard a woman scream and shouts for the people closest to the doors to get the hell out of the way.

The Cutlers and the members of the media around them stayed right where they were.

"I've heard of drumrolls," Cutler said, without missing a beat, "but this is ridiculous."

There was a ripple of nervous laughter. Some of the reporters looked up at the ceiling. Others looked over their shoulders at the exit. None of them left, clearly afraid they might miss something, now that another show was beginning.

At this point Oliver Cutler stopped smiling and said, "How about we all stop screwing around here and get to it?"

There were two TV cameramen a few feet in front of him. He played directly to them.

"General Rivers might not be happy when he hears what I'm about to say," Cutler continued. "But what we're really talking about at Mauna Loa is the Big One. Capital *B*, capital *O*. It's why Mr. Takayama of Civil Defense reached out to Leah and me and why we came all the way from Iceland as quickly as we could on the plane that J. P. Brett was generous enough to send for us."

You son of a bitch, Mac thought. *You smug, self-serving son of a bitch.* But trying to stop Cutler at this point, he knew, would be like trying to stop a volcano from erupting.

"I probably shouldn't be saying this either," Cutler went on, "but we believe that if the army and the people in charge of the Hawaiian Volcano Observatory don't put our plan into effect, Hilo is in grave and imminent danger."

One of the few townspeople who hadn't left the building after the quake shouted, "That's not what the general said!"

"I have all the respect in the world for General Rivers, though I've known him only a short amount of time. But he is an army man. In fact, he is *the* army man. And because he is, he's practically duty bound not to tell you everything he knows. Unfortunately—or perhaps fortunately for Hilo—I'm not bound by the same rules."

Cutler stared directly into the cameras.

"You all need to know that Leah and I have had the opportunity to thoroughly examine the subvolcanic structure," he said.

Like hell you have, Mac thought, fighting the urge to get up and drag Cutler away from the cameras. He looked down and saw that he was clenching his fists.

But Mac knew that hauling Cutler away from the press would only make things worse for him and for the army—it would look like they had something to hide.

Cutler said, "At first I was hopeful that the Big Island was moving off what we call a magma plume. But it turns out that the plume, which is like the heartbeat of the volcano, has gotten much stronger over the past week, as we all just felt once again. It means that the magma is picking up the pace, and the volume of magma underneath Mauna Loa is moving into superplume territory, which explains why it continues to rock your world. And it's why Leah and I believe that we are now talking about more lava than any of us have ever seen before. And it's why there is a possibility, if we don't act quickly and decisively, that Hilo will not be the only area threatened."

Cutler took in a big breath and let it out.

"It's the entire island that's in harm's way," he said.

The reporters all shouted questions at him at once, and Cutler waved for quiet as Rivers had done from the podium several minutes before.

"That's all I've got for now," he said. "Leah and I will be working through the night as we continue to track these repeated and quite troubling seismic events. Quakes measuring at three-plus magnitude, which had been occurring every three days or so, are now occurring on a daily basis. And four- and five-plus quakes that had been occurring on a monthly basis are now coming weekly."

Leah took a step forward, her eyes directed at the cameras. "The magma that my husband described is not just ascending—it's ascending quite rapidly, forcing the ground around the volcano to swell to the point of bursting. It's why we have to act aggressively and act soon."

"Bottom line," Oliver Cutler said. "This might not be the Big One we're talking about here. It might be the *Biggest* One."

Once more, he paused for dramatic effect. Then:

"Maybe the biggest the world has ever seen."

CHAPTER 47

Mac waited until the media crowd had dispersed before walking over to where the Cutlers and Henry Takayama were standing in front of the stage.

"Got a few minutes for a quick chat before you leave?" Mac asked Oliver. "Think of it as information sharing."

"No problem," Cutler said. "Is in here okay?"

"How about outside?" Mac said. "I'll probably need only five minutes, tops."

"You got it," Cutler said. He turned to Takayama, whom Mac had acknowledged with only a nod. "Henry, why don't you and Leah head back to the villa. She and I will be working from there tonight. You can tell our driver that I'll be along straightaway."

Leah Cutler and Takayama walked down the center aisle and out the double doors, neither one of them looking back, the overhead lights in the auditorium reflecting quite nicely, Mac thought, off Leah's silver jumpsuit.

Outside, Mac looked around to make sure it was just the two of them in the darkened area near the back parking lot. Then he grabbed Cutler by the front of his jumpsuit, nearly lifted him off the ground, and shoved him so hard against the stadium wall that Cutler's head snapped back.

"Are you out of your goddamn mind?" Mac said.

"Am I out of *my* mind?" Cutler sputtered. "Get your hands off me, you bastard."

"I know what you're thinking, Ollie," Mac said. "Where are all your media friends when you could really use them?" He gave Cutler another shove, then released him. Dr. John MacGregor couldn't remember the last time he'd been in a physical fight, or anything close to one. Maybe not since junior high school. But he was spoiling for one right now.

His face was still close to Cutler's, which had turned crimson. But Mac could see in Oliver Cutler's eyes that he wasn't about to say or do anything to escalate the situation.

"Just what exactly did you think you were accomplishing in there?" Mac asked. "Other than maybe getting you and your wife fired, which is frankly kind of a dream of mine. I don't know why you and Leah are here. Maybe Rivers thinks that somehow the two of you can humanize this whole situation. Or maybe by the time Takayama invited you to the party, it was too late for the general to do anything about it. I don't give a shit either way. What I *do* give a shit about is *you* causing *me* problems."

"I was telling the truth," Cutler said.

Mac snorted. "The truth?" he said. "Maybe those suckers in the media bought your garbage about 'examining the subvolcanic structure.'" Mac raised his hands to put air quotes around the words, which made Cutler flinch. "But we both know better, don't we? You and Leah are no seismologists, and I know you don't employ any, because you're just lava chasers. I happen to know every place you've been since you arrived on this island. And Mauna Loa wasn't one of them. Neither was the HVO data room."

"You're having me followed, MacGregor?" Cutler asked.

"We try to keep an eye on loose cannons," Mac said. "Even ones dressed like space-age cheerleaders."

Cutler let that go. "People have a right to know what's going on inside that mountain," he said. "And by the way, I don't take orders from you. I report to General Rivers, same as you."

He slid along the wall to create some space between himself and Mac. It was still just the two of them behind the auditorium.

"You act like I volunteered for this," Cutler said. "I didn't. I was asked to come."

"Yeah," Mac said, "by that clerk Takayama, like I said. He decided you could be useful, except that all you did in there was act like a useful idiot."

"You better figure out a way to work with me," Cutler said, "because my wife and I aren't going anywhere."

Mac took a step toward him, but Cutler managed to stand his ground.

"No, Ollie, you've got it wrong," Mac said. "You're the one who needs to find a way to work with me. Or I will bury you."

He let the words hang there in the night air, then got into his car, slammed the door shut, and drove off. He was so focused on getting far away from Cutler that he didn't notice the pretty, dark-haired woman running across the lot from the other side of the building, frantically waving at him to stop.

CHAPTER 48

Hawaiian Volcano Observatory, Hawai'i
Time to eruption: 60 hours

What's Rivers going to do when he finds out what Cutler told the media?" Rebecca Cruz asked Mac when they got back to HVO.

"Hopefully rip *him* a new trench," Mac said.

The immediate task for Mac's people and Cruz Demolition was to determine the steepest and safest descent path they could create for the lava, working off their original plan for targeted bombing on the ground. At daylight, Mac and Rebecca would head over to Mauna Loa to decide where to place the explosives that Rebecca would detonate remotely once the lava came.

"We'll need the exact locations of as many lava tubes as we can find so we can use them effectively," Mac told the group, who were once again seated around the long table in the conference room. "We also need to find places in the rock where we can safely dig deep enough to plant our bombs. Obviously, the wisdom on that will come from our experts from Cruz Demolition."

"We'll need to fast-track putting bombs into heat-protected casings," David Cruz said.

His sister grinned. "Premature detonation," she said. "Never a good thing, right, guys?"

"If that happens, do we even want to know what's next?" Jenny Kimura asked.

"Not so much," Rebecca said. "But I'm sure you can guess."

"Do I want to guess?" Jenny said.

"Not so much," Rebecca said again.

No one spoke for a moment.

Finally, Mac said, "We good for the time being?"

There were nods all around. Rick and Kenny and Pia Wilson went back to their stations to check the latest seismological reports. Rebecca Cruz and her brother and their cousin Leo said they were going to the map room to go over schematics.

Rebecca said to Mac, "What's on your agenda right now?"

"Jenny and I are going to take a ride."

"We are?" Jenny said. "Do I get to ask where?"

"The Ice Tube."

"Does the army know we're coming?"

"I thought we'd surprise them," Mac said.

"Yeah," Jenny said. "I'm sure the big guy just loves surprises."

"You're driving very fast," Jenny said to Mac when they were in the car.

"I always drive fast when I'm trying to save the world," Mac said.

"Well, when you put it like that," Jenny said, holding on to the dash as the car swerved. "But I'm not going to lie, MacGregor, I've had better dates."

They had called ahead to Sergeant Matthew Iona; Mac put the phone on speaker. Iona said he would be arriving at the Ice Tube soon and informed them that he was now checking the canisters every few hours.

After Mac hung up, Jenny said, "You ever wonder why they call it the Ice Tube instead of what it really is?"

"You mean a toxic-waste storage facility in a volcano next door to a much bigger volcano that's about to explode?" Mac asked.

"Yeah," Jenny said. "That."

"Did I forget to add *secure* toxic-waste storage facility?"

"Fingers crossed."

"Maybe the sign of the cross would be better," Mac said.

They arrived, signed in, and made their way to the locker room, where their heat-resistant suits were hanging. Their helmets were on top of the lockers. They changed and went back outside to the army jeep Iona had made sure would be waiting for them.

Mac drove more slowly up the narrow mountain path. He looked over at Jenny at one point and saw her smiling. She had both their helmets in her lap. "Why do you look like that?" Mac asked.

"Like what?"

"Like you're happy, which is strange, considering our current circumstances."

"I'm just glad to be doing this with you," Jenny said. "Honored, actually, without sounding too highfalutin. I'm also hoping General Rivers realizes how lucky he is to have you running point on this thing."

"Am I?" Mac asked. "Running point, I mean?"

"We both know you are," she said.

"I don't want to be the one to break it to Brett and the Cutlers."

"I frankly don't know why Rivers would want them involved," she said.

"I'm not sure he would have brought them here on his own," Mac said. "But now that they *are* here, they play nicely into what I've always felt is one of the first rules of command in the military."

"What's that?"

"Cover your ass whenever possible," Mac said. "The more people there are on the general's team, the more people to share the blame if something goes wrong."

"What happened to 'The buck stops here'?" Jenny asked.

"Sometimes it stops over there too," Mac said. "And also over there. But look at it this way, Jenny. If something does go wrong, there won't be anybody left to blame."

"Or anybody left, period," Jenny said.

They spoke again about the trust Rivers had placed in them, about the secret they were all keeping. Jenny wondered if he'd told them about it out of respect or necessity, and Mac said it was probably a little bit of both. He might not have trusted Mac, Jenny, and Rebecca Cruz completely. But Rivers had made it clear that he absolutely did not trust J. P. Brett or the Cutlers.

They rode in silence for a few minutes.

Jenny finally spoke, her voice soft. "We got this—right, Mac?" she asked. "Tell me we got this."

He grinned. "In my case," he said, "the buck does stop here."

"No shit," Jenny Kimura said, and they both managed a laugh.

Mac pulled the jeep to a stop next to Sergeant Iona's jeep;

they were maybe a hundred yards from the lights at the entrance. They would walk the rest of the way from here.

But as he and Jenny got out of the jeep, helmets in their hands, they saw Sergeant Matthew Iona sprinting down the hill toward them as men in hazmat suits ran past him toward the entrance to the Ice Tube.

CHAPTER 49

Outside the Ice Tube, Mauna Kea, Hawai'i

Mac and Jenny stood right where they were, next to the jeep, and waited for Iona to get to them.

They heard the roar of more jeeps behind them and found themselves in the middle of the bright lights from their high beams; they actually had to jump out of the way to keep from being hit by the jeeps whizzing past them.

These jeeps carried more men in hazmat suits, and as soon as the vehicles stopped, the men ran inside, all of them holding LED spotlights and what looked like large handguns but that Mac knew were Cold Fire extinguishers.

A minute later an army fire engine arrived, two soldiers in the cab and one standing in the open back door next to a water pump, hose already in his hands.

The fire engine pulled up next to the jeeps; the soldier in back was already on the ground, hauling the hose toward the entrance.

Iona reached Mac and Jenny, out of breath, chest heaving beneath his yellow suit. When he took off his helmet, Mac could see the sweat pouring down his face.

"What's happening?" Mac asked.

Iona tried to speak, but he was still breathing too hard. His eyes were fixed on the entrance and the smoke now pouring out of it.

"Iona!" Mac said, grabbing him by the arm and pulling him close. "What the hell is going on up there?"

"There...there's been a spill," he said. "One of the broken canisters...we're basically trying to flush it."

"What do these men think they're attempting to flush?" Mac asked.

"Decayed nuclear waste," Iona said. "Spent waste from navy vessels and private power plants they've been told has been here for thirty years. Even some solidified waste." Iona looked around. It was just them. He lowered his voice anyway. "We've made them take the same precautions they'd take if they knew what was really in that container," he said.

Mac said, "You're sure it's just the one container?"

"Yes," he said.

Mac stared past Iona, wanting to get a closer look. He told Jenny to stay where she was and ran up the hill; he got maybe ten yards inside the cave before one of the men in hazmat suits stopped him. The soldier's voice was tinny and nearly inaudible behind his mask when he said, "That's as far as you go." He stepped in front of Mac.

"I work for General Rivers," Mac said.

"Same," the soldier said.

Beyond him, Mac could see the black stain near the entrance, as if an inkwell had been turned over.

CHAPTER 50

If Mac had been wearing a hazmat he might have tried to get closer, but he was not. He wasn't sure what the black stain meant, but it had gotten his attention.

He walked back down the hill to Jenny.

"What could you see?" Jenny asked.

"Something that scared the shit out of me," he said. He told her about something he'd heard when he arrived at HVO, about an incident at the botanical gardens and army men in hazmat suits showing up there and leveling part of the place.

"I tried to find out more," Mac said. "But there was no real record of the event."

"You think what happened there is somehow connected with what's inside those canisters?" Jenny asked.

"What I know," he said, "is that we are about to move heaven and earth to keep a lava spill from coming anywhere near here."

"We have to assume they know how to contain this," Jenny said.

"It was the army that created this goddamn problem in the first place," Mac said.

Ten minutes passed.

Then twenty.

Most of the hazmat suits were inside the Ice Tube now. It was eerily quiet out here after the initial rush of noise and activity from the other jeeps and the fire engine.

He stared at the entrance. Now no one went in or out. Mac wanted to know what was going on inside. He hated not knowing. Sometimes not knowing was the only thing in the world that frightened him.

Thirty minutes.

Forty.

"What on earth are they doing in there?" Mac asked.

Jenny gently took his hand. "Breathe," she said.

"Make me."

The sound of a vehicle shattered the silence outside the cave again. They turned to see it was another jeep heading right for them, Colonel Briggs at the wheel. He brought it to a sudden stop a few yards away, spraying lava rock and dirt. A single cargo truck followed the jeep.

General Mark Rivers himself was in the jeep's passenger seat.

Rivers was in full uniform but wore no protective gear. He walked past Mac and Jenny without a word and marched into the cave.

Briggs ran to keep up with him.

More minutes passed. Mac and Jenny stayed where they were. Then slowly one hazmat suit after another began to file out. The fire engine pulled away, then the other jeeps. The last three jeeps left were Mac and Jenny's, Iona's, and the one Briggs had been driving; it was like they were the last part of the parade.

Briggs came out of the cave, Sergeant Iona beside him.

The last man out was General Mark Rivers.

He walked briskly to Mac and Jenny, his posture militarily erect, as always, as if he were about to inspect the troops.

He stopped directly in front of Mac.

"Was it just the one canister?" Mac asked him.

"It was contained," Rivers said.

He told Mac and Jenny they could leave and let the army finish up here and added that he was about to leave himself.

Seconds after Mac and Jenny left, a soldier in a hazmat suit came running down the hill toward Rivers. "You need to come with me, sir," the soldier said. "But first you need to put on one of these suits." Rivers got his protective yellow suit out of the back of the cargo truck and quickly put it on. Colonel Briggs, also in a hazmat suit, was waiting for Rivers with three other soldiers inside the Ice Tube.

The body at their feet was also in a yellow suit. The suit was ripped along the right arm. His gloves were gone.

The right hand was already turning black.

One of the soldiers said, "He must have torn it on a jagged part of the wall." The man paused, then added, "He was one of the first ones in here."

Rivers said, "It happens this fast."

"Not always, sir," Briggs said. "But it can. And it did."

Rivers said, "What's his name?"

"Sergeant Lalakuni," Briggs said. "Tommy."

Rivers stared at the exposed hand. "Family?"

"According to the men, his wife died last year in an automobile accident in Honolulu," Briggs said. "Parents, both from here, are deceased."

Rivers took a step closer to the body.

"Don't touch anything, sir," Briggs said.

"Who took the glove off?" Rivers asked.

One of the soldiers said, "He did. He said he felt like he was burning up."

The lights were bright enough that they could see Lalakuni's face beginning to turn black behind his mask.

No one said anything for a few seconds, all of them staring at the body. "Sergeant Lalakuni died in a lava accident," Rivers said.

He waited, moving his eyes from one face to another.

"Is that understood?" he said.

They all seemed relieved to be looking at anything that wasn't the body. They nodded.

There was another silence, longer than before, in the eerie quiet of the cave.

Finally, one of the soldiers asked, "What are we going to do with him?"

General Mark Rivers didn't hesitate.

"I saw shovels in the back of that truck," he said. "Go get them."

"Where do you plan to bury him, sir?"

"In here," Rivers said.

CHAPTER 51

U.S. Military Reserve, Hawai'i
Sunday, April 27, 2025

When the cleanup inside and outside that cave was over, Sergeant Noa Mahoe was one of the first out and back to the military base. He'd been a good soldier and done his duty, but he had plans.

Noa had a date.

And not just any date. He was meeting Leilana Kane at Hale Inu Sports Bar, their favorite spot. They had planned to meet there at eleven, after she got off work—she was a hostess at the Ohana Grill—but when Noa heard about the spill at the cave, he'd called her to say he was going to be late.

Before tonight Noa had never been inside the cave known as the Ice Tube. All he knew about it was that it was some kind of top secret storage facility. When the alarm sounded, they all got into their gear, drove up the mountain, and cleaned up the mess, but no one gave them any information about what they were cleaning up.

Their problem now, not his.

His problem was getting off this base and into town, and he was going to do that before the rest of the guys who'd been inside the cave with him even made it back to base. He knew what the protocols were: Leave the protective suit in a pile with the others in what they called the Haz Hut. Shower with the special disinfectant soap. Change into clean clothes. Go through the dose detector, at which point you got your hand stamped.

All because they'd been near some kind of waste that had been stored inside that cave since the 1990s, or so they'd been told. Then they were told that everything that had happened tonight was classified and not to be discussed with civilians, including family.

But Noa didn't have time for that whole process, not tonight. Leilana was waiting and her roommate was out of town and this was the night.

So he slipped back into his boots, threw on jeans and a white T-shirt, went back to the deserted barracks, took a fast shower there, and headed for the front gate. Even after his shower, for some reason, he was sweating like crazy. He worried that he was going to walk into the bar with sweat stains all over his shirt. He felt hotter now than he had inside the hazmat suit, inside that cave, which had felt like an oven.

Maybe his body thought he was still back there. Maybe it was because his heart was racing. *You're just on fire because of Leilana*, he told himself.

As he approached the gate, the guard called out his name. "You must have been in the first wave," Sergeant Ulani Moore said. "A lot of the guys aren't even back yet."

"Yeah," Noa said, "they wanted to get us out of there tonight. It's late."

"You got your stamp?"

He moved closer to her. The two of them had enlisted at the same time. She was probably his best friend in the army. He said in a low voice, "Listen, I did everything I was supposed to do, but the thing is, I've got a date."

That got a smile out of Ulani. "So miracles do happen."

He told her who the date was with and where he was going and how late he was already. "Can you do me a solid and let me out without the stamp just this one time?" Noa said.

Ulani looked around. "Go," she said.

She opened the gate for him and Noa broke into a run as he headed down the road toward the civilian parking lot.

Still on fire.

Thirty minutes later, Ulani Moore was in an office in front of General Mark Rivers. If she hadn't been a sergeant in the U.S. Army, a female sergeant who prided herself on being as tough and strong and capable as any man on the base, she might have cried.

She felt a combination of fear and intimidation. She had made a grave error in judgment, and she had gotten called on it fast. And not just by her own commanding officer but by pretty much *the* commanding officer of everybody everywhere.

"I've seen the video of you opening the gate," Rivers said. "But because the young man wasn't in uniform, we couldn't identify him. So you're going to do that for us, aren't you, Sergeant?"

He wasn't yelling, but somehow Ulani felt as if he were.

"Am I going to be discharged over this, sir?" Ulani asked. "I have to tell you, all I've ever wanted is to be a soldier. Sir."

Rivers either hadn't heard what she'd just said or simply didn't care.

"Who was it?" Rivers said.

"He's my friend."

"I won't ask again." His whole body was completely still, Rivers's cold blue eyes fixed on her, as if they were frozen in place.

She told him.

"Did he tell you where he was going?"

"Is it important, sir?"

"A lot happened after he left that cave," Rivers said. "And he should never have been allowed to step off this base. And I'll just leave it at that."

Ulani Moore told him where Sergeant Noa Mahoe had said he was going.

"You're dismissed," Rivers said.

"What's going to happen to him?" she asked.

"Not your concern."

"Permission to speak freely, sir?"

"If you're absolutely certain you want to," Rivers said.

"What was I supposed to do?" she asked, unable to help herself from laughing nervously. "Shoot him?"

The blue eyes didn't blink.

"Knowing what I know now?" Rivers said. "The answer is yes."

CHAPTER 52

Hale Inu Sports Bar, Hilo, Hawai'i

They were seated at a table against the wall underneath one of the TV sets, holding hands and acting as if there were no one else in the crowded bar.

Noa thought Leilana looked more beautiful than ever, if such a thing were even possible. When he'd first seen her at the Ohana Grill, he had thought she was out of his league. Was sure of it. But now here they were.

"Did you run all the way here?" she asked. "Your face looks sunburned." She touched his face with cool fingers. "God, Noa," she said. "You're burning up."

His mind took him back to the base, to the shower he didn't take, to boots he hadn't changed.

He told himself he was being crazy. What he was feeling was the rush of adrenaline that had gotten him here, the excitement of being with her.

"I would have run if I'd had to," he said. "I was afraid you wouldn't wait for me."

She asked what the big emergency had been. He told her as much as he could, making it sound like some sort of *Mission Impossible* plot.

He smiled. She smiled. They had both finished their first glasses of Big Island beer. Noa already wanted another one, another cold one, to see if that would cool him off.

What he wanted to do in this moment was just press a frosty mug to his forehead.

"Is the eruption going to be as bad as they're saying?" she said. "There's a headline on the *Star-Advertiser* website calling it 'The Biggest One?'—with a question mark at the end. Can that possibly be true?"

"Don't worry." He grabbed their empty glasses and headed for the bar. "I'll protect you."

He told himself he really was Tom Cruise tonight. Noa got up to the bar, waved at the bartender. He noticed that the back of his hand was bright red. The hand without the stamp on it.

He was staring at his hand, almost mesmerized by the color of it, wondering if something was terribly wrong, when men wearing the same kind of hazmat suit he'd left on top of a pile back at the base came charging through the door.

They made Noa think of the Star Wars stormtroopers.

And they were coming straight for him.

"Sergeant Noa Mahoe?" the lead man said from behind his mask.

"Yes," Noa said. "Yes, sir."

More than ever he felt as if he were burning up. Everyone's eyes were on him, including Leilana's, but what he felt was more than embarrassment; he was sure of that.

"You need to come with us," the man growled at him. "*Now.*"

Another man yelled, "Everybody else, stay where you are and do not try to leave."

The crowded bar had gone silent, but not for long.

"Fuck you, Iron Man," a big guy standing at the bar, a native in a floral shirt, said.

"You don't want to make trouble, sir," the first stormtrooper said.

"How do you know?" the big guy asked.

He tried to shove a couple of the stormtroopers, but they knocked him back hard, right into Noa. It was like getting hit by a car.

They both went down.

Noa heard yelling all around him. Somebody else went down. There were more shouts; Noa thought he could hear more men coming through the door.

There was a scuffle above him and then somebody fell on Noa, knocking the last air out of him. He struggled to get himself out from underneath the men pinning him to the sawdust-covered floor.

As he twisted his body, he could see the table where he'd been sitting with Leilana.

She was gone.

Sergeant Noa Mahoe's last thought before he passed out was that he felt like someone had set him on fire.

CHAPTER 53

Hawaiian Volcano Observatory, Hawaiʻi

Mac thought about the canisters constantly.

Mostly he wondered how the army could do everything it was doing and build everything it was building at Mauna Loa and Mauna Kea and yet not have been able to figure out a way to get the canisters the hell out of here.

He thought about the canisters when he and the team were trying to devise one final set of schemes to keep the contents from escaping into the atmosphere if the lava reached them, but they were as helpless to stop that as the rest of planet would eventually be.

A planet whose inhabitants had no idea what might be about to happen on an island in the middle of the Pacific Ocean.

No matter how old you were, you grew up fearing that a nuclear war would blow up the world. *This*, Mac thought now, *is that.*

He vaguely remembered learning in Catholic school about the ten plagues of Egypt in the Old Testament, how some of them had destroyed certain groups while sparing others.

But this plague would spare nothing and no one in the end; it would destroy all the life on the planet. At first, it had been impossible for Mac to wrap his mind around that fact, make sense of it in a rational way.

No longer.

The end. Mac thought that the real Ice Tube was the one inside him; knowing the magnitude of the situation as the clock continued to relentlessly wind down was like a cold grip on his heart.

His sons—they were his heart.

He stared now at one of the pictures of them on his desk, a black-and-white photograph in a small silver frame of his boys and him on a fishing trip in Montana. When he looked up, he was startled to see Jenny standing in the doorway.

"Hey," she said. "You okay?"

"Not even close."

She came around the desk and looked at the photo in his hand.

"I know how much you miss them, Mac," Jenny said.

He put the framed picture down gently, as if it might break if he weren't careful. "What if I never see them again?" he asked.

"You will."

What came next seemed to explode out of him; there was nothing he could do to stop it.

"You don't know that! No one does!"

He knew how angry he sounded and knew it had nothing to do with her, his best friend and his wingman and whatever else she was and might not ever be if they couldn't keep the lava away from the cave.

But she was Jenny. If he knew these things, so did she.

"Sorry," he said.

"You know you don't have to apologize to me."

"Yeah," he said. "Yeah, I do."

She sat down on the edge of the desk.

"I can't do this," he said, his voice not much above a whisper.

She smiled at him. "Then we really are screwed," she said.

He could not make himself smile back.

"I come in here sometimes and close the door and sit down behind this desk and try to think of what I might have missed," he said. "And then, just like that, I feel as if I want to drive a fist through one of these walls." He looked down and saw his fists clenched in front of him.

"I didn't sign up for this!" He didn't care if the people out in the bullpen heard him.

"None of us did," Jenny said softly. "And yet here we are. And all I'm going to ask is that you don't let anybody else see you like this. Because this isn't you, and we both know it."

"I'm allowed to feel like this, Jenny," Mac said. "And I'm allowed to tell you that right now I feel like there's not a snowball's chance in hell that we can pull this off."

She went behind him and reached down to the bottom drawer where she knew he kept the bottle of Macallan and two glasses. She poured them each a shot.

They drank, and Jenny made a big show of wiping her mouth with the back of her hand.

"Now please shut the fuck up and get to work, because that's what I'm going to do," Jenny said. When she got to the door, she added, "You're always telling me that if these jobs were easy, everybody would do them."

And she walked out.

* * *

Mac could hear the strain in Briggs's voice when the colonel called and said Mac needed to see something right away. It was as if Briggs's voice were stretched as far as it could go, and the next thing he said might snap it like a rubber band. He told Mac where he was—in a remote cabin at the end of Pe'epe'e Falls Road, near a succession of bubbling pools known in Hilo as the Boiling Pots area.

"Make sure to stop at the base on your way and pick up your hazmat suit," Briggs said.

CHAPTER 54

Briggs was waiting for Mac in front of what looked like an old-fashioned log cabin set back in the woods above Peʻepeʻe Falls Road, at least a mile past any lights Mac had seen as he slowly drove along a dirt road just wide enough for his jeep.

There were soldiers there, also in suits, training powerful flashlights on the area in front of the cabin.

Mac could see immediately that the shrubs the locals called Hawaiian cotton had turned black, like they'd suffered some kind of internal oil spill. The banyan trees on either side of the front door had also turned black and begun to wither; the branches were as thin as matchsticks. It smelled like a forest fire, except there was no smoke from the woods surrounding the cabin. There was only the scorched earth all around them.

"Follow me," Briggs said.

Battery-powered Nomad scene lights illuminated the single room, just some chairs set around an old butcher-block table covered with beer cans and empty whiskey bottles and ashtrays filled with cigarette butts.

The three dead men were on the floor, all of them with eyes and mouths open, as if they had died gasping for breath.

That wasn't the worst part.

Their faces and necks and arms and hands and feet had turned as black as the shrubs and trees outside. The dead men looked as if the jeans and T-shirts they'd been wearing were burned off their bodies in a fire.

Except there were no signs of fire in the old wooden cabin.

Mac wanted to look away from the bodies but could not. His eyes kept shifting from one to another. He could hear his breathing getting faster and shallower inside his mask. He was afraid he might be sick.

"We got a call about an hour ago," Briggs said, staring at the bodies himself.

"From who?" Mac asked.

Either Briggs was lost in his own thoughts about the scene around them and didn't hear him or he was just ignoring the question.

"What the hell happened here?" Mac asked.

"Black death," Briggs said.

He paused, then added, "In all ways."

He told Mac about the dead body in the Ice Tube belonging to Sergeant Tommy Lalakuni, and the rip in his protective suit, and how he had died the way these men had obviously died. The remnants of their clothes already looked like ash at the bottom of a grill, like what they had seen outside underneath the bushes and trees.

"Looks like this was some kind of crash pad," Briggs said.

"Crash-and-burn pad," Mac said quietly.

He did not want to be in this room near these bodies. The urge to flee was overpowering; the smell became stronger, even though he was wearing his mask. He wanted to be outside *right now*. But Briggs wasn't leaving, so neither was he.

"Do you have any idea who these men are?" Mac asked.

"Ours," Colonel James Briggs said. "They were on the

cleanup crew at the Ice Tube." He paused. "And then they didn't go through the proper protocols for cleaning themselves up as they were ordered to do."

Mac turned back to the bodies, which seemed to have gotten blacker as he and Briggs stood there.

Mac said, "When General Rivers came out of the cave, he said the spill had been contained."

"He thought it had been," Briggs said. "That was before he knew about the body inside the cave."

Then Briggs quietly said, "I've seen pictures from Vietnam. This is what napalm did."

They finally went back outside. One of the trees that had still been standing when Mac arrived was gone, reduced to a pile of ash. In the cool night air, Mac could see a faint steam lifting off the shrubs as they began to collapse in on themselves.

Briggs said there was another soldier, this one still alive, at the infirmary, currently under quarantine and armed guard until they could move him to the hospital in Hilo. He had come back from the Ice Tube and then snuck off the base without being scrubbed down and checked by radiation monitors and before he knew what had happened to Sergeant Lalakuni.

"So it turns out that this sergeant of ours wasn't the only one," Briggs said. "These three must have gotten past security too. Maybe they thought they needed to have a few…one of them tried to call the base when they…when they realized what was happening to them."

"Could there be any others?" Mac said.

Briggs hesitated. Mac didn't like that at all.

"We don't know," Briggs said, staring at the ground.

"How the fuck can you not know?" Mac shouted.

"Because we don't," Briggs said. He looked at Mac. "This is

what we're up against if what's in those canisters gets out," Briggs said.

"A plague that could be running through Hilo right now," Mac said.

Briggs nodded.

"Whatever you need to do to protect that cave, whatever you and your people *think* you're doing, you need to do more," Mac said. Then: "Does Rivers know about this?"

"He's the one who told me to call you," Briggs said.

"I need to get to work," Mac said.

Mac and General Rivers weren't scheduled to meet until six a.m., but it had to happen sooner than that. It wasn't easy to run in a hazmat suit, but Mac managed to stay upright as he went down the road to his jeep. He grabbed his phone, called Rivers, and told the general he'd see him in his office after he'd scrubbed himself down.

"That sounded like an order," Rivers said.

"Only because it was."

"You're still working for the army," Rivers said.

"And how's that working out for me so far?"

CHAPTER 55

U.S. Military Reserve, Hawai'i

In the office the general had taken over for the duration, Rivers said nothing about the situation on the ground involving dead soldiers who'd basically exited the Ice Tube under a death sentence.

And who might have made a stop or two before they arrived at their party cabin in the woods above Hilo.

"I fought wars in the Middle East," Rivers said. "I lived in a world of IEDs and lunatics with explosives strapped to their chests. And I sit here now knowing how close this eruption is, and I feel like this whole island has become a potential roadside bomb."

He put his elbows on his desk and his face in his hands.

"And now, on top of that, because some of the people in my command thought the rules didn't apply to them, I might have a budding pandemic on my hands," Rivers said. "Except with this one, you get burned to a fucking crisp."

Mac had changed back into his sweater and jeans. His hazmat suit had been collected. He had been checked and rechecked for radiation and pronounced clear.

For now, he thought.

"Do we tell the others about what I just witnessed?" Mac asked Rivers. "And do you tell them about the body in the cave?"

"Not even at gunpoint," Rivers said.

"I hate keeping things from my team," Mac said.

"They need to focus on what's about to happen at the top of that mountain," Rivers said.

"You're right."

The smallest of smiles crossed Rivers's lips. "Had to happen eventually." He got up and went to get more coffee. "I'm bringing boats into the Port of Hilo starting this morning," Rivers said. "We need to evacuate as much of the town as we can."

"The entire town?" Mac said.

"We don't have enough time for that," Rivers said. "We're using your schematics, going through the areas that we think are most vulnerable and telling people they need to leave. The way they do on the mainland when there's a hurricane coming."

"I can't disagree with that," Mac said.

Rivers shrugged. "Martial law," he said. "And I'm the marshal."

"You're doing what you need to do," Mac said. "I assume you always have."

The general sat back down and said to Mac, "I need *you*, Dr. MacGregor, now more than ever. Maybe even more than I thought I did." Before Mac could respond, Rivers held up a hand. "I'm a fast learner," he said. "Always have been, all the way back to the academy. First in my fucking class. I'm a smart bastard. But *really* smart bastards know what they don't know and know when they're out of their depth." He smiled, barely. "You see where I'm going with this?"

"Tell me what you need from me," Mac said.

"For the rest of this day and for as long as it takes, I need you to be the one calling the shots on how we protect those death canisters," Rivers said. "Although I want it to look and sound as if I'm the one calling those shots."

Mac needed to get out of here and get with Rebecca. But he knew this was important too. Now Mac was the one smiling. "You *are* a smart bastard."

"We'll still be speaking with one voice," Rivers said. "I want to make that clear."

Mac could see how difficult it was for a man who was so powerful, a man who had command and authority encoded in his DNA, to give up control like this.

To subordinate himself like this.

"But that voice will be your voice, starting right here and right now," Rivers said.

The general stood and reached across his desk. Mac stood and shook his hand, feeling in that moment as if he were saluting.

"Now you tell me what you need from me," Rivers said.

And Mac did.

CHAPTER 56

County of Hawaiʻi Civil Defense Building, Hilo, Hawaiʻi

The microphone stand was set up at the end of the long driveway that went from the main building down to Ululani Street.

Local television stations and newspapers had sent out email blasts about Rivers's press conference, not speculating as to why he would be out here this early in the morning, or what news he had to offer beyond what he had said at the auditorium the night before.

The TV trucks were lined up about a block away from where uniformed soldiers had set up crowd-control barriers in front of the media. A sizable crowd of onlookers were organizing themselves behind the reporters and photographers.

Mac and Rebecca were at Mauna Loa placing red flags where they planned to bury her explosives once they'd coordinated the locations with the army, but they stopped to watch on Rebecca's phone when Rivers stepped to the microphone.

Rivers spoke quickly, almost as if he didn't want the scope of what he was saying to sink in. He talked in broad strokes about ground explosives and aerial bombing and trenches and walls and the Army Corps of Engineers. If Mac hadn't known better, he would have sworn the chairman of the Joint Chiefs was reading from a teleprompter.

"These are extreme but necessary steps proposed by our team of experts," Rivers said. "Some of them, particularly aerial bombing, are unprecedented. But I want to stress to you: None of this would be undertaken if we didn't believe it would work."

There was a question shouted by a TV reporter, but neither Mac nor Rebecca could make it out.

Rivers put up a hand, like a crossing guard stopping traffic. "There will be time for questions later, because our work is about to begin in earnest," Rivers said. "Again, I am here today in the interest of transparency and to deliver the message that we're all in this together." He paused.

Mac said to Rebecca, "That can't be all of it."

"Wait for it," she said.

"These are extraordinary circumstances, I think everybody realizes that now," General Mark Rivers continued. "In so many ways, and I don't use this reference lightly, Hilo is about to be under attack the way Pearl Harbor was in 1941. The difference is that that time, we didn't know the attack was coming. This time, we *are* forewarned, and so we are going to be forearmed."

Rivers looked down, then back out at the crowd.

"For all of these reasons and others too numerous to list," Rivers said, "I have decided to place Hilo under martial law."

"Boom," the demolition woman next to Mac said.

CHAPTER 57

Inside Mauna Loa

Minutes after Rivers stepped away from the microphone without taking questions, Mac and Rebecca entered a lava tube on the southeast flank of the mountain.

Mac felt the same way he had for days: like there was a gun pointed at his head.

Mac and Rebecca each carried an LED flashlight as they advanced into the darkness underground. Mac hadn't even known this particular tube existed until Rick Ozaki discovered it the night before.

Rick and Jenny Kimura had come up here on their own because, they said, they were tired of staring at their screens. Rick had brought with him a gravimeter, which he used for surface detection because an empty tube read as lower density due to the absence of rock. After they returned and showed Mac what they had, Mac had pulled Jenny aside.

"It was your idea for you and Rick to go up there, wasn't it?" he asked.

"I just did what you would have done," she said.

"You're one in a million, you know that?"

Jenny smiled. "Just as long as you know," she'd said.

Now, about fifty yards into the tube, Rebecca Cruz asked, "Is it safe in there?"

"Define *safe*," Mac said.

"I was afraid you'd say something like that," she said.

The terrain was rough, nearly impassable in spots. They both stumbled and fell more than once. At one point, Rebecca made a startled noise as they felt the ground underneath them tilt; it was like the cave was being turned on its side.

"It happens like that sometimes," Mac said. "Nothing to worry about."

"Am I also not supposed to worry about how freaking hot it is in here?" she asked.

"I told you to dress light," Mac said. "Day at the beach." He shrugged. "So to speak."

As they walked deeper into the tube, Mac said, "This is all our way of trying to run an elaborate con on the lava. We want it to think it's going where *it* wants to go while we're actually making it go where we want it to go after those nifty bombs of yours are in place."

Rebecca said, "And we also want to keep it from going where we sure as hell don't want it to go."

"Near those canisters," Mac said. "And right through downtown Hilo."

She stopped and faced him. "You know, Dr. MacGregor," she said, "up till now you've only spoken to me in general terms about why we have to do everything humanly possible not to let the canisters blow."

The weird light was all around them; the beams of their

flashlights reflected off the lava rock. The inside of the tube seemed like the quietest place on earth.

Mac finally said, "Is there a question here?"

"I'm asking if there could be some kind of explosion that would mean the end of life on this island," Rebecca said.

"Not just the island."

"So we need to get the placement of these bombs exactly right."

"And even if we do," Mac said, "we have no idea if they're going to work the way we want them to."

They were more focused than ever when they were back outside, sometimes making multiple measurements and calculations before they marked a spot. Mac stressed how important this area was, how they couldn't afford to make a single mistake.

CHAPTER 58

Near the Hilo Botanical Gardens, Hawai'i

Rachel Sherrill looked out the window of her hotel room and saw the helicopters in the distance, which made her think back to the day, years ago, when helicopters had appeared over the botanical gardens.

She had finally turned off the television, having watched all the local reactions to General Mark Rivers's announcement about martial law; all the reporters were anticipating demonstrations in downtown Hilo and perhaps even at the Military Reserve.

Rachel sat down at her desk and fired up her laptop and saw that Rivers's decision was being covered by all the cable news networks and the major newspapers on the mainland. And #martiallaw was the number one trending topic on social media.

They're declaring martial law because of an eruption? Rachel thought.

She checked her watch.

If they hadn't been delayed on their way from the airport by the first demonstrations, they should be here any minute.

She fixed herself another cup of coffee from the minibar setup and took it to the terrace. The helicopters were gone from the sky, perhaps off to invade Oʻahu.

Maybe Oliver Cutler, that grandstanding gasbag, had been right. Rachel had seen him on the news once she got back to her room after trying in vain to catch up with John MacGregor. Maybe this eruption was going to be the Biggest One, and that was all there was to the story.

But by now, Rachel Sherrill's paranoia levels were high, especially when it came to anything involving the United States Army. It didn't take much to make her flash back to the blackened banyan grove. This time it had been the helicopters.

She heard loud knocking on her door.

When she opened it, she saw a young man and a young woman. The guy had shaggy hair and a beard and wore a T-shirt underneath his wrinkled sport jacket. The young woman wore a white summer dress and reminded Rachel of Halle Berry.

"Rachel?" the guy asked.

Rachel grinned. "I have a feeling you know that already."

The guy said, "Hey, we're from the *New York Times*. We know everything."

"Even when it's not fit to print," the young woman said. "May we come in?"

CHAPTER 59

Hawaiian Volcano Observatory, Hawai'i
Time to eruption: 48 hours

Mac was working on his laptop while construction crews descended on Mauna Loa like an invading army of their own. Jenny came in and walked around his desk and put a hand on his shoulder. Mac looked at it, then up at her, and saw her smiling at him.

"We're all scrambling here," Mac said. "The general included."

"And we might all be about to die no matter what we do and no matter how righteous we think our plan is," Jenny said.

"You're starting to sound like me," Mac said.

"I get to say what I'm thinking sometimes, just like you," she said. "And I'm allowed to be scared."

Mac knew how tough Jenny was; he often complimented her on it. But now she looked like she was about to cry.

"Hey," he said. "Take it easy."

"You first," she said.

They looked at each other until she made a quick motion with her hand, as if she were brushing away a tear. She started to say something, stopped herself, and left him sitting there.

He went to his social media accounts then and found a meme that showed lava flowing through a living room where J. P. Brett was standing like Moses parting the Red Sea, except he was stopping the lava.

He was about to call Brett and ask if he had anything to do with that when Betty Kilima, who'd given up her duties as librarian to run interference for Mac, gave a quick rap on his door and poked her head in.

"There's a couple of people out in the lobby who want to speak with you," Betty said.

"Tell them I'm busy."

"They say they're from the *New York Times*," she said.

He called Rivers immediately and asked what he should do.

"What I would," Rivers said. "Lie."

CHAPTER 60

U.S. Military Reserve, Hawai'i

J. P. Brett and General Mark Rivers were in a small private dining room at the military base. Normally, Rivers took his meals in the commissary with his officers. But not today.

Brett was the one who had requested the meeting, a way of trying to get himself on familiar ground, even if he hadn't put it that way to Rivers.

He was here to do some hard selling.

Of himself, mostly.

"I don't have a lot of time" was Rivers's greeting before Brett even sat down.

"Completely understand," Brett said. "I appreciate you making time for me at all." Brett thought: *Nobody fakes sincerity better than I do.*

He was here to do something he considered essential to the task at hand: cutting Dr. John MacGregor off at the knees.

There were several business principles to which J. P. Brett had adhered in the building of his brand and his empire. But there was one to which he clung more fiercely than he did to any of the others: Be the last man in the room whenever possible.

"I'm happy you didn't find my little show objectionable," Brett said.

"Hardly little, Mr. Brett."

"I don't do small very well, General," Brett said. "I'm not wired that way and never have been. It's the modern world, after all. The TikTok world, if you will, even if the Chinese hijacked that one. Presentation is everything. The truth is, it was like one of those old-fashioned infomercials, and it gave people a little taste of our might and even our will."

"Well, mission accomplished, as somebody once said. So why *are* we here?"

"So I can state plainly that I believe the only two people with the vision and balls to carry out this particular mission and save this island from imminent destruction are the two of us," Brett said.

"You have my attention, if not my agreement."

"We need to eliminate the middlemen, sir," Brett continued. "And the middlewoman. I'm not suggesting you freeze out Mac-Gregor and my dear friends the Cutlers. But it has to come from you that going forward, you and I speak with one voice."

"And what would you have us saying with that voice, if you don't mind me asking?"

"That my plan is not only the most comprehensive but the only one we need and the only one that will work," J. P. Brett said. "And the only one that can save this island."

"You've made clear your feelings about Dr. MacGregor," Rivers said. "But I was under the impression that you and the Cutlers were a team."

Brett chuckled. "I'm the team," he said.

"I have to say that MacGregor has impressed me, in a very short time, as being both smart and capable," Rivers said, "even though he doesn't appear to be much of a team player."

"He is smart and capable, don't misunderstand me," Brett said. "But in the end, he's a by-the-numbers, by-the-book guy. He can't help that; he's a scientist. Scientists take chances only as a last resort. I should know—I've dealt with enough of them. But by the time he and the Cruz woman finish setting their explosives in what they consider to be the absolute perfect spots, Hilo will be underneath a goddamn tidal wave of lava."

Brett leaned forward and lowered his voice, even though it was just the two of them in the room. "General, we need to bomb the east side of Mauna Loa as soon as it's feasible, bring the lava out in what I expect will be a biblical gush, then spray it with so much seawater it will be like we're using the ocean to drown it."

"MacGregor thinks that's reckless, even if it results in only one errant bomb."

"MacGregor is just covering his ass, General," Brett said.

"In what way?"

"In *every* way. He's holding back intel from the army and we both know it," Brett said. "You need to order him to turn over all of his internals right now. All of his maps, all of his seismic imaging for both the south and east sides of the volcano. I've had my drones photographing the area and doing 3-D renderings; my image processors are interpreting the data. But that goes only so far. MacGregor has been studying the damn mountain a lot longer than we have. He's been studying *all* of these mountains, has witnessed major eruptions. He's holding back information because he's threatened by me. Which is a pretty shitty reason, considering the stakes." Brett shook his head. "I run into a lot of that."

"Of what?"

"People being threatened by me." Brett grinned. "Just ask my ex-wives."

"I've made it clear that I don't need a turf war here, Mr. Brett. Especially not with the turf we're talking about and the consequences if we screw this up. Dissension like that doesn't just breed distrust. It breeds chaos."

Brett slapped the table, rattling their mugs. *"Chaos is my specialty!"* he said, no longer attempting to keep his voice down. "I'm the captain of chaos—it's why I'm here, General Rivers. I'm not looking to *cover* my ass. I'm willing to put it on the line right next to yours."

Brett paused.

"I'm just asking you, respectfully, to let me do me, sir," he said. "And I can't do that with John MacGregor in my way and constantly trying to convince you that his plan is the best one. Because it's not, unless you want the lava getting as close to Hilo as it did back in '84. And if that happens, the world will see it happening in real time and wonder why the U.S. Army couldn't protect a city it just put under martial law."

They stared at each other, each man waiting for the other to blink. Brett felt he had positioned Rivers as best as he could. But he still wasn't sure Rivers would see it his way. The general's face, as usual, told him nothing.

"I guess what I'm really asking is if you want to be the one to tell MacGregor to step aside or if I have your permission to handle this myself," Brett said.

"I'll need to consider this," Rivers said. His cell phone, on the table, buzzed. Rivers checked the caller ID but didn't answer it.

"I assumed you would need some time, sir. But as you know, we don't have much of that."

Brett didn't tell General Mark Rivers that he was already well on his way to handling things.

On multiple fronts.

CHAPTER 61

Hawaiian Volcano Observatory, Hawai'i

Mac made the *Times* reporters wait a little longer so he could sit in his office and have a few minutes to himself.

He was rarely alone these days, and he needed solitude to do his best thinking.

Linda, his soon-to-be-ex-wife, had told him once in the middle of an argument that she thought solitude was her husband's natural state.

Mac had the new seismic profiles—detailing both the volume and movement of the magma—spread across his desk. There were maps of the two rift zones at Mauna Loa's summit caldera, extending to the southwest and to the northeast; most of the volcano's eruptive fissures and vents were there. Hypothetically—and historically—the summit caldera provided a topographic barrier protecting the southeast flank of the mountain from normal lava flow.

Which was all well and good, except the coming flow would be anything but normal.

Normal, Mac knew, was whatever would happen when their world exploded sometime in the next forty-eight hours. He sat there and looked at hourly projections about the lava flow they could reasonably expect this time. Mac knew from his research that there had been upward of five hundred lava flows at Mauna Loa, starting as far back as thirty thousand years ago, all originating from the summit area, rift zones, radial vents. All their current estimates and projections were based on what had happened in the past.

But nothing like this had happened in the past, here or anywhere.

He was certain that an insane amount of lava was coming this time, so much lava that it might ultimately be impossible to divert all of it no matter how many channels they dug and how many bombs they set off and how many vents they used between now and the day after tomorrow.

Rebecca was on her way back to HVO from Hilo International. The military transport planes carrying her explosives from Cruz Demolition had finally arrived; Rebecca and her brother David had supervised the loading of the boxes onto the army trucks that would transport them to the Military Reserve. If everything went as scheduled, they'd be putting them in place by the end of the afternoon.

What he saw from the latest charts and graphs was that vents that had been so useful in the past were being plugged on an almost hourly basis by the volcano's initial underground rumblings. Not all. But too many, in his view.

He pushed back from his desk, put his feet up on it, tipped his chair back, and closed his eyes. Then Jenny and Rick came blowing into the office, both of them clearly on fire.

"Did they text you too?" Jenny snapped.

"Did who text me?" Mac asked.

"Those weasels Kenny and Pia, that's who," Rick said.

"I have no idea what you guys are talking about."

"They just went to work for J. P. Brett," Jenny said. "For Brett and the Cutlers."

She was breathing in big gulps, her chest heaving, her face red. Mac imagined steam coming off her. Jenny prided herself on her loyalty, and she hated disloyalty almost as much as she hated politicians.

"I just checked their stations," Jenny said. "They took their work with them, and their hard drives."

"How much of their work?" Mac asked.

"I misspoke," Jenny Kimura said. "I didn't mean *their* work. I meant *our* work. And they took all of it, Mac."

CHAPTER 62

The woman reporter was named Imani Burgess. The male reporter was Sam Ito, and he wasted no time informing Mac that he'd been fascinated by volcanoes his whole life.

Ito said that his family had moved from Maui to the mainland when he was an infant and that his father had studied volcanology at Caltech, where he now taught.

Mac said nothing, just leaned back with his fingers clasped behind his head.

"Took some undergrad courses on it myself at the University of Wisconsin," Ito said.

Mac almost told him how happy he was for him but decided to just stare at him instead.

Imani Burgess smiled. It was, Mac had to admit, a winning smile.

"The scouting report on you noted that you're not really the chatty type," she said.

"Who told you that?"

She held the smile. "I can't reveal my sources."

"Are you of the opinion that I should open up to two reporters

I just met?" Mac said. "In what world would that be a good idea?" But now he smiled.

"Are we getting off on the wrong foot here?" Sam Ito asked.

"You're the reporters," Mac said. "You figure it out."

"We haven't gotten much sleep the past twenty-four hours," Imani Burgess said. "Anyplace around here where a girl could get a cup of coffee?"

"There is," Mac said. "But without sounding rude, you won't be staying that long."

"Gee," she said, "why would anybody think that was rude?"

"We're not trying to make trouble for you, Dr. MacGregor," Ito said.

"Sure you are," Mac said.

"Excuse me?"

"My experience with reporters, Sam—may I call you Sam?—is that, whether the reporters are from the paper of record or not, they generally don't come around to help me."

Mac knew he was being a pain in the ass but couldn't stop himself.

"Why did you agree to see us, then?" Imani Burgess asked.

"Maybe I wanted to interview the two of you," Mac said, "before returning to my current problems with Mother Nature."

"Who I hear is one tough mother these days," she said.

Before Mac could respond, Sam Ito said, "We've spent a fair amount of time today talking to our sources in the military and getting a sense of what you plan to do about the lava once it comes. And we've spoken to a lot of the locals too. It's kind of fascinating, really, the way they talk about the volcano and the goddess Madame Pele, the force behind volcanic eruptions. But they say that what you're trying to do, divert the lava, is like trying to dim the light of the moon."

"But I'm sure, being as fascinated by volcanoes as you are,"

Mac said, "you know how effective diversion can be if it's done right."

He saw Imani Burgess nodding. "Etna in 1983 and 1992," she said. "The diversions saved Catania and a bunch of other towns on the east coast of Sicily." She opened her reporter's notebook and flipped through some pages. "Massive engineering effort," she continued, studying her notes. "Gouged-out channels, earthen walls, tons of workers on the front line. The fire department finally sprayed massive amounts of water on the lava and on the bulldozers, because they had to cool them down. Pretty heroic efforts, all in all."

"They usually are," Mac said. "That first effort, I'm sure you know, cost about two million dollars, and that was over forty years ago. But what they did there saved more than a hundred million dollars' worth of property. Maybe more. And they basically did it all with bulldozers and the judicious use of explosives."

"Is that what you're planning to do here?" she asked.

Mac looked at his watch. "You already know that, and I know you know that. But that's not really why you're here, is it?" He smiled again. This time neither one of them smiled back at him. It was official, he thought. They *had* gotten off on the wrong foot.

But Mac still didn't know why the two of them were sitting across from him.

"So how about this?" he said. "How about we all stop fucking around here?"

"You don't suffer fools gladly, do you, Dr. MacGregor?" Imani Burgess asked.

"Actually," Mac said, "I thought that was exactly what I was doing."

No one spoke. Mac was comfortable with the silence, but it turned out that so were they.

"We're here because we got a tip," Sam Ito said.

"A tip about what?"

"We're hearing some chatter that the eruption might not be the only threat to the island," Burgess said. "And that there might be concerns about Mauna Kea too."

"Do you know something about an eruption there that I don't?" Mac asked. "Because as far as *I* know, there hasn't been an eruption on Mauna Kea in four thousand years, give or take."

"The tip wasn't about an eruption," Imani Burgess said.

She casually reached out, placed a micro–tape recorder on the desk between them, and pushed what Mac assumed was the Record button because he saw the green light go on.

He picked it up, checked the buttons, and hit Stop. The green light promptly disappeared.

"If the tip wasn't about an eruption, what was it about?" he asked.

"Our source didn't know," Sam Ito said. "He'd just heard that there was some kind of emergency there. What the natives refer to as *ulia pōpilikia*."

"I know what it means," Mac said.

"Was there an emergency?" Ito asked.

He leaned forward. "At this point in time, I am basically working for the U.S. Army," he said. "And I'm not supposed to talk about things they don't want me to talk about, which is practically everything. Especially not with two reporters from the *Times*."

"How about if we're talking about the public's need to know?" Imani Burgess asked.

"When the public needs to know something, General Rivers will tell them," Mac said. "If you've got more questions going forward, you should probably ask him."

"We tried," Sam Ito said. "He won't talk to us."

"I know."

"General Rivers tell you that himself?" Ito asked.

"It's more something I intuited," Mac said. He shrugged and

stretched his arms out wide, a gesture of helplessness. "Sorry I don't have more for you."

"Actually, you didn't give us anything," she said.

"I know," Mac said sadly. "I know."

He stood. They stood.

"One more question," Sam Ito said. "Do you happen to know anything about some incident at the botanical gardens a few years ago?"

"What kind of incident?"

Ito shrugged. "Just another tip. Some kind of chemical spill, is what we heard."

"Well, good luck with that," Mac said.

"One more from me," Imani Burgess said. "Think of it as a Hail Mary. Do you know anything about a bunch of hazmat-suited army guys dragging a soldier out of a Hilo bar?"

"Can't help you there either." Mac walked over and opened the door for them. They left, and he was alone again in his office until Jenny came back. He told her he'd spent most of the past half hour bobbing and weaving.

"You think they know more than they were saying?" Jenny asked.

"They almost always do."

"You think they know about the canisters?"

"Not yet."

"You think they're going to give up?"

"They hardly ever do," Mac said.

They sat and talked about Kenny and Pia selling them out, and Mac let Jenny vent about them in increasingly colorful language. She told Mac he couldn't let this go. Mac said she had to know him better than that by now.

"Kenny and Pia did what they did," he said. "I'm not after them."

"Don't tell me," she said. "You're after Brett."

He nodded. "He's so worried about targets, he doesn't realize there's a brand-new one as of today."

"Where?"

"On his back."

Mac's phone buzzed. He picked it up and nodded when he heard the voice at the other end of the line. "I'm on my way," he said.

"Where are you going?" Jenny asked.

"You know what they say," he said. "If the mountain won't come to MacGregor…"

"Is that what they say?" she said, grinning at him.

Mac told her where he wanted her and Rick to meet later and headed for his car. He found himself wondering what new surprises the goddess of fire and lava, the one the locals called Madame Pele, "She Who Shapes the Sacred Land," had in store for him today.

Little did he know.

The ground underneath him had not shaken today, although the magma continued its steady rise on a timetable only it knew and maybe even it couldn't control. Over the past twenty-four hours the magma, thicker and more viscous than ever, had been thwarted, briefly, by the various blocked chambers it encountered above the subduction zone.

This was happening as the lava above it was receding below the water table, and the volatile mix of water and magma was turning to steam and beginning to eat away at the crater area.

They were less than two days from when they were convinced the eruption would come, and Mac was becoming more concerned by the hour that it might come sooner, before they could finish enough of their guardrails. More vents near the summit were being blocked. Mac wasn't sure how many.

Only the volcano goddess knew that.

Only she knew in this moment how quickly the increasingly combustible combination of steam and blocked gases and solid lava, known as cinder, was rising up within the Earth, ready to show them all that she still ruled the Big Island the way she always had.

And the unseen clock on the ticking bomb continued to count down.

Mac kept trying to focus on the work, distract himself from the reality of the situation with the volcano and the canisters, email his sons at least once a day, keep assuring the members of his team that they could only do what they could do in whatever time they had before the eruption that could destroy the island if the lava found the death inside the Ice Tube and inside the canisters and released it into the atmosphere...

Mac always stopped himself there. Dwelling on the consequences of their schemes not working, the devastation that would follow, got him nowhere, except to darker places.

Last week, when he was on the phone with his sons, Charlie and Max, Max had asked if everything was going to be okay.

"A-OK," he'd said.

When the boys were born, he'd promised himself he'd never lie to them. Now it was almost as easy as lying to himself.

When he began to make his way on foot toward all the men and women in their hard hats, the ones operating the heavy machinery and the ones directing it, holes being dug and rock and dirt being moved, he felt the first small quake underneath him, like a rug being pulled out from under him, making his knees buckle and nearly bringing him down.

But he did not go down.

One foot in front of the other.

When he looked up ahead, he could see that the work between him and the sky continued without interruption, making him wonder, with all the noise and activity and pieces of the mountain being moved around, if they had even felt the earth shift underneath them.

But it had. Again.

Dr. John MacGregor had stopped being so alarmed about quakes. He told himself this latest one was nothing out of the ordinary and slowed his pace just long enough to put on his hard hat.

Then he put his head back down and kept going.

CHAPTER 63

Mauna Loa, Hawai'i

By now Mac knew the zone maps for the lava as well as he knew his email address, knew that all the information he was getting, almost moment to moment, was based on the best empirical data and geologic mapping his team had available to it.

His team minus Kenny and Pia, of course.

He had studied the hydrologic modeling of the previous downhill lava flows from previous eruptions. He was fully aware that a flow path as immense as this one was would ultimately be defined from the point source of the catchment, following as closely as possible the steepest line of descent.

That was the plan, anyway.

But he knew the earth-eating goddess Pele had her own plans, with her rift zones and cones and scattered ramparts and what looked like a million ground cracks and everything that was happening right now in unseen lava channels.

Mac knew that in the end, the area covered by the lava would be a function of the duration of the volume of magma, how quickly it left the volcano—a fact as unknowable as anything they were dealing with—and its various angles of descent, how many and how steep.

No matter how often he told himself that the world had survived volcanoes before, he knew that the reality was that it would not survive this one because of the death contained in the canisters stored inside the Ice Tube.

This time both man and nature would lose...

The ground shook again. It didn't startle him as much as the loud voice behind him.

"You said you wanted to talk," J. P. Brett said. "So let's talk. I've got things to do."

Mac turned to face him. He felt a sudden and powerful urge to knock the smirk off Brett's face, this rich and powerful asshat who thought this was some kind of game, just like the Cutlers so clearly did, all of them more worried about the way things looked than the way things actually were, realizing what was on the line here, for all of them.

He wanted to ask them how being famous would help them when everyone and everything was gone. He wanted to scream at them that all of them might be about to die.

But before he could say a thing, there was an explosion from the summit. It sounded as if a bomb had gone off up there, as if the aerial bombing had already begun.

Another explosion followed that one.

Then a third.

Mac and Brett stared at where the noise was coming from and saw rocks rocketing up in the sky as if they had been shot from below the surface by some unseen cannon. Then a hailstorm of lava rock and ash rained down on them.

The vehicles came to a stop. The hard hats on all the crews

up the mountain began to scatter in all directions, men and women diving for cover, some of them going underneath the metal blades of the bulldozers, some of them crowding into the cabins, all looking for some shelter from the sudden storm.

Even from this distance, Mac could hear their screams.

Mac watched as a rock as big as a bowling ball hit a man squarely in the back and saw the man go down and then not move.

Another man raced down the hill toward Mac and Brett as if trying to outrun the storm; a jagged piece of basalt hit his hard hat and sent it flying, and he went down.

Mac turned to see if Brett was all right and saw him diving into the front seat of his Rivian R1T truck just as a rock came crashing into his windshield.

Mac ran up the mountain to the army man lying face down and motionless. He rolled him over and was relieved to see he was still breathing, although blood poured out of the wound on the side of his face.

In the next instant Mac smelled the rotten-egg odor of sulfur dioxide; the rocks kept raining down.

A rock slammed into Mac's hard hat, knocking him down and nearly out. He rolled over in the dirt, trying to cover up, and heard a different kind of roar above him. Mac looked up and saw a drone the size of a small plane spinning out of control, about to come crashing down from the sky on top of him.

For days he had been obsessed about the end being near.

It had been nearer than he'd thought.

CHAPTER 64

Hilo Medical Center, Hilo, Hawai'i

Jenny and Rebecca were waiting for Mac when he stepped out of the hospital and onto Wai Ānuenue Avenue.

They both knew what had happened up on the mountain by now, the crippled drone that had missed Mac by less than twenty yards. One of the soldiers from the Corps of Engineers had seen the whole thing, come sprinting to his aid, and driven him straight to the hospital despite Mac's protestations that all he had was a bump on the back of his head.

"Fortunately," Jenny said to Rebecca, "the rock struck the hardest part of him. So he caught a little break there."

"I *was* lucky," Mac said.

Jenny smiled at him.

As he told them about the various injuries people were being treated for in the medical center, from broken legs to fractured cheekbones, Jenny put a hand on Mac's shoulder. She let it rest there, and Mac saw Rebecca see her do it and then quickly look away, as if she were somehow intruding.

"You're sure you're still up to this meeting?" Jenny asked.

"Well, you call it a meeting," he said. "My understanding is that in the Mafia, they refer to them as sit-downs."

Rebecca Cruz smiled. "I'll put our mob up against Brett's any day of the week."

Lani was a native word for "paradise." It was also the name of a new hotel located in Hilo. The rival to the city's new Four Seasons turned out to be owned by one of J. P. Brett's holding companies. Mac wondered if Brett, as obsessed as he was with trying to be the star of it all, had considered the possibility that his new luxury resort might be a death trap if their calculations about the diversion of the lava, including some that had come from Brett and the Cutlers, were even a little bit wrong.

But they had found out today that all of their plans and schematics and projections, all the pretty pictures that had been drawn on various computers—none of that had been worth a bucket of spit when the rocks and ash came shooting out of the earth like some angry geyser.

Now they were in a ballroom on the second floor of the Lani, all of them: Mac, Jenny, Rebecca, the Cutlers, Brett. General Rivers was on his way back from visiting the injured at Hilo Medical Center.

"Glad to see you're all right," Brett had said to Mac when he arrived about ten minutes after the others.

"Are you?" Mac asked.

"Fortunately, I'm fine," Brett said.

"Not what I meant."

"What did you mean?"

"Just a general observation of how full of shit you are," Mac said evenly.

All eyes in the room quickly focused on the two of them, as if a fuse had just been lit.

"Hey, don't give me that," Brett said. "I was in the same danger you were in today."

"Except in your case, one of your drones didn't nearly take your goddamn head off."

"What was I supposed to do?" Brett said heatedly. "The drone was already in the airspace when the thing blew."

"Which means it's time for you to get your toys the hell away from the summit," Mac said. "If you don't have enough intel, then you're wasting your time here. And wasting mine."

"I wouldn't need more imaging if you'd share some of yours," Brett said. "You've been at this a hell of a lot longer than my team has."

"Wait," Mac said, "you mean the two people you just picked off from *my* team aren't giving you enough help? Holy shit, Brett, did you draft the wrong players?"

Brett smiled at Mac. "I don't see how you can blame them for wanting to be on the winning team when this is all over," he said.

Mac stepped closer to Brett. "You're out of line," Mac said quietly. "You've pretty much been out of line from the moment you arrived on this island."

"It's how I get things done," Brett said. "Over on my side of the line."

"What you're going to do is get people killed," Mac said. "For the last time, this isn't a competition. Are you not getting that, you arrogant prick? If we screw this up, maybe if we screw up any *part* of this, you're going to die along with everybody else. Unless you think you can somehow buy your way out of that too." Mac was breathing hard. "The competition is against the goddamn volcano!" Mac yelled, unable to keep himself from shouting.

Brett shook his head in either disgust or disappointment. "Do you not understand that *everything's* a competition, MacGregor?" Brett said. "And people who don't want to compete need to get the hell out of my way."

"You're the one who needs to get the hell out of Dr. Mac-Gregor's way," Rivers said from the back of the ballroom, as imposing as ever. "Starting right now."

CHAPTER 65

Sam Ito asked the admitting nurse at Hilo Medical Center if there might be a patient at the hospital, a soldier possibly in quarantine, named Mahoe.

Sergeant Noa Mahoe, he told her.

The nurse told Sam to wait a moment and walked away from her desk.

The soldiers came out of the elevator less than five minutes later. Both were young and built like football players. Or bouncers, Sam thought.

"Please come with us," the taller and slightly wider of the two said.

"Where am I going?" Sam asked.

"Somewhere other than here," the second soldier said.

Sam Ito looked up at both of them from his seat in the lobby.

"As the nurse over there probably told you, I'm a reporter," Ito said, adding, "From the *New York Times*."

"Wow," the first one said flatly.

They stared down at him with blank expressions.

"I'm just telling you that I have rights," Ito said.

"Not nearly as many rights as you had before our boss put martial law in place on this island," the first one said. "Now, either you leave peacefully or we arrest you."

"Arrest me on what grounds?"

"I'm sure General Rivers will think of something," the second one said.

As the first soldier reached for him, Sam Ito put up his hands in surrender and stood.

"To be continued," Ito said.

"I will look forward to it," the second soldier said.

Sam Ito walked outside and got his phone out and called Imani Burgess at J. P. Brett's hotel, the Lani, to tell her that he'd been unable to locate Sergeant Noa Mahoe. Neither one knew that they never would.

While Imani Burgess waited for their source, or at least someone they hoped would be a source, she sipped a white wine and thought about Dr. John MacGregor and her interview with him, if you could call it that.

She was certain that MacGregor wouldn't have been as dismissive as he had been if she and Sam weren't onto something. Imani just didn't know what, exactly. She was convinced that Dr. John MacGregor was hiding something. She was also convinced the army was hiding something, and not just about the eruption.

Imani was about to check her phone again to see if Sam had called when a familiar woman slid onto the stool next to her and apologized for being late. Rachel Sherill, the botanist.

"You said in your email that you had a story to tell me," Imani said.

Rachel Sherrill nodded and motioned to the bartender.

"A horror story," she said, "about the United States Army."

Just then the lights went out.

CHAPTER 66

Lani Hotel, Hilo, Hawai'i

Rivers and Brett were still going at each other when the lights came back on in the ballroom.

"How could you go behind my back this way?" Brett snapped.

"If you look at the big picture," Rivers said, "you're the one who thought he could go behind *my* back, and Dr. MacGregor's, poaching two of his people at a time when he needs all the help he can get."

"I do what I have to do."

"So do I, Mr. Brett," Rivers said. "So do I."

Brett wasn't backing down. "Sometimes I ask myself what I'm still doing here."

"Sometimes, Mr. Brett, I ask myself the same damn thing."

Brett stood, nearly knocking over his chair as he did. "I don't have to listen to this shit."

"We both know you're not going anywhere," Rivers said.

"Now sit your ass back down and listen to what Dr. MacGregor explained to the president a little while ago about the additional steps we have to take to save your ass and this island."

Mac stood up and walked to the front of the ballroom.

"Okay, I'll get right to it, we've clearly wasted enough time here already," Mac said, looking directly at Brett as he did. "This thing might happen sooner than we thought, judging from the events of today. It's why the first thing we need to do, and I mean first thing in the morning, is start covering as much territory near the Military Reserve as we can with metal sheeting."

Brett laughed suddenly. The sound came out raw and harsh.

"Perfect," he said sarcastically. "You're going to turn this island into more of a firetrap than it already is if the general lets you. Just how hard *did* you get hit in the head today?"

"Let him finish," Rivers said. "Or you *can* leave."

"It's going to have to be material with an extraordinarily high melting point," Mac continued, ignoring Brett. "My team and I"—Mac paused—"or at least, my *original* team, gamed this out early on. Tungsten melts at six thousand degrees Fahrenheit. Titanium is right around three thousand degrees."

Rebecca raised a hand. "You know this whole area better than anyone," she said. "So that means you know how many square miles we're talking about."

"Trust me, I do," he said. "But I believe the job is doable with the full backing of the army. Just one more thing we're throwing at the mountain and hoping sticks."

"Full backing, and cost be damned," Rivers said. "There are no titanium reserves in the National Defense Stockpile, so the president has authorized me to do whatever is necessary to get this job done. We've purchased titanium from Japan and even China to go with the small amounts we've already brought in from mines in Nevada and Utah. It's not as much as we need, but it's all we're getting on short notice. The president is more aware than ever of what we're up against and the unimaginable consequences if our mission fails."

Mac walked back to his table and picked up a folder filled with colored maps.

"Look at the highlighted areas," he said, passing the maps around. "If this works," he said, "we can still bury the bombs and get rid of most of the dirt and rocks in the time we have left before the eruption. Questions?"

"Just one," Brett said. "Have you lost your fucking mind?"

Mac shrugged. "Probably."

CHAPTER 67

Palace Theater, Hilo, Hawaiʻi

The loud, fiery town meeting that Hilo residents had demanded Henry Takayama call had been going on at the Palace Theater on Hāʻili Street for an hour.

The theater was a grand centerpiece of the town, roughly a hundred years old, and it did look like a palace inside, with its ornate walls and red velvet seats. Lono watched from a seat in the very back as people lined up in the center aisle, waiting to walk onstage to the microphone set up next to the one in front of Mr. Takayama. Like all of them, Lono had come because he wanted to know what was going on with his town. Mac hadn't returned his calls for a couple of days. School was canceled because the gym and cafeteria were being set up as evacuation shelters. The one time Lono had tried to go to HVO, he had been turned away, told that only "essential" personnel were allowed inside the buildings.

So he watched and listened to all the shouting, like this was a different kind of show at the theater. Like one of those Housewives shows his mother liked to watch.

As soon as someone new stepped to the microphone and began talking about how they were all in the dark about what the army was doing without their consent, the place would be thrown into an uproar all over again. Even though there was no debate tonight; they were all on the same side.

Us against them, Lono thought, *when it's really supposed to be us against the volcano.*

A short, white-haired native man made his way slowly up the stairs to the stage.

"I was born in this town and I will die in this town!" the white-haired man shouted into the microphone. "And no stinking *haole* is going to scare me away, whether they are wearing a uniform or not!"

The crowd raised the roof in approval, making the old hall shake as if another quake had just rocked Hilo.

"Sometimes I worry about these men with their white faces more than I worry about Pele!" the man said.

Lono knew that Pele was the goddess of volcanoes, and her legend was as much a part of this town as the volcanoes and all the danger inside them.

The old man quieted the crowd with his hands.

"This is our *faka* city!" he shouted in conclusion, and the crowd cheered again.

A woman in a flowered dress was next, also elderly and just as feisty. "We cannot let them violate our graves!" she said, shaking her fist. "These men have no right to do that!" She turned and pointed a finger at Henry Takayama. Lono saw the man flinch, even though the old woman was half his size.

"Are you just going to stand by and let them do that?" she asked.

Lono watched Mr. Takayama, the boss of his best friend Dennis's mother. In that moment, he looked as if he wanted to be anywhere other than this stage, this theater, even if it meant moving closer to the heat and danger of the summit.

Takayama rapidly shook his head: No, no, no.

Then he leaned into his own microphone and said, "I will always stand with the people who live in our town."

"Then you start proving that, Tako Takayama!" the woman said, spitting out the words.

Even at his age, Lono knew how sacred these burial sites were, sites that his mother said had preserved the spirits of the *kupuna* for thousands of years. He had been raised on these legends, steeped in them, and he had strict orders from his mother to tell her if he ever found out about anyone, even his friends, violating these sites; she would call the police.

"This is why our people did not trust the *kea* from the beginning," the woman said.

Kea. Another word for "white."

Sometimes the ones using it made it sound like a slur.

The people in the theater were back up, stomping their feet, raising their fists in defiance, some waving their arms in the air and swaying, as if to music.

Lono had never seen anything like this. And he'd never loved Hilo more, as scared as he was.

Lono was about to go outside and call Mac again, tell Mac about what he had seen tonight, when the soldiers came through the double doors. More appeared in front of the first row of seats.

Lono ran.

Lono was long gone when, a few minutes later, Mac and General Rivers walked across the stage to the microphones. The soldiers had stationed themselves at various points around the theater.

"By now, most of you know who I am," Rivers said. "Basically, I'm the *haole* who made this night necessary."

"You don't belong here!" an angry voice called out from the audience.

"As a matter of fact, this is exactly where I belong tonight," Rivers said.

"And why is that?" a woman in the middle of the theater yelled.

Mac handled that one. "Because we need your help."

It quieted the crowd for a moment; he had their full attention.

"Because we need you even more than you need us," he said.

CHAPTER 68

It had been Mac's idea for them to head over to the theater when Rivers got the call about what was happening.

They weren't there long; they told the crowd they had time for only a few questions because they were going to be working through the night. Mac ended up doing most of the talking. He told them how long he'd lived here with his family, then he told them how much manpower was needed to save Hilo and that they needed volunteers to work on the mountains, especially to help build the three dikes between the Military Reserve and the town.

"This isn't our island," Mac told the crowd. "It's yours."

He paused and looked out into the audience, squinting into the lights.

"You haven't felt as if you own it the past few days," he said. "But you do. And it's time for you to prove it."

The soldiers escorted Mac and Rivers out of the Palace Theater, and when they were in the back parking lot, getting into their separate jeeps, Rivers said, "I wanted to tell them more."

Mac said, "You mean the truth?"

"Exactly which truth are you referring to?"

"That we might all might be dead in two days?" Mac said. "That truth?"

Rivers told him about the dead body now buried in the Ice Tube.

The next morning, a few minutes after five in the predawn darkness, the townspeople of Hilo showed that they had gotten the message—they were lined up for a mile outside the military base, ready to go to work.

By then Mac and Jenny and Rick were already in the Ice Tube. Underneath the 360-degree LED lighting the army had provided, Mac oversaw the layering of the titanium around the rock walls, making sure it didn't block the ongoing digging of the canals and trenches.

Rick had gone off somewhere, and for now it was just Mac and Jenny. Mac had brought a thermos of coffee, and he poured some for the two of them.

He saw her staring at him, smiling, only half her face in the light. "What?"

"Can I be honest?" she asked.

He smiled. "When are you not?"

"I don't want to die, Mac."

"And you're not going to," he said. "Not on my watch."

"You're starting to sound like a general."

"Think of it as a battlefield commission."

"Tell me it's all going to come out right."

"It is," he said.

"You sure?"

"No."

She reached over and touched the side of his face.

"Glad we cleared that up," she said.

* * *

At almost the same moment, J. P. Brett and the Cutlers were at Hilo International preparing to board the Hungarian military helicopter that Brett had purchased in France a couple of weeks before, an Airbus H225M. There were only three dozen of them currently in the air anywhere, as he told anyone who asked. And several who didn't.

They would be joined on the flight by two Italian scientists that Brett had had flown into this same airport the night before, although he hadn't bothered to inform Rivers or John MacGregor. The Cutlers had worked with these scientists a few years back, at Mount Etna.

As Leah Cutler watched the two Italians walking toward the helicopter, she asked Brett, "Didn't they get into some trouble with the law after we made our heroes' exit from Sicily? I seem to recall something like that."

"They cut a few corners—what can I tell you?" Brett said. "But the bastards got things done. And the two of them have forgotten more about lava diversion and blowing shit up than MacGregor and Cruz have ever known, even if the two of them have convinced General Hard-Ass that they exist on some higher intellectual plane than the rest of us."

Brett added, "You know who I want on *our* dream team? Guys who aren't afraid to cross the line."

"Didn't Rivers tell you last night he wanted the airspace near the summit clear?" Oliver asked.

Brett grinned. "My Italian friends have told me they need to see *la grande immagine*—the big picture. After they've come this far, who am I to deny them? And it will be a short trip."

"You had to have felt those quakes all night long," Oliver said. "Leah and I barely slept, waiting for the next one to hit."

Brett raised an eyebrow. "You're not getting wobbly on me, are you, Oliver?"

"Never," he said.

"Keep it that way," Brett said.

"Our deal with you is the same as always." Oliver smiled his TV smile. "We're with you, win, win, or win."

Brett climbed up into the helicopter; he was followed by the two Italian scientists; Morgan, the videographer; and Oliver and Leah. The door to the cockpit was open, and Oliver stopped when he saw the pilot. Earlier, Brett had instructed him not to contact air traffic control at the airport. The pilot had pointed out that they would be breaking the law with this flight.

"Think of this as my own form of martial law," Brett had said.

"Wait, don't I know you?" Cutler asked the pilot now.

"Well, I was all over the news not too long ago," he said.

"You were in the crash with that TV cameraman," Cutler said.

"And lived to tell about it." The pilot reached out his right hand, which was bandaged. "Jake Rogers."

"Oliver Cutler."

"Now that the meet-and-greet is over, let's get this baby in the air and over to the rift zone!" Brett called out.

The helicopter lifted into the air, free from monitoring by air traffic control because the pilot hadn't called in the flight for clearance. Rogers worked the controls, the door to the cockpit still open. He gave his passengers a thumbs-up and yelled, "Okay, folks. Let's see what this baby's got!"

"How close can you get us?" Brett yelled back.

"Close as you want!" Rogers hollered over the noise of the engine and the blades.

J. P. Brett, one of the richest men on the planet, looked like a kid on Christmas morning.

"Remember that old movie *Joe Versus the Volcano*?" Brett yelled happily. "You all know my first name is Joseph, right?"

CHAPTER 69

Leah Cutler screamed as fluorescent orange streaks shot up out of the summit and rocks hit the state-of-the-art helicopter like artillery fire. Although the chopper had been built with war in mind, no one inside could tell how much damage was being done.

"What's happening?" Brett yelled.

"Incoming!" Jake Rogers yelled from the cockpit. "Lava bombs!"

They were flying through the darkness created by the ash and smoke from the volcano; the sun had risen, but the only light around them came from the streaks of orange and red that occasionally flashed up from the mountain.

"Lava must have reached the water table!" Oliver said. "When the lava is rising, rocks break off and plug vents. Water starts to boil, and the pressure builds." Oliver stared at the scene below, trying not to show the fear he was feeling. Oliver was as scared as his wife was; he just wasn't screaming. "The result is what we're experiencing!" Oliver added, still yelling to make himself heard over the engine and the storm.

"Not the Big One?" Brett said.

"Big enough," Oliver Cutler said.

Jake Rogers said, "I gotta take us up."

"*Not yet!*" Brett said. "These pictures are unbelievable. Keep shooting," Brett said to the Cutlers' cameraman, Morgan, who was lying on his belly, a harness strapped firmly to his leg, leaning out the open door even as rocks kept flying around the helicopter, occasionally crashing into it. It was as much a rock fight as a firefight.

Morgan had told the Cutlers once that his specialty was doing crazy shit, and that's what he was doing now. He was nearly halfway out the door. "My pleasure!" Morgan shouted, his camera focused on the incredible scene below them.

Jake Rogers was a career daredevil himself. It was why he'd nearly died up here with that wimp cameraman from CBS. Now he was frantically trying to get the helicopter under control and out of the special effects all around them.

They think this is a movie, Rogers thought.

He was almost directly over Mauna Loa, knowing he was too low, when the explosion occurred.

The helicopter dropped suddenly and violently, losing altitude when Rogers knew he needed to be gaining it, despite what that crazy bastard Brett said.

It was as if the Airbus H225M had a mind of its own.

Rogers was a veteran pilot and knew that when the battle was man versus machine, the machine almost always won.

"This isn't just a lava storm!" Rogers shouted over the noise of the blades and the big engine. "There's ash all around us, for fuck's sake! I gotta get out of here before it damages the rotors and this thing drops like one of these rocks."

"Are you kidding?" Morgan yelled and kept shooting. "This view is freaking awesome."

The Airbus lurched and dipped again, more violently than before.

"Oliver!" Leah Cutler screamed. "We need to get out of here. *Now!*"

But she could see the same wild-eyed excitement on her husband's face that she saw on J. P. Brett's. And she understood with great clarity why they were really here. It wasn't a sense of honor or duty that had brought them to Hawai'i. Despite the clear and present danger all around them, Brett and Oliver were here for this crazy roller-coaster ride through the sky, even though it felt to Leah like the planet was exploding around her. Before, no matter where on the globe they'd been, she had seen storms like this, explosions of color, only from a distance.

But now she was in the picture, and she was afraid they were going to die.

The Italians next to her were speaking to each other in their own language, looking as frightened as Leah Cutler, leaning back as far as they could and trying to tighten their seat belts.

The Airbus dipped another few hundred feet. Above the holler of the engine, Leah Cutler heard the pilot cursing. The scientist named Sparma murmured, *"Gesù, Maria, e Giuseppe."*

Jesus, Mary, and Joseph.

Somehow Morgan leaned out a little farther.

"You feel that?" Morgan shouted, pointing down at the scene below them.

They were quickly descending toward the fire, and the lava kept hitting them; one rock glanced off the side of the copter a few feet from Morgan's camera.

The combat-ready helicopter began to shake, as if being swallowed up by turbulence.

"Now or never!" Rogers yelled.

"Just a few more seconds!" Brett yelled back at him.

Morgan held on to his camera with his right hand, gave Brett a thumbs-up with his left.

Rogers knew how dangerously close to the summit they were, but he also knew that the man who had hired him didn't care.

"*Great!*" J. P. Brett said as the helicopter dropped again.

"That wasn't me!" Rogers yelled back. "The ash is sticking to the blades. Pretty sure the combustion chamber is starting to melt! I'm about to lose control of this thing!"

He seemed to be working all of the controls at once. "I need to find a place to put this down!" he said. "Nearly died up here once. Not risking it again!"

The lava was coming closer, and Jake Rogers knew better than any of his passengers that they were out of time.

Finally, J. P. Brett said, "Okay, pull out."

Rogers managed to turn the copter sharply left, away from where the ash and steam and smoke and rocks were shooting into the sky, throwing his passengers sideways.

When Rogers came out of the turn, Morgan the cameraman was gone.

CHAPTER 70

Mauna Loa, Hawai'i

Rebecca Cruz watched in horror as the figure fell out of the helicopter and into the lava stream below.

She had been down-mountain, making a final check of some new bomb locations, when she'd heard the explosion from the summit and saw the spray of lava rock filling the sky, along with what looked like fireworks.

So many things had happened quickly then: The helicopter came out of the suddenly orange sky; the quake knocked Rebecca and her brother David to the ground; the copter made a sharp, almost violent turn to its left.

Then the man—she assumed it was a man—fell from the helicopter, silhouetted against the morning sky like a cliff diver, like a movie special effect.

Except this was terrifyingly real.

"*David, let's go!*" she yelled. She got back on her feet and ran toward where she thought the man had landed.

David stayed where he was. "Go *where?*" he yelled. "There's no way someone could survive a fall from that height. And we need to get out of here before that thing blows again."

But Rebecca was sprinting ahead, stumbling occasionally over the new lava rocks littering this side of Mauna Loa. The one time she did go down, she broke her fall with her hands, popped right back up, and kept going.

"There's a crater lake over there you can't see!" she said over her shoulder, waving him to come along. "Maybe he fell into it." She looked down briefly, saw blood on the palms of her hands from where she'd skinned them on some jagged rocks.

Mac had shown her the lake when he'd first brought her to this area, told her that lakes like this were formed from an accumulation of rain and groundwater.

"What are the odds of him landing there?" David called out. "It looked like he was falling directly into the lava."

But reluctantly, he followed her.

Rebecca was a runner and hiker. Her brother was not. The distance between them grew as they made their way across the rough, uneven terrain.

"We need to find out!" she said.

The volcano had quieted, and the only sound in the sky, in the distance, was the helicopter.

Rebecca picked up her pace, as if this were some kind of crazy race, not stumbling at all now, not running for her life, just running for whoever had fallen from the sky.

"*We have to go back for him!*" Leah Cutler said to Jake Rogers.

"We *can't,*" he said. "The ash is sticking to the blades—I can feel it! I need to get us back to the airport before we end up like Morgan."

Brett got out of his seat and crouched down next to Rogers.

"Turn around," Brett said.

Rogers, eyes fixed on the summit to their left, said in a low voice that only Brett could hear, "There's no point, Mr. Brett. I'm sorry, but we both know he's dead."

"Go back," Brett said, "and find a place to get us on the ground."

"Mr. *Brett*," Rogers said, "that eruption just now might have been only an appetizer."

"It wasn't a request," Brett said.

"*Dude*, listen to me," Rogers said. "It's not just the blades not working the way they should. Listen to the freaking engine. There's something wrong with it too." He shook his head. "I'm telling you, it's time to cut our losses."

"Turn around and go back *now*," Brett said. "Or get out of that seat and I'll fly it myself. Because I can."

Jake Rogers hesitated, reviewing his options. He realized that the rich man taking the controls would be the worst one.

So he banked the Airbus H225M hard to the east.

For now, the activity and the light show at the summit had stopped. He didn't know how long that would last, though. None of them did, including Brett. The sudden quiet probably meant that the water that had caused the brief but violent eruption had cooled or begun to evaporate or both.

He was hoping the quakes would stop long enough for him to put J. P. Brett's bird safely on the ground near the locus of the eruption, since that was clearly the plan now; there was nothing he could do to change Brett's mind.

Rogers had a general idea of where they'd been in the sky when they lost Morgan, but he didn't know the precise location, partly because so much of the terrain looked the same—like

Mars, some pilots said—and partly because he'd been occupied trying to keep the helicopter in the air.

Morgan is even crazier than I am, Jake Rogers thought. *Or he was.*

Rogers flew to a crater lake on this side of the volcano. Above the lake was a containment pond the army must have built in the past couple of days; he could see it was already filling with lava.

Leah Cutler, looking out her window on that side of the helicopter, was the first to spot Morgan.

She started screaming again.

CHAPTER 71

Rebecca and David Cruz stared down into the containment pond that was perhaps a hundred yards south of the crater lake. It looked deeper somehow as it began to fill with lava.

They had made it here just as the body of the man from the helicopter came floating along on the orange and red stream of lava emptying into the pond, exactly as the Army Corps of Engineers had intended, although they hadn't known it would be needed this soon.

It was as if the man from the copter had come down a giant slide. Or were riding a wave the color of fire.

She knew why the man, whoever he was, had not disappeared below the surface of the lava. Mac had explained to her that lava didn't behave like other liquids, that it could be two or three times denser than water.

"He fell out of a helicopter. How did he not sink?" David asked, both of them staring helplessly at the man, his eyes lifeless, on his back below them in the pit.

"You float on lava," Rebecca said quietly.

Somehow, as much as she wanted to, she could not avert her

eyes from the terrible scene. She watched as the man's face and hands started to become the color of the lava underneath him.

Steam began to rise up off his body.

"His lungs burned up already," Rebecca said. "He was probably gone within a minute. Maybe two." She could hear Mac's voice in her head explaining the science of his world. "Even if he'd survived the fall somehow, he immediately began burning from the inside out."

"What the hell was he doing up there?" David asked, pointing at the sky. "Before he ended up down here."

A few seconds later, as if in answer to his question, a video camera came bobbing along on the last of the lava and into the pond. At the same time, the helicopter from which the man had fallen landed between the crater lake and the containment pond.

"Probably doing his job," Rebecca said, then added, "just like the rest of us."

The large helicopter, BRETT written in huge letters across the side, was on the ground, close to the crater lake, a few hundred yards up the mountain.

J. P. Brett was the first one out of it; he ran toward what looked like a steep cliff overlooking the opposite side of the containment pond.

David and Rebecca slowly made their way in that direction. A second helicopter, this one a U.S. army helicopter, not as big as Brett's but big enough, appeared out of the sky from the east.

It landed, and General Mark Rivers jumped out as soon as its side door opened; his boots sprayed dirt and rocks as he ran straight at Brett like one of Rebecca's Houston Texans looking to make a tackle.

Mac was the next one out of the army copter, running right behind the general.

CHAPTER 72

By the time Rebecca and David reached the patch of the mountain between the helicopters, both rotors still, a small crowd of their passengers had formed: Brett, Rivers, Mac, the Cutlers, and two men Rebecca didn't recognize who were speaking Italian.

The two pilots hung back near the copters, trying to stay out of the line of fire.

"Congratulations!" Rivers said, jabbing a finger into Brett's chest.

"For what?" Brett said.

"We told you that you were going to get somebody killed, and you just did, you son of a bitch!" Rivers said.

Rebecca had never heard him raise his voice before.

"You arrogant, pigheaded son of a bitch," Rivers said.

"Everything happened at once—the eruption and my helicopter having to make a sudden turn and then..." Brett shook his head as he looked down at Morgan's lifeless body. "An avoidable tragedy? Yes. But still a tragedy."

Jake Rogers was leaning against the side of the Airbus, and Rivers wheeled on him. "Was it your decision to fly that close to the summit at a time like this?" Rivers asked. "And not clear it with the tower or with the goddamn army?"

Rogers said, "I just work here, General. By the time I got this baby under control, the only option I had was to make the sharp turn that I did and try to get out of Dodge." He shrugged. "I thought the guy was strapped in."

"Well, you were wrong about that, weren't you, hotshot?" Rivers snapped. "All of you were wrong. This godforsaken volcano has already claimed its first victim, and it hasn't even started trying to kill us all."

Oliver Cutler was standing next to Brett. Rivers turned back to face them.

"Shame you two didn't have a backup cameraman," Rivers said. "Imagine the kick-ass pictures you would have had of the death dive."

"Morgan knew the risks of coming here just like we all do," Cutler said.

"You're all a bunch of cowboys," Rivers said. Before either Brett or Cutler could respond, Rivers added, "I hate fucking cowboys."

He looked around and said, "Questions? Comments?"

Brett took a small step forward, as if he were afraid he might step on a land mine. "I have just one comment, General," Brett said. "If you tell me to leave, I will."

"No," Rivers said. "You're staying. I need you more than ever, Mr. Brett."

CHAPTER 73

Outside of Hilo, Hawai'i
Time to eruption: 24 hours

It's like General Mark Rivers has gone back to war, Mac thought. *Or is looking to start one.*

He'd told Mac that earlier today he'd laid things out for the president and informed him about the soldiers who had been exposed to the black death, sparing none of the details about the way they had died.

"I told the president that we all grow up hearing about the war to end all wars," Rivers said. "Well, this is it."

Rivers had asked Mac to accompany him back to the base, and the two of them bounced around in Rivers's jeep, stopping where the dikes were being built between the base and Hilo.

The tremors, great and small, continued throughout the morning. Even when big ones hit and the men felt as if they could see the mountain shaking, the work went on, the energy all around them kinetic and powerful, as if the crews here were trying to build a whole new suburb of Hilo in a single day.

And because Mac had convinced the townspeople at the Palace Theater the night before that the more they pitched in and helped the army's effort, the safer their town would be in the end, the size of Rivers's workforce had doubled this morning, maybe even tripled.

J. P. Brett was supervising the caravan of tanker trucks bringing the seawater from the bay to Mauna Loa. "I'm curious about something," Mac asked Rivers as they were driving around. "How did he make that many trucks just appear? Magic?"

"He's Brett," Rivers said, as if that explained everything. "He might be a pirate, but for now, he's my pirate. There's not enough time to lay pipe from the water to that goddamn volcano, so we're doing it this way. He's not lying when he says he gets things done."

"And gets people killed," Mac said.

"At least we were able to pull the body out of that lake," Rivers said.

Rivers, in fatigues and a hard hat, was acting more like a foreman than the most powerful figure in the military. Sometimes he climbed right up into the cab of a bulldozer to show the driver where he wanted him to go and what he wanted him to do, making it clear that it needed to happen in five minutes or heads would roll.

When the Caterpillar bulldozers with the drop-deck trailers in front couldn't get close enough to the dikes, the volunteers who had shown up before dawn formed a human chain and passed rocks from one person to another like some old-fashioned bucket brigade.

"Would you rather be with Ms. Cruz at the bomb sites?" Rivers asked Mac when they took a water break. "If so, take the jeep."

"I want to be where I can be most useful," Mac said. "Neither one of us wants to die on this island because we didn't do every-thing that needed to be done to the extent it needed to be done."

Rivers tipped back his hard hat, studied Mac thoughtfully. "Do you think we *are* going to die here?" Rivers asked.

He didn't sound like a general, didn't sound like the big brass that he most certainly was. They were just talking man to man, as if one of them were in the line passing rocks to the other.

"We might," Mac said. "I think all the things we're doing will work to some degree. It just makes me crazy not knowing which ones will work best. I think Rebecca's explosives will work; I think dropping bombs will work; I think the titanium and the canals and the seawater all make sense. It sounds like a perfect plan."

He smiled at Rivers. "But you know that old Mike Tyson line, sir: 'Everybody has a plan until they get punched in the mouth.'"

There was another quake, biggest of the morning so far; it knocked both of them back against Rivers's jeep.

"Bottom line?" Mac said. "We might win the battle against this thing and still lose the war if we can't protect those canisters. In which case we're doomed no matter what we've done to get ready."

He added, "The road to hell really will be paved with good intentions."

It got a grin out of Rivers. "Don't sugarcoat it, Dr. Mac-Gregor."

"You ready to go back and take one last look at the dike clos-est to town, see where they are with it?" Mac asked.

Rivers nodded.

Suddenly Mac extended his hand. "I'm honored to be fight-ing alongside you, sir. I just want you to know that."

Rivers shook his hand.

Mac said, "I'm trying to remember who said that failure wasn't an option, but for the life of me I can't. Too much else going on inside my brain."

"It's a line from *Apollo Thirteen*," Rivers said. "Gene Kranz, the NASA flight director, says it."

Rivers clapped Mac on the back and then jumped behind the wheel, looking in that moment as if he were having the time of his life, as if the prospect of dying somehow made him feel more alive.

Mac got in the jeep, and Rivers drove like a madman toward Hilo; another quake nearly knocked the jeep over, but Rivers laughed and kept going. A song kept running through Mac's head. He couldn't remember who sang it, only that it was an oldie that'd had a recent resurgence on Hilo's classic-rock station.

The end of the world as we know it.

They heard Rivers's phone ring on the console between them, the ring volume obviously turned up as loud as it could go.

The general picked it up. "Rivers!" he yelled into the phone. He nodded as he listened. "On our way," he said. He hit the brakes hard, made a sudden U-turn, and sped forward; Mac was glad he'd remembered to fasten his seat belt.

"We need to get back to the base," Rivers said, driving even faster now.

"What's going on?"

"Another eruption," Rivers said.

CHAPTER 74

U.S. Military Reserve, Hawai'i

Brett and the Cutlers arrived at the conference room next to Rivers's office about fifteen minutes after the general and Mac did; Jenny and Rick Ozaki came in right after. The Cutlers had been in the air when Rivers had the base contact them, in another army helicopter, pinpointing the lava tubes that they wanted hit.

"So where's the fire?" Rick asked, trying—and failing—to sound casual. The time for that was long past, and they all knew it.

"The Galápagos Islands," Rivers said. "There has been what our people are calling a major event at the Wolf Volcano there."

Rivers put on his reading glasses and picked up the top sheet of the stack of printouts in front of him. "I got the call on it about forty-five minutes ago from Baltra, our air base there," he continued.

Mac knew a lot about the Galápagos Islands, had made

several visits to the volcanic archipelago six hundred miles off the coast of Ecuador. The cluster of small islands exhibited almost constant seismic activity. Three years ago, he had spent more than a month there when Wolf Volcano—Volcán Wolf, to the locals—had erupted for the first time in seven years, emitting rivers of fiery orange lava that were visible from space.

He had heard a prediction a few weeks ago about a possible event at the Galápagos Islands' largest and tallest volcano. But his focus since then had been here on the Big Island, the intense and all-consuming task at Mauna Loa.

"The good old Galápagos Islands," Jenny Kimura said. "Known for great big volcanoes, great big tortoises, and good old Charles Darwin."

Mac grinned. Sometimes he wondered how things would be between them when the world was normal again. If it ever did return to normal.

"Okay, let's focus, people," Rivers said. "The last time the Wolf Volcano erupted was three years ago, and the ash blew out over the Pacific for fifty miles or so. Now it's happened again. It wasn't unexpected—the signs have apparently been there—but no one anticipated it would have this much force, with lava emerging from at least three fissures on the eastern and southeastern slopes flowing through tubes and burning shrubs and grasses in its path."

If not for the situation here, Mac would have been in constant contact with the volcanologists and the people at Baltra, some of whom he'd met during the 2022 eruption. Maybe he'd have been on his way there. "They're controlling it for now," Rivers said, "or as much as you can control something like this."

"Interesting," Brett said. "But what does what's happening there have to do with what's happening here?"

"They're using the military to combat it there, from the air and from the sea," Rivers said.

"Wait," Mac said. "From the sea?"

Rivers tented his fingers underneath his chin and turned to face him. "They've brought in Zumwalt-class destroyers," Rivers said.

"Battleships," Mac said.

"Preparing to fire short-range ballistic missiles from where they sit in the Pacific, directly targeting the lava tubes with the most modern precision available."

"So they're trying to bomb their volcano back to the Stone Age," Brett said.

"They are," Rivers said.

"Thankfully, the eruption is happening on the opposite side of the mountain from where the endangered pink iguanas live," Jenny said.

"And they think this will work?" Mac asked. "As far as I know, missiles have never been used to attack volcanoes."

"They're about to find out if they work," Rivers said, "most likely before the day is out. Which is why I want our people there when the balloon goes up, as we like to say."

"Leah and I can go!" Oliver Cutler said, eagerly raising his hand like a kid in class who thinks he has the right answer.

"Anxious to get off *our* big little island?" Rivers asked.

"No, sir," Cutler said quickly. "My wife and I have never run from trouble. We just want to show you, despite your misgivings about us and what you see as our grandstanding, that we're willing to do anything that helps the cause."

Rivers turned to Mac. "Who do you think should go, Dr. MacGregor?"

Mac didn't hesitate. "Jenny and Rick."

Rivers said, "Any reason why you think that?"

"Because they're smart, they're brave, and if they see

something flawed in the army plan there, they won't bullshit you, General. Or waste time we don't have."

"Are you okay with a mission like this, Dr. Kimura?" Rivers asked Jenny.

"If Mac is, I am," she said.

"Then I'll arrange a plane," Rivers said.

Mac said, "Small problem, sir. I've made that trip more than once. The Galápagos Islands are forty-five hundred miles from here. That's at least eight hours by plane, even with a tailwind."

"Not my plane," J. P. Brett said.

CHAPTER 75

Hilo International Airport, Hawai'i

The fastest private jet on the planet was the Peregrine, and Brett had flown one into Hilo.

Mac stood with Jenny and Rick on the tarmac as the pilots went through their final checks before departing for the Galápagos. Brett had promised they'd land at José Joaquín de Olmedo International Airport in just over five hours. The copilot had collected their two small duffel bags; Jenny and Rick were traveling light, hopeful that they'd be in the Galápagos for only a few hours.

Rick gave Mac a quick hug.

"Your bride happy about this little adventure?" Mac asked him.

"What do you think?"

The Peregrine's engine fired up; it felt like another small tremor was running through the ground underneath them.

"Do *not* die on me while I'm gone," Jenny said. "Because you know how much that would piss me off."

"Well, now, we can't have that, can we?" Mac said.

Over Jenny's shoulder, Mac saw the copilot at the top of the airstairs.

"Dr. Kimura," he shouted over the roar of the engines, "just about time for wheels up."

It was unclear whether Mac or Jenny initiated their embrace, but they suddenly had their arms around each other.

"You take care of yourself," Mac said softly into her ear.

"Don't have your first scotch until I'm back," she said.

Mac gently kissed the top of her head and stepped back, his hands on her shoulders. He smiled.

Jenny nodded and smiled back. "I feel the same way," she said. She shrugged his hands off her shoulders, stepped toward him, and kissed him so quickly and lightly, it was almost as if their lips hadn't touched.

Then Jenny Kimura turned and walked toward what she was already calling the Brett Jet. She climbed the stairs and disappeared through the door without looking back.

Mac stood at the window in the terminal and watched Brett's fastest-in-the-world personal-jet taxi take off, the backdrop of its steep ascent the summit of Mauna Loa.

He went back to the army jeep Rivers had assigned to him exclusively. He planned to meet Rebecca and her crew back at Mauna Loa—the volcano permitting, of course—so they could finish burying the rest of her explosives. After that they would meet with Brett and the Cutlers and review the latest map for the aerial bombing.

All of that bombing would be contingent on what Jenny and Rick observed once they arrived in the Galápagos Islands, having traveled there by what would probably feel to them like the speed of sound.

It was just another way, Mac thought, of trying to beat the big clock.

He sat behind the wheel, not yet putting the key in the ignition, thinking of his goodbye with Jenny and wondering if he should have said something more to her. But then, he spent a lot of time wondering if he should be saying more to her about his feelings.

Maybe he would when he understood them better. He hoped there would be plenty of time for that.

The buzzing of his phone brought him back.

The caller ID read New York Times.

Mac wasn't remotely surprised that the reporters had his number. *Wait for it*, he thought.

A minute later he heard the ping that meant he had a new voicemail message. It was the woman reporter.

"This is Imani Burgess. I hope you can return my call before Sam and I file our story so we can get a comment from you about a source who's suggesting there's some sort of toxic-waste dump on the island and some dead soldiers who might have been contaminated by it."

There was a pause.

"We're on deadline," she said. "So the sooner you get back to us, the better. We'd really like to give you the chance to respond to what we have, especially if you know anything about the soldiers."

Mac played the message again.

Then he pressed the Delete button, put the key in the ignition, and drove out of the parking lot.

Then he placed a call of his own, but it wasn't to the *New York Times*.

CHAPTER 76

Above the Galápagos Islands

The eruption had ended by the time they arrived, less than five hours after they'd taken off from Hilo International, even faster than J. P. Brett had promised, aided mightily by a powerful Pacific jet stream.

As they flew over Isabela Island, where Volcán Wolf was one of six shield volcanoes, Jenny saw one of the most amazing sunsets she had ever seen, as bright orange as a lava waterfall. It was still in full force and view as they began their descent.

"So they did exactly what they wanted to do," Jenny said. She and Rick had watched the live stream of the event on her laptop.

"Turned the side of the volcano into a sieve," Rick said.

"More like they did a geologic cesarean," Jenny said. "They just took the baby early."

What they'd done here over the past month, under advisement from some Japanese scientists the Ecuadoran government had flown in, was depressurize magma chambers by guiding missiles deep into Volcán Wolf, as far down as ten kilometers. The passive degassing they'd implemented had relieved much of the pressure that had built up before the eruption, which they had pinpointed almost to the hour. The successful result had been a calculated, synchronized release of pressure through vents created by the short-range missiles.

The summit of Volcán Wolf disappeared as the pilot banked the Peregrine toward the airport.

"So our work here is basically done," Rick said.

"Not quite," Jenny said.

Lieutenant Abbott and his superior officer, Major Neibart, had plainly told Jenny there was no way, none, that they would allow them to fly to Isabela Island, even if the army had built an airstrip for its own use between the Wolf Volcano and one named after Charles Darwin.

"No way," Lieutenant Abbott, a hard-ass, had said. "Not happening."

But then Jenny had stepped outside Abbott's office and called Mac. Mac had contacted General Mark Rivers, who outranked pretty much everybody except the president of the United States. Now here they were on the island, having been flown over there by a young army pilot who pulled the four-seater nearly up to the front door of a Quonset hut that served as a subbase.

There were a couple of jeeps parked outside it.

"Does anybody live here?" Rick asked the pilot.

"Wolf Volcano giant tortoises," the pilot said. "They're pretty proud of the saddleback shells in these parts." Then he added, "I was told to inform you that if you're not back on this plane in an hour, you better hope you can get an Uber from here."

Jenny had the map of the island in her lap. She insisted on

determining exactly where the magma chambers had been and how close to them the vents were located—that way they could see for themselves how the bombing had controlled the lava flow so effectively. Rick drove the jeep up the steep 5,580-foot mountain, the elevation changing rapidly as they made their way to the summit.

"Tell me again why we're doing this," Rick said.

"Boots on the ground," Jenny said.

"Great," he said. "I'm riding around near an active volcano with GI Jane."

They got as close to the eastern flank of Wolf Volcano as they safely could, close enough for them to see the lava streams. Even from here, they could tell that the streams were beginning to slow as they flowed toward the ocean.

"Damn, they figured out a way to make the lava go exactly where they wanted it to go," Jenny said when they were out of the jeep. "If they can do it, so can we."

"*If* we can figure out how to do it the way they did," Rick said. "In the day or so we've got left."

"Can we get a little closer?" Jenny asked.

"No."

"We've come this far."

"Yeah, *too* far," he grumbled, but he parked the jeep and followed her up the mountain.

Eventually they reached a small but solid promontory that provided the best view they were going to get of the holes that had been blown in the Wolf Volcano, which was a quarter mile or so from where they now stood. The smaller streams of lava were still flowing out of them, south of where the most powerful stream flowed from the summit.

Rick had brought a Canon camera with a telephoto lens from the base, and he was shooting away. After a short time, he told

Jenny they needed to wrap this up because he was about to run out of light and space on his memory card.

"Just a few more," she said, "and then we're out of here, I promise. You know this footage is going to help Mac a lot."

"Oh, thank God," Rick said.

He got down on one knee to get a better shot. Jenny stood next to him.

The earthquake, sudden and violent and unexpected, hit Isabela Island with a force unlike any quake Jenny had ever felt, even in the run-up to the eruption back in Hilo; it was as if the whole world had exploded.

They looked around for cover, but there was no place for them to hide, no place for them to run. The sky suddenly went dark, as if night had fallen that quickly.

They looked back just in time to see much of Wolf Volcano falling toward them like a building collapsing; at the same moment the cliff on which they had been standing disappeared.

Then they were the ones falling.

CHAPTER 77

Hawaiian Volcano Observatory, Hawai'i

Mac left Rebecca Cruz in his office and reluctantly went outside the main building at HVO to have a face-to-face with the two *Times* reporters; they'd said they weren't leaving until he came out to talk to them.

There was another woman with them; she introduced herself as Rachel Sherrill.

Imani Burgess got right to it. "You'll be happy to know that the paper isn't going to run our story," she snapped. "Or maybe you knew that already." She made no attempt to hide her anger.

Rachel Sherrill added, "So the U.S. Army strikes again."

"I don't mean to sound rude, Ms. Sherrill," Mac said. "But who are you?"

"Someone hoping you might cut the shit," she said.

"Rachel was working at the botanical gardens several years ago when the army appeared out of the sky to clean up some kind of toxic spill," Burgess said. "Then they buried the story and, presumably, the waste along with it."

Sam Ito said, "They deliberately covered it up then, according to Ms. Sherrill, and our sources indicate something similar is going on now."

"And lo and behold, we're being called home," Burgess said. "They say at the paper it's because of the eruption. But we all know better, don't we, Dr. MacGregor?"

"I could have stayed inside," Mac said. "You guys don't need me. You already have all the answers."

"We figured you called Rivers as soon as you got Imani's message," Ito said. "After that we figured the general called the president of the United States himself. Who then called the managing editor of the *New York* freaking *Times* and told him that his two reporters in Hilo were about to put people's lives in danger with baseless allegations about the army."

"Except," Rachel Sherrill said, "you're the ones putting lives in danger, aren't you, Dr. MacGregor?"

"I'm trying to save them," Mac said. "Which, frankly, I can't do out here."

"Stop me if you've heard this one," Ito said. "But the people have a right to know."

"Not everything, they don't," Mac said. "Get over yourself, kid."

"I'm not a kid," Ito said heatedly.

"You are to me," Mac said.

"You don't get to decide what people do and don't have a right to know," Rachel Sherrill said. "Especially with stakes like these."

Mac said, "Please don't lecture me on what the stakes are here, Ms. Sherrill."

Rachel was breathing hard, her face red, fists clenched. She reminded Mac a little of Jenny when she thought that she was right about something and that he was dead wrong.

"This isn't over," she said. "Even though these two are leaving, I'm not going anywhere until I get some answers."

"Then I guess there's no point in my telling you to have a nice flight," Mac said.

They all stood there in silence. Mac was comfortable with it. He knew they had a lot more they wanted to say to him and a lot more they wanted to ask. But the three of them finally turned, went to their car in the visitors' lot, and drove away.

As Mac walked toward the building, he felt his phone buzzing in his pocket. He stepped to the side of the front door, leaned against the wall, and answered it: "This is MacGregor."

The reporters and Rachel Sherrill were too far away to hear the mournful wail that came out of Dr. John MacGregor then, the sound of a wounded animal; they didn't hear him scream *"No"* again and again, scream it until it was as if all the air had left his body.

He slid down the wall, phone still in his hand, and felt as if the world had ended already.

His and everybody else's.

Rebecca finally headed outside to look for him. There was still work to be done tonight, or there would be as soon as Jenny and Rick called in their final report from the Galápagos and transmitted the pictures Rick had taken, which they'd probably do when they were back in the air on Brett's fancy plane.

She and Mac had heard from them an hour or so ago, right before they'd landed on Isabela Island. Before Mac went out to meet the reporters and Sherrill, he'd said that if Jenny and Rick hadn't called by the time he got back to the office, he was calling them.

Rebecca stepped outside and saw Mac, sitting on the ground outside the door. He was motionless except for the heaving of his chest, his eyes fixed blankly on some point in the distance.

His phone was in his hand.

His eyes were red, and as hard as this was for Rebecca to believe, it looked like John MacGregor had been crying.

She started breathing hard, her chest constricting. She walked over and crouched down next to him.

"Mac, what's wrong?"

It was as if there were a delay between when she spoke and when her words reached him.

Finally, he looked up at her.

"Jenny died," he said. "And Rick too."

CHAPTER 78

Rebecca was still with Mac, sitting next to him on the ground.

"There are people I need to call," Mac said.

"There will be time for that later," she said.

He swallowed hard. He needed a drink. "There was no warning—that's what the pilot who brought them there said," he told her. "That side of the mountain just...it was like some kind of avalanche. They're speculating that the missile strikes might have caused the seismic activity, but at this point they're just not sure." He took a deep breath. "Either way, knowing won't bring them back."

Now he turned to her. "I was the one who asked her to go," he said.

"If you hadn't, she would have volunteered," Rebecca said. "She was on a mission."

"For me."

"Mac," she said, "we're all on the same mission. And we're as fierce about it as Jenny was, because we know we're running out of time."

"The difference is," he said, "Jenny and Rick have already run out of time."

He told her to go get some rest, even if it was just on a couch somewhere. Rivers wanted them all in his office the next morning at six. She promised she would sleep after she went over her maps one last time.

"Liar," Mac said quietly.

Rebecca went back inside. Mac made no attempt to get up. He'd put his phone down in the dirt next to him. When it began buzzing, he forced himself to pick it up and see who was calling.

His wife.

"Rick's wife called to tell me," she said as soon as he answered. "Mac, I'm so sorry."

He'd spoken to Linda a couple of times over the past week, Mac explaining the situation here in the broadest possible terms. And he'd called the boys a few times and exchanged emails. Linda hadn't told them how much danger their dad was in; there was no point in scaring them. But she knew, even with as little as he was telling her.

"Not nearly as sorry as I am," Mac said.

She knew most of what had happened on Isabela Island from what the army had told Rick's wife, Eileen. Mac and Linda spoke for a couple of minutes, then he asked if he could talk to the boys.

She put the phone on speaker so the boys could hear him. They asked if he was okay. He told them he was. They said they were sad about Aunt Jenny and Uncle Rick, and Mac said that he was too. Charlie asked, his voice breaking, if Mac was going to die. Mac told them both that he was fine and that they shouldn't worry, he'd be seeing them before they knew it, and what had happened to Aunt Jenny and Uncle Rick had happened thousands of miles away.

He squeezed his eyes shut and tried to hold it together, not allow himself to think this might be the last time he'd ever talk to his sons.

"Both of you..." His throat felt tight. He covered the phone and cleared his throat and went on. "You both know how proud I am of you, right? How proud I've always been?"

Max said, "Dad, you tell us that *all* the time."

"I can never tell you enough," Mac said.

Charlie said, "You tell us that too."

Mac covered the phone again. Cleared his throat again. "The best thing that has ever happened to me is being your dad," he said finally. He could feel the tears on his cheeks and was grateful he wasn't on FaceTime or Zoom. "I love you both so much," he said. The tears kept coming.

"Love you too, Dad," they said in unison.

Then Charlie said, "Talk soon."

Talk soon.

Linda took the phone off speaker.

"The boys wish they were with you," she said.

"Well, we both know that's not going to happen any time soon." *And maybe not ever.*

Neither one of them spoke for a few moments. Mac was used to that by now with the woman he already thought of as his ex-wife. By the end, before she'd taken the twins and left, the only way they'd communicated was with extended silences like these.

"I'm so sorry," Linda said finally.

"I know how much you liked them both," he said.

"I meant I'm so sorry about *us*, Mac," she said. "I'm so sorry we couldn't make it work."

He wasn't sure what to say to that, so he didn't say anything. All he knew was that he no longer wanted to be on this call.

"I know I'd sound like an idiot if I told you to stay safe," she said. "But you can at least take some consolation in knowing that the boys are safe."

He wanted to start screaming again in that moment, the way

he'd screamed his throat raw when he'd gotten the call from the Galápagos.

He wanted to scream at her that their sons weren't safe and she wasn't safe whether they were on the mainland or not, because no one was safe no matter where in the world they were.

But he didn't say that.

Not because he'd promised Rivers he wouldn't tell anybody.

He didn't say that because he couldn't bring himself to.

There was one last silence before Linda said, "I love you, Mac."

He acted as if he hadn't heard, as if the call were already over. He was about to go back inside when the phone buzzed again.

A single word on the caller ID:

Rivers.

CHAPTER 79

Outside the Ice Tube, Mauna Kea, Hawai'i
Time to eruption: 16 hours

Mac drove to the Military Reserve as if running from the night; he parked his jeep there and walked up to where Rivers was waiting for him.

Thinking the whole way about how little time they had left and how, if their projections were correct, the Big Island might be a different place by noon tomorrow.

We're moving up on high noon, Mac thought, imagining what was happening inside Mauna Loa, how fast and how powerfully the magma was rising toward the summit, operating on the only timetable that mattered to the volcano—its own.

The magma moving toward what Jenny had insisted on calling "the big bang."

Jenny.

After Rivers called him, he had started to hit Jenny's number on speed dial, by reflex.

Jenny, who'd been brave.

When Mac was finally standing next to Rivers, a hundred yards or so from the entrance to the Ice Tube, he saw more flatbed trucks stacked with more titanium sheets. More lights all around them. More men working to protect this fortress with the canisters inside, some unloading the titanium, some putting another layer of it in place.

More noise than ever up here, he thought, *more urgency, if such a thing is possible.*

No uniform for Rivers tonight. Hard hat and fatigues again. He seemed delighted to look like a grunt, even if he was the one barking out orders.

"I want to tell you again how sorry I am about the casualties," Rivers said, his words clipped.

Casualties—the language of war. But he can't help himself. "I know you are, sir," Mac said.

"You were right," Rivers said. "They were brave."

Then he said, "Another layer of titanium can't possibly hurt."

"Agreed," Mac said. "And who knows? It might make all the difference in the end. We should definitely go for it."

Mac pointed in the general direction of Mauna Loa as more soldiers and more townspeople appeared above them and began unloading the titanium.

"It's twenty miles, give or take, from here to there," Mac said. "If our diversion works, we won't need to shield the cave any more than we already have. And if it doesn't?" Mac shrugged. "We just have to hope that what you call our side-walling buys us time until the lava flames itself out."

They heard what sounded like gunfire from where the first dike was being built, on another part of the mountain.

A minute later a soldier came running up, waving his phone at General Rivers.

"There's trouble, sir," the young guy said.

"Were those shots I just heard?" Rivers asked.

"Warning shots, sir," the soldier said. "Because of the protesters."

"Protesting what, for fuck's sake?" Rivers yelled.

"Somehow they found out we've been digging up some of their burial sites."

"I have to take care of this," Rivers said to Mac.

Mac nodded. "You're way better at crowd control than I am. I've got a few things to do myself."

Rivers ran down to his jeep, got behind the wheel, and sped off.

Mac was behind the wheel of his own jeep when he got the call from Lono.

"I need to see you bad, Mac man," the boy said.

"Where?"

"Meet me at our beach."

Mac drove even faster than usual.

CHAPTER 80

Honoli'i Beach Park, Hilo, Hawai'i
Tuesday, April 29, 2025

Mac got to the beach first. He parked his jeep where he always had in much better times than these, grabbed his gear, and made his way down toward the water. When he felt the sand underneath his feet, he felt, for a moment, as if he were home.

He used to come down here on Akua, the one night in every month when the moon was at its fullest and biggest and brightest and appeared even rounder than usual, the waves dancing in its amazing light, as if the dawn had arrived early.

Tonight, there was just a crescent moon. Mac stood in the sand and took it all in and thought how perfect the world looked from here. The only sounds were the lapping of the waves in front of him and the occasional call of a nightbird. He felt like the last man on earth.

This is what we're trying to save, he thought. *What we* have *to save*.

Beauty like this was as much a force of the natural world as the volcano; it took the breath out of him.

He looked in the direction of the volcano and thought: *You cannot have this.*

He heard someone behind him making his way through the foliage. Mac turned and saw Lono, this boy who just seemed to keep growing—Mac joked sometimes that he could almost *hear* Lono growing—carrying two surfboards under his arm.

"I thought you had forgotten me," Lono said, putting out his hand for a fist bump.

"It would be like forgetting one of my sons," Mac said.

"Here, I brought you a board, just in case," Lono said.

They sat down on the boards and looked out at the water, neither one of them speaking, as if they were in church.

And maybe in a way they were.

"It's gonna be bad, isn't it?" Lono said finally.

"Worse than bad," Mac said.

"You think my mom and me should be looking to get off the island?" Lono asked.

He felt the boy's eyes hard on him. Mac turned and met his eyes.

"I can't explain this to you in any detail, because I gave my word," Mac said. "But you have to trust me when I tell you that even if you could find a boat or a plane, it's too late."

Lono hesitated, then said, "I do trust you, Mac. With my life."

So did Jenny and Rick.

"The volcano isn't the only ticking bomb, is it, Mac man? This is about something inside the White Mountain, isn't it?"

It was what the natives called Mauna Kea.

"Where did you hear something like that?" Mac asked him.

Lono shrugged. "Some woman, a *haole*, was at Civil Defense trying to see Mr. Takayama again. She told Dennis's mom that the army was keeping secrets that could end up wiping out the whole town and that if Mr. Takayama wasn't going to tell people, she was going to. Something about how she wouldn't let Mr. Takayama do something to her again."

Lono looked at Mac. "The *haole* woman knows things, doesn't she?"

Mac said, "She only knows what she doesn't know."

Lono sighed. It came out of him as sad as a blues note from a horn.

"Heard about Jenny," Lono said. "And Rick. They were good dudes."

"Not just good. The best."

"You okay?"

"Someday, maybe. Just not today, kid."

Another sigh came out of the boy. Then he said, "I gotta tell you, Mac, it was *me* got the word out about what was happening at the burial sites." He paused and then quickly added, "I didn't mean for there to be trouble."

Mac smiled. "You sure about that?"

"I maybe wasn't sad to cause a little bit of *pilikia*."

"No matter. General Rivers stopped them in their tracks."

"I heard." Now Lono smiled. "That's a bad, bad man, the general. But in a good way, no matter how much he pisses off people around here."

"Not just good," Mac said again. "The best."

"I've got a big mouth," Lono said.

"You always have." Mac punched his arm lightly. "But this is your island, not ours."

The sun was rising. They could see the big morning waves beginning to build in the distance. Without another word, they ran to the water, got on their boards, and paddled out.

Being in the water only made the world more beautiful, Mac thought. The light seemed to be coming from the ocean as well as the sky.

"I don't have a lot of time," Mac said.

Lono said, "You're the one who always told me that you had to make time for the things you love."

"Then let's ride, cowboy."

Mac wondered, briefly, if this might be the last ride for both of them.

A few minutes later they were up on their boards, the two of them maybe fifty yards apart, maybe more, the water as warm as bathwater, both of them catching the first great wave at the same moment.

Mac heard Lono whoop and laugh with joy as they both glided toward the beach.

Mac took in the whole scene, the boy and the water and the morning sky, and thought again: *This is what we're trying to save.*

CHAPTER 81

U.S. Military Reserve, Hawai'i
Time to eruption: 6 hours

They still hadn't found the Kane girl, the one who'd been with Sergeant Noa Mahoe at the bar the night of the leak at the Ice Tube. The girl or girlfriend.

General Mark Rivers didn't want to hear any more excuses from Briggs. It wasn't as if they were trying to find a missing person in New York City, he'd said.

"Find her!" Rivers roared, then dismissed Briggs with an irritated wave of his hand.

The girl was a loose end. He hated loose ends.

Sergeant Mahoe, that dumb-ass, was still in quarantine. In quarantine and under twenty-four-hour armed guard and possibly recovering from exposure to the radiation, although in the pictures Rivers had seen Mahoe looked like a napalm victim. The doctors wouldn't say that he was definitely going to make it, just that he had a chance. They wanted to know more about his exposure.

All Rivers cared about was that this dumb-ass horny kid had taken his exposure with him off the base that night and without permission.

He needed to know if the girl was infected and whom she might have infected.

Goddamn, he hated loose ends.

Mark Rivers rubbed his forehead so hard he was afraid he'd break the skin. He wondered if the girl even knew Mahoe was sick, wondered if she might be some sort of carrier even if her skin wasn't starting to fall off her in black flakes.

What if we all survive the eruption, what if we control the lava in the end at the same time a different kind of black death starts to seep across the island like a plague, all because of a sergeant under my command? Rivers thought.

On how many fronts was he expected to fight this war?

What if something just as deadly made its way across the Big Island before the lava began to flow like a tidal wave from the top of the mountain about which they were all obsessing?

God, he needed sleep.

Or a stiff drink.

Maybe both.

Patton had slapped soldiers under his command during the Sicily campaign, and Rivers thought he might've had the right idea. Rivers would've considered slapping Sergeant Mahoe now if he hadn't been afraid of catching what Mahoe had and causing his own skin to rot.

His landline rang. The soldier at the front desk informed him MacGregor, Rebecca Cruz, Brett, and the Cutlers were here.

All of the available intel, all of the science at their fingertips, said that the eruption would happen today, perhaps even before the morning was over. The quakes were coming more rapidly now, the way contractions did when a woman was about to give birth.

Birth, he thought. *Beginning of life.*

This might be the opposite of that.

Rivers looked down at the Hawaiian words he'd scrawled on the pad in front of him:

Ka hopena

The end.

Now his satellite phone was ringing. Rivers was using this, not his cell phone, now—the way all military personnel were.

Briggs.

"I think we might have eyes on the girl," Colonel James Briggs said as the walls of the military base began to shake again, harder than ever.

Leilana Kane tried to blend in as best she could with the crowd moving toward the piers at the Port of Hilo, all the people ahead of her and behind her trying to get on one of the small ferryboats that had begun evacuating people from the island the previous afternoon. These were the residents of Hilo who had chosen to leave rather than work with the army, some of them not knowing when they would return or what shape the Big Island might be in when they did.

Some residents with enough money had been chartering small planes to get them to one of the other islands, wanting to be anywhere but here when Mauna Loa exploded with a force they had been hearing about for days, a force the likes of which their island had never seen.

Leilana had been on the run since the soldiers had dragged Noa out of Hale Inu Sports Bar like he was some sort of criminal;

Leilana had managed to slip out the back door moments before the army closed the place down.

She had given up trying to reach Noa on his phone, especially after some of her friends told her that men from the army were calling around and asking if anybody had seen her or been in contact with her. She'd stopped using her phone at all, afraid the army or the police might use it to track her.

After she left the sports bar, she'd gone to the macadamia farm where her grandparents on her mother's side had raised her after her mother died of cancer. The next morning soldiers had shown up at the farm, a postcard-pretty place off Saddle Road not far from the military base. Leilana had gotten away again, but not before telling her grandparents to tell the soldiers they hadn't seen her and didn't have any idea where she was.

Last night, Leilana had slept on the beach. She was used to being on her own, sometimes feeling as if she'd raised herself, and she had never been afraid, not in Hilo, to sleep on the sand and under the stars.

Maybe she could come back after the eruption, when the island was safe again, and find out what happened to Noa, but now she wanted to be anywhere except here, like the other people in the line.

There were soldiers and police showing up at her friends' houses, saying it was urgent that they find her, that she was in danger.

But in danger from what?

Before Leilana stopped using her phone because it was a tracking device, one of the girls she worked with, Natalie Palakiko, asked, "Did you break the law, Lani?"

"God, no," Leilana said.

"Because I got the feeling that if they find you, they want to arrest you," Natalie said.

"Arrest me for what?"

"I don't know," Natalie said. "But before they left my house they told me that if you contacted me and I didn't immediately contact them, I might be in trouble too."

Leilana told herself she would sort it all out later. For now, as the ground kept shaking, causing occasional screams from the people moving slowly toward the piers, she just needed to make herself gone. She pulled her HILO VULCANS hat farther down over her eyes.

When she briefly stepped out of the line to see how close she was to the front, she heard a loud voice she recognized call out, "Leilana Kane! You bagging this piece of rock too?"

She turned and saw Sherry Hokula, a girl she'd gone to high school with, wildly waving.

"Leilana!" she said, louder than before. "That you, girlfriend? Over here!"

When Leilana looked at the front of the line, she saw two soldiers making their way toward her from the dock area.

One of them was on his phone.

Leilana ran, ran from the army again, sprinting back to her motorbike in the long-term parking garage on Kuhio Street; she looked back once and saw the soldiers break into a run too.

Her only thought was to make it back to the farm and her grandparents.

There was nowhere else for her to go, nowhere to hide.

She didn't know why she was on the run. But she was. Running harder than ever.

The sun was finally up, usually such a beautiful time of day in Hilo, one she loved watching from the beach.

Just not today.

The walls were closing in on her before the volcano did.

Leilana was very fast; she had been a sprinter at Hilo High.

She raced past the garage now, then circled back on side

streets. When she finally reached the garage, the soldiers were nowhere in sight.

She got on her small motorized bike, eased it out onto the street, and headed out of town, making sure not to drive too fast. She drove until she ran out of gas, maybe half a mile from the farm.

She left the bike in the brush on the side of the road that was just wide enough for her grandfather's rickety old truck.

Just before she reached the farmhouse, she stopped.

Something was wrong.

Something, she could see, was very wrong.

She stared at the small cluster of macadamia trees to the side of the ranch house, the beginning of the modest orchard that had been in her family for generations.

The trees had turned completely black—they looked like they had been drenched in ink.

Or burned in a fire.

In addition, she could see small black circles leading from the trees toward the front door, as if holes had been burned into the lawn.

Leilana Kane felt as if she could not breathe, as if a shadow had fallen on her grandparents' beautiful, innocent world.

She moved to the other side of the house, to where she had always been able to find her grandmother's pride and joy, the jacaranda tree whose blossoms were almost too lovely to bear at this time of year, the one that her grandmother had told Leilana had grown up with her, because she had planted it the day Leilana was born.

Now it looked as if someone had set fire to it; the remaining leaves on the tree were completely black, the trunk withered. If she walked over and touched it, Leilana thought, it would simply turn into a pile of ash.

But she was afraid to get closer to it, much less touch it.

She kept moving around the house, afraid now to go inside, hoping that her grandparents were anywhere but here.

Her grandmother's small vegetable garden in the back, the one she grew her beloved tomatoes in, looked like soot; it had turned black along with everything else outside the house.

She took a deep breath, wondering what toxins she might be breathing, and walked back to the front of the house.

The windows were open, the curtains billowing softly, as they always did on mornings like these. Her grandmother said all the air-conditioning she needed was the breeze off the bay.

The front door was open. Her grandparents never locked the door. They had told her, for as long as she could remember, that Kū-kā'ili-moku, the god of protection, was all they needed to watch over them and keep them safe.

She called out as she opened the door.

"Kūkū?" she said.

It was the shorthand she'd used for both her grandparents since she was a little girl.

She stepped into the room and a strangled cry came from somewhere deep inside her.

Both her grandparents were dead on the floor of their tiny living room, their skin the color of coal as if they had been burned alive, though there was no sign of fire.

Leilana was startled by the sound of a car coming closer. Or maybe a jeep. Or a truck.

She wanted to look out the front windows, see who it might be.

But she couldn't stop staring at her grandparents.

Ka hopena.

CHAPTER 82

The walls of the Military Reserve's conference room were shaking every five to ten minutes now. The general, Mac, and Rebecca were at the long table. None of them even acknowledged the tremors anymore.

"So by everyone's calculations, today is D-Day," Rivers said.

Or doomsday, Mac thought.

Rivers said, "So the question is, what do we do in the hours we have left other than wait?" He paused. "I mean, the hours left before the eruption."

Mac shrugged. "We keep digging as long as we can," he said. "Lay as much titanium near the cave as we can. When the eruption comes, Rebecca will be in her bunker at Mauna Loa Observatory, working her remote detonation system to set off a coordinated series of explosions via electromagnetic signal. At the same time, sir, you can put your bombers in the air, and they can wait for your command."

"We could start bombing right now," Rivers said. "Why are we waiting?"

"We need to see the direction of the lava," Mac said. "If we get lucky and Rebecca's explosives work, as we're pretty certain they will, we might need only minimal aerial support."

There was a knock on the door, and Colonel Briggs stepped into the room. "A word, sir?"

The two of them went out into the hallway. Mac watched them through the window of the conference room. Briggs was doing most of the talking. Rivers stood impassively, arms crossed.

Finally, Rivers nodded.

The general came back in, sat down, and said, "Change of plans."

"About when we start the bombing?" Mac asked.

"We're going to remove the canisters from the Ice Tube and transport them to a safe location."

Mac couldn't help himself. "Where?" he asked. "The moon?"

No one spoke as the walls shook again, rattling the windows, spilling coffee out of the cups in front of them.

"It's too late to move the canisters, and you know it, sir," Mac said. "There's no feasible way for that to happen."

"It's already happening," Rivers said. "And frankly, Dr. Mac-Gregor, it will be too late when I say it is."

They were both seated, but Mac felt as if he and Rivers were standing toe-to-toe.

"Don't tell me that," Mac said. "Tell the volcano."

"I don't need your permission," Rivers said.

"No one said that you did."

Rivers looked down at his big hands clasped in front of him, then back up at Mac.

"Lead, follow, or get out of the way," he said quietly. "Isn't that what they say?"

Mac could see that Rivers was scared whether he admitted it or not. He wondered if anything else had ever scared this man, and he also wondered how far he could take this with the chairman of the Joint Chiefs.

"Sir," Mac said, trying to regain his composure. "It was too late for moving those canisters when you arrived here. Colonel Briggs told all of us it was a four-week job at the very least, not the four days we had at the time." He shook his head furiously, not believing what he'd heard. "I'm going to remind you how many of those canisters there are," Mac said, plowing ahead. "And now we've seen with our own eyes what happens when what's inside them gets out. We have no idea how many of them are damaged," Mac continued, "but all of them are sure as hell filled with deadly radwaste herbicide that is essentially the most lethal weapon in the history of this planet. And now, at this stage of the game, we're simply going to load them up and move them away in—I must have mentioned this—four fucking hours?"

"There is a platoon of my men in hazmat suits on their way up the mountain as we speak," Rivers said, ignoring everything Mac had just said and acting as if the hazmat reinforcements were all they needed.

"Something has obviously changed your thinking," Mac said. "We have a right to know what that is, General Rivers."

Now it wasn't simply fear Mac was seeing in Rivers's eyes.

It was more than that.

What he was seeing now was panic.

"What changed?" Mac said again.

"People started dying," Rivers said.

CHAPTER 83

Outside the Ice Tube, Mauna Kea, Hawai'i

The eruption at Mauna Loa came as Mac and Rivers pulled up to the Ice Tube in General Rivers's jeep.

From the side of Mauna Kea, they could see the smoke and flames, orange and red and blue, the color of fire, against the blue sky. Mac knew what was happening, even from here: the caldera was covered with lava that was beginning to travel from the rift zones.

They would find out soon—how soon depended on the speed of the lava—if the canals and trenches, all of the diversions, all of their plans, actually worked.

In the distance, they heard the sound of sirens from the All-Hazard Statewide Outdoor Warning Siren System, signaling that the Big Island was essentially under attack.

Our Pearl Harbor, Mac thought. *Just no sneak attack from out of the sky this time.*

The ground underneath them shook again; this quake lasted longer than the others and felt more serious.

Rivers yanked off his helmet, ran to the entrance, and began yelling at the men in the hazmat suits to get back into their trucks, waving at all of them to get back down the mountain.

"*Go, go, go!*"

Two of the men in hazmat suits hadn't heard him over the sound of the sirens, and they continued to move toward the entrance.

Rivers ran after them, grabbed one man by his shoulders, and spun him around.

"*Go!*" Mac heard again.

In the distance Mac saw a sunrise-bright glow from the summit.

The fireball outlined against the sky grew bigger, and then another violent quake shook Mauna Kea, upending one of the trucks; the men inside managed to dive out before the truck crashed to the ground and rolled over.

Mac saw Rivers pitch forward maybe fifty yards from the entrance to the cave, the fall so sudden that he couldn't catch himself with his hands, and he landed face down in the dirt and rocks. The earth underneath them would not stop shaking.

Rivers was still.

Mac ran to him, rolled him over, saw blood coming from a big cut on his forehead. But both of the man's eyes were open and he was breathing.

"We need to get you out of here," Mac said.

"Not until the others are out," Rivers said.

Mac got him into a sitting position, wiped some of the blood away with his sleeve, helped him to his feet, and pulled him toward the jeep.

Rivers's chest was heaving. In the jeep, he touched his

forehead, then looked at the blood. "Is this it?" Rivers said. "Is this the one we've been expecting?" He sounded dazed. "Good God."

"Let's hope He's good to us," Mac said.

He got behind the wheel, pulled ahead of the caravan of trucks—the ones still upright, anyway—and headed back to the base.

He gave one quick glance back at Mauna Loa, more afraid than ever of what was coming next.

And where.

Mike Tyson was right: Everybody had a plan until they got punched in the mouth. Mac drove faster, ignoring the bumps, sometimes feeling as if the jeep were flying, feeling as if the volcano were already chasing them.

Rebecca Cruz was in the war room alone when Mac and Rivers returned.

"Where are the others?" Rivers asked. "Brett and the Cutlers were supposed to be here too."

"Brett and the Cutlers are gone, sir."

"Gone where?" Rivers said. "I need them here, goddamn it!"

"I assume they're in one of Brett's helicopters," Rebecca said. "He wants to film the eruption himself."

"Why?" Rivers asked.

"Because he can," Mac said.

"He's crazy," Rivers said.

"That too."

CHAPTER 84

Summit Cabin, Mauna Loa, Hawai'i

The army had taken over the Summit Cabin, on the rim of the large summit caldera, Moku'āweoweo, with its sweeping view of the true summit. An army helicopter had just delivered Mac and Rebecca to this temporary command post so they could determine when and where to begin detonating the first of Rebecca's explosives.

"To do it right," Rebecca had told Mac and Rivers, "I need to have eyes on the target."

The pilot told them to contact the Military Reserve to arrange for their pickup. "How soon?" he'd asked Mac before he left.

"Soon."

Mac and Rebecca stared across at the summit when the pilot was gone.

"I need to get set up," Rebecca said finally.

"And then we wait," Mac said.

Mauna Loa was still at an uneasy rest.

But not for long.

Another quake hit. Mac had stopped measuring one quake against another. Today they *all* felt big, as if the volcano were firing a round of warning shots.

They took refuge inside the cabin. That was when they felt the walls and windows begin to shake and heard an unmistakable sound.

Eruption.

They ran outside and looked toward the summit of Mauna Loa. Through the thick, dark smoke of an ash cloud, a fireball burst, setting the sky ablaze.

CHAPTER 85

Mac and Rebecca stood and watched the fire shoot into the sky.

The first lava appeared in crashing waves that seemed to flow in all directions—to the north and east, as Mac had expected, but to the south as well.

Mac had witnessed multiple volcanic eruptions, sometimes at very close range, all over the world. He had imagined this particular moment for this volcano, had obsessed about it, had told himself he was prepared.

He was not.

"The flow is bigger than we thought," he said.

Mac realized Rebecca was gripping his hand tightly, almost as if to steady herself.

She said, "I need to get to work."

Within moments Mac heard and felt a bomb blast behind him, the noise and force powerful enough to cause a concussion; it was as if Rebecca had detonated one of her explosives next to the cabin.

When he got to his feet, he saw the huge hole in the caldera known as Mokuʻāweoweo.

He saw the vent and saw lava now shooting out of it, a tight geyser flowing across the helipad the army had built and heading directly for the Summit Cabin.

The fire was coming for them now.

The summit continued to explode in streaks of orange and red and even black, not just into the sky but down the slopes of the volcano.

Even with all the eruptions he had seen, he had never seen lava like this.

As he ran into the cabin, he heard the chop of helicopter blades. But even if the army had sent a copter back for them, it was useless now because there was no place for it to land.

CHAPTER 86

Above Mauna Loa, Hawai'i

Brett and the Cutlers were in a replacement Airbus 225 newly purchased by J. P. Brett, and they were preparing to give the world a front-row seat to the biggest volcanic eruption in history.

"Shit!" the pilot, Jake Rogers, yelled as the helicopter bucked and jerked and then dropped a few hundred feet in a couple of seconds.

Rogers had just banked the Airbus in a wide swing around the summit and was now bringing them back to Mauna Loa from the southwest.

"Wind shear?" Brett asked.

"I fucking wish," Rogers said.

Leah Cutler looked out the window, wondering what the pilot was seeing. Her husband, acting as his own videographer for this flight, kept his camera focused on the top of the mountain, waiting for the perfect moment to start filming.

"Is there a problem, Jake?" Leah Cutler said.

"The lava's already spitting out of vents down there," he said. "*Hard,*" he added.

The big helicopter bounced like a small boat in a rough sea.

To Brett, Rogers said, "You told me the lava would be on the other side!"

Before Brett could respond, the helicopter jerked again even more intensely than before, as if a ground quake had reached up and taken a swing at them.

Rogers fought the controls. "Shit, shit, shit!" he yelled.

"What is the problem?" Brett yelled back.

"It's happening, that's what the problem is!" Rogers said. "She's about to blow!"

"Get ready, Oliver!" Brett slapped Oliver Cutler on the back. "The pictures are going to be incredible." To Rogers, Brett said, "Get closer."

"You don't understand!" Rogers said. "We're already too close!"

"Keep shooting, Oliver!" Brett said.

"Are you insane?" Rogers shouted at J. P. Brett. "We can't be here right now."

"Are *you* insane?" Brett said. "This is why we came here!"

Rogers looked down, knowing he had flown too close to this side of the mountain, the side that was supposed to be safe enough for them to be in this airspace.

Another vent opened to their right, the force of this explosion more powerful than the first; the molten rock and gas shot at the helicopter like a small missile trying to take them out of the sky.

Rogers felt it spraying the underside of the Airbus 225, rocking it again.

"We're getting out of here *now!*" Rogers shouted.

He had flown around here for a long time. Had taken far too many chances, even if he had lived to tell about them. Had taken some in Brett's other beast of a copter.

But even he wasn't prepared for anything like this.

"My only choice is to take her up!" Rogers said.

"Get me out of here!" J. P. Brett said to Jake Rogers.

Not *us. Me.*

Leah Cutler was screaming hysterically, the way she had when their cameraman had fallen out of the helicopter.

Rogers reached for the cyclic, the stick that controlled his horizontal thrust, and altered the tilt of the rotor disk. As he did, he felt rocks hitting his blades.

Leah Cutler kept screaming.

"Will you please shut up!" Brett snapped at her.

"Go to hell!" she snapped back.

"Guess what," Rogers said. "That's where we're all going if I can't get us out of here."

They were at least gaining altitude, even with what felt like shrapnel hitting J. P. Brett's newest fancy helicopter, which was now bucking wildly.

Rogers was fighting his own controls. He realized now that there was no way they were making it back to the airport or even over to the Military Reserve at Mauna Kea. The best he could hope for was to get over the summit to the other side of the mountain and the new helipad the army had built near the Summit Cabin.

The pilot felt as if he were trying to push the Airbus up this side of Mauna Loa himself.

Come on, baby.

Almost there.

In the next moment, Mauna Loa erupted, underneath them

and all around them. The Airbus bounced up high in the sky and then began to drop like a stone.

Jake Rogers was blinded by the flashing lights all around him and he thought how beautiful they were as the helicopter was sucked down into the summit.

The screaming stopped then.

CHAPTER 87

The White House, Washington, DC

The president of the United States, who took great pride in staying calm in any crisis, could not get his heart to stop beating like a jackhammer.

He looked around, afraid the others in the Situation Room might actually be able to hear it, waited for them to turn and stare at him.

The president remembered the famous pictures of Barack Obama in this same Situation Room the night they had taken out bin Laden, remembered how calm Obama had looked.

Obama's national security team had been there with him. Vice President Joe Biden. Hillary Clinton, Obama's secretary of state. All of them watching and waiting for the kill shot on bin Laden.

This was different.

This time the enemy wasn't a terrorist who had blown up some buildings.

This time a volcano on the other side of the world was the terrorist, and if they couldn't stop it in time, it would destroy the world.

"Rivers says it's even more powerful than they thought it would be," the president said quietly.

His mouth was dry. He drank some water. It took all of his willpower to regulate his breathing.

His heart kept pounding, even as he tried to appear in charge and in control.

"It looks like that doggone mountain is on fire," said the vice president in his Louisiana accent.

"They have to stop it before it gets there," the president said.

They all knew what "there" meant.

They continued to watch the images they were getting from the military jets that were flying over the volcano Mauna Loa far enough away to be safe but close enough to capture the brilliant colors shooting out of the volcano like ground-to-air missiles and the lava that continued to spread in all directions.

But the only direction the president of the United States cared about was northeast, where those goddamn canisters were stored in that goddamn cave. He imagined them like ducks in a shooting gallery.

General Mark Rivers had just told him that bombing would commence shortly, as soon as the lava got closer to the military base and to Hilo; the people from Cruz Demolition were already detonating their explosives to divert the lava, the way the bombers would.

The president kneaded his forehead and thought about all the crises he'd faced, often on a daily basis. Terrorism and the Middle East and Russia and China and whatever new virus had popped up that day. His job was to defend this country against all of it, with aggression when necessary. He had promised to leave a better and safer America to his successor than his predecessor had left him.

And he believed he would.

Until now.

He sat there, starting to sweat, and found himself thinking about the pressure Truman must have felt before dropping the bomb on Hiroshima.

This was a different kind of pressure, pressure unlike anyone who had ever sat in this room had ever encountered, because there was nothing to do but watch.

And wait.

On one of the other screens in front of him, he watched the evacuation of Hilo continue, passenger boats arriving and leaving the port constantly.

The president turned to his secretary of state.

"Rivers tells me that the fastest-moving lava ever measured in Hawai'i was on Mauna Loa and it traveled sixty miles per hour," the president said. "At that speed, the flows could get from the summit to the coast in one and a half to two hours."

The secretary of state asked, "How far away is the Ice Tube from the summit?"

"Twenty miles," the president said. He had his eyes fixed on the volcano again, unable to look away.

He kept thinking of Truman.

Imagining a new and more deadly mushroom cloud, one that might be about to cover everyone and everything.

CHAPTER 88

Summit Cabin, Mauna Loa, Hawai'i

Rebecca was at the front door of the cabin, staring at what looked like a gaping wound in the outside wall of the caldera.

When he saw her, Mac shouted, "Did you do this?"

She shouted right back at him, "Are you crazy, MacGregor? The volcano did this!"

She moved quickly to where Mac was standing and watched the flow of lava get closer. Nothing in their imaging had indicated the vents on this side of the caldera were in any danger of being breached when Mauna Loa erupted. The data was wrong.

They could feel the heat from the ground inside their boots. Before they came up here, Mac had thought about wearing thermal suits. But he'd rejected the idea.

The ground shook again.

There was even more fire in the sky above the summit. The summit cairn was just under two miles away from where they stood, but they were in far more danger from the caldera, which was morphing before their eyes.

Rebecca noticed the helipad, a hundred or so yards away from the cabin, completely engulfed by smoking lava, part of a rising river of it.

Moving directly toward them, like the tide.

Rebecca Cruz said, "What do we do? The helicopter can't come back here now, and the observatory is miles down the mountain."

"We move as fast as we can to stay ahead of the lava," Mac said.

He watched as the lava made a slight turn on its way toward the trail behind them, as if diverting itself without any need for explosives or help from them.

There was another blast from the caldera, and another vent blew open.

More lava coming at them now.

Mac and Rebecca ran.

Anyone who'd ever hiked up here, and Mac had, had been warned against running on this trail, even when heading back down the mountain; a careless movement could easily break an ankle.

They ran anyway.

CHAPTER 89

Nāʻālehu Police Station, Nāʻālehu, Hawaiʻi

Captain Sam Aukai, chief of police in Nāʻālehu—Hawaiian for "the volcanic ashes"—was inside the station a little before eleven o'clock in the morning when he heard the sirens: 121 decibels of boom-box sound rocking the southernmost town in the United States and the island's sweetest, quietest garden spot.

The sound, Sam well knew, came from the All-Hazard Statewide Outdoor Warning Siren System that broadcast from ninety-two towers installed in communities around the Big Island. The sirens told him there was a threat, but not where or how bad. Mostly Sam wanted to know if his town was safe.

There was one person who would know for sure. His friend Pia Wilson was the point person over at HVO for the volcano alert levels that charted the time frame of volcanic threats.

"Thank you for calling, Chief Aukai," said the woman who

answered HVO's main number and identified herself as Ms. Kilima, the librarian taking phone duty today.

When Sam and Pia had spoken a few days ago, Pia told him that the flow would primarily be to the north and east the way it had been in 2022.

"Can HVO verify what Ms. Wilson told me, that Nāʻālehu, just east of South Point, is still safe from the lava flow?" Sam asked Ms. Kilima.

"Ms. Wilson no longer works here," the librarian said, her words clipped. "She quit a couple of days ago."

Sam didn't ask why and didn't care. "Who took over for her on volcano alert levels?"

There was a pause. "A young woman named Jenny Kimura."

"Is she there?"

"She's dead," Ms. Kilima said.

The television in Sam's office cut to an aerial shot of the summit of Mauna Loa. Lava was spilling out of it, a tremendous amount of lava, much more than Sam remembered from the eruption of 2022.

And not just to the north and east, he saw.

Due south as well.

Toward them.

The crawl at the bottom of the screen was about lava speeds already reaching fifty miles per hour. Or more.

Captain Sam Aukai felt as if a cold hand had suddenly gripped his heart.

He took one last shot with the librarian. "Can you tell us if our status is still yellow?"

There were four stages of volcano alert levels. Green was normal. Yellow was advisory. They had been yellow in Nāʻālehu since last week.

Orange meant watch.

Red meant your area was in grave danger.

Ms. Kilima said she was putting him on hold. When she got back on the phone she said, "Nā'ālehu is red, Captain. Didn't anybody from this office alert you?"

Sam ended the call without answering, ran outside, and looked up at the rolling hills that fed down from the long mountain and toward his town.

The grip on his heart got tighter. He could already see the streak of orange moving as fast as they said it was on television, already close to Nā'ālehu. Sam knew the consequences if it kept coming this fast.

Even if the lava somehow bypassed the town, if it reached Route 11, the road that snaked its way around the southern tip of the island and all the way to Hilo, they would be trapped, as that road was their only way in or out.

He ran back into his squad room, shouting at the twelve men and women in his department about the imminent danger, telling them to get in their cars, turn on their sirens, and spread out.

"What do we tell people?" Sergeant Nick Hale asked.

"That they need to get out of here while they can," Sam Aukai said.

"What if they don't want to?"

"Tell them they can stay here and die," Sam said.

He ran back outside to where he'd parked his own car on Hawai'i Belt Road and looked up again at the lava. The fire had come much closer just in the time he'd been inside, as if it were picking up steam. The streak looked red to him now. Like the threat level.

His ex-wife was long gone from Nā'ālehu. His daughter was in her first year at the University of Hawai'i at Mānoa, outside Honolulu. He paused just long enough to call her. It went to voicemail. Probably in class.

He left a message that he loved her.

Then Sam Aukai got into his car and drove into town, telling himself he'd be the last man out if necessary. He had protected the people of the town in which he'd grown up. And he'd always felt protected here himself.

Not today.

He turned on his siren.

Somebody had dropped the ball at HVO and now the people on his watch could die.

CHAPTER 90

Honoliʻi Beach Park, Hilo, Hawaiʻi

All residents of Hilo had been warned to take immediate shelter. But the young guys from the Canoe Club had decided to head over to South Point anyway, transporting their two outrigger canoes on the flatbed owned by Kimo Nakamura's father.

"If this is the end of the world," said Luke Takayama as they unloaded their OC4 boats and paddles from the back of the truck, "I want to be on the water when it happens."

All ten of them, four paddlers and a steersperson in each boat—Luke the steersman in one, Manny Kapua in the other—agreed, taking their lead from Luke, as always.

Luke knew he would get into trouble with his father, the head of Civil Defense in Hilo, if he found out what they were doing. But Luke had barely seen Henry Takayama recently. He had been in his office all day and most nights in anticipation of the eruption at Mauna Loa.

The boys from the Canoe Club were out on the water, a few miles to the east of South Point, when they heard the sirens.

Luke was Henry Takayama's son. He knew what the sirens meant as well as anyone.

Eruption.

The rowers stopped. They all looked back then and saw the lava cascading out of the hills, rushing toward the beach like a wave about to crash there.

Lava that wasn't expected to come anywhere near here. Or them.

"We need to get to the truck and get out of here!" Luke said.

His friends began to row furiously back toward the beach, but they were in a different kind of race now.

"Everybody said it wasn't supposed to come this way!" Manny yelled to Luke Takayama. "That it *never* comes this way!"

Luke knew he was right. But he saw what they all were seeing, the rising tide of orange and red getting closer and closer to South Point Park. What had happened before did them no good now.

It *wasn't* supposed to come in this direction, not according to his father.

And never this fast. "Power up!" Luke Takayama yelled to both boats. "Dig in now!"

He knew that if lava was hot enough it could boil seawater and all the life in it; knew they needed to get out of the ocean before it got its chance.

"*Go, go, go!*" Luke yelled, his eyes fixed on the lava that was crossing the narrow beach and moving into the ocean.

Luke's boat was the closest to the shore, Manny's to his left.

Even as the boys cut their paddles into the water with almost blinding speed, they could see steam rising up like a marine layer all around them.

The lava was already across the beach.

Scalding water was splashing into the two boats. As the ocean waves suddenly rose up all around them, Luke was afraid the boats might *huli*, capsize, dump them all into water that felt as if it had just been set on fire.

"Luke!" Manny yelled. "What do we *do*?"

Before Luke could answer, he began to choke on the acid smell that was trying to swallow them up along with the waves; his throat felt as if it were scratched raw by the combination of steam and glass particles in the air.

All of them were gagging and choking now, eyes tearing up, not wanting to let go of their paddles even though they wanted to wipe their eyes so they could see their way through water now streaked with orange and red.

This was the volcanic tsunami that Luke had read about and knew could be caused by lava flowing into the sea, and now it was happening to *them*, in real and terrifying time.

They were nearly back to shore.

A few hundred more yards.

That close.

Too far.

They felt as if they were trapped in a burning building, these boys who'd come to this beach thinking the eruption would happen somewhere else on the Big Island, up near the sky.

But the eruption had followed them here.

Then the boats were flipping, turning over in the air, *huli*, the boys falling out of them; then they were all in the boiling water, seeing their skin turn the color of the lava, violently choking on gases and fumes suffocating them.

Kids who thought they would live forever, not believing something like this could happen.

Not to them.

Not here.

Luke felt as if he were drowning, though he managed to keep his head above the water that began pushing them farther away from the shore.

All around him, his friends were shouting, some of them crying, the ones still in the boats asking Luke what they should do even as the water in which they'd grown up, the water they loved, started to burn all of them alive.

CHAPTER 91

U.S. Military Reserve, Hawai'i

General Mark Rivers's war had officially begun.

People had already died, including some of his own. It's what happened in war.

And he knew this was only the beginning. Mauna Loa had finally erupted a couple of hours ago with a force and a volume of lava that had shocked not only him but the scientists, including Brett's Italians, who had announced they were going to watch the eruption from the Mauna Loa Observatory. Rivers had objected, but the Italians hadn't listened to him any more than J. P. Brett had.

Everything happened at once.

Brett, who hadn't listened to the end, and the Cutlers and their pilot had crashed into the summit moments after the eruption.

He'd gotten a call from a hysterical and almost incoherent

Henry Takayama, the head of Civil Defense in Hilo, that the burned bodies of his son and nine other boys, rowers, had washed up on the beach at South Point Park.

Ten kids at a beach on the southern tip of the island.

Word was that a town there, Nāʻālehu, was about to be flooded by lava, what the chief of police there described as a tidal wave of it coming straight for them.

"Is there anything you can do for us?" the chief said.

"Pray," Rivers said.

Rivers kept hearing the sirens even after they'd gone silent.

There was a rap on the door and Colonel Briggs entered.

"Please give me some good news," Rivers said.

"Sorry, sir," Briggs said. "The kid sergeant who snuck out to the bar?"

"Mahoe."

"He died just now in quarantine, sir." Briggs paused. "Died looking like the others over there at the cabin. It just took longer with him."

"Was anybody at the hospital infected?"

"Not that we know of."

"Did you find his girlfriend yet?" Rivers asked.

"Yes, sir, we did. I got the call on her right before the one about Sergeant Mahoe. They found her body with the bodies of her grandparents at their little farmhouse near Saddle Road."

"In the same condition as the others?"

Briggs nodded.

So add the black-death toll to the one from the eruption.

As much as they'd done to defend the island against the lava, they were finding out they needed to do more.

Needed a new battle plan.

That's what you did in war when the old plan wasn't working.

It was time to put the planes in the air and to begin detonating Rebecca Cruz's explosives without her.

"I can't wait any longer to hear from MacGregor and Ms. Cruz," Rivers said to Briggs. "When we think it's safe from that goddamn cloud...what do you call it?"

"Vog, sir," he said. "Gas and steam and even glass particles. It forms around volcanic vents."

"When conditions are safe, I'm going to send an EO-5C to look for them," Rivers said.

But that aerial reconnaissance was for later. For now, General Mark Rivers was ready to attack. *Wanted* to attack.

He picked up his phone, called his marshaller at Hilo International, Lieutenant Carson, told him to give the three F-22 Raptor fighters waiting there a thumbs-up. When the bombs started to drop, David Cruz—in an office down the hall—would begin to detonate in coordination with them.

"Go time, son," Rivers said to the marshaller.

He watched on another monitor as the first jet taxied up the runway. But even as he watched, Rivers kept thinking about John MacGregor and Rebecca Cruz, wondering if the volcano had already added them to the morning's rising death toll.

But if they are somehow still alive, where are they?

CHAPTER 92

Nāʻālehu, Hawaiʻi

What looked like a glowing avalanche was coming at them less than an hour after the sirens sounded, and there was nothing Sam Aukai or anyone else in Nāʻālehu could do to stop it.

Sam had educated himself on volcanoes when he got this job. Because of that, he understood what was happening: A phenomenon made famous by Mount Saint Helens and believed impossible in Hawaiʻi. It was called *nuée ardente*.

This fiery cloud filled with tumbling blocks of rock could move down even slight inclines faster than fifty miles an hour, sometimes up to a hundred.

Mauna Loa's defiant geology was what he was witnessing. Fiery rocks crashed through Nāʻālehu; the town disappeared under a dark cloud of ash.

In desperation, Sam Aukai had briefly tried to go door to

door through the Kau district, all the places that were part of the permanent geography of his life: Kamaʻāina Kuts, Kalae Coffee, Hana Hou Restaurant, Patty's Motel, the Nāʻālehu Theatre, and, perhaps the most famous tourist spot in town, the Punaluʻu Bake Shop, which advertised itself as the southernmost bakery in America.

But he knew he was too late, that he'd gotten word about the avalanche of fire thundering to the south way too late. The people trapped inside those establishments were going to die there.

Sam was still ahead of the lava when he reached his car at the edge of town. Before he got in, he turned around, and he immediately wished he hadn't, because he saw bodies floating toward him on top of the lava that followed the rocky tumult. He knew the people hit by the waves of ash, rock, and lava were already dead, burning up from the inside and the outside; their lungs had been destroyed almost instantly by the heat they'd inhaled.

Sam gunned the engine, thinking that if he could stay ahead of the volcanic debris long enough to get to Nāʻālehu Spur Road and then head west on Route 11, he would—he prayed—be safe.

"Serve and protect" had always been his code. Now he tried to protect himself.

But when he reached Route 11, all he could see ahead of him was stalled traffic; all he could hear was the constant blare of car horns. People were using both lanes to drive to Hilo; there were no cars coming back to Nāʻālehu from the direction of South Point.

It didn't matter.

The traffic had stopped, but the lava kept coming.

Sam's was the last car in the line.

Last man out.

He heard the ring of his phone, picked it up. One of his cops, Mike Palakilu, was calling from somewhere up ahead; he told him that a finger of lava had split off and completely blocked Route 11 on the outskirts of town.

"I'm running for the water!" Mike yelled. "Only chance I've got, Sam!"

Sam Aukai pulled his car onto the shoulder of the road. He didn't want to take another look back, but he did, saw the orange and red of the blocky *'a'ā* lava burning Nā'ālehu and drowning it at the same time.

The air was thick with heat and gas and the smell of a burning town, making it difficult for him to breathe.

Two more bodies floated past him, their hideous red faces already unrecognizable. Maybe Sam had known them. No way to tell.

People ahead of him were abandoning their cars and running toward the water, not knowing that the water wasn't safe either, that it was part of the hot zone.

Sam ran hard for the water anyway. Sam Aukai, once the star running back at Ka'ū High, imagining he was sprinting for daylight one last time.

Too late.

He was swept up by the lava and carried along by it, helpless. His lungs were burning up and his skin was on fire as he rode on top of the lava.

He thought of his daughter.

CHAPTER 93

Mauna Loa, Hawai'i

In Hawaiian, *Mauna Loa* means "Long Mountain," a fact Mac could not get out of his head as the lava continued to chase them down the trail.

It did not slow; it just kept coming.

They knew they risked falling if they ran too fast, but they had no choice; they had to stay ahead of the ropy pahoehoe lava or die. Some of it had begun to spill off the trail and down the fields of old lava from previous eruptions.

They ran harder, trying to ignore the thin air and the burning in their legs, spurred on by adrenaline and fear.

Mac thought it was too risky to move across the mountain and down the lava fields. He was unsure of the sturdiness of the open stretches, knowing that there were places on fields like this that could crack like eggshells and swallow them up, maybe into magma flowing below the surface.

There was no cell service, no way to call for help. He'd slowed long enough to check his phone with its dying battery. Cell towers were probably down all over the island.

Mac wondered what else on the island was down and where and how fast the rest of the lava was headed.

The observatory finally came into view, but it looked impossibly far away. Mac allowed himself a quick look back.

Shit.

As the trail got steeper, the lava came faster.

"We've got to get off the trail now!" Mac yelled at Rebecca. "We're going to have to risk cutting across the lava field."

"Is that safe?" she asked.

"As long as the quakes and tremors haven't weakened the old lava too much," he said. "But at this point, we've got no choice. The lava's not going to get tired. We are."

They hooked a sharp turn off the trail. The lava flows closest to them kept going, passing them, at least for now. Rebecca slipped and went down. Mac pulled her up, then he removed a tool from his utility belt, an infrared thermometer, and held it toward the rocky mass directly ahead of them, which was clear of lava for the moment. He found a long stick that had fallen from a koa tree and tapped it on the surface, checking for hollow tubes where lava might be pooling underneath.

"Feels solid," Mac said, "but the mountain's interior temperature is rising. It's about six hundred degrees now. Our boots won't melt until it's about eight hundred, so we can keep making our way down."

Rebecca, who had looked more surefooted than Mac initially, took the lead and nimbly began to weave around masses of lava rock.

Mac thought: *The ground is too weak. Right fucking here.* "Rebecca! Stop!"

A hole in the earth opened up a few yards ahead of Rebecca.

What had just appeared without warning was a skylight. When quakes and tremors made cracks and fissures in a lava field, the ground could split open like a trapdoor over an air gap with lava flowing beneath it.

But Rebecca didn't see it because at that moment she half turned and said something to him. Mac screamed, even louder, *"Stop!"*

Rebecca didn't hear him—she faced forward again, the skylight right in front of her, and tripped over a large rock.

As Mac reached for her, she started to fall.

CHAPTER 94

Mac was sure that he had reached for Rebecca seconds too late.

Her arms had flailed wildly as she searched for something to hold on to, then she'd pitched forward, toward lava that was just twenty yards below her.

Somehow Mac had managed to grab hold of her left arm and shove her away from the hole.

But that wasn't what had saved her.

Lava did.

Her boot was caught in a crevice.

Mac had shoved her to the left, but her left foot and ankle were firmly locked in place.

Rebecca screamed in pain.

"Pretty sure I just broke my ankle," she said.

She was on the ground, but she hadn't fallen through the skylight. She could plainly see the bright glare of the lava below, feel the rising heat of it.

"*Holy hell.*" She gasped.

Mac got on his hands and knees and told her to brace a hand on his back. He slowly unlaced her boot and gently pulled her foot out of it. He heard a sharp intake of breath from her as he did.

Even with the heat they were both feeling now, her face was the color of ice.

"I'm so sorry," he said.

She nodded at the approaching lava.

"I'm not," she said.

He carried her down the mountain toward the Mauna Loa Observatory under a sky completely darkened by the spreading cloud of vog—volcanic ash and dust.

There was no other way.

Sometimes Mac carried her in his arms, sometimes over his shoulder like a soldier carrying a wounded comrade across a battlefield.

Every hundred yards or so, he stopped and put her down to rest. Then he picked her up and they would set out again. It had been more than an hour since they'd seen the F-22 Raptors in the air to the east, heard the first bombs in the distance.

The cloud of ash and gas kept getting darker and more ominous, turning day into night.

At one point when they were resting, she told him to leave her there, go to the base, and have someone come back for her.

"No," he said.

"You know that makes the most sense."

He gave her a long look. "Not to me, it doesn't."

He put her back over his shoulder.

They heard a plane and saw a fixed-wing turboprop appear suddenly out of the dark cloud and head south. Mac recognized it as an EO-5C, an army reconnaissance plane.

In the next moment, it was as if the sound had been turned off. They could no longer hear the engine.

The propellers were no longer spinning.

Mac and Rebecca watched in horror as the EO-5C descended too quickly toward the observatory.

CHAPTER 95

U.S. Military Reserve, Hawai'i

The reconnaissance plane Rivers had put in the air to look for Mac and Rebecca seemed to be coming straight at him.

He watched the feed from the security camera situated at the northwest gate of the observatory. The last communication from the two pilots was a report that the cloud they'd tried to avoid had killed their engines, and the ash and glass particles had rendered the propellers useless.

It didn't matter to Rivers how it had happened. Just that it had.

The plane disappeared briefly into the volcanic smog and then came back into view.

Rivers listened to the pilots on the speaker in his office feeling as if he were in the cockpit himself.

"I want to shoot for that helipad outside the compound!" the pilot said. "But I can barely make out where it is!"

Rivers checked the screen showing the view from the north

camera and saw the different flows of lava were coalescing into one large flow, glowing red at the edges and increasing in speed as it moved toward the observatory.

"So much freaking lava!" the copilot yelled. "But it hasn't reached—"

The pilot cut him off. "Wait, I think I see—"

"I can try to direct you," the voice from the tower said. "Are you able to—"

"No time—"

"To the left, Ron!" the copilot yelled.

The speaker went silent.

Rivers continued to stare at the feed, helpless.

The plane didn't veer away.

One hundred yards now.

Fifty.

Its nose was aimed directly at the camera until everything went dark.

CHAPTER 96

NOAA Mauna Loa Observatory, Hawai'i

It was nighttime when Mac and Rebecca managed to make it to the observatory.

They'd witnessed the recon plane's crash from about a mile up the mountain. As they continued down, they'd seen a series of small explosions, but these had finally begun to subside when they approached the main gate.

The only light came from the smoldering wreckage of the plane that was spread across the compound.

Mac ran to the cockpit, which had split off from the rest of the plane. Flames still licked around its fuselage, which had broken in half. With the small flashlight on his utility belt, Mac could see the lifeless bodies of the two pilots still harnessed in their seats.

The strong smell of gas signaled that he needed to get away before there was another explosion.

He moved quickly toward what was left of the communications building. The plane had plowed through the structure, completely destroying its front half.

But if the observatory hadn't been evacuated after the eruption, there might be people in there.

Mac went inside, saying a prayer as he did.

It was ironic, Mac thought as he glanced around, because this looked like the kind of catastrophic damage a lava bomb from the closest vents would inflict. But the direct hit from the plane had done this.

There were broken bodies everywhere in the rubble: Three scientists from the Maunakea Observatories. Two men in army fatigues.

Mac moved to the back of what was left of the main room and saw death all around him. That was where he found Katie Maurus and Rob Castillo—two kids from HVO who'd wanted to monitor the sensors near the summit from here—next to their desks; a section of the roof had clearly crushed them. Rob's body was on top of Katie's, as if he'd been trying to protect her in the last seconds of their lives.

Mac felt as if he couldn't breathe, suffocated by the tragedy in this room.

To be sure, he knelt and checked for their pulses. They were dead like the others.

From outside, he heard Rebecca scream.

CHAPTER 97

Saddle Road, Hawai'i

Sergeant Matthew Iona was driving the last Caterpillar 375 Excavator near Cinder Cone Road, closer to Mauna Loa than Mauna Kea, south of the Saddle Road area.

They were doing new digging here now that they'd seen the direction the lava was taking. The lava had surprised even the scientists, according to Colonel Briggs, by suddenly pouring from radial vents close to the base of Mauna Loa on its eastern side.

A new perimeter was needed. Briggs had said they had the same deadline they always had with General Rivers: "He wants the new holes in the ground five minutes ago," Briggs told Iona.

Iona had become Briggs's man on the ground. Briggs had first designated him to work as closely as possible with Dr. Mac-Gregor and Rebecca Cruz—not just work with them but keep eyes on them. Iona was happy to do it, even if he'd occasionally felt like he was spying. He was always looking for ways to make himself indispensable to the colonel. An added benefit to Colonel Briggs was that Iona had grown up working on road crews in Hilo. He hadn't been involved with digging like this for a while, but he assured the colonel that he still knew how to do it.

Tonight, he was acting as a foreman for this small army crew, who knew the lava from the vents was headed their way. As soon as they finished, a line of explosives set by Cruz Demolition would be detonated, and that would—hopefully—redirect the lava flow into the new trenches and the one lake to the east of Cinder Cone Road that had, almost miraculously, been dug tonight.

The bulldozers from the Hilo construction companies were gone for now. It was just Iona and his excavator and two army bulldozers, all of them basically trying to make one more fork in the road.

They had seen the lava coming closer from the south, but then it seemed to blessedly veer off, disappearing into the cloud of ash and smoke that had made breathing increasingly difficult out here.

They were about to pack it in when Colonel Briggs called Iona. He was already shouting.

"Get out of there now, Iona! The lava has picked up speed in the last fifteen minutes!"

Then: "I never should have sent you over there!"

Iona said, "I thought the lava had split off—"

"Son, I don't care what you thought! Turn the fuck around and haul ass!"

Iona looked in the Caterpillar's rearview mirror.

There it was.

The orange-red streak, the only color in the darkness, had suddenly appeared just a few hundred yards away.

It was speeding at them like a lit fuse.

Or a bullet.

Sergeant Matthew Iona didn't hesitate. He jumped out of his cab with the bullhorn he'd been using to direct the others and pointed at the lava now lighting up the sky overhead. The two bulldozers were already moving out, the other excavator right behind them.

Iona jumped back in his excavator's cab.

He knew he didn't have much time to get the hell out. He gunned the engine. He was on a curve, and as he turned the wheel, the ground shook, hard, the first significant tremor since the eruption in the morning. Then another tremor hit, bigger than the one before.

The excavator tilted and went into a skid.

The brakes did nothing as the truck began to slip sideways into the eight-foot-deep trench he'd just helped dig. Iona was thrown hard against the steering wheel; he felt his ribs crack. The pain shot everywhere, like foot-long splinters.

Then he was pinned against the door.

The passenger door was too far away to reach. Every time he moved his right arm, the pain from his fractured ribs shot through him.

He had no way of knowing if his buddies in the vehicles ahead had seen what happened.

Somehow, he managed to get his window open. He caught his breath and felt he had a chance. He pumped the brakes again. And again.

The last thing he saw was the river of lava flowing right at him.

Coming way too fast.

Rolling fire, sparks and ash, screaming thunder.

CHAPTER 98

U.S. Military Reserve, Hawai'i

Get out of the truck! *Sergeant, get out now.*"

Rivers and Briggs watched helplessly on Briggs's phone as Matthew Iona's truck slowly disappeared under an orange-red wave of lava.

They watched the boy die on a satellite phone, the same way they'd watched those pilots die on the monitor.

A boy—that was how General Mark Rivers thought of Sergeant Iona. Not as a soldier; as a boy. A college-age kid. And he had died not just for his country but for the whole world. He just hadn't known it.

The soldier in the excavator a couple hundred yards ahead of Iona had started to go back. He realized it was too late but recorded the scene on his phone before getting back to his excavator and saving his own life.

Briggs stuffed his phone into a side pocket. This was hard to take. It was like war, only worse, because so many civilians were dying.

"I'm the one who sent him there," Briggs said. "Iona worked for me."

"And you work for me," Rivers said. "You were both doing your jobs. The men who went into that cave, they were doing their jobs too."

Rivers and Briggs waited to see if the lava would move in the direction they wanted it to, toward Waimea. If it did, that would be some consolation.

"Do you think the worst is over?" Briggs asked.

But they both knew that the death toll from the town on the other side of the island, Nāʻālehu, would keep rising. It might take days or weeks to find out how many victims there were. Likely the whole town was gone. So were countless marine creatures who'd lived in the waters in and around South Point.

They already knew approximately how many had died at the Mauna Loa Observatory. The vog had cleared enough for them to send a helicopter, and it had landed ten minutes before.

The pilot found no one alive.

A day and night filled with death and dying and unimaginable suffering.

"No, Briggs," Rivers said. "The worst is yet to come. Go do your job."

Rivers was alone in the cafeteria, a mug of steaming coffee in front of his face, needing to get away from the monitors, not wanting to watch anyone else die today. He looked up and saw Dr. John MacGregor standing in front of him. The scientist looked sick to his stomach.

"Another eruption is happening," Mac said. "It's going to be worse than the first one."

CHAPTER 99

Mauna Loa, Hawaiʻi

Overnight, hour by hour, minute by minute, pictures of the eruption lighting up the Hawaiian sky had circulated around the world. The intense stories accompanying the pictures told of the most massive eruption in Hawaiʻi's history.

Thousands and thousands of pounds of rock had been blown into the sky. Fragments had shot hundreds of feet straight up. Clouds rose miles in seconds. Lightning lit a range of immense pyrocumulus clouds.

The world had also learned of what was being described on social media platforms as the tragic and heroic deaths of J. P. Brett and Oliver and Leah Cutler, all of whom had come to the Big Island on their own to help protect it.

Their doomed flight in J. P. Brett's helicopter was universally described as a "reconnaissance mission" the three of them had organized to aid the army's efforts to stop the flow of lava toward Hilo.

One of Brett's associates told the *New York Times* that before boarding the flight, Brett had said to her, "I'm going to help save this island or die trying."

Briggs had given General Mark Rivers a printout of that particular story; Rivers read it and said, "Who knows? It might even be true."

During most of those nighttime hours, Rivers had been busy mobilizing a mission to protect Saddle Road—which he'd taken to calling Apocalypse Road—trying to find a way to stop the smoldering river of lava before it reached the point of no return.

The Ice Tube. After that came hell on earth.

By the first light of day, he could see new canals and small lakes taking shape. It looked as if a whole new suburb had sprung up in the middle of the island. The work crews were doing their best to deepen the trenches and canals that had already been dug near where the canisters of deadly poison were stored in the cave.

"How much time do we have for the digging?" Rivers asked Mac.

"No time," Mac said.

They had combined the army's equipment and manpower with the equipment and employees of the twenty-some construction companies in Hilo. Mac was the foreman for Hilo's civilian construction crews.

Rebecca had desperately wanted to be on-site. She'd hot-wired a jeep at the observatory, and they'd driven it back to the Military Reserve. "I'm good with wires," she'd told Mac with a shrug. She needed to begin redrawing her bombing maps, but Rivers clearly wasn't going to allow it.

Rivers had looked at Rebecca's broken ankle, now in a walking boot. He told her that if she tried to hot-wire another one of his jeeps, she would be placed under house arrest for the duration. *For the duration.*

Riding in Rivers's jeep now, Mac explained to the general that the lava flow was taking the same direction as it had in the eruption of 1843. It rolled over the great expanse of lava fields that ran parallel to Mauna Loa Road, north of the unfinished road to Kona, then made a rapid descent toward Saddle Road and Mauna Kea.

Their last, best hope was threading a needle and redirecting the flow northwest, across the grassy fields south of Waimea, then toward Waikōloa Beach and the ocean. If they succeeded, fewer would die. Big if.

The original digs close to Mauna Loa had worked as well as they could have hoped. The lava was pooling in the man-made lakes, and it was continuously sprayed by a fleet of Chinooks, each helicopter dumping three thousand pounds of seawater. The bright red viscous matter darkened as it finally began to cool and harden.

They jumped out of the jeep and hurried toward the massive number of soldiers and civilians using bulldozers and excavators and even jackhammers to dig trenches. Rivers shouted over the noise, "We're talking about a massive fire drill! That's until there's enough visibility to put the bombers back in the air. Then you tell me what to hit and when to hit it."

Mac looked at the summit. The bright orange and red cloud above it was growing, and the darkness of the vog was once again moving in their direction. The lava was coming faster and faster.

"Just one thing, General," Mac said as he handed Rivers one of the bullhorns they'd brought with them.

"What's that?"

"This ain't a drill," Mac said.

* * *

Every time the workers felt the tremors of another quake, they would turn toward the summit, then get right back to work. They had no idea how soon the lava would get here, how soon they all might die.

But the message Mac had given them was the same one he had given Rivers: *No time.*

"These brave men, women, even kids, think they're saving their town," Rivers said.

"They might be saving the world," Mac said. "What a thought that is." Mac's satellite phone rang. "I have to take this."

Rebecca was calling from the military base. "I've got bad news," she said.

"Don't need any."

"You don't have a choice."

"How bad?"

"I can't tell you," she said. "I have to show you. Sending you a screenshot."

She did and Mac looked at it. The sensors at the base and at HVO were recording the speed of the lava and reporting a disastrous change in direction.

Mac dodged an excavator and ran as fast as he could to Rivers. He reached the general as he was about to raise his bullhorn again. Mac grabbed Rivers's arm.

Rivers started to bark something but stopped when he saw the look on Mac's face.

"Talk to me," he said.

"We might have to sacrifice Hilo."

CHAPTER 100

U.S. Military Reserve, Hawai'i

Animals knew enough to run and try to find cover. Nēnē geese, the state bird of Hawai'i, fled first. Then came many domesticated dogs, cats, birds. Even bees deserted their hives.

But few people on Hawai'i knew how bad things had really gotten.

Colonel Briggs came back to supervise the last of the probably futile digging effort while Mac and Rivers raced to the base.

"With the story the sensors are telling," Rivers said, "I have to think about evacuating this compound."

"You have to do it in the next hour or so," Mac said. "Maybe even sooner than that."

"I can send people to Hāwī on the north tip," Rivers said, "if we don't think we can save the base."

"General," Mac said, "right now, saving this base is the least of our worries."

They found Rebecca and her brother huddled together in a conference room surrounded by monitors.

"How's the ankle?" Mac asked.

"Sucks a big one," she said with a grin that came and went. "But thanks for asking."

Mac studied the monitor closest to him, reviewing the data from the sensors one more time; it hadn't changed since Rebecca had asked him to interpret it. The amount of lava pooling underneath the summit would send voluminous flows from Mauna Loa toward Mauna Kea. That might prove impossible to divert. Even if the trenches held.

"Mac, that shit just keeps pouring out of the center of the earth," Rebecca said.

"We need eyes on it," Rivers said and made a call. The vog had cleared enough that he could order a reconnaissance plane into the air.

Mac walked to an easel propped against the front wall. He drew a crude map: the Ice Tube, Hilo, Waimea, and Saddle Road.

"The lava from the first eruption mostly ended here," he said, pointing. "That's the Saddle Road area. The volcano gods willing, we want it to go over *there*."

He pointed first at Waimea, then farther to the west at Waikōloa Beach.

"What if it doesn't?" Rivers asked.

"If it doesn't, and the new holes in the ground get overtopped, it's like I told you before," Mac said. "Hilo gets hit. I don't see any way around it. And that's probably the best case."

Mac cursed as his satellite phone rang again, this time with an incoming call from HVO. For a moment, he imagined that he'd hear Jenny's voice.

But it was Kenny Wong, who'd quit him to work for Brett. Bad career move.

"You lost?" Mac asked.

"Mac, we can talk about what an asshole Judas I was another time, or maybe never," Kenny said. "But I came back because I felt like shit for what I did to you. And also because I couldn't sit this out."

"So what you got?"

"I'm sure you know the lava is well past that unfinished road to Kona," Kenny said.

"And more coming hard behind it, right?" Mac asked.

"General Rivers needs to get people off that base, Mac," Kenny said. "And whatever you're going to do, you need to do it now. The lava is on a collision course with that freaking cave."

"The new digging might still do its job," Mac said. "If not, we're planning a second wave with the jets."

Kenny suddenly shouted, "Mac, *listen to me!* The pictures in front of me aren't changing! Those people need to haul ass out of that base and off the mountain before it's too late!"

Mac hung up. He told the general and Rebecca what Kenny had said. Rivers walked into the hall to make the call.

"What are we going to do, Mac?" Rebecca asked.

"We're going to do our best to bury that shit with air-to-ground bombs once and for all," Mac said. "Your explosives have done as much to help us as they can. But once the lava has passed Saddle Road, the bombs are going to be the whole ball game."

He took one last look at the map he'd just drawn, then glanced at the monitor showing the latest pictures of the lava that the reconnaissance plane had just sent them.

The lava was still heading north. If it kept going, that would mean the end of everything. The end of the world. What a concept.

Rivers came back into the room. "They're evacuating the base," he said.

"Got a question," Mac said. "If you decide to use bombers, do you have any besides Raptors?"

"What do you mean, *if?* I've got a squadron loaded with GBU-32 attack munitions ready to go."

"What else do you have?"

"Just a couple of F-15EX Eagle IIs, that's it," Rivers said. "Two-seaters. They're at Hilo International."

Mac knew the plane, an upgraded model of the F-15 fourth-generation fighter jet equipped with AMBER Storm-Breaker smart weapons that could see through fog and, hopefully, vog. He knew a lot about fighter jets, had studied them since he was a kid and watched *Top Gun* on what sometimes felt like an endless loop. As a high-school senior, he'd even considered applying to the Air Force Academy until he'd become more fascinated with volcanoes.

Lucky me.

"Perfect," he said to Rivers.

"Why perfect?"

"There needs to be a seat for me if we're going to do this right," Mac said.

"Define *right*," Rivers said.

"We don't need a squadron of bombers," he said. "We just need the one I'm in."

"What else do you need?" Rivers asked.

"Your top gun," Mac said.

CHAPTER 101

Hilo International Airport, Hilo, Hawai'i

The pilot Rivers chose for the mission was the best he had in Hawai'i, or maybe anywhere: Colonel Chad Raley.

He had first served under Rivers during the Second Gulf War, and five years ago, when Rivers had risen to chairman of the Joint Chiefs, they had worked together again. That mission, off the USS *Nimitz* in the Arabian Sea, was to "deter," as Raley put it, aggression from Iran.

"We did that—deterred it," Raley said, removing his sunglasses.

He looked the part of a top gun: Tall, broad-shouldered. Silver crew cut. Blue eyes that were so light, they were close to the silver of his hair.

Raley had volunteered to come to Hawai'i before Rivers had even explained why he needed him.

A man of few words, Mac thought. *No—a man of almost no words.*

"So, you're my copilot today," Raley said.

"More like a newbie bombardier," Mac said.

"You ever flown in one of these things?"

"Only in my dreams."

"The general isn't all that thrilled with you going up with me," Raley said. "But he says you know more than anyone on this island about where these bombs need to go."

"*If* they need to go," Mac said. "We don't need volume today. Too risky. We need pinpoint accuracy." Mac grinned at Raley. "He told me you were the man."

Raley said, "I am the man."

Ten minutes later, they were in the air. Raley banked the Eagle to the south. The flight plan took them up the middle of the island so they could quickly assess the situation on the ground.

As the lava came into view, Mac thought: *This is a fool's errand. So I must be a fool.*

"I know you're the volcano guy," Raley said through his aviation respirator. "But from what I see, not a whole lot of time before the lava reaches that cave."

Before Mac could answer, Raley said, "And I know all about those canisters, Dr. MacGregor. General Rivers told me."

Mac looked down and to the east at the homes in Kaumana Estates between Saddle Road and Hilo. There had to be people down there who hadn't evacuated. Had to be. The whole town couldn't have left on those ferries.

Mac's throat felt dry. He tried not to think that only a respirator protected him from the sulfur dioxide contaminating the jet's ventilation system.

He had the latest projections about the flow of the lava from both Rebecca at the military base and Kenny Wong at HVO. There was too much lava heading for the Ice Tube. They'd have to split the flow into two fingers, west and east. If they could.

But east meant toward town; it meant destroying the homes below them and more innocent people dying.

Mac looked down at Kaumana Estates and thought of his sons again. As the day went on, he had been thinking about them more and more, then forcing himself to stop and focus on the job at hand.

"I know someone who lives down there," he said to Raley.

The colonel didn't respond. He was all about concentration. Raley got them low enough that Mac could even see the famous formation of lava known as Charles de Gaulle's profile. The new stream of lava was past the unfinished road to Kona, relentlessly pushing toward Saddle Road and the Ice Tube.

Mac fought the urge to squeeze his eyes shut so he wouldn't have to confront the scene below, the reality of it, the looming tragedy. But he couldn't look away because he knew exactly what was about to happen, or what he and Colonel Chad Raley were hopefully about to make happen; there was no margin for error and no guarantee that what they were attempting would work.

Mac said, "If it gets much closer to the cave —"

Raley finished the thought for him. "Game over," he said. "I get it."

Mac took a quick look at his map, even though he knew where the bombs needed to fall. They had to split the lava even if that meant redirecting it toward Hilo.

He saw the lava angle slightly to the north.

Not enough space.

They had circled for a second look at the target area. Mac glanced down again at Kaumana Estates.

He prayed that the boy and his mother had left.

"Can you get me even lower?" Mac shouted.

He knew he was trying to buy himself a little more time before he had to make his choice.

Raley gave him a thumbs-up.

"I need to be sure!" Mac said. "I need to see!"

Then they couldn't see anything because the vog blowing from the west swallowed them up.

And no one could see them.

CHAPTER 102

Kaumana Estates, Hawai'i

Lono stood in his backyard and watched the sky. He was afraid to blink. He'd heard the jet and gone running outside. He saw right away how close to the ground the shape was flying.

It was an army jet.

A bomber.

Mac had gotten him interested in planes, just like he had gotten him interested in so many things. Mac had made him a reader, an honor student, and a better surfer.

Lono felt as if he were flying blind right now. He had no internet. No way for him to get into the HVO computer system and find out where the lava was after the second eruption he'd heard and then seen on this day from hell.

His mother, Aramea, had stubbornly refused to leave their home, refused to get in the line with her friends at the Port of

Hilo, refused to board one of the boats that would take them to Maui, even though she had a sister there.

"The goddess has always provided for us," she told Lono. "It is Pele's will at work now. Not mine or yours. Not your friend Dr. MacGregor's."

"Are you saying it's her will for us to stay and die in this house?" Lono asked.

"You must have faith," she said. "You were raised in the ways of the natural world, and you were also raised in the ways of the spiritual world."

But I'm growing up in the world of science, he wanted to tell her. *In the* real *world.*

But he didn't say it. There was no point. She wasn't leaving this house, the only one Lono had ever known. And Lono wasn't leaving her. Even if that meant they would die together.

He looked behind him and saw her sweet face pressed against the kitchen window. He knew she was looking at the summit in the distance, the swollen clouds, the flames licking the sky, looking at Mauna Loa like it was some kind of deity.

Lono's eyes returned to the jet. It made a long turn to the east, came back around, and headed right for him.

Lono watched, his head craned back, and found himself wondering if the goddess of volcanoes could protect him and his mother from the army's bombs.

I don't want to die like this. I don't want my mom to die.

But that bomber was so close.

CHAPTER 103

U.S. Military Reserve, Hawai'i

The Military Reserve was empty except for a few last holdouts, General Mark Rivers and Rebecca Cruz among them.

They had stayed to monitor the flight path of the F-15. Air traffic control at Hilo International was still broadcasting over one speaker. Rivers and Rebecca knew that Mac's plan had been to wait until the last possible moment to deploy the missiles, and only if it came to that.

Rivers felt the moment was coming at them at the speed of sound.

The general's man in the control tower was Lieutenant Isaiah Jefferson. "There's a problem, sir," Jefferson said.

"What problem?" Rivers snapped.

"We just lost them," Jefferson said.

"You mean over the radio?" Rivers asked.

"Not just the radio. It's like that black cloud that blew in from the volcano made them disappear." Jefferson paused for a moment. "Sir, we just found out yesterday what clouds like that can do. You get inside one, it's like you're taking enemy fire."

There was another pause and then Jefferson said, "They could go down the way the reconnaissance plane did."

Across the room, Kenny Wong was staring at the image on his laptop.

"I've never seen vog this thick," he said. "During the 2022 eruption, it spread two hundred fifty miles, but it had far less of an effect on visibility."

He walked over to General Rivers.

"Never this much lava, never this much vog," Kenny said. He shook his head. "This is our perfect storm."

They were flying blind; the window of the cockpit was abraded by the hot sandstorm of tiny glass particles and pulverized rock embedded in the ash.

Chad Raley knew he had to get them out of here. He just didn't know in which direction, at what altitude, or at what speed, given the skewed readings on the airspeed sensors. They were in serious trouble; the ash eroding the blades of the engine compressor was as capable of bringing the Eagle down as an enemy missile.

The plane rocked again—another direct hit. Chad Raley had been shot down one time, in the Arabian Sea. He had survived, mostly by dumb luck.

Now he thought his dumb luck was running out.

A pilot survived one crash like that.

Never two.

* * *

"What the hell was that?" Mac asked after the plane passed through a driving cloud of ash and glass and rocks.

"That," Raley said, "was the sound of us losing our right engine."

The beautiful morning sky they had flown into had become blackened by a volcanic storm cloud.

The jet began to buck as if caught in hurricane-force winds.

Another loud *crack*, this time on the left side of the plane. Then what sounded like gunfire hit the F-15.

"Now the rocky ash is coming for the left engine," Chad Raley said, looking out the side window of the cockpit. "The engine is glowing with heat."

The plane dropped what felt like a thousand feet in a couple of seconds.

"How long can we stay in the air?" Mac yelled.

"We shouldn't still *be* in the air!" Raley yelled back.

Even with the sudden loss in altitude, he couldn't see anything except the cloud that was all around them.

"Got a question, Dr. MacGregor," Raley said. "You willing to die to save the world?"

Raley didn't wait for an answer.

"Because I am."

The plane dipped again and turned on its axis, the motion giving the men the feeling of flying sideways.

The Chinook carrying Rivers and Rebecca touched down on the pad at HVO. While they'd been in the air, Rivers had remained in contact with Lieutenant Jefferson, who still hadn't been able to reestablish contact with Mac and Colonel Raley.

Rebecca had been on the satellite phone with her brother and Kenny Wong as they monitored the flow of the lava almost yard by yard.

They told her it was past Saddle Road now.

Still on a collision course with the Ice Tube, with very little deviation.

Now Rivers shouted at Jefferson that he needed to talk to Mac and Colonel Raley immediately. "I don't care how they get them back. Just get them back!"

"Believe me, sir. Everyone here is trying. We're on it."

"They need to deploy the missiles now!" Rivers said.

"Not if they can't see the ground, General," Jefferson said. He paused. "Provided they're still up there."

"Have you even gotten an emergency squawk code?" Rivers asked. Squawk 7600 established that an aircraft had lost communication and needed direction from aviation light signals.

"No, sir. Nothing."

"I'm heading inside," Rivers told Jefferson. "I want to know the second you can see them. And I mean the *second*!"

CHAPTER 104

Somewhere Above the Big Island

They couldn't shake the thick volcanic smog. It kept washing over them in blinding, grainy waves. The wind buffeted the jet, tossing them in every direction, threatening to rip the plane apart or smash it to the ground. The ash blocked airflow to the engine, sending it toward a stall.

Then Mac felt the Eagle lose thrust. His heart nearly stopped.

"Left engine's compromised," Raley said before Mac had a chance to ask. "Ash and glass particles. Must be melting the components."

The F-15 dropped another few hundred feet.

"We need some sky," Raley said, "so I can see where the hell we are."

The plane was hit again by glass and rock, even harder than before.

"What was *that*?" Mac said, his voice going up an octave.

"That was our left wing," Raley said. "The rocky particles destroyed the outer surface of the fuselage where the wing connects to it."

Mac looked at his hands. He was squeezing his knees; his knuckles were the color of chalk. "Are we going down?" Mac asked.

"Not until we do what we came up here to do."

There was a brief patch of blue, there and then gone. But it lasted long enough for them to see another eruption at the summit and feel it in the F-15. It was as if the earthquake had suddenly reached up into the sky.

Somehow Chad Raley got control of the wounded plane. He leveled it off and said, "This shit is disabling the jet one piece at a time."

In the next moment, they saw the ground again. It was so fucking close.

Smoke and steam were rising up from the lava, but it was clear how fast and how far the lava had traveled while they were bouncing around in the cloud.

Raley said, "That thing you talked about doing before we took off?"

"Creating our own avalanche of fire?"

Raley nodded. "We need to send it toward Hilo while we still can." He gave Mac a hard look and said, "Whether you want to do that or not."

"With one working engine and one wing?" Mac asked.

"Who said the other engine was working?"

They heard the crackle inside their headsets and assumed radio contact with the tower at Hilo International was back.

It wasn't the tower.

The next voice they heard belonged to General Rivers.

"You're out of time," he said. *"Deploy!"*

Quietly and calmly, Colonel Raley said, "Not yet."

One last time, even as he felt them losing more altitude, Rivers's top pilot banked the F-15 to the south.

He didn't stay in open sky for long.

Raley circled back and aimed the jet at the even bigger cloud that had just appeared between them and the Ice Tube.

Flew directly into it as the sky turned black—black flecked with specks of fiery ash.

In the communications room at HVO, Rebecca Cruz locked her eyes on the radar screen in front of her. She was seeing the same pictures they were watching at air traffic control.

"What's the pilot doing?" she asked Rivers.

"Completing the mission."

Rebecca's eyes didn't leave the screen. "They're going to die, aren't they?"

CHAPTER 105

They were flying blind again. *Maybe for the last time*, Raley thought.

He looked down at the Eagle's damaged left wing and the volcanic ash still swirling around it.

All those years in the Middle East, Raley thought. Now an enemy like this, with more firepower than he'd ever encountered, was about to shoot him out of the sky, finish the job the bastards over the Arabian Sea hadn't been able to.

One more minute.

That was all he needed. He and Mac.

Maybe less than a minute.

They came out of the cloud, looked down, and saw that the lava had overtopped one of the last trenches to the north of Saddle Road.

Raley called to Mac in the copilot's seat. "Now?" His pale eyes were fixed on the horizon.

Mac didn't speak.

The plane began to shake violently. This was it, wasn't it?

"I asked you a question," Raley said.

Mac stayed silent.

"Now?" Colonel Chad Raley asked again.

The plane went into an even sharper descent.

Mac remembered the reconnaissance plane crashing into the observatory while he and Rebecca watched.

The lava was too close to the Ice Tube and the canisters inside. If the lava reached them, the effect would be like detonating a nuclear bomb.

They had to direct the lava toward Hilo. There was no other choice. "Now."

A moment later, Chad Raley said, "The ejector rack is jammed."

The bombs wouldn't deploy.

Somehow Raley was able to pull the plane out of the dive, veer to the right, then veer back to the left toward the target.

"Now we are out of time!" Raley yelled.

"What do we do?" Mac yelled.

"There's one way to create that avalanche of fire," Chad Raley said.

"How the hell do we do that without bombs?"

Raley looked at Mac and said, not yelling now, his words measured and eerily calm, "By crashing this plane."

"Do it," Mac said.

CHAPTER 106

The Ice Tube, Mauna Kea, Hawai'i

A camera installed over the entrance to the Ice Tube showed the approach of the F-15.

"They're going to crash," Rivers said. "It's too late for him to pull out."

They patched into the cockpit again.

They heard Colonel Chad Raley's voice: "Preparing to deploy" was all he said.

Suddenly the Eagle disappeared in the cloud. Everything in the room was quiet.

Colonel Chad Raley pulled the plane out of its dive with only precious seconds to spare before this mission became a suicide mission. They had been ready to do what they needed to do to keep the fire below them away from the Ice Tube and what was inside it, even if it meant death and destruction flowing into Hilo as well as their own deaths.

It was a sacrifice they had both been willing to make.

"Oh…my…God," Mac said when he was able to speak.

"There is one after all," Raley said.

They could clearly see the ground, and they looked down at what they realized was a miracle.

Because of Mauna Kea.

The other volcano.

Mauna Kea hadn't erupted in over four thousand years. But the thick lava that had hardened and cooled long ago near its base was functioning like a natural wall to divert the flowing lava.

A natural and impenetrable wall, perfectly positioned and stronger, better, than any the army and the construction crews from Hilo could build.

Mac and Raley watched in wonder as the glowing molten lava fresh from Mauna Loa hit the solid, ancient topography of Mauna Kea—and made a sharp westward turn, flowing across the grassy plains south of Waimea on its way to Waikōloa Beach and the Pacific Ocean.

The action was both unexpected and unpredictable, as if, in the end, the volcanoes had made the only life-and-death choice that mattered.

And they had made the choice for Raley and Mac.

Raley shook his head, eyes wide. "Tell me what just happened down there."

Mac waited until he was finally breathing normally again.

Then Dr. John MacGregor, man of science, smiled at the pilot.

"Nature just happened," he said. "Isn't that something. I can't believe what we just saw." Then Mac let out a whoop. So did Raley.

The Eagle was flying on only one engine, but it was enough for Raley to land the plane safely.

In the end, it had been lava that saved the world.

EPILOGUE

Four Weeks Later

CHAPTER 107

Colonel James Briggs had correctly predicted that, working around the clock, it would take four weeks to pack and remove the 642 canisters from the cave.

One less than when they had started their mission.

Throughout the process, no one had said the words *Agent Black*. No one dared.

Not even now that its lethal threat, having gotten out on the island, was once again contained.

The soldiers who had begun the original cleanup inside the Ice Tube had been transferred stateside. That left a small emergency crew in hazmat suits working the crane on one of the army's fleet of specially cushioned Heavy Expanded Mobility Tactical Trucks.

The last load of canisters would be transported the way the others had, via the Nimitz-class aircraft carrier USS *George Washington*, currently docked off the Port of Hilo. The ship from the U.S. Seventh Fleet had left Japan and was headed to a scheduled docking in Bremerton, Washington, providing the perfect military cover story: the *George Washington* had stopped here for repairs before continuing its journey to the mainland.

Even the sailors in the warship's hazardous material division did not know what chemicals they were transporting across the Pacific.

General Mark Rivers and Mac watched from down the hill as the last of Rivers's soldiers made their way out of the cave. They had just completed one final blasting with flamethrowers. Every inch of the lava tube had been scrubbed down and tested for radiation.

"You're really not going to tell me where those canisters will be stored?" Mac asked Rivers.

Rivers squinted into the morning sun, then grinned. "What canisters?" he said.

Mac turned and shook Rivers's hand.

"It was an honor serving with you, sir," Mac said, surprised at how emotional he felt.

In the end, it was as if they'd been through a war together.

Rivers continued to smile. "The honor was mine, Dr. Mac-Gregor."

Rivers got into his jeep and drove away, following the transport vehicle. Before Mac got into his own jeep, he took one last, long look up the hill. Then he reached into his wallet and pulled out two pieces of folded-up paper.

The notations General Arthur Bennett had made in his hospital room that night in Honolulu were now in Mac's possession, thanks to Colonel Briggs.

Mac examined the one with Bennett's drawing on it: a lopsided circle surrounded by a series of shaky, arc-shaped lines.

Then he looked at the other one. Some of the letters were still hard to make out: *I-C-E-T-U-B-B.*

CHAPTER 108

Mac and Lono stood on the still gorgeous beach at Honoliʻi, their backs to the water and the four- and five-foot breakers. During the second eruption, the beach had split open to the north. At one point, the ocean had gone as smooth as glass for a long moment that no one on the island would ever forget.

Now, all over the Big Island, the rebuilding and recovery went on; the local government said that some of the restoration might take years. With the assistance of the army, officials were still searching for casualties at Nāʻālehu and in the Waikōloa Beach area, where the lava that had been diverted to prevent a disaster—the scope of which the residents of the island would never know—had added to the death toll on its way into the Pacific Ocean.

"You were ready to drop those bombs of yours near my house, weren't you?" Lono asked.

"What bombs?" Mac said.

The boy smiled. "It's funny," he said. "All my life, my mother told me that Pele would provide. And in the end, that's exactly what she did."

Mac had told Lono how the hardened lava at the base of

Mauna Kea formed a wall that had saved the island. He didn't tell the boy that it had also saved the world.

"Mothers are always right," Mac said. He'd leave it at that.

They stared at the summit of Mauna Loa, as majestic as ever but once again still.

Until the next time.

"Your time at HVO is really up?" Lono asked. "You're leaving us?"

"You know I was moving toward the door before this all happened."

"And then what will you do?" Lono asked. "You know the next time we have an eruption, you're gonna get all *lōlō* wanting to be here."

"I'm thinking that maybe I might want to teach something other than surfing," Mac said.

There was a brief silence.

"I miss Jenny," Lono said.

"So do I, kid," Mac said. "So do I."

He and Rebecca were on the same afternoon flight, through Los Angeles to Houston. But he didn't tell Lono that.

Instead, he walked over to where they'd left their boards and picked his up.

As he walked toward the water, he thought:

Just another day in paradise.

CHAPTER 109

Since the second eruption of Mauna Loa, only army personnel were allowed close enough to the base of Mauna Kea to see the construction work that had been going on there for the past week.

Three days before, the USS *George Washington* had left the Port of Hilo with little fanfare. There had been no fanfare at all for the building of this one last wall, which completely covered the entrance to the cave formerly known as the Ice Tube.

When the last truck pulled away, the base of Mauna Kea looked the same as it had for centuries.

The effect was largely the same as when, years before, an incident at the Hilo Botanical Gardens, now forgotten, had briefly closed that park:

It was as if nothing had ever happened here.

ACKNOWLEDGMENTS

First and foremost, I would like to express my love and deepest gratitude for my late husband, Michael Crichton, who created this astounding and fascinating playground in which we play, and to our amazing son, John Michael, who inspires my daily efforts to help him to know his father and to reflect on the extraordinary man he was.

To the incredibly talented James Patterson: My profound gratitude for collaborating on this project. I knew from the moment we connected that I could trust you to bring this exceptional story and Michael's brilliant ideas to life. It has been a joy, a privilege, and an honor to join hands with you on this fantastic journey. You amaze me with your masterful storytelling and your ability to weave together every element so impeccably. Both you and your wife, Sue, have been so generous and kind; I am truly grateful. Thank you for honoring my husband by completing this book.

I am indebted to my remarkable manager, agent, and friend, Shane Salerno of the Story Factory: This project would not have come to light without your infinite passion for Michael's legacy. Thank you for your vision, drive, and perseverance to honor and share the worlds of Michael Crichton with new audiences and generations. You have an undeniable way of making magic happen, and I am in awe of all that you do.

I would also like to thank Richard Heller, Ryan C. Coleman, and Steve Hamilton.

Organizing the extensive volumes of research left behind by Michael that were necessary for this book would not have been possible without the exhaustive archival efforts and support of Laurent Bouzereau and my assistant, Megan Bailey. Thank you.

Deepest gratitude to the very talented and dedicated members of our Crichton/Patterson publishing family at Little, Brown and Company. Thank you for believing in this amazing collaboration from day one.

I want to personally acknowledge and thank Michael Pietsch, Bruce Nichols, Craig Young, Ned Rust, and Mary Jordan for their support and creative partnership.

—Sherri Crichton

Special thanks to Denise Roy, my patient, tireless, hugely talented editor. Denise is also my mentor and occasionally my therapist. *Eruption* wouldn't be the novel it is without her keen oversight and insights.

And to Dr. Elisabeth Nadin—associate professor, Department of Geosciences, University of Alaska Fairbanks—an expert and enthusiastic guide to the unique geology of the Big Island of Hawai'i, as well as to N. Ha'alilio Solomon from the Kawaihuelani Center for Hawaiian Language for his help with the dedication.

—James Patterson

A BIT OF BACKSTORY

by Sherri Crichton

The Black Zone, Michael's working title, was based on subject matter that captivated him for many years. Michael rarely spoke of his ideas or projects, not even to his family or closest friends; however, he frequently spoke of his volcano project, and when we were traveling through Italy, we made a special excursion to Pompeii so that he could further research the story he set in Hawai'i. After Michael passed, I came across the unfinished partial manuscript in the archive, and I couldn't believe how he'd brought the story together in his inimitable way. Unearthing this treasure inspired an intensive research project that involved scouring his multiple hard drives and papers, finding all relevant material.

Though Michael was meticulous in his research and organization, cross-referencing and updating his files across numerous locations was no small feat. What this work unveiled, however, was remarkable: his story was brilliantly laid out. He had extensive volumes of scientific research, notes, and outlines—even video footage of himself on location conducting interviews with a volcanologist. How exciting! What Michael created needed someone of his brilliance to complete. For years, I considered possible collaborators, holding off for that perfect partner to come into view. I would simply wait patiently for someone who could honor my husband's work and continue his story.

Then I was introduced to James Patterson.

Jim, you have been the perfect partner.

I am forever grateful.

ABOUT THE AUTHORS

© Jonathan Exley

MICHAEL CRICHTON remains one of the most popular writers in the world, best known as the author of the global phenomenon *Jurassic Park*. His books, which have been translated into 40 languages and adapted into 15 films, have sold more than 250 million copies worldwide. He wrote a number of global bestsellers, including *The Lost World: Jurassic Park, The Andromeda Strain, Congo, Sphere, Rising Sun, Disclosure, Airframe*, and *The Great Train Robbery*. His influence and creativity extended far beyond books—he was the creator of the landmark television series *ER*, which ran for 15 seasons, won 23 Primetime Emmy Awards, and received 124 Emmy nominations. He cowrote the screenplays of *Jurassic Park* and *Twister* and wrote and directed the film *Westworld*, which served as the basis for the HBO series. Crichton is the only writer in history to have a #1 book, #1 film, and #1 television series at the same time, and he did it twice.

© David Burnett

JAMES PATTERSON is the most popular storyteller of our time. He is the creator of unforgettable characters and series, including Alex Cross, the Women's Murder Club, Jane Smith, and Maximum Ride, and of breathtaking true stories about the Kennedys, John Lennon, and Tiger Woods, as well as our military heroes, police officers, and ER nurses. He has coauthored #1 best-selling novels with Bill Clinton and Dolly Parton, told the story of his own life in *James Patterson by James Patterson*, and received an Edgar Award, ten Emmy Awards, the Literarian Award from the National Book Foundation, and the National Humanities Medal.